Still Guilty

Pat Simmons

URBAN
CHRISTIAN

www.urbanchristianonline.net

Urban Books, LLC
78 East Industry Court
Deer Park, NY 11729

ISBN 13: 978-1-60162-851-0
ISBN 10: 1-60162-851-X

First Printing April 2010
Printed in the United States of America

10 9 8 7 6 5 4 3 2 1

Distributed by Kensington Corp.
Submit Wholesale Orders to:
Kensington Publishing Corp.
C/O Penguin Group (USA) Inc.
Attention: Order Processing
405 Murray Hill Parkway
East Rutherford, NJ 07073-2316
Phone: 1-800-526-0275
Fax: 1-800-227-9604

PRAISE FOR PAT SIMMONS

About Book II: Not Guilty of Love . . .
This follow-up to Guilty of Love will speak to anyone whose friends and loved ones do not understand their faith. The characters are well drawn, and Simmons has a real ear for dialogue. A great read!
Dee Y. Stewart
RT BOOK Reviews

Simmons has written her best work with this sequel to Guilty of Love. The richness of the characters and foundation of the word not only brings the story to life, but will encourage you while renewing your faith in God. This is a Christian fiction work of art.
Deltareviewer
Reviewing for Real Page Turners

The author provides great lessons for someone going through any aspect of their life in terms of health, relationships, bearing children, and family values. She truly deserves an encore for this story as she distinctively uses faith as her theme for the book. I look forward to the continuation she has in store!
EKG Literary Magazine

About Book I: Guilty of Love . . .
The author really outdid herself with this novel . . . as her first novel you can be sure that her gift is of God. I would have expected this work to have come from a more experienced author. A sequel is a MUST!

Idrissa Uqdah, AALBC.com Review Team

Pat Simmons has written a solid and satisfying story that will keep you glued until the last page. The characters are colorful and seem familiar. It describes friendship across racial lines, brotherly love, family issues, and religion in a non-preachy format. Pat Simmons is a fine writer. I look forward to reading more of her work.

Reviewed by R. M. Jackson for The RAWSISTAZ Reviewers

About *Talk to Me . . .*

It shows you how God can guide you to a better place in your life, no matter your situation. When Noel told Lana a scripture, he said "Our own righteousness is like filth unto God." Wow! I always believed in my own righteousness, but that verse really humbled me. I enjoyed this book . . . it is well worth it!!!

Jacqueline Janse, reader from Philipsburg, Sint Maarten

You will not want to put it down. When you turn your life over to God, nothing is impossible and that shows true with the story of Noel. Pat Simmons did an exceptional job with balancing romance and scripture. It shows how you can overcome any roadblock as long as you have God on your side.

Reviewed by Jackie for Urban-Reviews

Acknowledgments

Since God is awesome, I give Him all the praise. He opened the windows of heaven and poured out abundant blessings and my cup runneth over. Hallelujah! It's in Malachi 3:10.

Writing *Still Guilty* was a challenge. I had folks going to jail, characters having babies, and all kinds of comedy and drama. The end result wouldn't have been possible without the assistance from the following:

Terri and Mark Schuler for allowing me into their family.

The Honorable Judge Michael T. Jamison: thank you for accepting my calls, answering my questions, and not putting me out of your courtroom.

The Honorable Judge Michael Burton: thank you for reading all my emails and taking the time to clarify scenarios. I appreciate you!

The Honorable Judge Sandra Hemphill.

St. Charles County Prosecutor John Devouton: thank you for breaking down procedures and responding to my emails.

For the readers who will enjoy this book, I thank my dedicated, professional, and sweet-spirited editors: Urban Christian Executive Editor Joylynn Jossel for the extensions, and freelance editor extraordinaire, Chandra Sparks-Taylor.

Judy Mikalonis for negotiating *Still Guilty*'s contract.

The "village people" for your prayers and encouragement.

Acknowledgments

My family on my genealogy tree: Coles, Wades, Carters, Wilkersons (Wilkinsons), Simmonses, Sturdivants, Browns, Carters, Jamiesons, Palmers, and so many others. My mom, Johnnie Cole, and siblings, Kim Eastern and Rossi Cole III.

A shout out to readers who have picked up a book in the *Guilty* series and sent an e-mail to let me know how much they enjoyed it.

To my very best friend, husband, chauffeur, and "travel agent," Kerry Simmons

Pastor James Johnson for all the in-depth Bible classes and Sunday sermons. First Lady Juana Johnson, who knows how to boost a person's confidence.

To all others I have failed to mention, THANK YOU!

CHAPTER 1

How did my life become so complicated? Parke Kokumuo Jamieson VI wondered. He was the firstborn son in the tenth generation of descendants of Paki Kokumuo Jaja, the chief prince of the Diomande tribe of Côte d'Ivoire, Africa. Parke was destined to procreate the eleventh generation.

It was an honorable task that Parke had relished fulfilling, until he met Cheney Reynolds. He had tossed caution, common sense, and responsibility to hurricane-strength winds. Cheney was his destiny, and Parke was determined to have her even after being advised that she was sterile. Addicted to her strength, determination, and beauty, Parke proposed anyway—more than once.

Six feet without heels, Cheney's height complemented his six-foot-five frame. Her long lashes and shapely brows were show-stoppers, but it was Cheney's delicate feet that were his weakness—after her hips, of course. Her feet were always manicured and soft, and they seemed to nurture a slight bounce to her cat-walk.

Cheney's skin held a touch of lemon coloring, and her lips were a temptation for kisses. Within a year of their marriage, God performed a miracle against medical odds. Cheney became pregnant twice. Both times, they lost: the first through a miscarriage, the second—a precious son—delivered stillborn.

Late one night, while studying his Bible, Parke petitioned

God for a sign as to whether a son would ever come through his seed. He stumbled across Genesis 16—the story of Abram; his wife, Sarai; and Sarai's handmaiden, Hagar. Parke read the passage three times. "What are you telling me, God?"

With his sharp intellect, Parke interpreted that Cheney portrayed Sarai. Although Parke had just turned thirty-six, he prayed his reproduction bank wasn't as dormant as Abram's, in order for God to perform a miracle. He wasn't asking for anything major like the parting of the Red Sea; just something on a smaller scale. Maybe there was hope.

Closing his Bible, he slid to his knees and prayed, then climbed into the bed and wrapped his arms around his wife. As he reached to turn off the lamp, he wondered, for argument's sake, if he was Abram and Cheney was Sarai, then who was cast as Hagar?

An answer from God came the next day when his private investigator called. "I hope you're sitting down."

Sipping his cup of coffee, Parke stood, leaning against the kitchen counter, when he was eating breakfast on the run. As a senior financial analyst, he was mentally contemplating his workload for the day. Clients were clambering for his attention to review their personal portfolios and make recommendations concerning safe investments. Parke didn't answer him right away. "Nope. What's up?"

"If I'm lying, I'm dying, and God knows I'm not ready. What are the odds that I've found your son?" Ellington "The Duke" Brown stated then paused. "I think."

The hunt had actually started two years earlier. Parke had initiated a search after a social worker who was screening him and Cheney for the foster care program questioned the name similarity to Park Jamie, a toddler somewhere in the system. The woman had risked disciplinary action or termination for breaching client confidentiality. "I feel God wants me to say something to you," she had explained.

Parke contacted his longtime friend and Lincoln University Kappa Alpha Psi frat brother, Ellington, the CEO of Brown Investigations. The last time they had spoken, Ellington had basically told Parke the rumor was unfounded.

Now, seven hundred and four days later, Parke froze—his hand, mouth, and breathing—as his heart collided against his chest. Once he was able to thaw, he spewed coffee across the counter like a wayward water sprinkler. Dumping his cup in the sink, Parke used all his strength to gulp pockets of air. Somewhat composed, he sniffed as his vision blurred.

He stretched his hands in praise, forgetting about the cordless phone in the mishap. It tumbled to the floor. "Yes! Thank you, Jesus. Praise God—"

"Wait, Parke. Parke!" Ellington screamed repeatedly until Parke picked up the phone.

"Whew. Sorry about that. That's good news, Ellington." Parke grinned. He couldn't help it. "Thank God for Hagar, whoever she is," he whispered.

"Ah, there's a slight twist I should tell you. If he is your son, you're no longer his father." Ellington cleared his throat. "Your parental rights have been terminated. He's been adopted."

"What?" Parke shouted. As the words sank in, visions of his life seemed to appear in slow motion, before some internal fury raced to the surface. He glanced around the room, searching for any moveable object that Cheney wouldn't miss if he threw it "When? Why? Who?"

Ellington told Parke what he had learned, and Parke didn't like the answers as he began to clean up his mess.

***

Fast forward almost three weeks later, and Parke wasn't any closer to getting his son. "I'm tired of waiting. If I need to prick my finger, rub a swab in my mouth, pee in a cup, or pull out a hair sample, bring on the DNA test," Parke barked, anchoring his cell phone on his shoulder and thumb-steering his new Escalade Hybrid as he swerved around a pothole.

The vehicle's brakes suffered the abuse of Parke's frustration. He squinted at the clock on the dashboard and increased his speed to pick up his daughter. Racing through traffic on Chambers Road, Parke calculated the minutes to his destination—Mrs. Beatrice Tilley Beacon's house on Benton Street in Ferguson, Missouri, a suburb of St. Louis. She was his wife's former neighbor, a surrogate grandmother who answered to Grandma BB only if she liked the person, a reliable babysitter, and the only alleged suspect in the shooting of Cheney's father.

A traffic light snagged him. He huffed, venting, "Ellington, I'm capable of doing two things at one time, but arguing while driving isn't a preferable combination. A cop is right behind me, and I'm not up to hearing the wrath of my little diva if she's late for her martial arts lesson. That girl has a mean left kick."

"I'm not scared of your four-year-old. As a matter of fact, Kami loves me. Anyway, you're not paying me. The last time I checked, I quit after you fired me the second time."

That was true. Parke hadn't really meant to briefly lose control or sidestep the Holy Ghost. When it came to anything remotely Jamieson-related, his emotions often overrode his sensibility. "I was hoping you had forgotten about that—or at least, hadn't taken me seriously. You didn't, did you? I'll double my last offer."

"You can quadruple it, buddy, but four times zero is still nothing, so stop harassing me," Ellington retorted. "You asked me to check out a rumor that you had a son in the foster care system. Do you know how long that took?"

Too long, in Parke's opinion, but he didn't voice it. He shrugged. It was a good thing Ellington couldn't see his nonchalant behavior.

"I located a Park Jamie. His mother was a petite Latina who died in a car crash—"

"I don't need a summary of your report. I remember Rachel Lopez. God help me if I could forget that woman's legs—yeah." Parke shook himself and refocused. "I want Parke Kokumuo Jamieson VII." He scowled. "As his birth father, I have a right not only to see my son, but to take immediate custody."

"Parke, the child was adopted two months ago . . . and his name was changed. Even if the judge grants a paternity test, you'll have to prove you didn't voluntarily give up your rights as a parent," Ellington tried to console. "You can't bake a cake and have a clean pan, too."

"What? You know that didn't make any sense, right?" Parke frowned, irritated.

"It didn't, did it?" There was silence. "My point is you're an adoptive parent. You know the process. What if Kami's parents had challenged her adoption?"

That wasn't the same. Kami's natural family was so dysfunctional they probably didn't notice her missing when she was placed into the system. With a blink of an eye, the teenage mother and father had signed the papers, dissolving their parental rights.

"Listen, man, I'm just your friend/amateur shrink /professional investigator. You're at the end of the road with me. Call your attorney."

"I did. Can you believe he removed himself from the case then hung up on me?" Parke snarled.

"Yup. I'm not surprised. What did you do or say?" When Parke told him, Ellington exploded with untamed laughter.

"That makes how many attorneys—two? I'm telling you, you should've called Twinkie, my cousin, the first time. Don't let the name fool you. She's more than a sweet little snack. The girl squashes her competition. If there's a loophole in the law, she'll widen the gap. Until then, wait on the Lord, as you always tell me. Quote a scripture or something and you'll be all right."

Parke grunted then disconnected without saying good-bye. He was tired of waiting.

CHAPTER 2

Dr. Rainey Reynolds didn't understand his twin sister, Cheney Reynolds Jamieson. She was sleeping with the enemy—not in bed, but she was guilty by association. He was seconds away from demanding to know where her family allegiance lay as they engaged in a fierce stare-down duel.

They were outside their parents' palatial home, which was tucked behind a tree-lined block on Westmoreland Avenue in the Central West End, an affluent area within St. Louis city. The fifteen-room, three-story stone-and-brick mansion was daunting. Once a person entered, the feeling of being swallowed up wasn't an exaggeration.

Rainey hovered four inches over Cheney, but that didn't intimidate her. Not much of anything did. Naturally beautiful, people wouldn't believe she was as tough and stubborn as she was.

"Remember the family pact?" He blinked, losing the battle.

Frowning, Cheney squinted. "Nope." She jutted her chin higher and folded her arms, indicating she had time for an explanation.

"The unspoken rule," he stated, hissing. "If somebody talks about your mama, it's fighting words, or if someone jumps your sister or brother, we all fight."

"We're thirty-three years old. I've long ago put away childish things." Cheney turned to terminate their conversation. As she began to step down the brick-covered circular steps, he reached out and stopped her, causing Cheney to teeter on the edge.

Glancing over his shoulder, Rainey double-checked their privacy. He wanted to make sure their bickering hadn't summoned their parents' housekeeper, Miss Mattie, to investigate the disturbance.

"It's the same concept, twin. We should stick together in this crisis." He interlocked his hands. "Traitor," he bit out with venom then added a few profane words, which forced Cheney to blink. Tilting his head, Rainey gave her a look that was meant for a burglar to think twice about breaking and entering. "You don't get it, do you? If my so-called friend hurt one of my family members, it would be over, and my cut would be clean."

Cheney sighed and offered a strained smile. "Ever heard of forgiveness?"

"No." Rainey wanted to shake his sister until her dead brain cells came alive or fell out. She saw nothing wrong with befriending a woman who wanted their father dead.

He didn't care that Cheney had moved next door to Mrs. Beacon, who fabricated a lie that their upstanding father was a hit and run driver who mowed down her husband. Who knew that Mrs. Beacon would take it a step further and try to harm their father? Now, their father had to go on trial for an alleged hit and run fatal accident, which was ridiculous. It was mind boggling that Cheney still maintained a friendship with the lady.

"Not when it comes to my enemies, Cheney. I happen to be selective about extending amnesty." Rainey tried to control his temper and non-existent high blood pressure, a condition that would surely surface once the trial portraying his father as a murderer was over.

"God's trying to get someone's attention. No, make that a whole lot of folks' attention." She waved her hand in the air, stepping closer.

"Well, the Lord's got it, because every media outlet in the area is probably enjoying this." When she reached out to touch him, he moved back, disturbing a pillar of flowers.

"Rainey, this is not about you."

He grunted in disgust, jiggling keys to his black metallic BMW. The jiggling was a habit that annoyed others; still, he allowed the nuisance to fester when he was irritated. "That's where you're wrong, twin. This is about the Reynolds family, our reputation, and integrity. I will not believe our father intentionally ran over Mrs. Beacon's husband with his car and then cowardly left a man to die. Not only can he lose his medical license, he can go to prison for something he didn't do. It's a good thing that bullet grazed his shoulder, or he would've been dead."

Cheney scrutinized her brother from his leather designer shoes to his troublesome thick, wavy curls. His face was smooth except for a thin mustache and a goatee. As toddlers, people had doted on them, calling them cute. Now, standing regal, Rainey's looks could only be described as breathtaking, heart-stopping, and eye-bucking distinguished. His convictions—right or wrong—were tighter than matted hair.

His intellect was exceptional, and his career was soaring as one of the most sought-after new orthodontists in the St. Louis area. Being the son of the assistant director of obstetrics and gynecology at St. James West Hospital had its privileges. Rainey's style of dress was a war between conservative and contemporary. The result was his signature collection.

"Judgmental doesn't compliment you." Cheney shook her head.

"We're talking about some serious allegations here. You're way beyond rational." He balled his fists, jiggling his keys again.

"I have every right to be angry. It's going to be a media circus around the courthouse."

"Don't you think I know it?" Cheney folded her arms and tapped her shoe. "I know you're not blaming me for stirring the pot." This time she backed up, sidestepping the matching pillar of flowers. "You don't have to say it. Your eyes reflect your thoughts."

She gracefully planted her hand on her luscious hips, as her husband described them. She lifted a brow and exhaled. She counted to two-and-a-half before she was about to release her fury.

The power of life and death is in the tongue, God intercepted with a portion of Proverbs 18:21.

"I love you, Rainey," she said so unexpectedly, she surprised herself.

He frowned, clearly caught off guard. Forgoing an endearing reply, Rainey dared one last jiggle, shook his head, and opted to march away. He followed the stone path outlined with red petunias to his sedan parked in the semicircular drive. Before he disengaged his alarm, he looked back. "See you in court."

Cheney sighed. That didn't go well, she admitted, watching him rev up his motor. Rainey barely waved good-bye before he sped off. Cheney stared until his BMW disappeared. As she shrugged in defeat, the Lord dropped a chorus of an old church song, "Victory is Mine," in her mind. It managed to lift her troubled heart.

She strolled to the opposite end of the driveway to her Altima. Yes, she was walking a fine line between a natural bloodline and spiritual kinship, but she loved Mrs. Beacon almost as much as her father. Emotionally torn was too mild to describe her present state of mind.

Earlier, Cheney had stopped by her parents' home to prove

her solidarity before the start of her surrogate grandmother's trial. She was just as upset as her family about the shooting, but they didn't believe her. Despite talking to God before she arrived, it didn't take Cheney long before she had to escape the suffocating silence from her family. It was as if they were having a prayer meeting without praying. She hadn't made it an hour before she announced she was leaving.

"That's probably best, Cheney," her mother, Gayle Reynolds, agreed, standing to signal the end of Cheney's visit.

Cheney would never accept the mean streak that possessed her mother's spirit. Gayle could disconnect herself from Cheney without batting an eye. Her mother had not always been that way. Their relationship changed when she found out about Cheney's abortion in college. Cheney had thought all that was behind them. Gayle had embarked on a closer walk with God, confiding in Cheney that she wanted to rebuild their strained mother-daughter relationship.

Some fell on stony ground, where it had not much earth. And immediately it sprang up, because it had no depth of earth, God's voice echoed Mark 4:5 in Cheney's head.

The bottom line was that her mother wouldn't let forgiveness take root. Finally, what little Bible knowledge she had embraced, Gayle quickly discarded. Cheney refused to give the devil the satisfaction by giving up hope.

Her father didn't try to intervene in her dismissal as he sat quietly in his La-Z-Boy Crandell recliner. His movements were non-existent; he gazed with a frozen stare, as if he were contemplating his next chess move. The strong black man with a warm personality had become an old, broken man in a matter of months.

Cheney's older sister, Janae, a shorter and darker version, rocked her sleeping three-year-old son, Alex, in her lap. Most times, she didn't acknowledge Cheney's presence, unless she uncoiled her tongue to lash out at her. As expected, Janae didn't react to Cheney's announcement with a weak wave good-bye or exaggerated nod.

"I love you guys," Cheney whispered, coming to her feet to leave. She swallowed the knot in her throat as she kissed her nephew's head then her dad's cheeks.

"Then act like it," her sister stated, purposely twisting her head so as not to accept Cheney's show of affection.

Suddenly, the spacious room was overpowering. Cheney felt as if she were being sucked into an abyss. She walked out of the room and didn't look back. Though Cheney had not requested an escort, Rainey trailed her to the door.

God spoke swiftly and fiercely: *You are responsible for bringing your family together.*

She gasped. "You're kidding me. Lord, not only am I not feeling that, I'm not seeing that either. I'm going to need some spiritual backup." Cheney had long ago shed the anger she felt at Mrs. Beacon for shooting her father, but it took some soul searching.

Ironically, to date, Cheney still struggled to forgive her father's trespasses against her. Roland had used his professional connections to gain access to her medical records in another state. Throughout the notes of the surgeon, anesthesiologist, pathologist, and medical staff, the only phrase that doomed their father/daughter relationship was *complications of an elective abortion.* The guilt trip he put on her for a very personal decision was almost unbearable.

Mrs. Beacon's actions were entrenched in loneliness, bitterness, and retaliation. The widow constantly reminisced about Henry, the love of her life. Her husband had been in his late fifties when he was killed by a hit-and-run driver. Twenty-seven years after the accident, Roland confessed to Parke that he had been the one behind the wheel; then he talked to Mrs. Beacon. Cheney was the last to know, but under the advisement of his attorney, Roland formally entered a not guilty plea.

Cheney discovered there was more behind Rainey's steadfast disgust. It was a deep-rooted hurt. Ten years earlier, Rainey's then girlfriend, Shanice, who was four months pregnant, aborted their baby. She boasted it was her payback for him dating other women.

When Rainey found out what Shanice had done, he was beyond ballistic. He still harbored ill feelings on the topic of pro-choice. Where Shanice purposely destroyed their relationship, Cheney's reason to undergo an abortion was to save a relationship. In the end, Cheney and her college sweetheart split anyway, and the doctor who performed the procedure massacred her womb. It was a matter of time before Rainey transferred his hostility to her. She loved him too much to return the sentiment.

Her brother and her husband were one of a kind. Both, contrary to public misperception about black men, welcomed fatherhood; both were cheated.

When Roland uncovered the truth about why Cheney made excuses about coming home, he maliciously leaked bits and pieces and hints. Soon Cheney's entire family had put the puzzle together. Roland's rage against Cheney had been his cover-up, fearing his sins might be exposed.

After the initial shock that their father would commit such a heinous act, Cheney defended herself, stating she was responsible for only her sins. She refused to bear the punishment for someone else, as her brother fully expected. That was the purpose of the cross.

Cheney disengaged her alarm and slid behind the wheel. She

took a deep breath. It had been a long day. It seemed as if peace was about to take an extended vacation. Looking around at the estate, she often wished her life was as tranquil as her parents' lawn.

She noted the time on the dash. She had flown back in town a few hours earlier from Dallas for the start of the trial, after attending a two-day management seminar. Cheney was eager to see Parke and their daughter. Strapping her seat belt, she turned the ignition and said a quick prayer of thanks for the blessings and even the heartaches in her life. She drove away, leaving the city. Cheney was in North County and at Mrs. Beacon's house in less than thirty minutes.

Parking at the curb, Cheney sat in her car and stared at her former real estate investment—her first home. As therapy, she had restored the neglected house and lived there for almost two years before she met and married Parke. Afterward, she sold it to a dear friend.

Moments later, that friend, Imani Seagall, bounced down the porch's stairs. Born with a mischievous streak, Imani appeared suspicious. She bypassed her Mustang convertible in her driveway. Like a schoolgirl at recess, she did an impressive hopscotch across Mrs. Beacon's invisible property line onto her thick, chemically treated grass.

It was the first rule Cheney was forced to memorize when she moved on the block: the perimeter of Mrs. Beacon's front yard and the threat of relentless harassment if she came within inches of the boundaries. Cheney was positive Imani knew that too. Obviously, Imani was willing to take her chances.

Divorced and childless, Imani matched wits with Mrs. Beacon, who was also childless, but somehow earned the nickname Grandma BB from neighborhood children. The thirty-something and seventy-something women were worthy opponents.

Their daily mission was to outdo the other in the annoyance department.

When Imani noticed Cheney, she froze then laughed at her silliness and waved.

Getting out of the car, Cheney met Imani halfway. "Umm-hmm. I saw what you did, and I'm tellin'."

"Oooh." Imani shivered. "I'm scared," Imani mocked before they hugged. Cheney held on a little longer, almost collapsing in her arms before Imani nudged her back and squinted. "Hey, hey, it's going to be okay. Grandma BB going to jail may be a good thing." She paused then added, to Cheney's look of horror, "For the neighborhood, of course."

"Imani, this is serious," Cheney fussed after momentary speechlessness.

"I know . . . I know, but I had to say what some neighbors are probably thinking. Okay, I'm sorry." Imani rubbed Cheney's arms. "You know God has your back." Imani smirked. "I borrowed that line from you. That's what you always preached to me when I used to be a stewardess working those international flights."

Nodding, Cheney mustered a smile, remembering how Imani suffered from occasional panic attacks before boarding a plane. Imani wouldn't let her off the phone unless Cheney talked to Jesus on her behalf for at least five full minutes. Now Imani was out of the travel industry. Unfortunately, she had become a casualty of downsizing.

"If prayer doesn't work, I can always buy a lottery ticket."

Cheney sobered instantly. She would never let Imani get away unscathed when it came to God. "I thought we were talking about praying during the trial. How did you manage prayer and gambling in the same sentence?" She lifted a brow, twisted her mouth, and tapped a finger against her leg. "Maybe you haven't been listening to me praying."

"I have." Imani fanned her hand. "And every time I buy a lottery ticket, I pray to win, and you know what? It works. Sometimes a dollar. One time, I won thirteen thousand dollars. What's the saying? You can't beat God givin'."

"Which is not scriptural, but what does the Missouri lottery have to do with someone possibly going to jail? Plus, I've warned you about putting your faith in a number instead of God anyway." Cheney wasn't amused by Imani's bad imitation of slapstick comedy. "Here's a scripture you need to think about right before you hand over your money: 'What does it cost a man to gain the whole world, but lose his soul?' " Imani's slip of the tongue opened the door for Cheney to recite a portion of God's word. Imani always needed divine intervention, since she had yet to embrace salvation.

"Don't start. Bible class is not in session. Listen, I've got to run." Imani shifted her weight on what appeared to be four-inch stilettos. "If I didn't have these job interviews lined up, I'd be there too. Maybe by the time your dad's trial begins, I'll have another job with a flex schedule, and I'll be right there for you. Although it's a toss-up on whose side I'd root for. What a choice: your supercilious family, or your former—my current—wacko neighbor. Girl, you should've warned me."

Shaking her head, Cheney smothered a smile. "I did." Imani had painted accurate sketches of her loved ones.

"Too bad I didn't believe you. Good luck with Grandma BB. She's brought weird to a whole new level." Imani leaned close as if Mrs. Beacon had a magnified hearing device buried underground. "Besides wearing her army-polished Stacy Adams shoes, she's now modeling them with dashikis. I think she's lost it." She shrugged. "Anyway, I've got to go. Oh, and her houseguest moved in a few days ago. I think you'll like Joe. Bye. Love you. Smooches, and as you say, take Jesus with you, be blessed, and all that religious stuff you tell me." Balanced on her heels, she swayed her hips back to her car in case a good-looking man drove past them.

"Just when I thought the scriptures were sticking to her bones." Cheney proceeded to Mrs. Beacon's red-brick bungalow. It didn't have the height as some neighboring homes, but it was commanding as the block's snapshot postcard. It was larger than Cheney's old house, with an enclosed area connecting the main house and the garage. Three large dormers made the half story appear like a full second floor.

She refocused. Beginning the next day, Cheney would become a stickball between opposing teams—Reynolds versus Cheney and Reynolds versus Beacon—all in one courtroom. The scenario was sure to be repeated when it was her father's turn to go before the judge as the accused. When the rounds were over, there would be no winner, but she was praying for an acquittal, or both her dad and Mrs. Beacon could go to jail or maybe prison, depending on the severity of their convictions.

Cheney sighed and knocked. She knew her friend had a houseguest, but with so much going on, Cheney hadn't had time to introduce herself. Unfortunately, knowing Mrs. Beacon, it wouldn't be a surprise if it was someone of the opposite sex.

The door opened, and Imani's assessment proved accurate. Mrs. Beacon stood dressed in her customary Stacy Adams, a dashiki top, and pants. Cheney was familiar with Mrs. Beacon's idiosyncrasies, but the altered fashion statement hinted that a mental evaluation may not be a bad idea. Mrs. Beacon was going to plead insanity. Cheney was convinced.

"Friend or foe?" Mrs. Beacon didn't crack a smile. A Biblical David-size woman to Cheney's Goliath height, Mrs. Beacon was five feet in heels. She had wrinkle-free mocha skin, which was the envy of any makeup artist.

"Friend. You know that." Cheney stepped closer, but Mrs. Beacon didn't budge from the doorway.

"What are you going to be tomorrow? You know I can't stand any two-faced hussies," she challenged, folding her arms. She tapped her shoe to the energetic beat of Beyoncé's "All the Single Ladies," blasting in the background.

"I'm on Daddy's side and your side. Most importantly, I'm on Jesus' side. When everything is settled, we'll have to forgive."

"I don't have time for a group hug." Mrs. Beacon whipped a finger mid-air. "Last time I read it, the Word didn't say anything about forgetting." Cheney nodded as Mrs. Beacon sang, butchering the chorus, "If you like it, you shoulda put a ring on me. Oh, oh, oh. I'm a single woman, single woman . . ."

Cheney groaned as she whirled around and backtracked to her car. "Another song Grandma BB can't remember the words to." It was definitely praying time.

CHAPTER 3

The legal process intimidated Cheney. She had barely gotten enough sleep the previous night, fearing Mrs. Beacon wouldn't survive one day behind bars. Hardened criminals would skin the widow alive—or maybe not. As far as Cheney knew, the only infractions with the law that her surrogate grandmother had were complaints that she threatened trespassers in her neighborhood.

To make matters worse, Cheney was running late. It definitely wouldn't score any brownie points with her family. She arrived at the courthouse and parked in the garage. After Cheney cleared the building's metal detectors, she secured the purse strap on her shoulder. Cheney opted for the stairwell and hurried up the steps to the second floor.

Reaching her destination, Cheney opened the door and halted. As she sucked in her breath, Cheney momentarily became disoriented. Her effort to squeeze through the hordes of ladies in red hats was useless. "Excuse me, excuse me," Cheney mumbled to a couple of plump ladies decked out in red-and-purple attire. "Pardon me." When she stepped to the right, they shuffled to the left and blocked her path.

"Friend or foe?" the Munchkins demanded in unison.

Where did she hear that phrase before? Cheney frowned and shifted to the other side. They glided to match her move as if they were ballroom dancers. Cheney tried to hide her irritation, but she was wasting time. The sweet, old, grandmother-looking women were in her way.

"We repeat, friend or foe?" one interrogated.

Sighing, Cheney glared. "Look, you don't know me, and I don't know you—"

"Elsie and I already know that," the interrogator cut her off. "You're not in uniform, and there are no other courts in session on this floor, so you must be a foe," the unidentified woman stated matter-of-factly.

Cheney happened to favor the black or earth tones she was wearing. They were sounding too much like a Mrs. Beacon tactical unit. "Miss Elsie and Miss—"

"Vera, Miss Vera McDonnell, but not like the golden arches, young lady," she interrupted.

Cheney took a deep, calming breath before speaking. "Unfortunately, Grandma BB didn't send a memo on the dress code," she explained, glancing down at her business casual yet classy tan apparel for work. Cheney hoped to stop by her office at the telephone company later that day. As a manager, her schedule was somewhat flexible. "I'm definitely here to support her, but I'm already late." Her friend had organized an army of supporters.

"Not a problem, dear," Miss Elsie cooed. She reached inside her overstuffed purse and pulled out a red ball. Once it was released, the object sprang into a skull cap. "Here, put this on. Don't worry about lice. That doesn't concern us black folks that much. Besides, it's clean. I washed it last week in Suavitel. I love the way that fabric softener smells. Did you know Kmart always has it on a bargain?" she rattled on.

Reluctantly, Cheney accepted it from Miss Elsie and adjusted the ball of yarn on her head, smashing her curls. "There," she said, gritting her teeth. "The things I do for Grandma BB," she complained as the pair nodded their satisfaction.

Lifting her chin, Cheney added a bounce to her step and moved toward the end of the line to enter the courtroom. Ahead of her, three women and a man dressed in a red suit scooted closer to the door. The bailiff stepped in front of them and lifted his hand. "Sorry. There aren't any more seats available. You'll have to wait outside."

Behind the closed doors, Cheney could hear the roar of laughter before the deafening sound of the judge's gravel pounded the desk. Without Cheney witnessing it, she feared her beloved Grandma BB was putting on a show. That was bound to get the woman locked up before her trial began. She had to get inside.

Outraged, the women, minus the male, pushed forward as if they were about to stampede the bailiff. He smirked. Crossing his arms, he rippled his biceps, which danced to a secret beat. His actions mesmerized the group. The ladies almost swooned. The lone gentleman stood straighter, as not to be undone.

The fascination ended quickly as Mrs. Beacon's supporters murmured and grumbled as they broke up their orderly line. In a split second, they made beelines to the nearest vacancies on crowded benches.

"That ain't right," Cheney heard one say.

"The busload from Kankakee hasn't even gotten here yet," a whining voice complained.

"Elsie, did you bring your cell phone? Call the team in Springfield, Missouri. Tell them to turn around."

"You're not the boss of me, Vera. What are you going to do?" Miss Elsie huffed as she dug inside her bag to do as the other woman had ordered.

"Humph! Your boss? You better be glad I'm your best friend. So that you'll know, I'm going to send out a mass text. Maybe it's not too late for our Little Rock team, which had a late start to turn around. The society from Bowling Green, Missouri, should be here any minute once they find a parking spot for a chartered over-the-road bus . . . ."

Cheney tuned them out. Surely, as part of the plaintiff's family, she would be allowed inside. "Excuse me, sir." The bailiff huffed, annoyed. He glared at Cheney, but didn't answer. "My father is the victim. I got separated from my family, but I know they're saving me a seat." She hoped God was going to make a way.

His voice came out as a growl. "I have been instructed not to let another person enter, and that means you."

Cheney had no choice but to patrol the door until someone came out, so she could go in and snag their spot. It was an even exchange she was sure the wannabe warden wouldn't mind. If Plan A didn't work, Plan B would be to get Miss Vera and Miss Elsie to call a cease-fire long enough to take down her name and pass it on to Mrs. Beacon. Any explanation to her family about her absence wouldn't be acceptable anyway.

Cheney was about to patrol near the door when a tall woman who could only be described as majestic caught her attention. The stranger was five-ten, give or take an inch. She wore the red uniform. The dress was simple, but her head wrap was a twisted combination of a red cloth and purple ribbon. It was as unusual as it was beautiful. Her skin glowed, but Cheney couldn't determine if it was a gift from God or a cosmetic counter. She didn't appear to be old enough to be part of the "society." Nosy, Cheney detoured in the woman's direction.

"Hi," Cheney said, holding out her hand. The woman accepted it. "My name is Cheney Jamieson, and I'm—"

"I know who you are. Mrs. Beacon—I mean, Grandmother B—told me all about you, Mrs. Jamieson. I'm glad you could make it. She will be pleased," the lady said, speaking in proper English. Her eyes sparkled with delight.

Cheney had two questions: who was this woman, and how did she know so much? "Grandmother B? I'm sorry for asking, but you are . . .?" Cheney leaned forward, her mouth open, waiting for the woman to fill in the blank.

She gave a polite chuckle. "My name is Josephine Yaa Amoah."

Neither the woman nor the name seemed familiar. Cheney thought a few minutes before she guessed. "Oh, so you're Grandma BB's houseguest, Josephine. Thank you, Jesus. For a moment I thought she had a man . . . never mind." Cheney patted her chest in surprise.

As Josephine spoke, Cheney cataloged her poise and features: flawless coffee-rich skin, enviable slanted eyes, and a nose that seemed to be finger-pinched below her eyes then expanded to her nostrils. Her smile was so perfect that Cheney's orthodontist brother would want to take the credit. "May I ask your native country without being offensive?"

She nodded, resting one hand on top of the other. "Of course, you may. Ghana, Africa."

Cheney's eyes widened. "Really? Please tell me you didn't leave your continent for Grandma BB's trial."

She shook her head. "Oh, no. I'm a candidate for a master's degree in library science. I'm taking classes at various locations, but primarily at the University of Missouri at St. Louis, and Mrs. Grandmother B graciously offered me free room and board in exchange for sharing my culture and providing her company. She's a lonely widow, you know."

Cheney released the hinges on her jaw as her mouth dropped open. *Lonely? Right, and these ladies are here to sightsee.* Cheney did her best to contain a smirk. The woman didn't know the real Grandma BB.

She eyed Josephine's head wrap. "We call her Grandma BB, and the university, UMSL."

Josephine's quick frown and stiffened posture was faint.

Cheney couldn't determine if she was offended by the correction or not.

Moments later, Josephine's full lips spread into a warm smile as she fingered her head. "Mrs.—I mean, Grandma BB insisted I represent her in my native garb." She chuckled. "This is not my usual dress."

They shared a laugh. Josephine had a calming effect, but Cheney couldn't linger. She had to call Parke and tell him not to bother leaving his meeting only to be turned away when he arrived at the courthouse. "I'm late, but I'm determined to get into that courtroom to support my father and defend Grandma BB. If that makes any sense."

"You need not fret." In a surprising move, Josephine whispered, "All things work together for good."

Cheney stepped back. "What did you say?"

"I'm quite sure you've memorized Romans 8:28, so love Him, and walk in His spotlight," Josephine instructed, nodded, and moved on to speak with someone else.

What were the odds of a Bible-quoting woman from Africa living in the house with a professed gun-toting backslider? Cheney quietly finished the quote: *And we know that all things work together for good to them that love God, to them who are called according to His purpose.* She couldn't wait to see how this was going to play out. With a satisfying grin and a deep breath, Cheney whirled around to reclaim her post near the door. She didn't see the bailiff, but she met the scowl on Rainey's face.

From Mrs. Beacon's flamboyant getup to her overdose of arrogance, Rainey was ready to roar his frustration. While she carried on as if she were a celebrity, prosecutors were collecting evidence to paint his father—a doctor—as a criminal for an upcoming trial. Rainey had saved his sister a seat, but she hadn't come. He wondered if her response for not choosing sides was to not show up. Would she come when her father took the witness stand?

Rainey did not take off work for entertainment. Mrs. Beacon's hat was fire engine red and shaped like a bell; the rim was wide enough to set place settings for dinner. It appeared Rainey caught on to Mrs. Beacon's hand signals at the same time as Judge Kendall. When Mrs. Beacon pointed her red glove-covered hand to the right, she glanced back at her bull pen of supporters. In a synchronized move, they would lift their purple fans and swish it once.

"Hold on, counselor." Judge Kendall interrupted the opening statements. Her facial expression gave away what was about to come. "Mrs. Beacon, my courtroom is not the place for theatrics. Armed criminal assault is a serious charge. I'll overlook your choice of attire, but keep up with your shenanigans, and I'll have no problem having you disrobed and thrown in jail."

Mrs. Beacon leaped to her feet despite the efforts of her two attorneys at her side to restrain her. "Your Honor, in all fairness, I didn't interrupt the man. You did." Mrs. Beacon turned to her group and they nodded in sync. "I'm harmless and old enough to be your grandma. I'm—"

"Enough!" Judge Kendall slammed her gavel. "If you don't behave, today won't be your best day. Now, sit down and take off that hat. This is a courtroom, not the Kentucky Derby."

"But Your Honor, I feel naked without my bonnet—" She didn't finish, as her attorneys wrestled her to her chair. One had an arm wrapped around her waist, while the other was brave enough to cover her mouth while apologizing to the judge. When Mrs. Beacon bit down on his finger, he released the muzzle.

Rainey had enough. He got up from his seat as the judge added more charges to Mrs. Beacon's slate. Exiting the Barnum and Bailey arena, Rainey exhaled to release the jumbled emotional mess from thirty minutes in Mrs. Beacon's presence.

Outside the courtroom, the scene was just as maddening. The number of people had swelled. It was as if Santa's elves, topped off in red hats, were scurrying, doing nothing. As he tried to head to the restroom, a bunch of old women refused to let him through, mumbling something about his name wasn't on Mrs. Beacon's list. What list?

"I've heard of a key for access to the men's room, but a list. I just walked outside this courtroom." Rainey was dumbfounded.

"Hmm-mmm. That's what they all say," a woman with a long face and Jay Leno chin argued.

"Excuse me again, but this is a public building," he had politely informed them, trying his best not to yell.

"Exactly, young man, and we are here to enforce the building code. You'd make one person over the mandatory limit. We need all the space we can get. With so many women here, we've taken over the men's restroom. Sorry. Just hold it a little while longer," one cute little woman advised. "Whatever you do, don't drink any more water. Coffee, teas, and soda could also act as diuretics."

He was losing patience and about to forgo his impeccable upbringing when he spotted a woman who seemed to garnish his attention as if he were a tourist admiring the Statue of Liberty. The ladies' ramblings faded as he zoomed in across the room, filtering out those in his line of view. Cheney was chatting up a storm with the woman, instead of being inside the courtroom. He was willing to test the effectiveness of his bladder to find out why.

Rainey was tempted to push his way through their barricade when Cheney turned around, smiling. Since it wasn't considered a day of celebration, why was she so happy? Cheney left the woman and headed his way. He cursed at the missed opportunity for an introduction and a beautiful diversion. He couldn't believe his mood swing from disgust to intrigue. Maybe it was the poison from his bladder getting to his brain.

Somehow, Cheney's acquaintance stood out in the sea of red. Even the ridiculous rag on her hair didn't distract from her allure. Rainey was used to attractive women, but he didn't trust them. At one time, he wanted it all: to be a third-generation doctor, have a loving family, and to live a satisfying life. As far as he was concerned, two out of three goals achieved weren't bad, although he was becoming less and less satisfied.

Rainey shook himself. Cheney was right. The moment wasn't about him, but his dad's trial, which was tearing apart his only family. Since Shanice, he felt a relationship wasn't worth developing, and there wasn't anything satisfying about not having a soul mate. So, how could a woman yards away, separated by a mob of busybodies, beckon to him without batting an eye? He didn't know the answer, and was weary about finding out.

Cheney walked up to him, and in a surprising move, hugged him. Rainey had no choice but to begrudgingly return her embrace. Briefly, he basked in their carefree affection, but that didn't change the reason why they were there. Once she released him and stepped back, they engaged in a stare-down again. Rainey wanted to recall his anger, his purpose for being down there, but the best he could muster was a kitten-size meow instead of a lion's roar.

"How's it going in there?"

"Aren't you feeling guilty that you're not inside, but talking to your friend over there?" he baited her, expecting a confession.

"Nope," she replied with a white, perfectly aligned smile, an asset Rainey couldn't claim his medical training assisted. She was born that way.

Clearing his throat, Rainey dismissed the temporary distraction. He was not in his office doing a consultation, but in a
courthouse, facing his father's accuser. "How come you're not
in there watching her proceedings?"

"Look around you," she said, sweeping her hand in the air.
"There's no room, but Josephine assured me Grandma BB is
well represented inside."

Josephine. He rolled the name in his head, trying to remember if he had ever known a Josephine. The conclusion was if
he had, they never looked like her or held her immediate magnetism. Suddenly, the day wasn't as doom and gloom as it was
when he came out of the courtroom.

"You can have my spot. I needed some fresh air while your
friend is putting on a show." Rainey remembered his bladder.
Maybe Cheney could get him a pass to the restroom. He dropped
the idea because he didn't feel like the hassle.

As Rainey turned and led the way back to the room, the bailiff
sabotaged their pathway.

"Sorry, you can't go in there." He folded his arms and
frowned at Cheney as if he recognized her.

"I don't think you understand; we're part of the family, and
I just came out a few minutes ago."

"That's too bad. As the saying goes, you move, so you lose.
Now, I think the ladies set up a table for cookies and punch. You
might want to help yourself."

Rainey groaned. He was back to his sour mood.

CHAPTER 4

Three times, Parke circled his neighborhood before deciding he wasn't going home. He didn't have a near-death excuse to explain to Cheney why he didn't make it to the courthouse on the first day. His doghouse was getting smaller; all because he didn't call his wife. How inconsiderate. His secretary had pulled him out of the conference room in the middle of an important meeting to take a call from his new attorney. The rest of the day was a blur. How did he get himself into these situations?

This is not of your doing. Only I can work all things for the good to those who love me, the Lord had spoken earlier that morning.

"How, Jesus? Make a believer out of me."

You will know by the trying of your faith, God reminded him, referring to James 1:3.

Groaning, Parke wished God had a daily limit of trials per person. He felt he had reached his when a judge informed Twinkie that his possible son's adoption was a done deal. The news couldn't have come at a worse time, as he strolled into his office to do some paperwork before heading to the courthouse for Mrs. Beacon's trial for shooting Roland.

"But I could be the father. I probably am the father. Don't I have a say?" Parke yelled into the phone, delirious with grief.

"Would you calm down? Give me time—"

Parke rubbed the back of his head and took a deep breath. "Twinkie, I don't have time to wait. My son could be getting his driver's license. For two months, he's been calling a stranger Daddy."

"Listen to me." His attorney raised her voice. "First we have to prove he's your son; then we have to have justification why he never should've been adopted. Do you have time now to go over everything you've told me?"

"Of course." Parke didn't glance at his watch. However long it took, he would make the time. Locking his office door, Parke listened as Twinkie verified his story.

More than once, Twinkie forced Parke to elaborate on details: dates, places, and conversations. When the call ended, he had a pounding headache. Opening his desk drawer, he pulled out a bottle of Tylenol and downed three gelcaps. Gagging, he raced to his adjoining bathroom for a cup of water.

He returned to his desk in a daze. "Okay, God, you are try-ing me. I hope my heart holds out." Regaining control, Parke rolled his shoulders. Booting his computer, he pulled client files from the drawers and scanned their portfolios, noting the mar-ket change. He was about to sign off when Twinkie called again. Her probing questions made Parke recollect more things about the woman he once dated.

Glancing at his watch, Parke figured he had time to get to the courthouse before the judge adjourned the court for the day. He couldn't risk turning off his phone and missing another call from Twinkie.

As the hours passed and the morning turned into afternoon, Parke called Twinkie for an update. Fifteen minutes later, when she didn't respond, Parke texted her twice, followed by one more frantic call. Before he knew it, his assistant was locking up her desk and saying good evening. Suddenly, he wondered if God didn't skip a few hours in his day. Parke's energy was zapped, his stomach complained, and his spirit was downcast. He had been so preoccupied; Parke had forgotten about his wife's needs.

When Parke had left the house, Cheney hadn't stirred. He took pity on his wife. She was exhausted after Kami kept them up most of the night, complaining of nightmares. Family programming wasn't all it was cracked up to be. There was always an antagonist who either looked creepy or issued petty threats.

Parke had gotten out of bed, showered, dressed, and left the house with good intentions. Throughout their four years of marriage, they had always, always been there for each other. He didn't even take time for his customary morning prayer or a cup of coffee.

Now, late evening, Cheney had probably been home for a couple of hours. It was his routine to communicate with his wife several times throughout the day by text, e-mail, or phone. They hadn't spoken, which was definitely a bad sign. In his mind, that was reason enough to bypass his house.

Less than a half hour later, Parke pulled into a different driveway that lacked any blemishes. The manicured lawn had the fingerprints of his younger brother, Malcolm. The neatly planted flowers bordering the shrubbery had the trademark of Malcolm's wife, Hallison. Stepping out of his SUV, he followed the short path to a porch with an explosion of colorful flowers in clay pots on both sides of the door.

Parke nodded his approval upon further inspection. Since childhood, each Jamieson brother always tried to show up the other. Parke believed he and his brother Malcolm were the models for television commercials, where neighbors outdid each other with better lawns, bigger houses, or more expensive gadgets.

When Parke purchased his Cadillac SUV, Malcolm got a top-of-the-line sports car, fully accessorized. After Parke bought and tackled the restoration of a historic house in older, nostalgic area of Ferguson, Malcolm helped design and had a new home constructed in historical St. Charles, which was the state's first capitol before it was later relocated to Jefferson City. Parke got married; months later, Malcolm proposed to Hallison, who turned him down until he surrendered his life to Christ. Besides the strong brotherly bond, their love and mutual respect were apparent.

Self-proclaimed local, state, and African-American history fanatics, they were also die-hard family genealogists. If they didn't know answers off the tops of their heads, they utilized every waking hour researching for information or at least clues. They attributed their passion to family documents dating back almost three hundred years that proved the determination of their ancestors.

To irritate his brother, Parke pounded on the stained-glass and dark wood door. To Malcolm, a doorbell was a musical instrument that should be appreciated for its harmonious or quaky sound to announce visitors. Parke wasn't a guest. He was family.

Malcolm flung open the door, standing barefooted and shirtless in late autumn. *Hmm,* Parke snickered at the younger version of himself and the possibility of interrupting newlywed activities.

"What do you want?" Malcolm didn't try to tame his rudeness.

"I was in the neighborhood." Parke shrugged, stuffing his hands in his pants pockets and admiring the new home's stone-and-brick detail. "I thought I'd stop by."

"Really? Coming from work, you passed up your house, say five miles ago on the other side of the Missouri River." Malcolm folded his arms. "Are you lost? Do I need to call your wife? Better yet, let me write down directions back—"

The remark was a flashback to a time when Parke was fed up with Malcolm's disrespect for family gatherings because of a woman he dated. Parke had been so mad, he wrote down their parents' address in case Malcolm had forgotten. Now, Malcolm was throwing it back in Parke's face.

"Malcolm? Who is it, babe?" Hallison's hand snaked from behind her husband and brushed his tight abs. One inch taller than Parke's six-three height, and a drop of brown caramel darker than Parke, Malcolm opted for a five o'clock shadow to Parke's trimmed mustache. After months of marriage, Malcolm was still in shape. Give Hallison more time, and Malcolm's abs would readjust to her cooking, as Parke's had. Cheney's excellent culinary skills had done Parke in.

Hallison's eyes sparkled at her husband then wandered to Parke. "What are you doing here?" She squinted. Her attire was modest, but hinted of an evening without guests.

"Ah, nothing like feelin' welcomed," Parke mumbled, elbowing his way between them as he invited himself inside. Halfway through the marble-tiled foyer, he froze. He was definitely interrupting something. Candles were burning on the glass coffee table and plates were empty. A pair of sleeping bags was on the floor with a board game between them. Parke grunted. Ummhmm, he didn't believe that for one second.

Malcolm slammed the door, shaking the crystal bits of the overhead mini-chandelier. "All I ask is for some quality time with my wife. We haven't been married a year and already you're becoming a dreaded in-law."

"I'm your brother, so technically I'm not an in-law." Parke stepped over a sleeping bag and flopped on the couch.

"Whatever, man. Why don't you make yourself at home?" Malcolm suggested sarcastically.

"Baby, he already did," Hallison griped as she walked around the great room, blowing out the candles. She then proceeded to roll up the sleeping bags. "By the way, how did it go in court today?"

Parke plucked at the fabric on their sofa. "Ah, I didn't

make it." He avoided eye contact, answering faster than an announcer reading a ten-second radio commercial.

"What do you mean you didn't go?" Hallison's tone was barely controllable. When Parke had the courage to look up, Hallison folded her arms.

"Ah." Parke gritted his teeth. "I forgot."

"You what!" Malcolm and Hallison thundered at the same time.

Parke expected nothing less than that reaction. The Jamieson men were noted for their loyalty to their women. Cheney and Parke shared everything before they were married. Afterward, they truly enjoyed and operated under the vow of "one flesh" as instructed in Ephesians 5:31. Today was the first time he had failed his wife. Well, not the first time, but the first in a long time. At least two months. Well, maybe a month, but this would cost him big time.

"You insensitive, self-absorbed, and selfish—" Hallison fussed. She suddenly became Cheney Jamieson reincarnated.

Parke shot off the sofa as if he would attack. Instead, he huffed, pacing their floor. "Okay, I messed up. It wasn't intentional. I had planned to go into the office, work a few hours, and meet her at the courthouse. When Twinkie called about—"

"Who's Twinkie?" Hallison asked coyly, leaning against Malcolm as he perched on the arm of a chair.

Parke stopped and shook his head. "I mean Attorney Williams. We had to brainstorm my custody case."

"Go home, man. Cheney will understand," Malcolm instructed.

"Hold up." Hallison lifted her hand. "No, she won't. You did at least call her throughout the day, right?"

Parke shook his head.

Malcolm stood and reached for Hallison's hand. "You're on

your own, man." Fingers linked, the couple headed for the kitch-
en. Malcolm paused and looked over his shoulder. "The couch
is available."

Traitors, Parke thought. He would have to go home praying,
because there was no way he wasn't going to make peace with
his wife.

CHAPTER 5

"Mommy, are we still mad at Daddy?" Innocent, large brown eyes reflected Kami Jamieson's concern as they knelt to pray before Kami climbed in bed.

The child's bedroom was a playground: toys, stuffed animals, and electronic and board games were in abundance. Oversized white juvenile furniture accented in pastel green, pink, and lilac polka dots were an amateur's replica of *Alice in Wonderland*. Accent pillows occupied half of Kami's full-size bed. Sketches of ballerinas and child stars and animal photos claimed large portions of the wall. A large pink area rug protected the hardwood floor.

Cheney blinked. "What makes you think we're angry at your father?" Her heart sank as she delayed answering her perceptive daughter. Cheney and Parke were careful not to involve Kami in grown folks' business.

You may not be mad at him, Kami, but I'm fired up. Parke stood me up. Cheney was battling conflicted emotions: content that Mrs. Beacon had a contingency of supporters and burdened that her father was the accuser. What a mess.

When she left the daylong trial, Cheney was mentally exhausted. Her disappointment built as she picked up Kami from preschool, and Parke hadn't bothered to come or call. She had phoned him on his cell and left a message on his voice mail not to come. He never called back. When she called his office, she disconnected after being put on hold. Granted, the day hadn't been as disastrous as she had expected, but what was up with her husband?

When Cheney arrived home and Parke's Escalade was missing, her aggravation worsened and she barely held her peace. She evidently had not done a good job of hiding her frustration. Kami had a gift to interpret Cheney's moods since her last pregnancy.

If she dared tell Kami what any mother would say to comfort her child, Cheney, while on her knees, would be lying in front of the Holy Ghost. She didn't want the same fate to fall on her as Ananias and Sapphira in the Book of Acts. Soon after Cheney was filled with the Holy Ghost and read chapter five, she strived not to lie, so she wouldn't fall dead like that couple.

Becoming impatient, with her hands poised, Kami eyed her mother. "I need to know what to pray for, Mommy," she insisted with an angelic expression. Her resemblance to Parke was uncanny. Unless someone read the adoption papers, they would argue Parke was her biological father, but Kami was a product of teenagers: a white girl and a drug-selling black youth incarcerated for violating his probation.

Cheney bowed her head. "Let's pray for love. Pray for peace, pray for understanding . . . ."

"Mommy, that's a lot. I have to pray for me too."

Smiling, Cheney looked up. "We're not mad at Daddy," she forced out of her mouth and shuffled the words in her head to believe them. Lord, help her. He was charging her to bring the Reynoldses closer, but she hoped that wouldn't be at the expense of her family of Parke and Kami. Currently, her life seemed to have built-in roadblocks.

As Cheney prayed, she battled the devil as he tried to stack the bad times in her life for her demise: the elective abortion that doctors said left her sterile; the pregnancy that doctors called unexplainable only to end in a miscarriage; another miracle pregnancy whose outcome was a stillbirth; a loving, gentle father who secretly admitted to running over and killing a man. The devil added the neighbor who had become Cheney's surrogate grandmother and now an enemy of the Reynolds family; then Satan went in for the kill: Parke was forsaking her for a son she couldn't and didn't deliver.

The burdens were too heavy as she tuned out Kami's requests to Jesus: a dog, her BB not to go to jail, a computer for her room, and more. Cheney sniffed, but the tears were determined to come.

Hang it up, Cheney. God never meant for you to be happy, the devil taunted her.

God stepped in and rebuked the thoughts. Thus, began the spiritual battle, as unknown tongues convulsed from Cheney's lips. The words were unrecognizable and the speed uncontrollable. Kami was accustomed to high praise, and would continue talking to God, or sing along until Cheney quieted.

Amazingly, when Cheney finished praying, there were no tears to wipe away. She inhaled deeply and opened her eyes.

"Mommy?" Kami wiped back Cheney's silky black hair from her forehead.

"Yeah, baby?"

"God wants you to read Revelate 21:4."

Cheney frowned. "Revelation?"

Nodding, Kami leaned in to Cheney. "Yep. That's what God said. I'm sleepy now. Will you tell Daddy we love him and we're not mad at him anymore?"

"I'll tell him." Cheney chuckled. She stood and pulled back the thick, polka-dot print comforter. After Kami climbed in the bed, Cheney tucked her into a cocoon and kissed her forehead.

As a nightly routine, she wound the music box on the table next to Kami's bed. "Silent Night" serenaded Kami, whether it was Christmas or not. Then Cheney left the room and closed the door, wondering if God had given Kami the interpretation through her prayer tongues.

Minutes earlier, Cheney's spirit felt cleansed after talking to Jesus and knowing He not only listened, but had sent her a word. Cheney shook her head, amused. God had never used Kami before to communicate His message.

Once in her bedroom, Cheney scooped up her Bible and lounged on a jacquard silk chaise near the bay window sitting area.

Before she opened to Revelation, she glanced at her watch. Cheney refused to track down her husband. It wasn't the first time Parke managed to get himself in the doghouse by forgetting something important. He always seemed to have a good reason, so she couldn't wait to hear his story this time. Despite his imperfections, Parke was a good husband, father, and provider. Besides, Parke had few hiding places: his parents, Malcolm, or his frat brother, Ellington.

Ignoring any distractions about Parke, Cheney flipped to the end of the Bible. From Revelation 21:4: *And God shall wipe away all tears from their eyes; and there shall be no more death, neither sorrow, nor crying, neither shall there be any more pain: for the former things are passed away.* It was the scripture that every Christian longed for in the end in heaven. Until then, Cheney had to ask God for peace in the middle of conflict.

From that reflection, Cheney felt led to 1 Peter 5:7: *Casting the whole of your care, all your anxieties, all your worries, all your concerns, once and for all on Him, for He cares for you affectionately and cares about you watchfully.*

She concluded with Psalm 39:7: *And now, Lord, what wait I for? My hope is in thee.*

An hour later, God provided her some comfort in lieu of a total understanding of the mission at this moment in her life. She checked the mirror clock on the wall. It read nine-thirty. She yawned as her phone rang, expecting Parke. Instead, it was her sister-in-law.

"Hey, Hali."

"Do you know where your husband is?" Hallison teased.

Cheney didn't need to guess. The phone call said it all. "Will you put your brother-in-law out," she suggested, annoyed by Parke's mysterious behavior. What was going on with him anyway? That's all she needed was for Parke to go through some male hormonal change or pre-mid-life crisis now.

Hallison asked what happened in court, and Cheney summarized the day's event. They chatted for a few more minutes before disconnecting.

Knowing that her husband wasn't hurt or missing, but had a case of inconsiderateness, Cheney opted for a long, hot bath. She was too exhausted from lack of sleep over the past few nights to worry about him. Plus, she was determined to get inside that courtroom early the next day. Too bad she couldn't camp out. The morning would come soon enough for Parke to explain, apologize, and bring her flowers. The ultimate surprise would be something gift-wrapped with a red bow.

Good sign. The lights were out when Parke pulled into his driveway. The outdoor lighting illuminated his century-old, custom-built, mouse-gray home, which mingled with the other houses on the block that were listed on the historic registry. Once he locked his SUV and walked the short path to the front door, he took a deep breath. His wife had to wear two hats today: understanding Mrs. Beacon's actions while supporting her father. She deserved him by her side. Parke understood that, but he had a strange feeling that soon his needs would outweigh hers.

Parke unlocked the front door and punched in the security code on the wall pad. His attempt to walk softly so as not to disturb his family was fruitless, as a large object on his mahogany wood floor served as a booby trap and thwarted his quiet entrance. Tripping, he braced himself on a wall. He flipped on a floor lamp and discovered he had sabotaged himself with a misplaced size-thirteen tennis shoe, or a yacht, as Cheney called his walking attire.

Composed, he opened the hall closet and threw it inside. He proceeded upstairs to the bedrooms, careful of the squeaky spots. He was at the top landing when a plank squealed. Shushing himself, he walked down the hall to Kami's bedroom and opened her door.

His lips had barely brushed against her head when she stirred. Smiling, Kami's lids fluttered open. "I got you out of trouble, Daddy," she whispered.

"Thank you, Daddy's girl. I love you," he whispered back, but she had already drifted back to sleep. She had been protective of him since the first day she was a foster child in Cheney's home. Two years later and legally adopted, their bond hadn't weakened. He kissed the top of her head again, stood, and walked out of the room, closing the door. He prayed Cheney wouldn't stir.

Inside his own bedroom, Parke removed his shoes and socks then padded into their showcase bathroom. It was big enough for a nursery and then some. When they married, Parke had it updated with marble floors and walls, a side closet, plus a linen area, his and hers sinks, a vanity table, and a Jacuzzi tub.

Returning to their bedroom, Parke knelt, and stayed on his knees longer than usual, praying. He wanted to share his frustration and listen to hers, but he was tired. Slurring an Amen, he climbed into their California king-size bed. Thin netting draped from the ceiling encased the mahogany bedposts. Cheney didn't wake. As a matter of fact, she claimed his side. "Eighty-four inches wide and she's sprawled out on most of it," he grumbled.

He adjusted his body and snuggled around what available room Cheney had left him. Parke sighed and reconsidered his predicament. He was purpose-driven, a go-getter, and tenth descendant of Prince Paki. That was reason enough to focus on freeing his son. The heir was within reach, and despite everything else going on around them, they had to refocus. Parke rubbed a hand over his face. Reversing that adoption was a priority. It would trump any card.

God knew that Cheney wouldn't be able to have children, so He had Rachel Lopez—Hagar—waiting in the wings. Now, Parke understood the saying, "Making a way out of no way." That's why it was so important for them to be unified as they fought for custody. He had prayed all the way home, but a deep-soul, gut-wrenching prayer escaped him.

Carefully, he untangled Cheney's body from his. Parke got on his knees again, getting lost in time as he asked God for direction. He hated to pull rank, but God did give him authority over his wife and household. Before he could say Amen, God spoke from Ephesians 5: *I command you as a husband to love your wife as Christ also loved the Church and I gave myself for you.*

"I do love her," Parke whispered.

The test begins, God spoke, leaving Parke to struggle with the interpretation.

CHAPTER 6

The next morning, Cheney greeted Parke, who was already downstairs in the kitchen. He offered her a steaming mug of half decaf and half hot chocolate topped with whipped cream. Her eyes sparkled with gratitude.

"Thank you," she said, accepting it and brushing her lips against his.

Cheney chanced a sip and swallowed, closing her eyes as a sign he had perfected her weird blend of morning java. She moved around the kitchen, peeping through the white shutters, fingering small potted plants, and scanning the room. He stood impatiently as she waited patiently to carve an opening into the quietness.

As usual, she represented morning glory. He was well aware of her wardrobe. After all, shopping was a family affair. He and Kami would pick out an outfit for Cheney; then they were off to shop for him. Parke swelled with pride at allowing his ladies to choose his clothes.

Kami was last, and always added a little something extra in her shopping spree—a toy. Parke didn't recall seeing much of anything red in their closet. Yet, red was striking against his wife's fair skin tone. She was beautiful in her red top, skirt, and red nail polish glistening on her narrow toes exposed by her open-toed shoes. He exhaled, twisting his mouth in reaction to his wife's allure.

Parke drained the remains of his cranberry juice and cleared his throat. "Baby—"

"Honey—" she interrupted as she whirled around from the sink.

They shared an uncomfortable laugh. With three steps and one arm's reach, he encircled Cheney's waist and drew her closer. He lingered a kiss then stepped back and held up his hand. "Let me go first."

She obliged with a smile. Her eyes danced with merriment as if she were saying, *It better be good, and I'd like to see you dig yourself out of this one.* Cheney nodded, waiting.

Sighing, Parke began. "Yesterday was important to you, which makes it a priority for me. You expected me there, and I expected to be right beside you like I always have and always will—"

Cheney rested a finger on his lips. "I love you, too, Parke." She frowned. "Now, cut to the chase on why you couldn't make it." She lifted her face in a challenge.

"Twinkie is trying to convince the judge to request a paternity test. I've lost my rights without having them. Twinkie plans to file a motion to set aside a judgment. She advised we need to be as perfect as God—her words, not mine—and we need to be a united front."

She nodded. "I agree, but how are we going to do this? I overheard Grandma BB's trial could last a week, two tops." She shrugged. "Daddy's case will probably start not long after that. His lawyer doubts the judge will grant another continuance. If I believed in luck, I would say three trials in one year is extremely bad luck."

Lord, now what? His wife wasn't getting it. "Cheney, this is our priority. God has made a way for us to have our son."

Quietly, Cheney strolled to the sink. She took two gulps of the hot brew that she could bear then poured the rest down the drain. Meticulously, she rinsed out her cup. Parke stood waiting, and before a minute was up, he got it.

"I understand that, but emotionally, I don't have the capacity for any more drama at this point. I tell you what; we'll support each other in thoughts and prayers, so you can deal with that end, and I'll do the same on my side."

"Cheney, after all we've been through, this is it—our chance to have a son without the fear of wondering if we're going to have another baby or if that baby will live. I believe God wants us to pursue this."

"Mom, I can't find my Indian bracelet Grandma BB bought me!" Kami screamed with desperation from upstairs.

"Girl, stop yelling," Cheney shouted to the ceiling. She shook her head. "That may be, but I don't believe it has precedence over what's already underway."

"Daddy!"

Parke jerked his head in the direction of the stairs. "Princess, don't start calling me. You know I can't find anything in this house . . . and stop yelling," he yelled then exhaled. "Now, back to us, Cheney." His nostrils flared as he twitched his mouth. "What exactly are you saying? I don't want to demand you choose sides, Mrs. Jamieson."

She backed up and jammed a fist on her side. "My dear husband, I'm going to the courthouse today, tomorrow, and as long as they're in session. I have to be there. I'm bringing work home, and I'll remain on call throughout the day. This is my family—blood and surrogate. You know the saying about tragedy bringing a family together. Well, I'm living it. I hope for the better."

"I believe they would understand we have a life too." He raised his voice then softened it. He sipped a few deep breaths before rubbing his chin. "This is Parke the Seventh that I'm talking about, baby."

She tilted her head, causing a looped earring to dangle. Her naturally arched brows knitted together. She was gearing up for a fight. "Hmm. I thought we buried Parke the Seventh less than a year ago," she said, referring to the name they had given their stillborn son.

"Yeah, well . . ." Parke grappled for the right answer before his determination surged.

Cheney leaned against the cabinet and drummed her nails against the counter. "You are not renaming my baby."

"At the time, we didn't know about this other boy. This is too much of a coincidence for Park Jamie not to be mine. From the woman I dated to the child's age and my butchered name . . . everything about this kid says, yes, he's mine. Finally, God spoke to me about Abraham and Sarah when she couldn't conceive. God made a way through a Hagar. Rachel is our Hagar-type figure. This is our ram in the bush," he said, citing a ram God had placed in a bush so that Abraham wouldn't have to offer the son God had promised him as a sacrifice.

Cheney was silent as she inhaled. Her face became flushed, and her eyes raced across his face, starting at his eyes, moving to his lips then nose and ears, and starting over again. As Christians, they didn't participate in a marriage with bouts of physical or verbal abuse, but Parke stepped back anyway, in case she was considering it.

Folding her arms, Cheney twisted her mouth. "I'm not feeling this whole handmaid story, Parke. God made Abraham a promise. Has He made you one?"

"What is that supposed to mean? God's given all of us promises. We're supposed to be on the same page with this."

"I'm on a different chapter. I had hoped you would be there for me." Her nostrils flared, daring him to deny it.

"Cheney, I have been there for you from the beginning."

"Oh, so now we're keeping score?" She balled her fists. "Okay, since God has spoken with you, He also had a message for me. God has put me right dab in the middle of this mess to bring my family together. We're going to have to compromise. Now, are you coming to the courthouse today? It's a yes-or-no answer."

"No." This was the most important thing to Parke outside of Cheney and Kami, but he wasn't budging. As she retreated up the back stairs to the bedrooms to check on their daughter, Parke stormed out of the kitchen to the front door. Evidently, they had different messages from God. *Lord, what now?*

Sunday morning, the Jamiesons sat in the same pew in church with the same people—Malcolm, Hallison, Kami, and her doll— yet they were mentally miles apart. Physically, there was too much space between them. Parke and Cheney enjoyed the oneness concept of coming to church—the one mind to hear from God. Cheney missed Parke's arm draped protectively around her shoulders.

As Christians, how could they actually walk into church together, hear the same message, and walk out still apart? *It all depends on the message,* the antagonist whispered. Opting for on the sermon for a resolution, Cheney tuned out the nagging voice.

"It's God's will for us at some point or time in our lives to bear one another's burdens," Pastor Scott of Faith Miracle Church, instructed. "In the sixth chapter of Galatians, let us not get twisted by the word *fault*, which means defect, imperfection, failure, mistake, error, and on and on. Who, besides God, can judge sins? So, don't deceive yourself trying. Other faults can weigh us down—indecisiveness, mourning, affliction. All those things can be burdens. What does the Lord say?" He repeated, "Bear each other's burdens. Let's hold each other up, saints . . . ."

As the pastor stressed the definition of *faults*, Cheney struggled not to see herself as one who wasn't compassionate. She
chanced a glance at her husband, who was already waiting for
her to look his way. She blinked and mouthed, "I'm sorry."

"You know I love you," he mouthed back.

Yes, she knew it, but where was his apology? Did a lack of
one mean he wasn't backing down from his earlier demand? She
hoped for some revelations in the sermon, but an hour later,
when Pastor Scott ended his preaching, Cheney had no answers
from God.

With one arm stretched toward the congregation, Pastor Scott
stepped down from the pulpit. "You know another way to get rid
of your burdens is to give them to Jesus. He challenges you to
cast your cares on Him. He can handle it. C'mon. It's so easy.
Repent where you are, which means more than to be sorry for
your sins. You have to have a change of mind if you're going to
walk down this aisle. If you're truly ready to be set free, we have
baptismal clothes for you to change into and be baptized in Jesus' name; then we have workers ready to pray with you, so that
God can fill you up, and He'll give you the evidence to prove it."

Cheney bowed her head and closed her eyes. She heard the
message, read the scriptures, and still was clueless about who was
going to carry whose burden. *Lord, can I get a footnote?*

CHAPTER 7

Josephine. Her face never faded from Rainey's mind. Wearing a sleek red outfit, Rainey groaned with a wild imagination before he sobered. Rainey hoped he wouldn't see that society of Santa's helpers again today, or whatever the silly little group called themselves. Rainey eyed her a second time. Somehow red was becoming his favorite color.

As visitors shifted in line toward the metal detector inside the courthouse, he rocked the opposite way to observe her: shoulders relaxed, head held high, and her legs and other body parts weren't bad looking either. He completed his assessment with five people between them.

Josephine was really pretty. No, Rainey corrected, his long ago girlfriend, Shanice, was pretty. Josephine had an added touch of something, and from a distance, Rainey couldn't tell what it was, but he was curious. The sudden, unwanted, one-sided attraction unsettled him. She didn't know he existed, and on the surface, he didn't want to know her. Yet, the sight of Josephine made him want to forget the past wrongs against him and move on emotionally in a relationship; but one thing kept holding him back—the trust issue. Plus, Josephine was part of Mrs. Beacon's brigade.

The entrance's security checkpoint was in sight. Rainey waited impatiently as an officer instructed Josephine to strip off her jewelry to clear the detector. Folding his arms, Rainey actually smiled. Josephine seemed flustered. If she removed one more item, including her teeth, then he would hand her his business card and suggest that she make an appointment. Another person requested Josephine's permission to rummage through her knapsack-size purse. The man dug into the bag as if it were a bottomless pit. For some reason, Rainey should have been irritated for the inconvenience she was causing. Instead, he was amused.

When it was his turn, Rainey placed his keys and cell phone in a plastic bowl then strolled through security without a hitch. Discreetly eying Josephine, he clipped his cell phone back on his belt as she repacked her purse. She walked past Rainey as if he were a vapor.

"Josephine," he called as she made it to the escalator.

Already ascending, she glanced over her shoulder and looked down. Josephine scanned faces for recognition. With no acknowledgement, she turned back and prepared to step off at the landing. Once Rainey reached the top, he hurried to catch up then slowed his steps to a casual pace.

"Josephine."

She stopped and whirled around to face him. "Do I know you?" she asked matter-of-factly.

I'm planning on it. Her words were proper and saucy. Her demeanor was carefree. Rainey strolled closer, observing her under the hood of his lashes. He dared to admit Josephine was prettier than his twin sister. Very few women held that distinction, but Josephine's beauty was like a slow cooker. The more he saw of her, the more in awe he became. Of course, he trapped any compliments in his head.

"No, we've never met. I'm Rainey Reynolds." He offered his hand.

Lifting her chin, her eyes sparkled as she accepted it. "Ah. Correction, you're Dr. Rainey Reynolds, Cheney's twin and the only son of murder suspect, Dr. Roland Reynolds, who happens to be testifying against Grandmother B."

Rainey gritted his teeth. "Now, wait a minute. You can stop right there," he snarled. Initially, he was impressed with her knowledge, until the end.

"As you wish." Nodding, Josephine proceeded to the elevator.

Her nonchalant attitude irked him. The woman blew him off, flattered him, then called his father a criminal in one sentence.

"Hey!" He caught up with her. "How do you know so much about me? I don't know who you are beyond your first name."

She ignored him as she entered the packed elevator. Rainey followed. The squeeze was tight, but he managed to face her. Josephine was unable to move since he towered over her. She made a great effort to ignore him, but Rainey wasn't having it.

"By the way, you have the most beautiful skin." She didn't answer, but her cheeks rose in a strained blush. Rainey was taking pleasure in their brief close encounter. When the doors opened to the third floor, she stepped off. He trailed, assured they were headed to the same destination.

Unexpectedly, Josephine whirled around as if she were on a runway. Her murderous, thundering stare was a seduction. Angry never looked so good.

"My birth name is Abena Yaa Amoah."

Lifting his brow, Rainey held his breath, waiting for her to explain how that stood for or spelled *Josephine*, forward or backward. She disappointed him.

"Anyway, my roommate has given me a character sketch of all parties guilty by association. Of course, she's not holding anything against Cheney; just her father."

"Of course," Rainey mumbled. His nostrils flared as the woman continued to insult him with little regard. She had perfected the art of deflating a brother's ego. He swallowed hard to keep from snapping. "You actually live in the same house with that Mrs. Beacon?" Rainey asked incredulously, shaking his head. He was disgusted with himself for his attraction. She was way too opinionated for him.

"Yes, technically, she's my host family while I'm an exchange student. When I finish, I will return to my home country of Ghana." She paused. "I'm sorry, Dr. Reynolds, but I need to end this meeting. It appears the ladies are already lining up to go inside." She tilted her head. "May God be with your family during this trying time."

Turning, Josephine sauntered away, leaving Rainey's eyes to roam over her retreating figure. She disturbed his hormones while sidetracking his reason for being there. Plus, he would've enjoyed the view if it weren't for the arrogance that spilled from her mouth. As far as he was concerned, God didn't have a good track record intervening in crucial situations—not with Shanice, his father, or his sister. In all cases, no life had been spared. Now, he definitely wasn't putting faith in God on this one either.

Irritation replaced his attraction. Leaning against the wall, Rainey alternated between worrying his mustache and folding his arms. Besides him and Josephine in the lobby outside the courtroom, a handful of people milled around. He felt as if he were a boxer banned to his corner, waiting for the bell before returning to the ring. Presently, Josephine appeared to be his opponent, ready to throw more verbal insults against his family's character.

Across the lobby, Josephine was leisurely pacing as she talked on her cell phone, laughing. Rainey knew it was petty, but he wouldn't allow Josephine to ignore him. He was about to engage in more sparring when a bell rang, but not for another round. It signaled the arrival of one elevator car, followed by another.

Mrs. Beacon spilled out in another red outfit. Her choice

of accessories included large, dark sunglasses trimmed in a red frame. She didn't acknowledge him as she shuffled to Judge Kendall's courtroom. Her cluster of parasites brought up the rear. Once again, they were in red, including red hats, with the addition of dark glasses.

The clones made Rainey snicker. There was nothing sexy about these women in red. "Thank God cloning was limited to animals."

A third elevator dumped another group of Mrs. Beacon's copycats. Rainey lamented when another elevator car arrived. He expected to see more of Santa's elves. Instead, his family stepped out with determination stretched across their faces. They were dressed in black, except for Cheney, who chose brown as her choice of clothing. She had made a good choice.

Before the week was over, Parke's attorney was able to get a family court judge to at least hear his petition for the following Monday. That was more than the other attorneys had achieved. Twinkie gave him hope that Judge Davis in the family court division would understand his plight. It seemed as if nothing could damper Parke's good mood. Once the paternity had been verified, the judge should begin the legal process to return his son, and everything would be fine.

One Sunday, Parke and his family had returned home after church. The message had been stirring about people praying on one accord, then God making things happen, taken from Acts 2. Still, it seemed as if Cheney and Parke struggled with the message to penetrate their spirits. The trio prepared dinner together, allowing Kami to create her banana pudding masterpiece that had more wafers than pudding. They performed the task as if everything were okay between them. Later, they painstakingly helped Kami complete a three hundred piece puzzle.

Later that night, behind closed, locked doors of their bedroom, they allowed their disagreements to fade as their love resurfaced. "Baby, I don't want this to separate us," Parke said, brushing a kiss against Cheney's ear as she snuggled close to him.

Cheney sighed and looked up. She massaged his clean-shaved jaw, thinking before she responded. "It won't. God has already spoken to us, remember?"

Parke relaxed, relieved. There was nothing more to say. Hopefully, they were finally on the same page, unified and on one accord. He reached to turn off the lamp on their nightstand, mumbling, "Thank you, Lord Jesus," before he drifted to sleep.

Monday morning, they woke almost simultaneously; they kissed and slid to the floor to say their morning prayers. Afterward, he showered while Cheney woke Kami. When she showered, he dressed and started a breakfast of frozen waffles, turkey sausage, and instant oatmeal for Kami.

Cheney came down the back stairs, smelling good, looking pretty, and dressed in red again. He made note of her new color scheme. Kami appeared minutes later, also dressed in a red outfit. Parke praised the Lord he and Cheney had come to an understanding. Once seated around the table, they chuckled as their daughter entertained them.

"Can I have a puppy? God said it was okay," Kami asked Cheney, but she looked at Parke with an expectant smile.

Parke and Cheney attempted to restrain their amusement, but Parke failed. "Yeah, Mommy, didn't you get the memo?" he baited her.

Cheney's look issued a silent threat for payback for setting her up. "No, it was in shorthand."

Kami shook her head, perplexed. "I don't know how to read shorthand."

"Me either, baby." Cheney scrunched her nose at her husband.

When they were finished, Parke offered to load the dishwasher as Kami raced upstairs to get her backpack. Cheney grabbed her keys and strained her voice not to yell for Kami to hurry. It was ineffective. Cheney talked in a loud pitch.

Parke frowned. "Babe, we don't have to drive two cars. I can drop you back at work. I don't think the hearing will last long."

"I'm going to court first; then I'll head to work."

"Didn't we resolve this last night in bed?" His nostrils flared with irritation. Were they back to square one on opposing sides? He slapped his palm against the counter. "Cheney, I thought we were united on this. Look, woman, don't let me have to pull rank on this. I need you with me!" Parke gritted his teeth then bit his lip to keep him from saying more.

Glancing at her watch, Cheney slowly sat on a barstool and leaned forward. "Dear," she whispered sweetly, "you never have to threaten me. All you have to do is ask." She smiled and wrinkled her nose.

Relieved, Parke snickered. He loved that woman. "Okay, sweetheart. I'm sorry. Will you accompany me to court?"

She stood when Kami ran into the room, screaming, "C'mon, Mommy. My teacher plays games before the bell rings."

"All right, young lady." Cheney turned back to Parke. "I'll try to get there, but remember, if I'm not there in body, I'm present in love and spirit."

That wasn't the response he was expecting. Before Parke's temper flared, Kami and Cheney barreled into him with kisses and hugs then left. *Don't play with me, woman,* he wanted to scold. Instead, he rinsed out his mug, swiped his keys off the wall hook, and left.

An hour later, Parke was downtown in the St. Louis Municipal Court building. Apparently, his case was not the only one to be heard. There were pockets of people with their attorneys.

"All rise," the young bailiff ordered as a petite woman entered the courtroom and took her place.

Judge Davis's glossy silver hair was a contrast to her youthful face and the beginning of a warm smile that never quite made it.

Two cases were called before his. Parke was encouraged by the swiftness of the judge's decisions in them. She didn't appear to be swayed by the frills, but concerned with the facts. It boosted his confidence.

Finally, after scanning another file in front of her, the judge looked up and called his name. "Counselor are you presenting Mr. Jamieson?"

Twinkie nodded. Physically, she stood five feet, maybe, in her stilettos; Twinkie's mircobraids were long, but trimmed. Dressed in a black pantsuit, she looked more like Parke's adolescent daughter than a magna cum laude graduate from St. Louis University School of Law. "I am, Your Honor, and I'm petitioning the court for custody of a child who was erroneously adopted. We would like to request a paternity test to prove my client is the biological father."

"The fifteen-day limitation has expired," the judge stated as if she had memorized a handout. "Surely, you are aware of that."

"Yes, Your Honor," Twinkie responded, clicking her heels as if she were Dorothy from the *Wizard of Oz*, or answering to a drill sergeant.

"Are you aware that the adoption was finalized last month? Six months after he was placed in foster care with that family? Your parental rights were terminated." She turned to Parke and squinted. "Mr. Jamieson, is there a reason why, after five years, you want to be a father? Why should I order a paternity test? If you're not the biological father, then what? Will you demand paternity tests until you find the right child? That's ridiculous.

What's this all about?" Leaning back in a leather chair designed for comfort, she folded her arms.

"Rachel Lopez and I had a short fling . . ." Parke summarized their relationship in less than five hundred words, finishing with the shock of her death and the possibility of his son, Park Jamie. "So," he said, clutching his fist in his other hand as if he had caught a foul ball, "Your Honor, I'm standing before you as a possible wronged party and a deprived father. I'm sure you know that about one out of every three children live in a home without his or her natural father. I don't want that statistic to fall on my son."

Twinkie cleared her throat and shoved him. "Parke, stay focused," she hushed.

"Mr. Jamieson, your rights have already been terminated," Judge Davis reminded him.

Parke would never accept that. "Your Honor, I believe I can prove Park Jamie is my son through a paternity test. His rightful name should be Parke Kokumuo Jamieson the Seventh or the Eighth, depending on—anyway, the namesake spans ten generations."

Judge Davis unfolded her arms, counted a few times on her fingers then leaned forward. "Math wasn't my strong subject, so explain."

Parke's lips stretched into a lazy grin, ready to defend his heritage. "My tenth great-grandfather, Paki Kokumuo Jaja, was born in December 1770 in Côte d'Ivoire, on the Gold Coast of Africa. His name means 'a witness that this one will not die.' Paki was part of the Diomande Tribe.

"In the fall of 1790, he and his warriors were attacked by slave traders. They were severely beaten, kidnapped, and chained. He was among hundreds of thousands who were hauled to the Gate of No Return castle. As they waited, many captives prayed they would die, including my tenth great-grandfather, but thank God, he survived. They were unmercifully stacked together in the bowels of a ship. It wasn't the ironic *Good Ship Jesus* under the command of Sir John Hawkins, but the mighty *Snow Elijah* ship. The biblical reference is uncanny, isn't it?" He paused. "The Black World History Wax Museum in North St. Louis city has an unbelievable replica.

"Anyway, Paki's slave ship landed in Maryland, a state known for harsh slave laws. Because of his statute and strength, he was sold at the highest price of two hundred and seventy-five dollars to wealthy slave owner Jethro Turner. That purchase gave Turner exactly one hundred and thirteen slaves.

"My great-great-great—you know what I mean—was isolated from the other slaves because he refused to submit to orders. After all, he was a prince, and others did his bidding. The consequences for his disobedience were lashings, his clothes were taken away, or he was tied up for days without food.

"As time passed, the slave owner's seventeen-year-old daughter, Elaine, noted Paki's dignity was never compromised, and eventually she became his self-appointed protector. He was the best looking of all the slaves." Parke grinned. "I added that last part, but seriously, one afternoon, she witnessed him being tied to a tree and beat with cowhide. She ordered him down. After dark, she applied salve to his wounds. Later, Elaine snuck Paki clothes and food."

The judge didn't interrupt. She seemed genuinely engaged. Even the court clerk listened intently, but her fingers never stopped transcribing.

"Escaping and taking Elaine with him, he became a fugitive of the state and a dead man if he was caught." Parke pulled out a business-size laminated card from his wallet. I actually have a copy of the ad from the *Baltimore Star*. The caption read: FOUR

HUNDRED AND FIFTY DOLLAR REWARD. 'Ran away from subscriber. Negro man kidnapped only daughter, Elaine Turner. The said Negro is nearly black, between twenty and twenty-five years old, very good-looking, and tall, over six feet, and muscular. I hereby forewarn all persons not to harbor or employ the said man or woman at the peril of the law. Reward is for his capture, in the state or out, dead or alive. I want my daughter alive.' "

The clerk's eyes watered, but she didn't stop typing.

"Thank God they were never captured, especially since the journey was extremely hard on women. I guess you can call their relationship an uncommon-law marriage.

"Later, in a journal, Elaine wrote that Paki sobbed uncontrollably as he looked down at his firstborn son's bright yellow face. He lifted the child to his god, mumbling a native blessing: *Dankie, kind aansoek doen*—thank you, the child I had hoped." He paused and stood taller.

"They named him Parker Kokumuo Jamieson and every firstborn male each generation thereafter. Elaine and Paki had four more sons. Then, in 1867, a few years after slavery was abolished, the third generation Parker altered the name. He removed the last *R* to symbolize the first son who was removed from slavery." Parke would have continued if Twinkie hadn't kicked him.

Folding her hands, Judge Davis digested Parke's monologue. "I'm impressed, Mr. Jamieson, and I commend you on your family history. Are you married?"

"Happily," he answered swiftly, grinning. *Cheney, where are you?*

"Where is she?" Judge Davis glanced around the courtroom.

"Ah . . ." He took a deep breath, choking on air. He squinted as if he didn't understand. "Pardon me?"

"Your wife—you know, the love of your life, the little lady of the house, the—"

He grunted. "Cheney's not little. She's six feet and beautiful."

Growing impatient, the judge cleared her throat, tapping her pen on the folder. Twinkie nudged him.

"She's in court."

Judge Davis jotted some notes. "Don't tell me she's trying to adopt a daughter."

Parke shook his head. "Oh, no, we've already adopted a daughter two years ago."

"Why is she in court then, Mr. Jamieson?" When he stalled, the judge's impatience was visible in the scowl on her face. "Mr. Jamieson, you are under oath."

Nodding, Parke swallowed and said a quick prayer. "Well, Your Honor, her surrogate grandmother is on trial for shooting Cheney's father, who killed her surrogate grandmother's husband."

"Does insanity run in your genes?" The judge's expression indicated she was serious. "Your name wasn't listed on the child's birth certificate. It doesn't appear you signed a putative registry. There's no reason to believe you're the biological father."

CHAPTER 8

"What do you mean you have to register to have sex?" Ellington asked, hyperventilating at the thought. "Parke, please tell me you made that up," he stuttered. Laying his beer can on the floor, Ellington sat forward in his recliner.

The notion did seem ridiculous. If Parke didn't know Rachel was pregnant, then there wasn't a reason to register as the biological father of a mythical child. Parke couldn't believe there was a law on the state's books that encouraged men to sign up for the Putative Father Registry.

Parke laughed at the fear etched on his friend's face as he and Malcolm lounged in Ellington's game room, which was a combined living and dining room in his three-bedroom house. Ellington had purchased the property listed on Clemens Avenue when the block was undergoing a city neighborhood transition.

The two-story house was sparsely furnished except for the game room, which was stocked with every electronic gadget ever advertised on TV. The trio established the routine on biweekly Thursday nights when Cheney, Kami, and Hallison scheduled their hair appointments.

Ellington's bare essentials throughout the other rooms didn't equate tidiness. Unless friends requested a visit at least a week in advance, Ellington's house resembled the remnants of a frat party. Incredulously, his home office was immaculate. He could retrieve a file in five minutes or less, compared to forty-five minutes to locate the match to a sock.

Malcolm clicked off the TV in the middle of an argument between the commentators of ESPN's *Pardon the Interruption*. "What?" He frowned as if he hadn't heard right.

"Twinkie never mentioned it, or if she did, I didn't pay attention," Parke said, reclining in one of four black suede theater chairs and fingering his mustache. "I think it was created to protect the father and the child in case of an adoption. Can you imagine after every sexual tryst with a woman who we aren't married to, we run down to the county's vital record department and fill out a form in case a child is produced? That's too much like signing up for a lottery you don't want to win, but in my case, it might have helped."

Deep in thought, the three engaged in a moment of silence. The only sound was a soft snore from Penelope, Ellington's German shepherd mixed with mutt. Ellington stroked the sleeping dog's head absentmindedly. Finally, Ellington sighed and reached for his can of Budweiser. "That's messed up," he said before downing his beer.

Although Parke and Malcolm's visits were under the guise of get-togethers, when the Holy Spirit moved, Parke witnessed to Ellington about a lifestyle change. Ellington was a good man on the inside, but who can know the heart of men? So, God told Parke to be a light among men, which was more than a notion during Parke's present situation that was testing his own faith.

At thirty-five, Ellington's trademark dress code was a sleeveless T-shirt, slacks, and no socks. The T-shirt was purely for vanity purposes: to showcase his solid biceps and red-and-black racing car tattoo. Six-two and two hundred pounds, his self-professed stumbling blocks were women and drinking.

"That characterizes us as male prostitutes. The woman might as well have a clipboard to sign in before climbing into her bed." Ellington suddenly whipped out a BlackBerry from the back pocket of his jeans, which appeared to have more holes than material.

"What are you doing?" Parke lifted his bowed head and squinted.

"Good thing I've kept track of my women. Maybe I'll make some follow-up calls to see how my former ladies are doing and to make sure there are no little EJs crawling around."

"Eliminate the worry and fill out the form. You do need to have the woman or the potential mother's social security number. Good luck with that," Parke advised.

Malcolm flexed his muscles then folded them behind his head while rocking in his seat. "Whew! I guess it's a good thing I believed in monogamous relationships instead of one-nighters; although I had some close calls. After Hali and I broke up, I went on a mission to conquer. As the saying goes, I praise God for saving me before I could do any damage."

"Well, it's that B.C. slip-up that could turn out to be my blessing. The next generation of Parke Jamieson is within my reach."

"B.C.?" Ellington asked.

"Yeah, stuff I did *before* Christ." Parke shook his head.

Ellington grunted. "Whatever." With his beer can in his hand, he pointed. "See, that's where I have a problem with your religion. This whole wipe-the-slate-clean stuff after you commit to Christ is too simplistic. C'mon. Salvation isn't that easy."

"Actually, it is," Malcolm jumped in. "We're the ones who make it difficult." He thumped his chest. "And I know what I'm talking about. Ask Hali. The more I fought against Jesus, the more battle scars I reluctantly earned. You might as well say, 'Yes, Lord' right now. Save yourself some drama."

Ellington placed his beer on the floor next to Penelope. Lifting her head, the dog sniffed the top before she went back to sleep. Ellington sliced his hand through the air as he shook his head. "Hold up. I'm not in the mood for any prayer or preaching. Not tonight, my brothas."

Parke and Malcolm exchanged looks. They nodded their understanding. Parke never pushed Ellington.

"Okay, Parke, back to your sex registry thing. I know Twinkie's going to challenge that, isn't she?"

"Rachel didn't make it easy. She didn't put my name on the boy's birth certificate. Plus, if I had known—key words *had known*—I would've had fifteen days after my son—because I believe he is mine—was born to claim parental rights. If I had only . . . If I'd only known about the possibility." He paused to reflect on the different scenarios. "God told me He's got my back, but I keep glancing over my shoulder for confirmation."

"See, that's what I mean—"

Parke held up his hand. "Now, don't you start, man." Parke had to keep reminding himself he couldn't speak freely in front of his friend about the Lord because Ellington was looking for a loophole. "Like I was saying, Rach and I had been a couple for less than two months when I stopped feeling us." Parke thumped his chest near his heart for emphasis. "Our relationship was going nowhere. I called it quits. Rach wasn't happy about the breakup, as it was with many of my past flings, but hey, she agreed that if I didn't want to commit, then I should go. I went."

It seemed like a fair arrangement at the time to Parke. Years later, he was shocked to learn she had a child. The insult was Rachel had given the boy a butchered version of Parke's name.

Ellington rubbed his chin. "I would say it's not worth sleeping with a woman, but it's always worth it." He grinned.

"Down, coyote," Parke taunted. "I need a little help. If only I can get a phone number, address of the adoptive parents . . ."

"The adoption records are sealed. It was like pulling toenails trying to get the names of the adoptive parents." Ellington paused, shrugging. "All I know is Gilbert, and his last name is Ann. Sounds like his parents were confused, or cross-dressers."

Leaning over, Parke bumped fists with Ellington. "You are the man, besides the one upstairs. I knew I could count on you. Nothing slips under your radar."

The air chilled. Even Penelope ceased snoring. They tried to avoid the subject, but a case did slip under Ellington's radar, the most important one of his life—his twin brother. Louis Brown had been missing for years. Despite Ellington's high-tech skills, he hadn't come close to finding Louis.

Parke exhaled slowly. "Do whatever you can to track them down." Parke glanced at his watch. "My ladies should be about dolled up by now. I'd better head home."

Malcolm nodded and added a mischievous wink. He hadn't been home since work. He was the only one still dressed for the office in dark slacks, a starched shirt minus a tie, Sunday dress shoes, and silk socks. "Yeah, it's TLC night, and Hali's probably waiting for me."

"What?" Ellington evidently took the bait to change the subject.

"Thursdays are reserved for pampering in the bedroom, kitchen, or living room. A designated place is not a requirement. We've christened every room in our condo."

A loud noise caused Penelope to bark twice, but she didn't move to investigate. Malcolm jerked his head in the direction outside the front door. Parke leaned forward. "What was that?"

Ellington tilted his head, straining to listen. Suspicion caused his nostrils to flare. "You heard that too?" Standing, Ellington stomped to the window, angled his body as if he were on a covert mission, and peeked through a slit in the curtains. Without an explanation, he dashed to his office, almost tripping over a bowl of untouched cheddar popcorn.

"Where are you going? What's wrong?" Parke asked. He and Malcolm stood, alarmed.

"Somebody's trying to steal my truck. I'm going to get my gun," Ellington yelled from another room.

"Wait a minute before we get in a gun battle. Let's head outside first. Maybe we'll scare them off," Parke advised his friend. "It's probably a bunch of kids, testing their burglary skills."

Malcolm frowned. "The more reason I say call nine-one-one. I'm not putting my life on the line over your custom, fully loaded F-150 truck. I'm a newlywed, and if it's God's will, I've already mapped out a long, enjoyable life with my wife."

Parke shoved his brother. "C'mon. Let's see what's up. Be a man, not a hubby."

"Humph. The other option is much more rewarding," Malcolm retorted.

Ellington raced out of his home office with a gun stuffed in his waistband. The brothers followed. The driver of a monster-size tow truck had finished strapping the wheels to drag it off private property.

"Hey! Hey! What are you doing? Get away from my truck!" Ellington shouted, but the person kept working.

Parke's jaw dropped as he back-slapped Ellington across the chest. "Man, are you having money problems? You could've asked me."

"Shut up, Parke." Ellington marched down the steps to his truck. "Listen, man, I think you—" He halted when he noticed bright red lipstick. "The repo man is a drag queen? Great. Why use a gun when my fists will do?" he mumbled as he balled his hands.

The repo man held the clipboard away from his jacket. "Do I look like a man to you?" the woman snapped in a lethal tone that would've been sexy under different circumstances.

Ellington was blindsided. "You look like a thief," he argued, not deterred.

"If you paid your bill, I wouldn't have to come like a thief in the night. Back off. I'm just doing my job. You can settle your bill—"

"Imani?" Parke asked, surprised he recognized the sass behind her voice. It had been a while since he had seen Cheney's best friend, who was also Mrs. Beacon's neighbor.

She squinted over Ellington's shoulder and squealed, "Parke." Smiling, Imani sidestepped Ellington. "Excuse me." She hugged Parke. "Looking fine as ever, bro. How are my girls, Cheney and Kami?"

"They're good." Parke grinned then squinted. His eyes darted from the tow truck to her face. "What are you doing here?"

"You hang out with this guy?" Imani ignored his question as she slanted her head and popped her gum.

"Yeah, I do. We go back to our college days, but what are you doing here?" Parke couldn't connect any dots. So far, his one friend had a loaded gun. His wife's best friend had a tow truck with the motor running, he presumed, for a quick getaway. And Parke was waiting for answers.

Glancing over his shoulder, Parke shook his head. His brother wasn't kidding about not getting tangled up in any mischief. Unless Malcolm, Hallison, or the Jamiesons were in imminent danger, Malcolm wasn't going to bruise a knuckle. He would weigh his options for a best friend of anyone else. Keeping his distance, Malcolm sat on the steps and talked on his cell phone, probably to Hallison. Parke waved him over.

Parke turned back to Imani. "Wait a minute. You can't be . . . you're a repo woman?"

"Nope. I'm an auto recovery specialist." Imani beamed, showing all her feminine charm disguised under a worn baseball cap and an oversized denim jacket.

Throwing his arms up, Ellington mumbled something as he stalked to the driveway to inspect his truck. Imani ignored him as she continued. "I had to get out of the friendly skies. The airlines started layoffs, and I had to maintain my own lavish lifestyle, so I changed careers for a steady income." She leaned closer and whispered, "Not to mention my increased fear of flying. I guess the job was starting to get to me.

"It's my first hit tonight, and just my luck, I broke a fingernail because the stupid remote control to lift my hook on the tow truck wouldn't work. It took me longer than the estimated five minutes, or you guys never would've caught me." Imani winked. "You wouldn't believe how many cars I had to chase tonight already. I finally got one."

Parke smothered his amusement. A repo woman with legs; he had to smirk. Of course, they were hidden under her loose-fitting jeans, but if Ellington caught one look at her shapely curves, he might consider trading his worldly possessions, except for the truck, for one hour with Imani Seagall.

"Whatever he owes, I'll cover it." Parke reached for his wallet.

"No, you won't, because I don't owe a cent. You're not taking this—" Ellington gritted his teeth, storming back to Imani and pointing to his partially hoisted vehicle "—unless it's over my dead body." He barely contained his anger.

"Umm-hmm. Parke, call an ambulance in case he's still breathing. Otherwise, the medical examiner should be notified." Imani lifted the clipboard, removed her work gloves, and double checked her order. "This is fifty-nine thirteen Clemens, right?"

"Yeah," Ellington bit off.

"You're Dale Cochran, right?"

Ellington stood straighter and folded his arms. "Right address, wrong client, baby. He's two doors down with a GMC Sierra 1500—same color." He twisted his lips as his nostrils flared, expecting an apology.

Imani peered at her board and tapped her long nail on a line. "Oh, I guess I've got my numbers transposed." Without even a slight hint of embarrassment, she shrugged. "I'll release your vehicle. Next time, use brighter lights on your house. There could've been an emergency and no one would've found you." Turning around, Imani strolled to her wrecker.

The sway of her hips had Ellington salivating. As if knowing her effect, Imani whirled around. "Have a good night, gentlemen. Oh, and Parke, tell Cheney I'll holla at her later."

Malcolm cruised up behind them. Releasing a contagious hoot, Malcolm made his presence known. Parke followed as laughter rumbled from his stomach and spilled out of his mouth. Ellington huffed then gritted his teeth.

Imani wasn't through with her antics. "Hey, Dale's neighbor, you need to wash your truck. I've got a smudge on my designer boots."

Ellington growled like a mad dog, ready to attack. Fuming, he retreated into his house and slammed the door. The Jamieson brothers traded looks.

"You think he's upset?" Malcolm teased, stroking his beard.

"Maybe a little." Parke laughed. Despite the night chill, Parke and Malcolm remained rooted in their spots and watched Imani creep a few doors away and work her magic at the correct address. This time, she wasn't interrupted.

Hoping Ellington had calmed his temper, the brothers meandered back toward his home, still chuckling. When the knob wouldn't turn, Parke touched the doorbell. Cracking the door, Ellington silently communicated he wasn't in the mood for jokes. Parke and Malcolm bowed their heads, smothering their laughter as they entered behind him.

"I do not like that woman," Ellington practically growled, stepping over his useless dog that hadn't moved from her earlier spot. Ellington had admitted the mutt wasn't a compatible pet for investigating any ruckus. She would bark to alert her owner of pending danger then leave the rest up to Ellington.

Parke fought for composure, twisting his lips to keep a straight face. Crossing his arms, he snuck a look at Malcolm, who refused to make eye contact. "That's too bad, E, because Imani is Cheney's friend who she wanted you to meet."

"Humph. Forget it. Not only would I not sign a sex registry to get in her bed, but if she was hitchhiking on a dark road, I'd pick up speed. Plus, you know I prefer sistas, and she ain't one."

"If only you had seen her legs. You might've handed over your keys; and I know you're a leg man, so don't deny it. Didn't you think she was fine?" Parke asked incredulously.

"Not interested."

Parke and Malcolm shook their heads. "Fool," they said in unison.

Later that night at home, as customary, Parke and Cheney prayed together before getting in bed. Minutes earlier, Parke rehashed the scene at Ellington's house. Cheney couldn't control her giggles. He warned her they could wake Kami, and Cheney sobered before starting up again.

"Baby?" He kissed the top of Cheney's hair. The unrecognizable scent permeated his senses. Her soft feet caressed his ankles.

"Yes?" She snuggled closer.

"I guess you couldn't get away from Mrs. Beacon's trial today," he stated. "I needed backup in the courtroom this morning. That judge was a pit bull with lipstick." He sighed. "You do believe God is in this, don't you? I mean, we do agree that this is God's will." Parke lifted his head to look at his wife. He needed to make sure Cheney was coherent. "He has made a way for us to have our Parke the Seventh."

Whatever drowsy state Cheney had been under, she was fully alert now. Her eyes popped open at the same time her foot froze. Meeting his face, she squinted. "The Seventh? Parke, we buried him six months ago."

"Yeah, but technically, the boy I'm trying to get custody of, who no doubt is mine, would be my firstborn son. By birthright, he is entitled to that name."

She lifted her brow and calmly took a deep breath before scooting up in bed. "So, what do you suppose we do? Change the name on Parke the Seventh's death certificate?" She paused. "Say the right answer, Parke." Her words were soft, but her threat unwavering.

He glanced away. *Lord? This is one of those times when I need a hint.*

Resting on her elbow, Cheney reached out to finger-comb Parke's curly hair then guided his attention to her. "You're a creative soul, Parke. For ten generations, there has been some form of derivation in Paki's descendant's names. Your third generation great-grandfather started a new tradition by removing the *R* from Parker. I'll admit, I haven't given this much thought, but how about removing the *E* and *K* and adding a *C* for Parc? See, problem solved." She smacked a kiss on his cheek. "Good night." Yawning, she scooted next to Parke and fell asleep.

CHAPTER 9

Cheney had to skip court. She could no longer put off the work on her desk that needed her approval. She had just completed a conference call with other departmental managers when her mind drifted. She fought to focus, but she could only dwell on her ongoing family drama.

She constantly prayed that Parke would know in his heart that she was behind him more than one hundred percent. She would love his son as if she had birthed him, but in her state of mind, she couldn't deal with any more "baby" drama at the moment. She had too much craziness in her life. Cheney wanted to reach out and be there for Parke, but she couldn't take another devastating loss if it wasn't his son. Parke was stronger than she, because silently, Cheney was still mourning the loss of their baby—the one they had created together.

She gave herself a pep talk. "Enough! It's time for intermission from the pity party." Cheney reached for a stack of technicians' job orders as her phone rang. "Missouri Telephone Property Management. This is Cheney."

"Mrs. Jamieson, this is the Mothership Jamieson," Parke's mother greeted in her usual singsong voice, a sound that would cheer up the most despondent person.

Charlotte Jamieson stood on the sidelines when it came to interfering in the lives of her two sons and daughters-in-law; however, at certain times, Mrs. Jamieson teetered on a thread-thin line. Warm, genuine, and saturated with a sweet disposition, Cheney was convinced Mrs. Jamieson would be a perfect candidate to represent God's salvation. The woman seemed to love everybody.

When Cheney and Hallison broached the subject of salvation, Mrs. Jamieson's response was always the same: "I'm coming to the Lord, but I'm waiting on your father-in-law."

"The Bible tells us to save ourselves, Momma J," was always Cheney's standard reply.

Although Cheney couldn't afford the interruption, she welcomed the phone call. "How's my favorite mother-in-law?"

"I'll ask the questions," Mrs. Jamieson fussed good-naturedly. Both chuckled. "Now, down to business. Rumor has it that you're irritable and not that much fun."

"Kami." Cheney doodled her daughter's name on a notepad.

"Yep. She's our go-between for you and my son."

"She's a snitch." Shaking her head, Cheney snickered.

"Umm-hmm. She makes the best kind, but seriously, baby, I know that life hasn't been fair to you, but don't stop living one part of your life when another part is in turmoil. A person doesn't stop walking when one leg is broke. Your life consists of more than this senseless trial," Mrs. Jamieson sweetly scolded. "You need some girl time, and that's why I'm calling. Tomorrow, lunch is on me. Hali suggested Freddie's on Natural Bridge in the city, since it's midway between downtown and North County, and she's taking an extended lunch so she won't have to rush back."

When her mother-in-law laid down the rule to smother her family with love, standing her up was not an option. Cheney bowed to Mrs. Jamieson's edict, licking her lips at the imaginary taste of Freddie's wings. "I won't be late," she said and disconnected.

With renewed concentration, Cheney tackled her work pile—pending orders, vacation requests, and employee squabbles—in record time. "Take that!" She pushed back from her desk and stretched her arms over her head. She had put a dent in her paperwork, which left the remainder manageable. Her big bosses, who were flying in from Dallas, were sure to give her a glowing bi-yearly evaluation. She would prove to them nothing had been neglected despite her recent excused absences.

She was a card-carrying MBA graduate from Duke University's Global Executive program. After working four years at SAS, an impressive world leader in business analyst software and services based in North Carolina, she returned home to St. Louis. She accepted the management position at Missouri Telephone with the possibility of an advancement based on job performance. To ensure the level of competiveness, the phone company had enrolled her in property and facility management classes.

Without question, Cheney was certified to fully maintain her four office buildings and prove to the eight men she supervised that she was more than an affirmative action, strikingly beautiful—her husband's words—quota. Despite the havoc in her life, business-wise, she was still on top of her game.

The following day at noon, the three Mrs. Jamiesons strolled into Freddie's Fish and Chicken restaurant. The Jamiesons not only supported black-owned businesses, but were a grapevine for spreading the word about mouth-watering Southern cooking. A Christian brother owned it, and Fred spared no expenses on his menu to entice suburbanites to drive into the city for his soul food.

Cheney considered her mother-in-law's words of wisdom and concluded Mrs. Jamieson was right. Life didn't stand still during

a crisis. Cheney reminded herself of that for the second consecu-
tive day when she didn't go to the courthouse.

The restaurant's eating area was small, but customer service
made up for what the size lacked. The lobby was teeming with
customers placing takeout orders. Her mother-in-law never had a
bad thing to say about the catfish, and Hallison recently changed
her preference from jumbo shrimp to the wings, waffles, and
eggs. After telling the worker what they wanted, they chose one
of the red parlor-style tables.

Once they were comfortable, Mrs. Jamieson rested a delicate
hand on top of Cheney's. A petite woman with reddish-brown
skin the color of Oklahoma dirt, Mrs. Jamieson possessed bursts
of youthful energy. She passed on her thick, wavy hair and brown
eyes to her sons. Otherwise, Parke Jamieson V's trademark was
stamped on each of them: height, looks, and stubbornness.

"I know the trial must be hard for you."

"It is." Cheney nodded. "Grandma BB acts as if she doesn't
have a care in the world. I really believe she thinks she is invin-
cible. I can tell Daddy is uncomfortable facing Grandma BB as
the accuser and testifying against her."

While Hallison rummaged through her purse, Cheney observed their mother-in-law. Cheney was always in awe whenever
she was in the presence of the family matriarch. There were so
many other things for them to talk about besides her family
drama.

Charlotte and the elder Parke had been married for more
than thirty-five years. Cheney considered her father-in-law the
genealogist extraordinaire, but he hadn't been able to connect as
many dots on his wife's family tree to the shores of Africa. Since
only a man's DNA could be used to pinpoint her ancestor's tribe
or homeland, she asked her oldest brother to submit a sample,
and he consented. "It's a matter of time before these diehard

Jamieson sleuths break the code," she always stated with a laugh and twinkle in her eyes whenever she hit a limestone-and-brick wall.

Mrs. Jamieson had three great-great-uncles who were fathered by different men: slaveholder, slave overseer, and a male slave companion who was sold away. Charlotte's great-great grand-mother, Priscilla Ned, had been a young woman sold twice as a slave before she died free as a house servant. Somehow, the brothers, Armstead Jackson, Henry Wade, and Mandy Wright, found each other through the papers filed at the Freedmen's Bureau in 1870. By the 1880 census, the siblings were living in the same household.

As Cheney got to know and later fell in love with Parke, he explained how slavery was an inhumane period in world his-tory—not only in the Americas, but England, Spain, Portugal, and other countries who purchased human cargo. His mother's ancestors included one of many young wenches advertised in Virginia as good breeding stock.

Embarrassed that Mrs. Jamieson had been speaking, Cheney blinked. "I'm sorry, Momma J. What did you say? My mind was elsewhere." Her eyes darted from her mother-in-law to her sister-in-law.

The worried lines on Hallison's brown face spoke volumes as she reached for Cheney's other hand. Their food hadn't arrived, but when Hallison felt like praying, she didn't ask for permis-sion. As soon as the trio bowed their heads, Hallison finished with "Amen."

Shaking her head, Mrs. Jamieson tsked. "You and your five-second prayers."

Hallison shrugged. "That's all it takes when you know what to pray for. Jesus will take it from there."

When their orders arrived, they bowed their heads once more

and blessed their food before digging in. Finally, Mrs. Jamieson asked about her grandbaby.

"I try to keep Kami out of the loop, but she prays every night for her grandpa and BB. The next morning, she seems to wake up without a care." Cheney lifted a brow. "I had no idea that girl was crossing enemy lines." She made a sorry attempt at joking. The last thing she wanted to do was to stress out her little girl.

Hallison shattered the awkward quietness with a long sip on her lemonade. Smiling, she exaggerated a deep breath. "Hey, there's one bright spot. I mean, hopefully, you'll have a son very soon. No bottles, diaper-changing, or potty-training. That's good news, right?"

Cheney hesitated before answering. She scrutinized her sister-in-law under hooded lashes. Was that an undercover test question? It must be Cheney's overworked imagination playing tricks on her.

Cheney and Hallison had met and bonded as natural sisters while dating the Jamieson brothers. Cheney often referred to Hallison as her triplet. Hallison wasn't as tall as Cheney, but the woman was gorgeous without trying. God created her with brown hair that matched the shade of her henna eyes. Hallison's skin was flawless without artificial help aids, and there was no debate about her strong African ancestry.

When Cheney tangled with demons from her past, Hallison had been there. In turn, Cheney reciprocated her love and support when Hallison broke off her engagement with Malcolm over spiritual differences. Hallison and Malcolm would have lost each other if it hadn't been for God's will working in their lives.

Resting her fork on her plate, Cheney folded her hands. "Hali, I hope you and Momma J aren't judging me." She held their stare until they nodded. Taking a deep breath, Cheney continued, "I welcome any child of Parke's in our home, whether

I'm the birth mother or not." Cheney felt a thump in her chest after her admission. It seemed as if the devil grinned and taunted, *Really?* She ignored him. "If that boy is Parke's son, I'll love him and take care of him as if my blood runs through his veins." She paused and raised her hand. "But he can't replace the baby I miscarried, or the son I delivered stillborn."

Mrs. Jamieson shook her head. "Sweetie, we love you as a daughter, not a daughter-in-law. Once a Jamieson, always a Jamieson. No one is asking you to forget the babies that the Jamieson family lost—we all lost. Their memories will live on."

Cheney sniffed to fight off a crying spell. She desperately needed to confess her feelings and have someone understand. Cheney waited for Hallison's response as her sister-in-law finished the last of her chicken wings and wiped her mouth. Cheney discreetly watched Hallison toy with her napkin. "Hali?"

"It goes without saying; we'll always be there for each other." Hallison tilted her head as if contemplating her next words. "I know you're still hurting, and you've got more drama than a *CSI* episode, but don't let Parke go through this alone. You two have shared so much during your short marriage. He has never let you walk alone. Please don't desert him now, Cheney."

Offended, Cheney pushed aside her empty plate. She tapped her nail on the table. Hallison's disguised accusation stung. "Is that what you really think?" Cheney's mouth dropped open. Evidently Hallison didn't know her. She had been her best friend until a minute ago. "I can't believe you said that. You of all people," Cheney accused.

"Just because we're saints doesn't mean we don't fight off tit-for-tat issues. You know what I mean. 'I can't have my baby, so I don't want you to have yours,' like the woman in the book of first Kings," Hallison carefully explained.

"Are you crazy, Hali? Yes, my baby died like that woman's

in chapter three, but I wouldn't wish death on someone else's baby. King Solomon saw right through her when she agreed to divide a baby in half so she could have a baby." With her tears on standby, Cheney swallowed heavily and mustered a weak smile. "That woman was spiteful. God has already given me a daughter who looks so much like Parke it's as if he birthed her. Kami has thick eyebrows and long lashes like me. After that, it's all Parke—wavy black hair and skin coloring. I'm content, and somehow, she's developed Grandma BB's temperament. I tell you, God gave Kami everything she needed to be a Jamieson. I'm fulfilled," she defended as if she were trying to convince herself.

No one responded. Mrs. Jamieson tapped her empty cup on the table. At a loss for words, she appeared flustered.

"Boy, we can sure use a prayer." Hallison reached for their hands.

"Let me lead this one," Mrs. Jamieson stated. "Lord Jesus, I don't know you like my girls, but something has to give in my daughter's life. This is too much for me, so I know how heavy it is for her. I would appreciate it if you give her some mercy. Thank you." The three chorused Amens, sniffed, and laughed.

"Thanks, Momma J, for the prayer." Cheney blinked, guessing everything and every conversation happens for a reason. Cheney didn't see the moment for prayer coming from her mother-in-law.

"I knew she had it in her." Hallison beamed, pointing. "Time out for a commercial break." She put her hands together to form the letter *T* and waited for their undivided attention. Once she had it, Hallison took a deep breath and smiled. "Okay, Malcolm and I are pregnant."

"Yes." Clapping her hands, Mrs. Jamieson screamed her excitement before reaching over the table and gathering Hallison in a hug. "My second grandbaby!" Releasing Hallison, Mrs. Jamieson searched the floor for her purse before realizing it was on the table in front of her plate. She grabbed her cell phone, her fingers poised to punch in numbers.

Stunned and happy, tears sprung in Cheney's eyes. *So, my best friend and sister-in-law will do what I can't: produce the firstborn Jamieson grandchild,* Cheney thought. She had no reason to complain. Parke's parents treated Kami as the princess granddaughter. She had to believe what her mouth had just confessed about being content.

Failure, the devil shouted.

No, victor! She silently rebuked him, standing to round the table. She squeezed Hallison in a hug and sobbed. Parke's son was Cheney's only hope.

Frustrated that all she got were voice mails of those on her party lines, Mrs. Jamieson threw the device back in her purse and opted to regale them again with childhood tales about her triple threats: Parke the Sixth, Malcolm, and Cameron, who lived in Boston. Some of the stories Cheney had heard the first time she was pregnant, like Parke trying to set a trap for a pesky mole by using his father's dress shoe.

Hallison's face glowed with merriment and excitement, which was the driving force behind each of Cheney's smiles. Only when Hallison announced that she had to return to work did Cheney relax.

Hours later, Josephine texted Cheney with the news: GRAND-MOTHER B GUILTY OF SECOND DEGREE ASSAULT. SENTENCING NEXT MONTH. UP TO SEVEN YEARS IN PRISON. SHE'S TOO OLD AND FRAGILE TO GO TO JAIL. PLEASE PRAY.

It had been two weeks of torture, but the news made it the second blow of the day. Hallison's announcement was first. Cheney sighed. Mrs. Beacon wasn't fragile by anyone's measures, but she could age rapidly if she were to be incarcerated. She prayed Mrs. Beacon didn't celebrate by mimicking a church dance or something else to cause the judge to reconsider the punishment.

Anxiety seeped from Cheney's body. Hopefully, the seventy-something senior—Mrs. Beacon never disclosed her actual date of birth, stating her number was stuck on seventy—wouldn't serve jail time. "One down, one more to go." She wondered how long her father's trial would be once it started, and what would be its outcome.

That night, Cheney craved some quiet time to reflect on the day's events. She played dolls with Kami as Parke settled on the sunporch to manage the St. Louis Cardinals from his spot on the sofa. She couldn't get her mind off Hallison's pregnancy. Hallison had called her out about accepting Parke's son, but the biggest trial was accepting Hallison's fertility. Was it a coincidence that she referred to the Old Testament passage about the two women and the one baby? Did it foretell what her relationship would be with Hallison during her pregnancy, or was it more that she didn't want Parke to have what she couldn't have?

She would never be jealous of Hallison. *Never.* "Would I, Jesus?" she questioned god after putting Kami to bed and walking into her master bedroom. She welcomed the solitude as Parke remained downstairs, yelling at the television. The baseball game was tied, and it was already in the eleventh inning. Parke wouldn't leave his entertainment sanctuary until it was over.

Closing the door, she dropped to her knees. "Jesus, you can see through me. You know I would *never* be jealous. Would I?" she asked again. "Hallison and I are like sisters, not sisters-in-law. Am I deceiving myself?" Cheney prayed, not expecting an answer, but she got one anyway.

The heart is deceitful above all things, and it is exceedingly perverse and corrupt and severely, mortally sick! Who can know it, perceive, understand, or be acquainted with his own heart and mind? The Lord whispered Jeremiah 17:9 in her ear.

Cheney cried harder. Leave it to God to tell it like it was. Was she lying to herself? *Now what, Jesus?* She couldn't get 1 Corinthians 13:4 out of her head: *Love endures long and is patient and kind; love never is envious nor boils over with jealousy, is not boastful or vainglorious, does not display itself haughtily.*

"Lord, I know you grant the devil permission to put us through any trial, but Lord, surely you know this isn't a good time for me."

God didn't answer.

CHAPTER 10

"What!" Rainey knew he hadn't heard right as he stepped out of the shower. Securing his bath towel around his waist, he reached for the radio console mounted on the wall in his master bathroom. He turned up the volume.

"A jury has found the Ferguson woman accused of shooting Dr. Roland Reynolds guilty of second degree assault. The judge will decide if the elderly woman will serve time or be sentenced to community service," the announcer broadcast.

"Unbelievable. What is there to decide?" Rainey griped as he dried off. "If that woman doesn't do jail time, then the system is severely rigged." Without question, his older sister, Janae, would share his outrage. He wondered what Cheney felt. Was she relieved? If his dad did what Mrs. Beacon maliciously accused him of doing, did that give her justification to retaliate, instead of letting the judicial system work?

It was Sunday morning, and Rainey's routine was to enjoy brunch at one of the upscale hotel restaurants in St. Louis County. Instead of contemplating where he would eat, his mind returned to Cheney. He had grown accustomed to the rift between them since she relocated back home years ago. He had become bitter over the years, and he rebuffed her olive-branch attempts. The outcome of Mrs. Beacon's trial would determine how Rainey dealt with his sister in the future.

Walking into his closet off the bathroom, he rummaged

through his chest of drawers for his designer underwear then selected a T-shirt. Next, he slid into a pair of clean, but worn jeans. His mood soured; Rainey would fix his own breakfast.

If he called Cheney, would their conversation be strained? He didn't know how to get past the forgiveness Cheney extended to Mrs. Beacon, and he didn't want to be a traitor. Curiosity gnawed at him. Would Cheney attempt to ignore the subject altogether and joke about the antics of her adopted daughter or some other light topic? Unless he pushed her, Cheney would engage him in a safe banter, or inquire about the latest success of his practice.

Stuffing his hands in his pants pocket, he padded across his heated marble floor, an upgrade option when he had his home constructed. Rainey strolled to the hearth room off the kitchen and peeked out the French doors that opened to a private common ground and a manmade lake to enhance the landscape for a community of eight families.

His mind returned to Cheney and her subtle habit of trying to pull out some happy childhood memories. Rainey chuckled. He and Cheney hadn't been more than four years old when they decided to trick their parents.

"Twin, I've got an idea," Rainey had whispered into Cheney's ear.

Mischievous, Cheney was always a willing participant in any scheme. Her eyes had widened as she grinned, showing a missing front tooth. "What?"

"You know how twins fool their mommy and daddy because they look alike?"

"Yeah, so?" She cocked her head.

"I'll dress up as you and you can dress up as me in my clothes." Rainey had devised the plan, until Cheney explained he had to wear flowered panties and pee sitting on the toilet. Rainey immediately thought of another plan that didn't involve him wearing girls' underwear.

Rainey blinked and returned to the present. He couldn't resist laughing at the carefree life they'd enjoyed as children. Now, their adult life was far from tranquil. They both knew what buttons to push to set off an argument. Rainey sighed and walked away from the door.

He always seemed to self-destruct after any discussion that centered on their father and his current dilemma because of Mrs. Beacon. Cheney wouldn't back down in defending the woman—it was irritating and mind-boggling—nor would she bad-mouth their father. He couldn't figure out his sister. "Either you're for the Reynoldses or against us," he had challenged her before the trial began.

His anger rekindled at the thought of the criminal being set free, as if using a Monopoly "Get out of Jail Free" trump card. Rainey felt the need to vent, and with two siblings, he planned to talk to one of them. His decision was a no-brainer. He stomped the few steps to the cordless phone. Swiping it off the counter, Rainey speed-dialed his sister's number and waited for her to pick up. "You heard the news?"

"Yeah. Can you believe it? The only thing I've got to say is if that crazy woman gets off with a slap on the hand, then Dad better be set free," Janae stated. "She's probably doing her church dance by now."

He had to feed off Janae's fury in order to maintain the unwarranted bitterness toward his twin. "I'm tired of being mad about stuff that happened a long time ago, but somehow I don't know how to let it go."

"Rainey, now isn't the time to go AWOL. Justice has not been served."

***

What does a person say to the woman who tried to kill her father when the judicial system decides the crime isn't jail-worthy? Congratulations? Cheney was in turmoil. Her surrogate grandmother deserved some sort of punishment. Mrs. Beacon could have killed her father. Then, she couldn't accept the fact that her father had killed a man. It was a constant balancing act between two people whose lives were connected long before she entered the picture.

Cheney didn't have any lines rehearsed or congratulations to give to Mrs. Beacon. She planned to pay the woman a visit and see how they interacted from there. She would pick up Kami after school and take her as a buffer, if necessary. At least with her daughter, she and Mrs. Beacon wouldn't blow up at each other.

Later that day, Cheney drove to her old neighborhood. Although Mrs. Beacon lived only a few blocks away on the other side of Chambers Road, Cheney felt it was a treacherous journey through a forest of uncertainty, not knowing what she would face once she arrived.

It was a Monday, and Cheney couldn't fathom why side streets were packed with parked cars, occupying space that was always available throughout the week. Strapped into a booster, Kami peered from the backseat on the lookout. She pointed at the same time she yelled, "There's one, Mommy. Hurry, hurry before someone steals it."

It took three attempts and one bumper kiss, but Cheney had accomplished the mission to park her Altima. Since Kami started preschool, she advised her parents she was a big girl, so Cheney patiently waited as Kami climbed out of the car seat unassisted. Closing the door and activating the alarm, Cheney took Kami's reluctant hand and began a leisurely trek around the corner.

With temperatures in the low sixties, Cheney was thankful

for the warmth before cooler temperatures set in. As the leaves crushed under their feet, Cheney admired the magnificent houses that were pushed back from the sidewalk. By day, they were majestic; at night, they were scary. Cheney knew most of the neighbors from her old neighborhood and hoped none had suffered a death in the family. She said a silent prayer anyway.

As they got closer, Kami yanked on Cheney's hand, fascinated by the helium balloons bouncing in the air. "Look, Mommy."

Pulsating R&B music pinpointed the location of a celebration. Only one person on Benton Street would host a party at the beginning of a work week—Mrs. Beacon. Cheney read the large bed sheet–size banner: NO JUDGE CAN KEEP AN OLD WOMAN DOWN.

She wasn't out of the woods yet, Cheney thought as Kami broke free and ran wildly toward Mrs. Beacon's house. Once at the property line, Kami was careful not to walk on Mrs. Beacon's grass. Instead, she stared at the two wrought-iron black dog silhouettes attached to a "Doggy Don't" sign, a humorous warning to dog owners walking without a pooper scooper.

From her backyard botanical garden, Mrs. Beacon waved. "Hey, you two. Party over here." She snapped her fingers to an unrecognizable rap song as Kami and Cheney approached. "You heard the news?"

"No, I heard the music," Cheney answered sarcastically. "Of course I did. Why do you think I'm here?"

Mrs. Beacon shrugged. "For the food?"

"No. I came to check on you. What I did hear was you may not go to jail. I see you're celebrating already. I wish I hadn't come now." Cheney fanned her arm in the air. "Your party is a slap in my face."

"How did I know you were coming? This party was an R.S.V.P., but my basement wasn't large enough."

Cheney gritted her teeth and rolled her eyes. She tried to control her reaction in front of her child. "You don't get it, do you? This is one-sided. If God spares you, does that mean you're ready to forgive?"

Halting her moments, Mrs. Beacon squinted. "Wait a minute. You're putting stuff in my mouth, and it ain't my homemade spinach dip. I said nothing close to that."

Kami jumped up and down. "BB, can I have some dip?" She grinned with a hopeful expression. When Mrs. Beacon nodded, she sped off, bobbing her head to the music.

Cheney was about to yell, "Slow down," when she noted that most of the guests were the ladies in the red hats. She did a double take at the Stacy Adams on their feet. Cheney wondered if they raided thrift stores to find them. "Grandma BB, you've been my best friend, my confidant, and surrogate grandmother since I moved back home years ago . . . ."

Folding her arms, Mrs. Beacon tilted her head. "That's me. Go on."

Cheney searched the sky for a cloud or balloon for a distraction. She found neither. She sniffed. Now was not the time for a nervous breakdown or pity party. She concentrated to recall the previous day's sermon. Finally, Philippians 4:6 came to life: *Be anxious for nothing . . .* "Never mind."

Mrs. Beacon's expression turned serious. "Heney, come on and take a seat."

Cheney rolled her eyes at Mrs. Beacon's pet name and allowed the woman to steer her to a vacated grass-green Adirondack rocking chair.

"Talk—and fast. I'm the hostess, and I ain't dancing." Mrs. Beacon tapped one Stacy Adams shoe.

"He is my father." The music faded as Cheney fiddled with her fingers. It was amazing that even after Mrs. Beacon's short-lived salvation walk, Cheney could still discuss anything with her.

Mrs. Beacon had seen her go through good times and bad.

Her friend never called Cheney a hypocrite for not reacting to every situation as a perfect Christian. Although Mrs. Beacon was a self-professed hypocrite, Cheney needed a friend, a sounding board, a person of wisdom. Scratch that last part, but she was about to explode unless she talked to someone.

"Well, Daddy may not be as blessed as you. I know that's what you're hoping. God help me, because any other person wanting that I'd probably despise."

"Me too." Mrs. Beacon nodded with conviction. "If I were you."

Cheney ignored her. "But I'm praying for mercy on your part, and the judge's. God told me He granted this situation for me to bring my family closer, but that can't happen if Daddy is in jail. Please put aside your animosity against my father and think of me."

"Umm-hmm." Mrs. Beacon crossed her arms. "There's more on your mind. I can feel it in my bones, and it ain't arthritis."

"Parke and I are living in the same house, same bedroom, but it's like we're on two different planets."

"Umm-hmm."

Cheney sighed heavily before revealing the last thing. "Hallison is going to have the first Jamieson baby."

Compassion covered Mrs. Beacon's face as she reached for her hands. "Oh, no. I mean." She cleared her throat. "Congratulations, but how are you handling that, chile? If I didn't like Hali, I could send a few of my red hat girls to rough her up, but that wouldn't be nice, considering she's in the family way. But I know that news had to sting."

Without making eye contact, Cheney whispered, "I'm okay. I'm happy for her. I guess it's my turn to host a baby shower, the—"

"Girl, would you stop rambling? If this music doesn't give me a headache, your sorry excuses will. Leave it to Grandma BB." She pointed to herself and winked. "I know what will cheer you up." She stood, smiling.

Cheney groaned. She was scared to ask.

CHAPTER 11

"Maybe I should let it go," Parke mumbled after letting himself into his parents' Paddock Estates ranch home in North St. Louis County.

As empty nesters, and married for thirty-seven years, Parke V and Charlotte were almost inseparable. At the moment, they were cuddled in a cozy corner of a deep blue spacious sofa. It was barely mid-October, but Parke was convinced it was for romantic intentions that his father had lit a fire in the fireplace. In unison, they turned their heads as Parke entered the family room.

The welcoming expression on the elder Parke's face flashed then turned to concern at hearing his son's words. "What should you let go?" he asked, standing and helping his wife up. No one would doubt Parke was the elder Parke's boy. Except for gray patches in his hair and skin tanned from the years, the father and son were mirror images.

Parke shook his head and grunted. "Nothing. I'm talking to myself."

"You're in my home now, so talk to me." It wasn't a suggestion. Parke K. Jamieson V was a man who meant every word he said. His love was genuine, his interest authentic, and commands were meant to be followed, whether his sons were grown and gone, or living under his roof.

His parents waited as Parke slipped out of his leather jacket and laid it on a nearby chair. Taking a seat, he stretched his legs and exhaled. "I needed a pep talk, Mom and Dad," he explained with a weak smile.

They remained standing until Parke realized his mistake. He got up and crossed the room. Once he hugged and kissed his mother, she sat again. The elder Parke waited for his acknowledgement with a handshake and slap on the back. Satisfied, his father nodded and reclaimed his spot next to his wife.

"I'm this close." Parke squinted as he used his pointer finger and thumb to demonstrate the distance. He dropped to the sofa and closed his eyes. "Roadblocks are being built right before me. I cannot believe our legal system," he rambled; they listened. "The judge won't even let me prove I could be the child's father." He pounded his fist on his knee. "I don't need this," he said, gritting his teeth.

"Son."

"Yeah, Dad?"

"You asked if you should let it go. I can't tell you what to do, but I want you to separate yourself from what's going on for a minute." Shrugging, his father clasped his hands. "You have everything, PJ—a beautiful wife and daughter. What more could you ask for?"

Parke's mouth slacked, and his eyes widened. If words could drug, then he was doped up. Angling his head, he stared at his father. Charlotte also gave her husband an odd look. "A son, Dad. If he's mine, I want him."

Although the elder Parke encouraged his sons to be independent thinkers, he was always available as a sounding board to help them make the best decisions. The last time Parke had confided in his father, he had broken off his relationship with Cheney and was miserable. At the time, they both thought she was sterile.

His father nodded several times. "We all want that, but—" he held up his finger "—our ancestors, Paki and Elaine, had to fight battles along the way to survive. Don't think there weren't losses and sacrifices. That boy may very well have Jamieson blood running through his veins. We may never find out, but we have to obey the law. If he's ours, he'll find his path back to his bloodline."

Parke jumped from his perch. He twirled around. "And maybe he won't, or can't, Dad. How can you want me to let go without fighting to the end?"

Standing, the elder Parke matched his son's height. "I tell you what I do care about is the family you have now. You and Cheney have suffered enough heartache. I'm *advising* you to really think about letting it go, PJ."

"Dad, I respect you and I love you, but I can't and won't." Parke frowned. "I can't believe you are the same man who drilled into your three sons about the strength and dedication of our family roots."

Charlotte got up and pushed her way between them. "Honey, I'm even disappointed to hear you tell him to back off, but I'm with PJ on this. We can never have too many grandchildren."

Hugging his wife, the elder Parke reclaimed his seat and pulled her down with him. He urged his son to do the same. He took a deep breath and began explaining himself, using his hands. "Don't misunderstand or underestimate my fierce commitment to my family, but sometimes we have to let it go for the sake of what we have."

Tears cradled in Charlotte's eyes, but she remained quiet.

"Here's a question, PJ. Is this law any different from the laws of slavery? No, it's still a system with faults."

"I think I'm going to pray on it," Charlotte said, gnawing on her lip, deep in thought.

Parke's jaw dropped. He had never heard his mother openly

profess that she was, would, or thought about praying on something. His father didn't seem to notice the conviction behind her statement.

"By the way, did Cheney tell you the news?" Charlotte asked.

Racking his brain, Parke wondered what news. His heart pounded with a tinge of excitement. His parents had been teasing about letting it go, knowing there was good news ahead. Parke would play along as he prepared for them to say the judge granted the paternity test.

"Malcolm and Hali are expecting a baby," she said in her singsong voice.

His father's expression didn't change as he waited for his son's reaction. Parke experienced a moment of vertigo as he stood and grabbed his jacket. "No, Cheney never mentioned it."

Telling them good night, he hurried out the door. By the time he was behind the wheel of his SUV, his cell phone was already ringing Cheney.

"Hello?"

Parke's voice choked. Tears stung his eyes. "Why didn't you tell me about Hali?"

"I couldn't," she said, sniffing.

"I'm on my way home." Parke blinked, a tear dropped, and he made a decision. His wife was more important than the chase of proving a child was his. Suddenly, Parke didn't want to know.

A few nights later, as soon as Cheney opened the front door, darkness greeted her, while a Luther Vandross song serenaded her. She followed "When You Call on Me/Baby, That's When I Come Runnin'" to their bedroom, where the music grew louder.

Pushing the door open, she gasped. Parke walked out of their master bathroom dressed in his black silk pajama pants. Bare chest and solid ripples of muscles, he crossed his arms and leaned against the doorway. Her heart dropped when he smirked then winked. He knew she couldn't resist him when he winked.

"What's going on?" she whispered as she stepped inside.

His approach was slow and his focus unyielding. If any object was in his path, Cheney was certain he would maneuver around it without taking his eyes off her.

"Where's Kami, Parke?"

"Grandma BB."

Cheney lifted a brow and smiled. "Really? On a school night?"

"Yeah." He grinned. "Who was I to deny a moment of family bonding? Plus, it was free babysitting, and your daughter demanded a shopping trip to Gam-boy-ree."

Cheney chuckled. "Of course. The little diva rules."

Parke lowered his voice. "Notice anything?"

"Yes." She dropped her voice to match his huskiness. "I love what you did to the room." Cheney played dumb. Of course she recognized his black silk pajama pants. She had bought them. She held back a blush, thinking about what they shared behind closed doors whenever he modeled them.

"Listen, Miss Killjoy, you've got a God-fearing, extremely handsome, and sensitive black man standing in front of you. The bonus is I'm your husband."

Before she could blink, he moved swiftly and had her wrap-ped in his arms.

She laughed. "Hmm . . . and you smell good too. You're not in bad shape, but you're irresistible and conceited," she said, reaching behind him and pinching his hip.

"Ouch!" Parke pulled her closer, assaulting her lips with a strong, then tender kiss as Luther Vandross' song played in a continuous loop from the house's sound system.

Parke began a path of kisses from her cheek to her neck and shoulder. "I love you, Cheney."

"I love you too," she said breathlessly as her lids fluttered.

"Lately, it seems when you've called on me to be there by your side, I didn't run fast enough. I'm here now, and it has nothing to do with us finally getting Little PJ. Yes, he's been my obsession, but you are my possession. You deserve to be cherished and loved the way I promised when I said my vow," Parke whispered, undressing his willing wife. When she was stripped to one of her collections from Victoria's Secret, he scooped her up and carried her into their master bath.

Parke refused to let Cheney talk. It would be time for him to listen later. Their bath was long and unhurried. Once they were finished, Parke lifted Cheney, cradling her as if she were as light as Kami. On their marriage bed, the Luther Vandross song continued to entice them as Parke focused on fulfilling the needs of his wife. Within minutes, their lips were swollen from their passionate kisses. He wrapped Cheney in his arms and encouraged her to rest her head on his chest.

"Now, baby, talk to me about anything except for the jerk I've been."

She snapped her fingers. "Hmm. That was the first—"

He kissed her again. "Now, I promise I'll listen." He reached for the stereo's remote and turned off the music throughout the house, freezing the moment.

Cheney inhaled, but when she exhaled, tears followed. He stroked her hair. They had been through so much together and they had made it. If it wasn't the case against Mrs. Beacon, it was his quest for a son. Now, Hali was pregnant.

God, did you forget about us? This is too much to handle at one time, Parke prayed silently.

God answered, *My grace is sufficient for thee: for my strength is made perfect in weakness.*

Parke's breath stilled and Cheney's sniffing ceased. He wondered if she heard the Lord's voice too. He allowed the aroma from the scented candles to hypnotize him as he stroked her silky skin. Cheney's steady heart rhythm lulled him almost to sleep until Cheney's soft cries exploded into heart-wrenching sobs.

"Shhh, baby. Don't cry. Please tell me what's running around inside that pretty head of yours, especially since pleasing you took all my strength and I'm about to fall asleep." Parke didn't get her smart-mouth reply he had come to expect and enjoy. His statement only intensified her agony. "Sweetheart, I love you. I really love you. Since my kisses didn't make you feel better, talk to me, baby." He sat up and dragged her with him. "Remember when we first met?"

"Yeah."

"I gave you a small bottle filled with pieces of paper that I scribbled my commitments to you. It was a few weeks after I went missing in action when you told me you couldn't have kids. I was as devastated as you probably were when you first got the news, but look at God. I came back more determined to prove my love."

"You have, but I'm going through a pre-pre-menopausal minute," she strained with a hoarse voice. She snuggled closer as Parke pulled the thick comforter to cover them. "I don't want to be jealous of Hali because she could be the first to produce a Jamieson offspring through marriage, but in the flesh, I am, and I'm asking God to help me."

Parke kissed her head without interrupting. Cheney called herself jealous, but he would call it hurting. He hoped God's grace was sufficient to heal his wife spiritually and emotionally. He hoped God's grace was sufficient to be beside her in sickness and in health, for better and for worse. He hoped God's grace was sufficient to give him peace to accept whatever God's will was in his life. That was his last thought before he fell asleep.

CHAPTER 12

The boys were handsome, rambunctious, and mischievous. No one could tell the twins apart, except for, perhaps, another twin. Rainey could point out Peter from Paul by the slant of his eyes and the lift of the right brow; most noticeably, the difference in their imperfect teeth exposed by their childish grins. They were projects his expertise couldn't wait to tackle.

Peter Thomas's bottom teeth were crowded, causing his jaw to misalign when trying to close his mouth. He had already begun to complain to his mother about pain in his cheek and neck. Paul had the annoying habit of grinding his teeth. It started a year ago in his sleep, but now continued throughout the day. Their pediatrician referred them to Rainey.

"Dr. Reynolds, I got on your website, and the colored braces are cool," Peter said excitedly. The ten-year-old was younger by three minutes. "Does that mean you're going to paint my teeth too?"

"Rainbows are for girls." Paul shoved his brother and scrunched up his nose.

Neither boy had dimples, moles, or long lashes that were considered cute assets for boys. Yet, Rainey had a gut feeling once they matured into men, they wouldn't have a problem catching a few girls' eyes, especially with a winning smile.

He admired a barber's recent handiwork of edging their hairlines. Rainey remembered the days he sat in the barber's chair while his father was serviced in a chair beside him. Those were the times he bonded with his father.

Next he scrutinized the brothers' clothes. They were as different as the owners' personalities. If one wore white, the other wore black. Today, Peter was dressed in blue; Paul was decked out in green.

Rainey laughed. "If you two get the black ones, you can pretend to be pirates," he teased.

They shouted "Yeah!" at the same time Mrs. Thomas interjected, "No."

Rainey pouted with the boys before he chuckled. He loved his profession as a skillful artisan. By the time he finished his procedures, monitored the success, and reviewed dental hygiene guidelines, his patients walked out of his office happy clients.

When their mother winked, the boys grinned back. Mrs. Thomas shooed them out of his office into the lobby, which Rainey had stocked with inexpensive and easily replaceable electronic gadgets. "I need to talk to Dr. Reynolds." She looked worried.

Rainey tapped his pen on Peter's and Paul's files. "Mrs. Thomas, please don't lose sleep about the cost. After your insurance pays its portion, I'm giving you the twin discount." She relaxed. "If you're still concerned about the payment plan, I've already agreed to extend it indefinitely."

"That's not it, Dr. Reynolds." She squeezed her lips together, daring to show her teeth. Since her very first visit to his office, Mrs. Thomas routinely dressed casually and comfortably in various skirts, but her tops were always white. Her dark skin bore minimal makeup, and her hair was short and stylish. Mrs. Thomas and her husband were hard workers, who, despite working long work hours they did a great job rearing polite children.

"Please tell me I don't have food stuck in my teeth," he joked, but it didn't have the effect he sought. Leaning forward, he coaxed her to talk. "Mrs. Thomas, what's wrong?"

She sighed then looked up. "I'm praying for you, Dr. Reynolds."

Rainey strained a brow upward and sat back. He didn't know what was coming, but he was sure he wasn't going to like it.

"I don't watch much news, but one night I did. I'm sorry about what happened to your father. I hope he's doing better after being shot. The news says it was retaliation about something that happened a long time ago. I don't believe it. I'm sure he's a great man to rear a good son and doctor. I'm praying that justice is served against that lady, for him, and especially for you."

"Thank you." He nodded, not sure if he wanted to participate in this conversation. By sheer will, he didn't tear his eyes away to check his watch or glance at the wall clock. Rainey bet she probably wouldn't get the hint anyway. He grimaced, holding his breath that his next appointment would be early. Lucky for him, Mrs. Thomas said she had to get to work after she dropped her sons back at school. Rainey relaxed.

"Dr. Reynolds, I don't profess to be a prophet, an evangelist, a minister, or even a Sunday school teacher, but this morning while praying . . ."

His heart raced as he debated if he wanted to hear the rest. He threatened his body not to sweat, but it was getting hot in his office. Maybe he needed to check the thermostat.

"God placed your face before me and said, *Come to me, all of you who are weary and burdened, and I will give you rest. Take my yoke upon you and learn from me and you will find rest in your soul.* In case you want to read the entire passage in your Bible, it's in Matthew 11. You do have a Bible, don't you?"

"Of course." He did have one at home somewhere. God was starting to show up in too many people. Recently, a grocery store clerk had quoted scriptures to a customer who was ahead of him in line. Then, he had somehow programmed his satellite radio to a gospel station. Now, God had him cornered by using the mother of his patients.

Gathering her purse, Mrs. Thomas stood and shuffled to the door. Before leaving, she glanced over her shoulder and added, "Visitors are always welcomed at Redemption at the Cross Church in case you want to attend. We would love for you to be our guest."

"Have a good day, Mrs. Thomas. See you in a few weeks," Rainey politely dismissed her as he got up. Once she left, he exhaled. Going to church was too much like forgiving, and if he succumbed to that temptation, he couldn't face being a traitor to his dad, as his sister had become.

It was Friday night, which meant Kami ruled in the kitchen. She prepared the family meal under the auspices of Cheney.

"Okay, Mommy and Daddy, fold your hands and close your eyes—no peeping," Kami demanded with a toothy grin, barely containing her happiness after completing her duty. Their daughter loved to pray, mostly to ask God for harmless things.

"Lord Jesus, thank you for our food, but I wanted to talk to you about Mommy and Daddy. Please let them be happy, because I want a dog."

Parke coughed. Cheney cleared her throat.

"Okay," Kami whined. "Lord, help me be a good girl . . . and bless my hands that fixed the food and let it taste good. Amen."

"And bless our food, young lady. Amen," Cheney corrected.

When Kami looked at Parke for his reprimand, he winked. She bowed her head. "Sorry, Mommy. Bless our food. Amen."

The night's special was spaghetti. The meatballs were hidden somewhere on his plate. A pile of parmesan cheese was dumped on the side. The saving grace was Cheney's zesty sauce.

Cooking demonstrated Kami's feminine side; karate lessons were to reign in her aggressiveness. Parke felt sorry for the guy who fell in love with his daughter, in nothing short of forty years. That suitor would have to appreciate a Jamieson woman who called her own shots, and hopefully cooked more dishes than pasta.

After two mouthfuls, Parke was able to trap a meatball inside the spaghetti maze as the phone rang. "I'll get it." He wiped his mouth, got up, and grabbed the cordless phone off the counter.

Parke barely said hello when the caller blurted out, "You're going to love me."

"I doubt it, Ellington, but I'm listening."

"Remember you asked me to get an ID on the adoptive parents?"

Ellington had followed through. At the time Parke made his request, he was desperate. Now, hope leaped into Parke's heart, but he wasn't so sure if he wanted to keep hope alive anymore. "Ah, no, thanks, man. I'm tired of the hunt."

"What do you mean no thanks?" Ellington's voice was a notch below agitated. "Too late. I've already tapped into the system. What do you have to lose?"

Insanity, peace in my home and life. "Aren't those documents sealed?"

"Even plastic bags leak sometimes," Ellington teased. "I've got a name and number," he whispered as if he were making a drug transaction.

Chuckling at Ellington's antics, Parke's interest was piqued. He glanced over his shoulder. Kami was twirling spaghetti around her fork like a ballerina. Cheney eyed him suspiciously. "Oh, hold on. Let me go into the other room." On the sunporch, he sank into the sofa and hunched his back as he glued the phone to his ear. "Okay, what ya got?"

"You're in luck. Gilbert Ann lives in west St. Louis County. His number is . . ."

Parke didn't write down the information. He memorized the digits as they fell off Ellington's lips. After they disconnected, Parke took a deep breath. "Lord, I've gotten one thing I asked for. What should I do with it?" He returned to the dinner table without waiting for God's reply.

CHAPTER 13

Monday morning, Cheney called her pastor. It was unbelievable it took Mrs. Beacon, a professed and unashamed backslider,
to advise her to reach out to her minister. After all, Mrs. Beacon
had defected from the church not long after she joined, and she
had been resisting the notion of living an exemplified Christian
life ever since.

Of course, Mrs. Beacon had been right about contacting Pastor
Scott, but Cheney had rather bend her surrogate grandmother's
ear than consult the man of God. Sunday's sermon from Acts
15:28 sealed the deal that God was talking to her: *For it seemed
good to the Holy Ghost, and to us, to lay upon you no greater burden
than these necessary things.*

"Faith Miracle Church, where every day is a good day because
Jesus lives," the secretary greeted.

"Praise the Lord, Sister Ethel. This is Sister Jamieson. I was
wondering if I can make an appointment with the pastor,"
Cheney said as she doodled on her desk calendar.

"He's in his office now. Hold on. I'll connect you."

Whoa. Cheney wanted to make an appointment for a future
date, not talk to him now. When Pastor Scott came on the line,
Cheney didn't know why her composure exploded. She could
barely form a sentence as tears sprung up. Surprisingly, he patiently endured her angst. Finally, Cheney wiped her eyes and
calmed down. "I'm sorry, Pastor. That came out of nowhere."

"Now, now, Sister Jamieson, hurt and other emotions come from somewhere—the heart. What's on your heart and mind?"

Swallowing, Cheney went for it. "I know you're busy pastoring—"

"Hold it right there. God has called me for more than preaching. I'm instructed to pray without ceasing, for I am the shepherd of the flock. God has given me charge over you, and you better believe if you fall, I fail."

"I feel like the devil is pitching a fast ball at me every minute."

"Are you wearing your spiritual gear?"

When she didn't say anything right away, he answered for her. "Remember the breast plate of righteousness?"

Cheney shook her head and sighed. "I always forget about that passage in Ephesians 6."

"It was created specifically for the saints of God. When you put on your clothes in the morning, outfit yourself with something invisible to the naked eye. Only those wearing spiritual goggles will see it." He tried to drive home his point. "Our servicemen wouldn't dare leave their barracks without their armor. Neither should you leave the house without yours. Now, what's bothering you?"

Although Cheney's spirit had calmed and she didn't feel so overwhelmed, she was still unsettled. She cleared her throat. "So much is going on that I don't have enough energy to tell you, and I'm sure you don't have enough time to listen. I don't know if you heard anything about my father."

"Of course, I've heard, and I'm so sorry. I've been available, waiting for you to contact me in case you've needed counsel, and now you've come. I'm not here to judge your father, or the lady who shot him. God will do that Himself based on their repentance. I'm here to remind you of God's promises and the benefit clauses in His contract. Brother Jamieson is with you through all this, isn't he?"

Shaking her head, Cheney was suddenly ashamed. That was one more burden they hadn't shared with Pastor Scott. "No, sir." She explained Parke's legal fight for a paternity test to verify if a boy was his son. "It's too much at one time. We're trying to keep these situations from tearing us apart. I'm scared.

"Grandma BB—you might remember her as Sister Beacon—well, her trial is over, which means my dad's trial will start soon. I'm waiting to see what kind of sentence the judge is going to give Grandma BB. I'm praying for community service or something light.

"Another totally separate struggle is I'm ashamed to admit that I'm becoming jealous of every pregnant woman who comes near me." She didn't divulge her near barren condition was self-made and not a random act of God. "Yet, God spoke to me and told me I'm here to bring my family together." She sighed, exhausted from revealing her woes. "I don't see how I'm capable to carry out God's assignment. I can't see the blessings."

"Sister Jamieson, sometimes our blessings are delayed. Reread Daniel 10. As you continue to seek God for answers, remember the prophet. God dispatched the messenger, but the devil set up a roadblock for twenty-one days. During that time, God's army battled the devil's toy soldiers before getting to Daniel. I don't know how God is measuring your days in this instance, but believe God that your answer is near."

Cheney's understanding had swelled by the time she disconnected. Covering her face with her hands, Cheney silently prayed for a change of attitude. Taking a deep breath, she mentally forced herself to tackle the work on her desk.

She verbally checked her armor when a moment of humor surfaced. Cheney went through the motions of strapping a shield onto her chest for God's righteousness. Standing, Cheney acted as if she were stepping into armor-plated shoes for the preparation for the gospel. As a cartoon superhero, she patted her head as if she were positioning protective gear. Cheney swiped a pen from her desk and sliced the air as if it were a sword as her door was thrown open.

An angry employee picked that moment to storm into her office without an invitation. He offered a cautious nod before beginning his gripe. "I can't believe you let two people go on vacation in the same week. Do you know how much work that gives me? I'm going to grieve it to the union," the elderly white man threatened. Every week he had a different complaint about something he felt she wasn't capable of resolving to his satisfaction. The old-timer was convinced Cheney was hired for a quota system rather than for her credentials.

Watch the darts, watch the darts, she reminded herself. Instead of defending her actions, Cheney let him stew. She lifted her imaginary sword in the air, mimicking a *wshing* sound. Startled, he backed out of her office with a scowl. Chuckling, she blew on the tip of her finger as if it were a smoking gun. "Yep, I'm ready now."

Saturday morning, courtesy of Mrs. Beacon, Cheney was a complimentary guest at Cream of the Crop Salon. This was despite Cheney's protest that she had a regular stylist. Mrs. Beacon also insisted Josephine and Imani tag along. Hallison had to bow out at the last minute after a bout of morning sickness. The owner, Alicia Blair, unlocked the doors to her full-service shop almost two hours early to support Mrs. Beacon's cause—an extreme morning of vanity pampering.

"I'm not up to feeling beautiful. I'm still in the middle of a crisis, remember?" Cheney whined, slumping into a styling chair. She slapped her hand over her mouth, trapping further pessimistic phrases from escaping. She had managed her "crisis" much better after talking with her pastor, but every now and then she would absentmindedly speak defeat. The Bible wasn't kidding. The mouth was uncontrollable, as mentioned in James 3:8: *But the tongue can no man tame; it is an unruly evil, full of deadly poison.*

"How can I forget? I'll even say a prayer if that will help, but you know we all have to bear our own burdens," Mrs. Beacon mockingly censured.

Cheney squinted and pointed. "How is it you can quote scriptures when you want to?"

"As long as I don't have to live them, I can recite them day and night. Besides, once you ingest them, the scriptures are kinda hanging around dormant. Every now and then, they come out."

"Humph. Well, maybe you should come back to church every now and then," Cheney retorted.

"Listen, Heney." Mrs. Beacon fought with the plastic bib draped over her to free her hands. She leaned close to Cheney while gripping the arm of the chair so she wouldn't fall. "You better be glad I didn't take you to Chip's Place."

Alicia gasped. "What? I know you haven't been patronizing them." The woman frowned, twirling her shears on one finger as if she were about to perform a magic trick.

"Humph. Stop eavesdropping," Mrs. Beacon ordered over her shoulder. She continued with no shame. "Anyway, Chip and his dales—get it? Chippendales are at any woman's disposal. They are ten of the best looking African tribesmen I've ever seen. The foot massages, scalp massages, and body—"

"I don't want to hear it." Cheney pushed her hand in the air as a stop sign. "I'm a married woman—"

"And I'm not." Imani interrupted Cheney, fanning her face. "What time do they open? I'll get my things."

Mrs. Beacon smirked at Imani's eagerness. She didn't answer, just to aggravate her neighbor. She glanced at Josephine. "Okay, you're the tie-breaker. What's it going to be?"

"Me?" Josephine patted her chest. "I prefer to have only one man to touch my feet, scalp, and body. That would be my husband."

"You don't have one. Girl, you better live," Mrs. Beacon fussed at her houseguest, while Alicia tapped her foot, signaling her impatience.

"Grandmother B, I may not have one today, but who knows who God will send me tomorrow? Therefore, I decline. You are outnumbered." Josephine's smile was brilliant.

"Humph." Mrs. Beacon shifted her shoulders as she leaned back in her chair. "That's what I get for hanging around church folks. I'm going to get me some new friends."

"I wouldn't say that too loudly. God can make that happen in prison," Cheney advised her.

That reminder shut Mrs. Beacon's mouth, as Alicia swirled Mrs. Beacon's chair around to examine her hair, face, and nails. "Chippendales, humph," Alicia mumbled, tilting her head. For a few minutes, Alicia twisted her lips and squinted as if contemplating a major task.

"I want something sassy, smart, and short, but I don't want to look like I'm going bald."

"Umm-hmm. Anything else?" Alicia angled her hand on her hip.

"Yes, I don't want the designer nail extensions on my toes today, but I would like the same color nail polish on those corns to match my toenails."

Cheney's eyes bucked as hysteria circled the room. Imani cackled the loudest, with no attempt at censure. "No wonder you slip into those old Stacys to hide your polka dot–painted toes."

Gagging for breath, Cheney giggled until tears fell. Even Josephine covered her snickers with a hand; then realization hit Cheney that Mrs. Beacon wanted to chop off her long, lopsided ponytail. It was as much as a body landmark as her signature Stacy Adams shoes.

Alicia was glad to do Mrs. Beacon's bidding. She tied her client's silvery mane into a ponytail with a rubber band. With one clip, about eight inches was cut. Alicia handed the souvenir to Mrs. Beacon.

"Hey," Mrs. Beacon said, gawking.

"What's wrong now? You told me to cut it," she defended as she fluffed her client's hair, shaping a style before heading to the shampoo bowl. "You have plenty of hair left."

"Chile, if I need some hair, I'll buy it. I'm looking at these split ends." She pointed to her keepsake. "My hair was raggedy. What have you been doing every two weeks when I come?"

Rolling her eyes, Alicia took her shears. She reached over Mrs. Beacon's shoulder and snapped the uneven strands in the detached ponytail. "There. It's trimmed now."

"Hussy. Should've done that while the hair was on my head," Mrs. Beacon fussed as Alicia led her to another area.

One by one, Alicia gave each lady her attention. Before long, they all were lounging in chairs, waiting under plastic caps for the conditioners to work their magic.

Mrs. Beacon jutted her chin and eyed Cheney. "You know, I always liked Hallison. She's been a good friend to you. What I don't like is the fact she threw her pregnancy in your face like that," she said.

"She didn't." Cheney shoved one hand in the air. "Stop before you get started."

"Ah, don't defend her. That's your problem: always giving people the benefit of the doubt, and they'll cut you down at the first chance."

"Jesus gives us the benefit of the doubt every time He gives us grace. He does all the time," Cheney said.

"I'm on vacation from church, God, and if you keep it up, you too," Mrs. Beacon advised, biting her lip, "although I did thank Him for that lesser charge of second-degree assault. I guess it could've been attempted murder or something." She tilted toward Cheney. "You know my court-appointed attorney argued the sudden passion angle. The Lord's good for some things—like you, for instance—you need God all the time. Me, I'm more independent."

"Hypocrite should be your middle name. You act like you enjoyed going to court." Cheney shook her head in disbelief.

"You should've seen Grandmother B work her magic on the days you weren't there. She batted her eyes, and you should've seen him drooling," Josephine jokingly scolded Mrs. Beacon.

"He was cute. Who knows? He may moonlight as one of Chip's dales when I haven't gone." Mrs. Beacon bowed her head bashfully as she climbed into Alicia's chair.

"Who?" Cheney, Imani, and Alicia, who switched off the blow dryer she had just turned on, asked in unison. Alicia patted Josephine's face with a towel to catch the excess water trickling from under her plastic cap.

Josephine nodded. "He was a handsome and a very distinguished gentleman, but he was a bit intimidating at times. But I guess in a way, intimidation can be somewhat sexy. I mean, if he's your husband, of course."

"Excuse me," Cheney interrupted. "Who is handsome, distinguished, intimidating, and now sexy?" She thought the description fit her brother, chuckling.

"George, the bailiff. Of course, a serious relationship is on hold." Mrs. Beacon shrugged. "Conflict of interest, but after I'm cleared, we're going to the movies. It's still a good place for necking." Mrs. Beacon puckered up.

Cheney rolled her eyes. "Maybe George can bring you to church."

"If he tries, I'll put—" Mrs. Beacon sheepishly grinned before she cleared her throat. "Anyway, he had the nerve to tell me only one man in the relationship wears the Stacy Adams, and his are size thirteen."

"Good for him. Bad for you." So far, Cheney hadn't met a man who could possibly tame her surrogate grandmother. To Cheney, even God seemed to have backed off, which wasn't a good sign. A reprobate mind was a devil's stronghold, whether it was in regards to homosexuality or a proud, boastful spirit as mentioned in Romans 1. There was so much to pray for and not enough energy to do it, but God said she was responsible for putting her family back together. It appeared she would pick up strays along the way.

As the shop filled with regular customers, the conversation was a boomerang of topics before returning to Mrs. Beacon's plaything. Cheney tuned out the old woman's boasting. Every few minutes, Josephine smiled in amusement, never adding anything to Mrs. Beacon's commentary.

"For a moment back there, your description reminded me of my twin."

Josephine was quiet as she pondered what Cheney had just relayed. "Did it? You know, I've never noticed him in that way."

Cheney smirked. She knew her brother was so good looking, even a woman with cataracts could see it.

CHAPTER 14

Ten days later, the jury in the case of the State of Missouri vs. Mrs. Beatrice Tilley Beacon a.k.a Grandma BB had reached a verdict. Cheney sat in a row between her family and Josephine. She had hoped the seating arrangement would make her appear neutral. A contingency of Red Hat Society members colored the courtroom with their hats and contrasting purple attire. With linked hands, Mrs. Beacon's supporters formed a human chain in each pew. Cheney silently prayed.

The bailiff, George, accepted the note from the lead juror and passed it to Judge Kendall, careful not to make eye contact with the defendant. The judge opened the folded paper and read Mrs. Beacon's recommended fate. Her mouth didn't twitch, neither did her brows rise. For a couple of seconds, she gave nothing away; then she looked at the prosecuting attorney. "Does your client wish to have a say in the sentencing phase?"

Roland shook his head. "No, Your Honor." Gayle shifted in her seat as if she had plenty to say. Cheney assumed her father had restrained her mother.

"Very well. Mrs. Beacon, please stand." Judge Kendall waited while Mrs. Beacon's attorney assisted her. "I have observed you throughout this trial. Somehow, your demeanor suggests anything but remorse for your actions."

Cheney wasn't surprised by the judge's assessment. Mrs. Beacon hadn't fooled the judge, despite scuffling into the courtroom that morning aided by her bamboo cane. The woman was in better shape than some teenagers, and her mind was sharp.

Thank goodness she had left the Stacy Adams shoes at home. Mrs. Beacon's last-minute old-woman-barely-moving getup was turned against her. The large cross hanging from a chain around her neck didn't have an effect either. Her attorney had made an error, arguing dementia as her defense.

"The jury recommends a minimum sentence of three years in prison and a three thousand dollar fine for the crime committed." Judge Kendall paused. "However, I think considering your age, respect in the community, and a clean police record, that sentence may be too harsh."

"Thank you, Your Honor." She breathed a sigh of relief, beaming. "I guess I can go to Disney."

"Not so fast." She squinted at the defendant. "Missouri's conceal and carry law does not give you the right to fire at will. I think one year probation is more appropriate in your case, and one hundred and twenty days in jail, beginning immediately. The shock time will force you to think about the responsibilities as a gun owner." Judge Kendall hit the desk with her gavel, stood, and exited the courtroom.

Mrs. Beacon blinked. "What just happened?" she asked while George gently handcuffed her. Again, George refused to make eye contact with Mrs. Beacon as he carried out his duty.

Cheney gasped. She couldn't believe it. It wasn't a movie featuring Madea, or a screenplay written by Tyler Perry. Her mouth dropped open as she whispered, "Grandma BB is going to jail."

Numb was the only way Cheney could describe herself after she witnessed Mrs. Beacon being hauled away to jail. She didn't move as she stared ahead, while others scurried around her. Most spectators left the courtroom, chatting about the surprising sentence.

"Cheney, are you all right? Hey?" Josephine shoved Cheney to disrupt her physical paralysis. "God will take care of Grand-mother B. You know she makes a friend wherever she goes."

"I hope not in prison."

With encouraging words, Josephine coaxed Cheney to stand and exit the empty courtroom. Once in the lobby, Josephine gave her a Kleenex to wipe away her tears after a tight hug. When she was certain her friend was all right, Josephine waved good-bye. Sniffing, Cheney watched Josephine walk away as the crowd of Mrs. Beacon's red hat supporters thinned.

Her parents and sister were gone. She wondered how they felt about the outcome: jubilant that justice had been served, or disappointed that it wasn't life in prison. In the distance, Rainey lingered at the elevator. He didn't move as he stood there with his hands stuffed in his pockets. She couldn't see his expression, and neither seemed willing to make a move toward the other.

Rainey nodded and spoke to Josephine as she reached the el-evator. His interest in Cheney was lost as he pushed the elevator button and waited as Josephine entered first; then he joined her.

Punching in Parke's cell number, Cheney slid onto a nearby bench. She seemed to move in slow motion as her mind kept re-winding the image of Mrs. Beacon being led away in handcuffs.

"Yeah, baby. How did it go?" Parke asked as soon as he an-swered.

"Grandma BB is going to jail for four months. I can't believe it."

Parke was quiet after a heavy sigh. "Whew. I'm sorry. How are you doing?" When she didn't answer, he kept talking. "That's messed up, babe. I don't know what to say, except sometimes God allows Satan to bind us spiritually before He sets us free. Maybe God will work with her heart while He has her attention. Maybe she'll come out with a new attitude about salvation."

***

Exactly one month later, it was déjà vu for Cheney. The court-room was as packed as a church revival. The trial for the State vs. Dr. Roland Reynolds was underway. This courtroom experience was darker and more serious. It definitely had a more doom and gloom feel as compared to Mrs. Beacon's artistic production. Cheney wasn't prepared for the prosecutor's insidious attacks against her father's character. The prosecutors weren't going for her father's blood, but his soul.

"Your Honor, we have secured a photocopy from the Missouri Historical Society's archives. It shows the same neighborhood exactly one week prior to the night Henry Beacon was struck and killed. Here's a picturesque, tranquil, and inviting area," the at-torney, a large man, narrated. "There were no obscurities—not a tree or towering building. It's a picture of the crime scene a week later in front of a few storefront businesses, including Jolly Joe's Joint and Tavern, where a patron stumbled outside and discov-ered the victim's body. At dusk, the street lights illuminate . . ."

Cheney's heart sank. She didn't want to be privy to the sins of her father, or anyone else. The moment became surreal, as if she were watching an episode of *Law and Order*. A flash before Cheney's face caused her lids to flutter. God gave her a glimpse of Him reading the evidence against mankind in Revelation 20:12: *And I saw the dead, great and small, standing before the throne, and books were opened. Then another book was opened, which is the book of life. And the dead were judged by what was written in the books, according to what they had done.*

She briefly closed her eyes and the image vanished. Oddly, Cheney hadn't missed a word of the attorney's argument. Her heart pounded, and a premenopausal moment caused a sudden sweat from the prophetic vision.

Cheney had a bad feeling come over her. *Lord Jesus, I know we can't run or escape your judgment, but please show mercy. You said I am here to bring my family together. I believe you will keep my father out of prison to accomplish that. I believe, Lord.*

CHAPTER 15

By the end of second week of his father's trial, Rainey woke in a foul mood. It seemed as if he had spent more time in the courthouse the last few months than he had in his office. He cleared the security checkpoint at the courthouse entrance and took the elevator to the fourth floor. When the doors opened, he headed toward the courtroom. His older sister, Janae, and Cheney were nearby, involved in a heated discussion. He walked right into the crossfire. His mood wasn't getting any better

"What's going on here?" He expected a disclosure, but neither sister provided one.

"I'll never forgive you for this, Cheney," Janae continued with her fists balled. Five inches shorter than her younger sister's six feet, Janae never issued idle words. She spoke whatever was on her mind and never apologized for it. His anger, his sister's anger, and the family's strife were becoming tiring. It was one thing for him to carry an attitude on his back, but to be surrounded by it didn't give him any reprieve. He was beginning to suffocate.

Growing up, the Reynolds sisters always had a loving relationship, and he thrived on their lavished attention as the only brother in the family. The bickering started after Cheney went into hiding for five years in North Carolina right after she attempted to cover up her abortion. That act was a disgrace to the Reynolds name. As far as his parents were concerned, their children's business was also theirs.

Cheney met Janae's chiseled frown with a softened but determined expression. "I'm not asking for it. This is not of my doing. Daddy—"

"Don't blame my father for this mess. If you hadn't moved next door to that crackpot, none of this would've ever happened. At least she's in jail; just not long enough for me, after she ruined our family's good name. The media is here in full force to make sure of it. Why? Because of some stupid old woman's accusation. She probably can't remember her name from time to time."

Rainey's head played volleyball between them. He agreed with everything Janae said, plus some, but now he wondered if his words were coated with so much venom. If so, he needed to tone them down, because he didn't like the edge to Janae's voice. "Okay, enough." Rainey nudged them apart like a referee between two boxers. "Dad's innocent until proven guilty, and he's not going to be proven guilty."

"That's because there's no proof," Janae bit out, squinting at her sister.

Sighing, Rainey nodded. "You know it. Now, as a family, let's get through this so our lives can get back to normal," he instructed as if he were the oldest.

Janae snorted. "Normal? How can our lives ever be the same again?"

"Only God knows how all this is going to end," Cheney said, opening her arms for a truce. "I love you two."

"Humph." Janae manipulated a brow that wasn't quite as perfect as Cheney's and snarled, "You have a funny way of demonstrating love and loyalty." She turned to dismiss Cheney, but Rainey gripped Janae's shoulder and twirled her around until she ended in Cheney's outstretched arms.

"Group hug," Rainey announced as he swallowed them up.

A television journalist lifted his camera and pointed it in their direction.

Right about now, Rainey would have preferred sitting in Mrs. Beacon's courtroom again more than in his father's, listening to the lies against a man he didn't know. His dad was proud, strong, and compassionate. Roland didn't drink, swear, or have a sinful bone in his body as far as Rainey was concerned. He instilled right and wrong in his family and expected his children to live as respectable, irreproachable members of the elite society.

Posing themselves for the public's eye, they ended the hug in what outsiders might consider a team pep talk before the big game. In unison, they walked to the door; he opened it, and shoulder to shoulder, the sisters entered, smiling.

"Jesus, let your perfect will be done," he heard Cheney whisper.

Perfect? There is no such thing as perfection in the middle of turmoil. He grunted at the absurdity. Spectators had beaten them to seats, so they squeezed into rows far from the front.

Rainey happened to glance over his shoulder. He connected with Josephine's brown stare as she sat a couple of rows behind them. She was silently conveying a message he couldn't interpret, but her presence oddly relaxed him.

Parke's zeal to verify the bloodline of the boy had simmered down. Cheney needed him right now, because she had enough checkers still on the game board before a winner would be declared. He couldn't believe how fast months could come and go. As Parke and Cheney counted down the days before Mrs. Beacon's release—two and a half months—they prayed that her father's trial would end soon in an acquittal.

Mrs. Beacon had written twice, advising she was okay as long as no one jumped in front of her in the food line. On the other hand, Cheney's family turned up the heat on the blame game. Parke remembered what Cheney had said about her mission to mend the cracks in her family relationship.

"God, I need a whole lot of faith, because the fog is thick in this situation," Parke prayed one night while Cheney put Kami to bed. "Lord, this test is bigger than what's going on in the courtroom. Help me to be strong for her, because I feel helpless. We need you. I'm sending up my own S.O.S., Jesus. Amen."

The phone rang as he got off his knees. He answered it as Cheney walked through their bedroom door. Her smile was weak and her eyes tired as she headed to their bathroom.

"Parke, how's my girl?" Imani asked.

"About the same," he paused, frowning. "We could use your prayers over here, and I'm not talking about your quick ones you say when purchasing a lottery ticket."

"That's why I called with a plan, so stop fussin'. I need you to help me get her to a girl's night out."

"Imani, you know I love you, but my baby needs spiritual reinforcement. I'm sure whatever you have in mind isn't even close. Cheney told me about Grandma BB's Chip's Place, and ain't no man touching my wife. Nope."

"You know, it's a good thing my girl loves you, and I like you, but you are so wrong for calling me out like that. I only have three words for you: Josephine, gospel concert, and Cheney smiling. Okay, that's more than three, but you get the idea, and for your information, I've never been to Chip's Place. His first opening is three months away."

Parke shook his head. Where did his wife pick up her friends? Cheney hinted of matching Ellington with Imani as a way to keep them out of trouble. Knowing both of their personalities, Parke didn't think Cheney's experiment would be successful.

Josephine, on the other hand, seemed to be a godsend when

Cheney needed one. Since Cheney met her at Mrs. Beacon's trial, Josephine had practically become part of the family. To a stranger, she came across as snobbish, but according to his wife, Josephine was easygoing once a person took the time to get to know her. Parke liked her because Cheney did.

"You and Josephine tell me when, and I'll talk my baby into it, as long as it's Christian-themed."

CHAPTER 16

Cheney was trying to stay strong, especially since her family had practically banned her from coming to her parents' house during the trial. Their actions were louder than words. She didn't know hatred could be so thick among family members. She settled for talking to her father by phone to minimize her stress level. Her saving grace had been the simple, nightly home Bible classes with Parke and Kami, and the family prayers were priceless.

On Saturday, Cheney should have suspected Parke was up to something when he treated her to a day at the spa and shopping, while he and Kami had their own scheduled activities. When she returned home that afternoon, Parke revealed the scheme.

"Baby, I'm not in the mood for Imani. I was looking forward to an evening with you and Kami." Cheney practically pouted with disappointment.

"Trust me on this, because I'm trusting Josephine to keep Imani in line. Kami and I will be here when you get back. Go on, Mrs. Jamieson the Sixth. Enjoy yourself. Plus, I like to see you in that outfit."

Wrapping Cheney in his arms, Parke kissed her passionately then whispered, "After you return from the girls' night out, then be prepared for husband's night in."

"Hmm." She smiled. "What time does the concert start?"

Parke laughed. "Seven."

"Good. I'll be home thirty minutes after it's over."

The concert was held at The Pageant in the Delmar Loop in the city, a venue known for diverse concerts, political rallies, and comedy shows. St. Louis native Angela Winbush was the headliner.

"I'll have you know I gave up a Will Downing, Gerald Albright, and Lalah Hathaway concert for you. That man could've been serenading me with some serious love ballads by now," Imani teased Cheney.

"Right. God knew what He was doing with this gospel concert. You thought you were bringing me, but somehow, I think God turned the tables on you. Josephine and I are probably *your* chaperones."

An hour into the concert, when the band played BeBe and Cece Winans' rendition of the Staples Singers' "I'll Take You There," Imani was on her feet, singing along.

Cheney rolled her eyes when Imani shook her hips like Beyoncé, encouraging Josephine to follow her steps. Josephine laughed as she badly imitated the dance steps. Imani snapped her fingers.

"Ah, yeah. This is much better than drag racing down the streets of St. Louis to track down cars and trucks in default. I almost feel like I'm at a party."

Chuckling, Cheney shook her head. "And I thought this night was to cheer me up. Girl, don't you know ain't no party like a Holy Ghost party, where the saints dance all night long?" She bumped Imani with her hips.

After three more energetic gospel songs, the singers kept the crowd in praise mode with "How Great Thou Art." Cheney's hands were lifted in the air when her cell phone vibrated on her wrist. The wrist band for cell phones was a contraption Kami found during a flea market scavenger hunt a few Saturdays ago.

"Hello? Hello? Hold on." Cheney scooted past her friends, making her way to a hall near the restrooms. Once she had better reception, she recognized Rainey's voice.

"Where are you?" Rainey's tone was a toss-up between a demand and some concern.

"On a girls' night out. Why?"

"Where?"

Excuse me? Cheney gawked at the phone. "I'm at The Pageant with Imani and Josie. Why?"

His pause was lengthy. Cheney wondered if he had disconnected the call. "Josephine, huh? I see. Well, this is pretty important. Dad's calling a family meeting."

"When?"

"Now. We're waiting on you."

"I'm on my way." Cheney pushed END without asking any more questions. Her heart pounded as she entertained several scenarios and blinked back tears. In the past, their parents called meetings to prepare them for the imminent death of a family member, a private celebration, or . . . at the moment, she couldn't rack her brain for anything else. She grimaced. Lately it was just like her family to tell her something important at the last minute

Cheney backtracked to the auditorium, weaving between concertgoers. When she located her group, she was almost breathless. "I've got to go." Thank God she drove herself instead of riding with the pair.

"Why? Is everything all right? Parke and Kami are okay?" Imani halted her movements. Always on standby, Imani was ready to react to any situation, as if she were a marine. Her mid-thigh-length green dress wouldn't constrain her from any tomboy activities if need be.

Josephine's silent stare intensified as she waited for more information. She dug in the bottom pocket of her coatdress and jiggled her keys. Josephine's expression said she was ready to leave too.

"My brother just called. Dad's holding a family meeting," Cheney shouted over the music.

"Oh." Imani shrugged while waving her hand in the air, and briefly returned her attention to the musicians on the stage. "Hey, you need backup?"

Cheney shook her head. Leaving with Imani could result in a cat fight with her sister Janae. "By all means, please stay. I think you're already enjoying yourself."

"Go, Cheney. I'll be praying for you in Jesus' name. Something is going to give. Call us later if you need anything," Josephine offered.

Cheney's eyes misted at Josephine's compassion. She nodded, grabbed her purse, and left the building under the watchful eye of a security guard. Once inside her car, she immediately called Parke and relayed what limited information she knew.

"Baby, you want me to go with you?"

Cheney gnawed on her lip. "No, I think I'll be okay . . ."

Parke grunted. "I'll meet you there." He disconnected. Cheney's heart swelled with love for her husband, who could read between the lines.

When Cheney pulled into the Reynoldses' circular drive, Parke's SUV was already there. The night air was chilly but comfortable with a jacket. Leaning against his vehicle, Parke had his arms folded and feet crossed at the ankles. Cheney sighed. She always liked his natural pose, which reminded her of male models selling luxury cars. She couldn't resist the muscles that ripped through his arms. She hungered for those strong arms to wrap around her and convince her everything was going to be okay. His presence made a difference as he walked toward her.

"Hey, baby. I dropped Kami off at Mom's." Parke opened her door and allowed her to step out before kissing her cheek. He did as Cheney had hoped; he wrapped his arms around her and squeezed her gently. "It's going to be fine. We're in this together, okay?" he whispered then held her back to scrutinize her. "You sure do look pretty." He took her keys and activated her car alarm with little effort.

"Thank you, Parke."

"For what?" He frowned. "Supporting my wife, no matter what? I signed on for that, babe."

As Parke linked his fingers through hers, Cheney sniffed and swallowed, approaching the porch of her parents' home. "You're making me feel guilty."

"Am I?" Parke playfully pinched her hip. "Hmm."

She shoved his hand away. Their tit-for-tat ended after Cheney rang the bell and Miss Mattie opened the door promptly. She stepped back to allow them room to enter.

"Miss Cheney and Mr. Parke, I hope you've come to liven up the wake they have going on in there. I'm out of here. Have a good night—if you can," she said, swiping her purse off the table. Instead of leaving through the back door, which would require her to pass the study, she raced out the front, closing the door behind her.

Cheney exchanged perplexed looks with Parke. Shrugging, he rubbed her hand and nudged her forward. "C'mon, in the name of Jesus."

Nodding, Cheney inhaled and exhaled. "Yep, in Jesus' name," she repeated to combat the fear of the unknown trying to overtake her.

They strolled into the study. The housekeeper didn't exaggerate when she described the mood as sober. The soft glow from a half dozen wall sconces stood at attention, but the room was still too dark, which added to the eerie vibe she felt. Liquid swished in the brandy snifters held by Rainey, Gayle, and Janae's husband, Bryce. Cradling her sleeping toddler, Janae resembled a contented, loving mother. The scowl on her face told another story. She refused to meet Cheney's eyes.

It was not a good sign. Cheney wondered what had been her latest offense. She briefly recalled God's assignment to her.

Parke claimed a spot on a nearby love seat, guiding Cheney beside him. He traded a nod with Janae's husband. Bryce was a nice guy, but he allowed Janae to overrule many of his decisions.

"Okay, Dad, Cheney's here. What's going on?" Rainey asked as he laid his glass on the square granite coffee table then rested his ankle on top of his knee. Gayle Reynolds stood regal, dressed as if she were about to go out to dinner or shopping; instead, she was home, standing behind her husband. Roland sat posed in his overstuffed leather chair, staring into space.

Clearing his throat, her father glanced at his wife, children, and his sons-in-law. "This meeting is twofold. I wanted you all here for me to apologize for the disruption and deceit I've caused in your lives." His husky tone tested the waters for their reaction.

"Sweetheart, you have nothing to be sorry for," Gayle cooed and patted his shoulder. "It's Cheney's next-door neighbor's fault," she added in a clipped, accusatory tone.

Roland hushed his wife. He reached for Gayle's hand, and she elegantly placed it in the cushion of his strong one. "No, Gayle. Tomorrow, against my attorney's recommendation, I will enter a guilty plea."

Plopping her toddler son on Bryce's lap aside his three-year-old sister, Natalie, Janae leaped up. "What! You've got to be kidding me."

Rainey shifted, but didn't stand. Instead, he methodically brushed the fine hairs of his mustache and frowned. "Dad, you can't be serious. Have you thought of the repercussions of a false confession?"

"Roland, are you not feeling well?" Gayle gasped in horror. Her face turned a lighter shade than her already fair skin.

"I feel fine, Gayle. As a matter of fact, once I made the decision, the heaviness surrounding me seemed to lift." Roland got up. His stance was proud as he stirred about the room. He was a handsome and fit man who aged well. Stuffing his hands in his slacks pocket, he made deliberate eye contact with each of them. "The circus is over. It's time to release the demons and be truly set free from my secret."

He didn't break his concentration as he forged ahead. "Although none of you have ever seen me sip one drink, that wasn't always the case when I was younger. The night of the accident, I was drinking after my exams, and then got behind the wheel."

"Dad, it wasn't your fault. Mr. Beacon probably jumped into the path of your car," Rainey explained, grasping for straws. "From what limited knowledge I have of the law, prosecutors can't prove criminal intent because someone left the scene of an accident. You're innocent. Let them prove you're guilty. With your impeccable reputation, no judge or jury would convict you."

Roland nodded. "Yes, that is a possibility, but what about God?" He bowed his head and folded his hands as if he were praying, before looking up. "But I *was* responsible. I won't deny it."

With mixed emotions, Cheney's head drooped. It was a struggle to choose the appropriate emotion: relief that her father was willing to do what was right, or sadness that his life would never be the same. Roland was breaking the yoke to set his conscience free. Cheney knew that since he had made the first step with his confession, God could work with him. Cheney closed her eyes as Parke massaged her fingers.

He leaned over and whispered, "Pray."

"This is Cheney's fault." Gayle's voice shook with fear, piercing the stifled silence.

"No, Gayle, our daughter had no way of knowing what God had planned. We can thank her for helping me cleanse my soul."

"On the flipside, there could be a backlash from the community. The public could demand you serve some serious prison time, Dad," Rainey said, pleading for his father to reconsider.

"I'd rather serve it down here than down in hell." The conviction in Roland's voice was strong.

"Now what, Mr. Reynolds?" Bryce spoke for the first time. He and Janae were complete opposites in personalities. "What can we do?"

"Honestly, answers seem hard to come by, son-in-law." Roland shrugged. "Right now, all we can do is pray for God's forgiveness and ask for mercy."

Janae released her fury, piecing together one curse word after another. She seemed to spew every negative emotion known. Embarrassed, Bryce couldn't console her. Neither could Roland. When the profanity relented, her conversation was more understandable. "I can't believe my two children will have to carry the shame that their grandfather served time in prison."

"Janae, I can understand your outburst, but we have more class than that!" Gayle raised her voice in a dignified manner. "You will not talk like trash in our house or in our presence. Certainly, not in front of my precious grandchildren."

Their father's nostrils flared with anger. "Listen, young lady, I may have my faults, but you will not disrespect me." The sternness in his voice put everyone on notice that he was in complete control and was not to be crossed. No one else spoke. "This craziness has gone on long enough. I'm tired of the stress and tension. I need some peace. Cheney and Parke, do you mind saying a prayer?" He frowned at his family. "And no one leaves this room without joining in," he ordered.

CHAPTER 17

Parke was grateful the prayer wasn't a solo event. One by one, the Reynoldses uttered phrases like, *Spare my husband, Jesus. Save us, Lord. We need your Help. Forgive us.* When it could have been turmoil, the Lord manifested 1 Peter 3:22–*Who is gone into heaven, and is on the right hand of God; angels and authorities and powers being made subject unto Him*–before Cheney and Parke's eyes. The Lord brought every unsettling, combative, and weary spirit under His subjection.

Afterward, Roland spoke first. "My secrets have ripped my family apart. Cheney, I apologize for wronging you by invading your privacy. I know it was God who carried you during that dark period in your life. Right now, I'm in that dark hole and shamelessly, I've dragged my family through it with me."

"Daddy, God can fix this. I suffered so long because I didn't believe He could. I thought I fell in love with my college sweetheart. When I got pregnant, Larry was adamant about not keeping the baby." She dropped her head, but Parke took his finger and lifted her chin, silently reminding her that there was no condemnation in Christ.

Taking a deep breath, Cheney continued her testimony, admitting to misjudgments years earlier, which included pushing away her family. "I wasn't prepared for the consequences, but thank God for His redemption."

Although there wasn't a group discussion afterward, they had been attentive and respectful. Their expressions were mixed. Bryce seemed as if he wanted to reach out and hug her, but one glance at his wife, and Bryce thought twice. It was mind-boggling how Janae and Bryce got together in the first place then stayed married past the mythical five- year period when some people called it quits, blaming incompatibility. Janae and Bryce were the poster children.

"Yes, thank God, baby," Roland whispered.

"I never thought you would submit to peer pressure," Gayle censured.

"It wasn't pressure, Mom. I had a choice," Cheney explained. "For me, it was the wrong one."

Later that night, at home and in bed with his wife, Parke allowed Cheney to cry happy tears. "I had hoped . . . but wondered if I'd ever see the day where my family would pray together outside of a church setting," she confessed.

Parke hugged his wife. Although Parke didn't believe God was finished, the Lord had proven His Word to Cheney. She was mending her family in small steps. Parke must have misinterpreted God's message to him, because so far, he wasn't getting any breaks.

That Sunday morning at church, Parke praised God when Cheney rejoiced openly during praise and worship service. She barely tempered her spirit as Pastor Scott preached. A few times, her arm lifted involuntarily in praise. The rest of the afternoon and evening, Cheney and Parke obeyed Psalm 34 and continued to praise. When Kami caught on, she let out a string of hallelujahs.

Monday morning, Cheney kissed him before dropping off Kami at preschool; then she headed to court for her dad's confession. Alone for a few minutes, Parke suddenly reflected on the information Ellington had passed on to him. He had thought his decision was final. Now, Parke was beginning to question that decision. He was ready to resume his pursuit to rescue his son.

Call him, a voice whispered, but Parke couldn't distinguish the source: God or the devil. Of all times not to have a clear connection, this was one of them. *Call him.* Without any more stalling, Parke stole a deep breath and punched in the home number of Gilbert Ann in West St. Louis County.

Twinkie had advised him against contacting the child's adoptive parents, but he couldn't resist the temptation after Ellington gave him the information. "The Duke" reminded Parke he had eliminated one hundred and seventy-five G. Anns, Gilbert Anns, and other initials between the G and Ann.

After two rings, an authoritative male answered. Parke momentarily panicked, but swiftly recovered. The fate of the future Jamiesons depended on how gently Parke handled the conversation.

No, your fate is in the hands of Jesus, God spoke.

After the third impatient hello, Parke responded, "Mr. Ann, please."

"Speaking." The man didn't temper his apparent irritation.

"My name is Parke Jamieson the Sixth." He paused, waiting for Gilbert to stutter, gasp, or grunt an acknowledgment that he might be a connection to the child living in his house.

"How did you get my number?" Gilbert demanded, confirming Parke's suspicion.

"It's listed." Parke proceeded with caution, praying with every breath. At least that was true. If it had been private, then Ellington could have been in serious trouble. "I was wondering if we could meet—"

"For?"

Parke cleared his throat. "To discuss the possibility you may have adopted my son."

"You lost that right. Gilbert's my son now, and I'm not giving him up without a fight. I don't know what source you used to locate me despite a sealed adoption record; however, I'll warn you now, I won't be harassed, and I'll use legal measures to ensure that."

Parke rubbed his hair in frustration. *God, can I get a little help here?*

Acknowledge me in all thy ways, and I will direct your path, God instructed. Finally, the Lord was clear.

"Mr. Ann, all I'm asking is to meet for a cup of coffee, lunch, or dinner, please." Parke was a proud man. Despite his Christian commitment, he didn't take too kindly to asking for another man's permission for access to someone who could be related to him.

"Mr. Jamieson, I don't owe you the time of day, so understand my position to decline."

"All I'm asking for is an opportunity—a test to prove one way or the other that he is my son." Parke slowed his words so his rage wouldn't flare, but family meant everything to him, and he refused to step back now that he started the journey with the phone call.

He briefly recalled Friday's prayer with Cheney's family. At a time like this, the testosterone in Parke wanted to take matters into his hands. Without God in his life, that would be a fist, but God told him He had his back and to yield to the authority in Jesus the Lord. *You don't have to stick around and fight. I have the battle won,* God had spoken a while back.

"You had a chance to be a decent man and act responsibly where this boy is concerned and you missed it. I'll teach Little Gilbert how to be a strong man."

Little Gilbert? Parke's trained ear told him Gilbert Ann wasn't black. How could he show a black boy how to be a strong black man? That was Parke's responsibility—if he ever got a chance. No one would call him a deadbeat father who could care less about any child he sired unaware, an attitude that had thrust some black families into poverty. He was honorable and had the Lord on his side. *I will acknowledge your power and presence. Please help me, Jesus, through this.*

"Mr. Ann, my life is an open book. I'm listed in the *Who's Who Among Young Black Professionals*, I'm on the board of the Matthews-Dickey Boys' and Girls' Club, and I'm a financial planner for a Fortune 200 company. I'm—"

Gilbert huffed. "If I wanted your résumé, I'd Google you." His tone softened. "But I do have compassion. Although I would normally talk things like this over with my wife, I don't want to upset her, since Little Gilbert is already bonding with his new mother. I'll consider your request." Parke shoved his hand in the air. "But—and I do mean but—regardless of the outcome, you must agree to make no further contact with my family and take comfort in knowing we'll do what's best for Little Gilbert. If our son wants to contact his biological father when he becomes an adult, we won't stop him. Agreed?"

I will agree to no such thing, Parke thought, frowning. Gilbert? What kind of name is Gilbert for the descendent of an African prince? "Thank you," he said hastily before Gilbert changed his mind or read between the lines that Parke hadn't really agreed.

He won't change his mind, Jesus reassured Parke.

Grinning, Parke relaxed. "Whew." He sighed now that he had soared over one hurdle. "Great. How about later today? I'm free—"

"Nope. Little Gilbert has karate," he countered. "I have Wednesday afternoon open."

That was two days away. Parke was speechless. Was it a coincidence Kami was also enrolled in martial arts classes? It was as if Parke were going toe to toe and tit for tat, only Gilbert had no idea he and Cheney had made similar choices with their adopted daughter.

Parke swallowed the lump in his throat. Two days, forty-eight hours. If necessary, he would have his assistant adjust his appointments. Parke had been a successful financial planner for years. Most of his referrals had come after conducting financial seminars and speaking at clubs, schools, or businesses. Currently, he was backlogged with requests from clients who were panicking about their recent losses on Wall Street. He countered Gilbert with another date.

"You asked for this meeting, not me. Neither am I obligated. You can take it or leave it, Mr. Jamieson."

Gilbert wasn't bluffing. Parke had a feeling there would be no further negotiation. Parke had no choice but to have his assistant rearrange his schedule on Wednesday.

To his surprise, Cheney was behind his decision. She had said it was a different type of diversion to her drama. Parke was so close to finding out the truth he was about to lose his mind.

Enduring the wait, sleep evaded Parke like a bug eluded pesticide. He was easily distracted. When the time finally arrived, Parke broke out in a cold sweat after a hot shower. As he dressed, Cheney straightened his tie and patted his chest.

"Baby, you're close. We're close," Cheney said during her pep talk.

Taking her hands, Parke squeezed them. Never taking his eyes off his wife, he kissed her knuckles. "You know, babe, for years, I've been chasing a rumor, a dream. For months, I've been fighting to verify it. Now . . ." he said, sighing heavily, "I may be granted the opportunity to learn the truth. Then what? If he isn't mine, I'm dyeing every gray strand that I've earned while searching for the truth."

She laughed and rubbed his cheek. "Since we've exchanged our heartaches, it's my turn to be your backbone." Grinning, she cleared her throat. "Where's your faith? Now is not the time to let it expire. If the test proves he is yours—ours—are you prepared for a ruthless legal battle?"

Letting Cheney's words penetrate his soul, Parke's confidence began to surface. "Yes. With your support, I can do it." He chided himself for the moments of doubt, remembering God told him the battle was already won. It was now time for him to believe it.

"Parke, all these trials were dumped on us at one time, but you told me that God said He's got your back, so . . . what does part of Numbers 23 say? *God is not a man that He should lie.* He can't do it. It's impossible. That's Bible Lesson 101 for Christians." She winked and moseyed into their bathroom, patting his behind along the way. "You're a Jamieson. Jesus already knows the game plan, so go for it, tiger."

He lifted his brow and flared his nostrils. "Umm-hmm, you teaser." Whistling, Parke walked downstairs, grabbed his keys, and left. Although it was going to be a long morning before lunch, Parke was too worked up to eat.

Later, in his office, the morning crawled by and he got little accomplished.

Four hours later, Parke's GPS brought him to his destination, an affluent, newly constructed area of West County. Cheney had called him twice while he was en route, once with a scripture, Hebrews 11:1: *Now faith is a substance of things hoped for, the evidence of things not seen.* The second time when she phoned, it was with her declaration of love.

The area was sprinkled with a few African-American patrons. After parking and locking his vehicle, he strolled confidently inside Starr's Restaurant with the confidence God and his ancestors bestowed on him. Inside, the décor was plush and the hostess was dressed professionally.

He requested a table near the front and waited. Although he hadn't eaten anything, this wasn't a social call. He was all about business. Besides, his pent-up energy was his strength.

As the lunch crowd thinned, Parke scrutinized every man who entered. He had yet to be impressed. None seemed worthy to be a father to a Jamieson male. Finally, another white male stepped through the glass doors.

Not surprisingly, his suit shouted corporate money and several vacation homes. What was disturbing was his face. He had what many African-Americans would describe as a racist game face: a scowl, distrusting beady eyes, and an air of superiority. He didn't attempt a quick sweep of the restaurant. With one turn of his head, he made direct eye contact with Parke then headed his way.

"Mr. Jamieson, I'm Mr. Ann, GJ's father."

Now it's GJ, as in Gilbert Junior? He's trying to bait me. Parke lifted a brow and stood. "I don't want to get off on the wrong foot, but he may call you Dad, but if he's mine, I'm Parke's father."

Gilbert snorted and took a seat. "I'm going to save us some time. The adoption is final. What are you trying to prove after the fact?" He leaned forward.

Parke sat back and tapped his finger on the bare table. "If PJ is my son, I plan to fight for custody." He didn't blink.

Gilbert taunted Parke with a laugh that rebuked his statement. "I recall that you agreed to my conditions."

"I didn't."

"You're wasting your time and mine. No judge in the state will overturn the adoption based on an 'I didn't know' excuse." He leaned back as if he had trumped Parke's card. "This meeting had nothing to do with you, but was confirmation that I had made the right decision. I knew you were trouble the moment you called my house."

Relax your fist, Parke. Relax. Stop imagining his lip swollen. Parke could hear Cheney's voice.

They threw taunts back and forth as if they were riding on a seesaw. A waitress approached to take their orders and both waved her away. Now Parke was hungry. He had worked up an appetite, but he was focused on one thing only. "If I lose, at least my son will know his natural father wasn't a wimp or coward—that Parke Kokumuo Jamieson the Sixth was a man who loved his son, but was denied access. He will know I would spend every dime I had to secure his release."

"Ha!" Gilbert dropped his head back and laughed again. "Release? You make it sound as if he's been captured." He slapped his palm on the table.

Parke mentally tried to hum every gospel song he could remember, or recite scriptures he had read. He admitted he was in the midst of a serious ordeal. "In a way, yes, because regardless of who set the trap, God already has a plan of escape. My tenth great-grandfather was also captured in Africa, but he escaped slavery in the United States."

He switched to spiritual warfare. "You can't see them, Mr. Ann, but I came with backup. God has dispatched legions of His angels to help me. It doesn't matter what you or the law says. All I have to do is endure until the end. You game? Because I'm suited up." *Ah, that felt good to get out.*

Gilbert didn't respond right away. Parke hoped he wasn't snickering, because at the moment, he felt victorious. With the upper hand, Parke relaxed. Suddenly, he was famished. Parke signaled for the waitress. She appeared immediately with a pad.

"My wife can't have kids," Gilbert admitted, losing the steam behind his boldness. The hardness in his features disappeared.

Parke wondered if he had imagined their earlier conversation. "What?" Parke banished the waitress again.

"We're God-fearing people, and God promised us a child." He paused. "We believe God."

Parke grimaced. *God, you're making far too many promises.*

I can fulfill each one, God chastened him.

"I'm a man of meager means, but one thing my wife and I have is an abundance of love for Little Gilbert."

Parke cringed at the name change again. "Excuse me, but one word I wouldn't use to describe you is meager. From your necktie to your shoes, you seem to be living quite comfortably."

Gilbert smiled for the first time and blushed. "Do you really think I was going to meet a man who could possibly be my son's birth father dressed as if I was a construction worker, which I am? This is my best suit, which I usually reserve for church. Although the entire strip mall and the surrounding development are new and pricey, I live in one of the original modest neighborhoods."

Who turned the tables on whom? Parke's heart sank. He berated himself for his first impression of Gilbert. He had no right to judge another. Confessions were revealed, but the fact remained they both wanted something from God.

Parke sighed heavily. "My wife can't have children either. We've lost two babies trying. If otherwise proven, Parke would be my only bloodline."

"Can't you adopt?" Gilbert suggested, leaning closer. His green eyes reflected genuine concern about Parke's situation.

"I already have."

Unexpectedly, Gilbert chuckled and loosened his tie. "Parke, don't you see? I guess we're both even."

"No, we're not. I want to know." Parke scanned the restaurant, meeting the waitress's stare. She didn't move.

"Mr. Jamieson. He returned to the formality. You're already a step ahead of Harriett and me. We can't have kids either."

Harriett? Harriet, Hagar, Hag—it all sounded the same to him. They all began with the letter H. Parke recalled the scripture that set his obsession in motion. Parke was in trouble if he had misinterpreted God in His reference to Genesis 16.

Evidently, God wasn't referring to him as Abraham and Cheney as Sarai. Was God foretelling him that the child he sought would belong to Gilbert and his wife, Harriett, who could represent a modern day Hagar? Parke's head was spinning with too many scenarios.

Gilbert took a moment to reflect what he had just admitted. He sighed heavily and waved his hand in the air as if he were signaling a bartender to refill a drink.

The waitress didn't appear to fall for the summons. She remained rooted as she continued to scrutinize them.

Suddenly, Parke was feeling sick in his stomach. He hoped Pepto-Bismol was on the menu. "What a mess. We're not even, and I want to prove it."

"I'll agree to the DNA test, but you still can't have my son."

"I'll fight for custody," Parke warned. The battle resumed.

"I know, but you'd be the only loser. I won't allow, nor am I obligated to share joint custody with you. I won't stop him from searching you out, but there can only be two fathers in his life, not three." He thumped his chest. "Me and God."

It was praying time, Parke decided. God was the only judge, and Parke wasn't sure what sentence He would hand down. Nodding, Parke stood and handed Gilbert one of his business cards. Thanking him for the meeting, Parke turned and left, ignoring the waitress's odd expression. His proud swagger upon entering was reduced to slumped shoulders when he exited.

Moments later, Parke sat inside his SUV without turning the key. He couldn't move. He felt numb, beginning at his heart and migrating throughout his body. There was no emotion he could pull out. Closing his eyes, he placed his head on the head rest. God was speaking to him, but he seemed to misunderstand every message.

A Marvin Sapp ringtone alerted Parke that Cheney was calling. He didn't open his eyes as he pushed ON and placed it on his ear. "Yeah, baby?" He attempted to build a smile behind his words, but there was no solid ground for its construction.

"It appears your prayers may have been answered. You have a son."

He didn't respond. "Yeah, I may have a son, who, even if I prove it, I can't have."

"Parke, you were really a rolling stone. An old flame claims you are the father of her son, and she's seeking child support. Pretty soon, I'm going to feel like Old Mother Hubbard in the shoe. I've got so many children I don't know what to do—and none of them are mine." Her disconnect was sudden and quick.

"Ouch." Cheney knew of his philandering ways before they married. After four years of bliss overshadowed with heartaches, this was one more thing that could tear them apart. It was as if these women from his past had coordinated their efforts to torment his marriage.

Tears dampened Parke's face as he mumbled, "God, have you forsaken me?"

Let your conversation be without covetousness; and be content with such things as ye have: for he hath said, I will never leave thee, nor forsake thee. God spoke Hebrews 13:5.

The ringtone interrupted his moment of despair again. Startled, Parke jumped, realizing he'd had a nightmare in the middle of the day. "Hello."

"So, how did it go?" Cheney asked expectantly.

CHAPTER 18

This was it, the Reynolds family's day of reckoning. The court-room had its regular crowd of spectators and media presence since the trial had begun. No one had any idea what was about to happen.

At the bailiff's order, everyone stood when Judge Wells en-tered. Once he settled in his chair, the judge's alert, neutral expression couldn't completely mask his body language, which read boredom as the State vs. Reynolds trial continued.

Roland's attorney, Marshall Newsome, and the prosecutor ap-proached the bench to confer with the judge.

"Your Honor, against my advisement, my client would like to enter a guilty plea."

The admission had everyone's attention. Judge Wells's inter-est seemed to pique. "Mr. Reynolds, do you understand this court will not accept a guilty plea if it believes the defendant is innocent?"

He nodded. Caught off guard by the new development, the prosecutor recovered and recommended a five-year sentence. Roland's attorney countered with a fine and probation. Since he decided to forgo a jury trial, the judge listened intently.

Rainey had braced himself for this moment. He even planted himself between his sisters in case Janae wanted to lash out at Cheney. Their husbands were on either side of them. As they linked hands with their mother at the beginning of the row, the trail of tears began. Gayle's shoulders shook with grief. Fighting the humiliation, Rainey lifted his head, impeding a tear's journey to the edge of his chin.

Judge Wells accepted the plea, gave Roland two months before sentencing, and dismissed the court. Instantly, murmurs began to circulate. The media was ready to pounce on them. One by one, the Reynoldses stood. Cheney suggested they pray before leaving the courtroom. Traumatized, they reluctantly agreed and gathered closer.

"Father God, in the name of Jesus," Cheney began. She paused, unsure of what to say. Rainey, Janae, and Gayle Reynolds waited. Rainey squeezed her hand at the same time as Parke, encouraging her to finish.

"This is hard for our family, Jesus. We're hurting, and we all love Daddy. We're concerned about him. I ask that you to spare him, but whatever is your will, give our family peace to accept it. Amen."

"Humph," Janae said, replacing "Amen."

Gayle's silent grief intensified as Rainey reached over Janae and took his mother's hand. *Now what?*

If peace came in a bottle, Rainey would be the highest bidder. The shock still lingered after his father's admission of his deliberate involvement in the death of an innocent man; yet Rainey had to respect Roland for wanting to rectify his past mistakes. It had been almost two weeks, and his family was still in limbo as to what would be his father's fate.

Rainey's Saturday afternoon was free, but he was scheduled to attend a fundraiser for the Sickle Cell Foundation later that evening. In the meantime, he was restless and nothing, so far, seemed to pacify an unnamed craving that almost made him not want to be alone.

Janae had convinced their mother, who was becoming more withdrawn, to spend time with her "only" grandchildren—though technically that wasn't true. It was Janae's jab at Cheney's inability to have her own children and adopting Kami. Rainey loved his sister, but he wasn't up to enduring another gripe session, blaming Cheney for all their woes. As a matter of fact, if Rainey was honest with himself, Janae was becoming a person he didn't want to become. It seemed as if he barely knew her anymore. The bitterness was taking over. That was something Cheney could pray about.

Cheney? He took a few minutes to convince himself; then he dialed her cell. "Hey," he said, opting for an informal greeting. After all, it was his sister.

"Hey yourself, twin," she replied with a warm reception.

"If you're not doing anything, how about hanging out with your big brother?"

She mumbled, "Thank you, Jesus," and laughed. "Hah. Only by four minutes. When were you thinking about getting together?"

Rainey strained his ears as if he were a K-9. "Today. It's a nice day. Maybe we can even do something with my little niece." Rainey held his breath.

"I'm at Ferguson Library with your niece. Kami enjoys story time, so I'm camped out here for the next couple of hours."

He snickered then released a smile as he checked his watch. He wondered if Josephine was working. "Story time. I don't think I've been to one of those since . . . since you and I were in the second grade," he said with awe.

"Fourth grade," she corrected.

He glanced back at the window, facing the lake. A father and son were perched at the bank, fishing. The idyllic scene made up his mind—almost.

"C'mon. It'll be fun. We might be able to find you a big people's chair."

There was no way he was going to stay inside—even a noon game between the rival St. Louis Cardinals and Chicago Cubs couldn't sway his decision. Laughing, he agreed. As he disconnected, he yearned for the child that his girlfriend had aborted—the missed opportunity of playing catch, watching sports together in high def, and wrestling in the house where his home rule would be to christen the furniture by breaking it first. He glanced back at the lake, thinking that fishing with his son or daughter would probably be safer. It did seem ridiculous that he allowed one woman to cheat him out of happiness then blamed the entire female species for her actions.

Since he had already showered, Rainey traded his sweats for a comfortable pair of black slacks and a black polo shirt. *Dangerous*—some of his female admirers always commented about that color on him. Would Josephine ever pay him a compliment? He completed his grooming in less than fifteen minutes. Once he was behind the wheel of his BMW, he picked up speed as his heart pounded in anticipation of a childhood memory.

It didn't take Rainey long to cruise to his destination. The Ferguson Library and its parking lot were small, a testament that it catered to its residents, most of which probably walked there. Unless a person knew the location, it could easily have been passed by, which Rainey had already done twice.

Rainey bit his bottom lip, annoyed at the inconvenience of parking elsewhere. He trekked across New Florissant Road to the front entrance. Rainey hoped he hadn't missed much of the story time. Opening the door, he sucked in his breath, surprised at the large gathering crammed in the back of the library. The real shocker was the storyteller. Josephine had her audience—young and old—spellbound. Momentarily, he forgot about scanning the crowd for Cheney and his niece.

He couldn't take his eyes off Josephine as he jingled his car keys a few times before slipping them into his pants pocket. Rainey hadn't been inside the library one minute, and already Josephine had captured him in her tale of tales. He gravitated toward her.

"Just like North America has fifty states, my continent, Africa, has fifty-three countries. Our desert, the Sahara, is larger than the United States. Come home to Africa with me and to the world's tallest animal, the giraffe, and the largest reptile, the Nile crocodile." She bent and made eye contact with one captivated girl and wiggled her finger. "I'll show you exotic wildlife, many customs, and food you will never forget. Come to Africa with me, and I'll . . ."

Rainey's breathing deepened. If she kept beckoning like that, he would go home, pack, and program the destination in his GPS.

"Come to Africa and enjoy our festivals, move to the beat of the drums, and taste our dishes. Come to . . ."

Josephine was casually dressed in brown and green earth tones that blended with her brown complexion. The skirt wrapped around her body like melted wax from a burning candle. She was tall and moved like a dancer. Simply, Josephine was a woman any man would notice with her dark, silky skin, and expressive brown eyes.

When a phone at the reference desk rang, Rainey frowned at the annoyance. He almost answered it himself. The African woman was articulate, fascinating, exciting, and she exasperated him. Fantasizing, Rainey didn't recall the moment she stepped out of the world of Africa and opened the floor for questions.

"Why is your country poor?" a black child asked, raising his hand. He sat cross-legged on the floor in the front row.

Josephine's smile was warm; her reply gentle. "Which one? Remember Africa has fifty-three countries, and we aren't all poor. Somali, Sudan, and Ethiopia have been run by bad people, and the land can't provide . . ."

A man wearing a large Stetson didn't raise his hand, yet he bullied his question into the conversation. "Hey, since so many of the countries have been conquered and industrialized countries have colonized Africa, don't you feel slavery was justified? I mean, even the Bible tells slaves to be obedient." He shrugged, chagrined. "Hey, I'm just asking."

As a hush came over the room, Rainey was ready to leap over the group and strangle the wrangler for his apparent arrogance. Josephine's body language didn't give away anything. Rainey wondered if Josephine was angry, offended, or combative.

Scanning her audience, Josephine's face expressed tenderness. Her inviting eyes briefly locked with Rainey's before moving on and finally resting on Mr. Cowboy. Her head was poised and her shoulders straight with confidence.

"The first man was created from the dust of African soil. God cursed the land, not the people. Africans weren't the only slaves. The Israelites were also sold into bondage, but we know that God is for the underdog. Isn't it amazing how God performed miracles to bring them out of Egypt and slavery? God instructed slaves to basically be content until He comes; not to worry about a plan of escape because He had it already in place. The moral of the Bible story about the Israelites held captive under Pharaoh is to not let anybody trick the former slaves back into bondage. Does that answer your question?

"By the way, many American slaves were shipped back to Africa, which is present day Sierra Leone. We were meant to be free, and I think the slaveholders had to finally accept that."

With so many scowling faces directed at the man, he had no choice but to mumble a thank you.

To trump the antagonist, a pale white woman raised her hand and stood to be acknowledged. "I want to say I've never seen so many beautiful faces from Africa—Miss Universe Ghana Pearl Amoah, the first Black African to win the Miss World Beauty crown in 2001, Agbani Darego—or fashion icon Otunba Francesca Aina," she gushed. "I must say between your vacation destinations and rich and diverse cultures, Africa is definitely the world's hidden treasure."

Rainey couldn't answer for others, but he was impressed by Josephine's class. Although he attended medical school with exchange students from Africa, he never put forth an effort to get to know them. He definitely had missed an educational experience.

"You are very informed. Thank you, Miss—"

"Please call me Katie Jo. I've been there several times," she said before taking her seat.

Suddenly, a woman with the library staff, possibly the moderator, rushed to Josephine's side. Her slanted eyes nervously spied the audience, purposely overlooking a few hands. "Well," the woman said with a sigh of relief, "that ends our story time for this month. Did you enjoy yourself today? Let us thank Miss Yaa Amoah."

The applause was deafening, but none of the library patrons seemed to mind the temporary disturbance, because they were also absorbed in the tale. Even Rainey stuck two fingers in his mouth and whistled. Locating the source of the piercing noise, Josephine met his eyes with a censuring frown. She smirked before dismissing his presence.

As the crowd dispersed, Rainey was fuming with her annoying habit of brushing him off. When he was about to bring that to her attention, Kami blocked his path. Cheney further restricted his view by pulling his head down for a kiss to his cheek then a bear hug.

"Rainey, I'm so glad you could come. Doesn't it bring back memories of Saturday mornings in the summer?" Cheney stated. Her eyes sparkled. She was practically giddy with excitement, as if she had traveled back in time when their innocence was protected.

"Yeah," he agreed as she released her stronghold so he could breathe again.

"Wasn't Josephine amazing?" Twirling around, she looped her arm through Rainey's. "How about a sandwich from the Whistle Stop? Kami loves to watch the trains come by and wait for the conductor to blow his whistle."

Shrugging, Rainey nodded. "Why not? That sounds like . . ."

As Josephine strolled to her work station, Rainey became acutely aware of her movements, and her scent was intoxicating; yet, something about that woman irked him. "Ah, go ahead, twin. I'm right behind you." He didn't wait for Cheney's response as he trailed his target.

"Josephine." He leaned forward on the counter, waiting for her undivided attention.

"Dr. Reynolds." She barely acknowledged him. She proceeded to help a child check out a book about African animals.

Does she think I'm invisible? The thought irritated Rainey. Affluent and influential socialites surrounded him all his life. Their snootiness was part of the package of the privileged. He should know, yet he had a hard time digesting the air of superiority Josephine seemed to exhale. He would have to change tactics.

"Please call me Rainey," he reminded her. "You're really something," he complimented to pull her attention back to him.

"Thank you. God made me like that."

Dumbfounded, it was on the edge of Rainey's tongue to inform her that she tipped the scale of arrogance. "Listen, I know we didn't get off to a good start—"

"Which was a result of your bad manners," she scolded as a teacher would a naughty student. The reprimand came with a re-freshing smile that, if duplicated, would put him out of business.

Surely, she was teasing. He snickered. That was a point worth arguing, but at another time. "Umm-hmm. So, do you work here as part of a work-study program? You mentioned you were an exchange student." He barraged her with questions.

"Dr. Rey—Rainey, those are not questions that I can answer while I'm on duty."

"Of course. Then I guess you're going to have to go out with me." He stuffed his hands in his pants pockets, confident she had fallen into his trap.

"Only if I am properly asked."

He grinned. She wasn't. Her frankness was fresh and almost insulting. "My apologies. Josephine Yaa Amoah, will you have dinner with me on Friday?"

She shook her head. "I'm sorry. I've already accepted an invi-tation from your sister. It's family night, you know."

Rainey didn't know, but he would find out. A growing line of impatient patrons dashed his comeback with a plan B or C. Rainey stepped out of the way. "Perhaps another time."

"Perhaps."

Discarded one more time and not liking it, Rainey stormed out of the library. He didn't bother looking back. Josephine twisted his insides. She was as complex as she was beautiful, but no woman rejected his advances when he offered them. No woman. Did she go to sleep and wake up dressed in complexity?

Forgoing his car, he opted to walk the one block to Church Road. The Whistle Stop was hard to miss, rooted on top of a small hill beside train trestles.

Rainey shook his head. Cheney had built a picturesque life in a fairytale world. *How did Cheney move past her guilt and find happiness?* he wondered as a train conductor raced by the former train depot, tooting its whistle. Rainey heard excited children's muffled screams. He smiled. He was glad he had come.

CHAPTER 19

"It's show time," Parke yelled upstairs to Cheney and Kami. He crossed the living room to the front door before it rang again. He was looking forward to another game night, although it would mark one more family get-together without the acknowledgment of a son. Parke wasn't a long-suffering man, and the unknown was taking a toll on his spiritual walk.

God had spoken James 1:4: *But let patience have her perfect work, that you may be perfect and entire, wanting nothing.*

Sighing, Parke struggled to fully yield to God's reprimand. Presently, he wanted to stew in his human displeasure. If he found one more gray hair on his thirty-six-year-old head, he would purchase a box of Just for Men then buy shares in the company. As he waited for the okay to prove or disprove that Gilbert's adopted son was his biological heir, Parke welcomed his family as a respite from worrying.

Let patience have her perfect work, God repeated. *Let her work!*

"Yes, Lord. Please help me," Parke said with a huff. He had little choice but to accept God's chastisement. He quickly re-grouped, so he could enjoy this time with his family.

According to Parke's mother, the informal game night had become a traditional Friday family get-together since Parke and his brothers were snotty-nosed nuisances. As children, the Jamie-son boys couldn't wait for the end of the week—no chores, no school the following day, and no regularly scheduled bed time, courtesy of game night.

The rules were simple: no serious discussions of any kind for the next couple of hours. The board games were selected by majority votes. Educational and African-American themes were always encouraged. Now, three decades later, two married sons, one granddaughter, and no dog—despite Kami's pleas—the get-togethers thrived on a monthly family night schedule. Tonight, Parke, Cheney, and Kami were the designated hosts.

The aroma of Cheney's secret recipe for meatballs drifted in the air as Kami's footsteps thundered down the stairs. As Parke opened the door, one boisterous greeting led the chorus of others.

"Hey, Parke. What's up, man? Thanks for the invite," Ellington said, slapping Parke on the back. "Sorry I'm empty handed this time, but after I innocently brought a bottle of Chardonnay a while back and you refused to take it, I figured, why waste my money? I will volunteer to wash the dishes." He smirked, knowing they had purchased a Maytag built-in oversized capacity dishwasher.

Parke was about to remind his friend that his family's choice of drink was Kool-Aid, but his father was on Ellington's heels.

"Don't you shut that door, PJ," the elder Parke ordered jokingly as he and his wife, Charlotte, came in with bag-covered dishes.

Turning around, Ellington offered his help. "Oh, let me get that from you, Mrs. Jamieson."

Thinking the coast was clear, Parke closed the door. The bell chimed. He opened it and greeted Josephine.

Cheney appeared from the kitchen, evidently using the back stairwell. She always claimed she was too tall to be cute, but tonight he begged to differ. Six feet wasn't tall for a woman. When his father regaled him with stories about the late Phyllis Hyman, Parke was always mesmerized like he was now with his wife. She was so beautiful.

Parke's household wore matching royal blue polo shirts bearing the "Jamiesons Rule" logo. Kami modeled hers partially hidden by a khaki jumper. Cheney opted for a khaki skirt, and Parke had slipped on tan Dockers.

Cheney smiled when she saw Josephine. "I'm so glad you could make it."

Josephine laughed; her eyes danced with mirth. "Invitations are extended to be accepted."

As Cheney made the introductions, Ellington shoved Parke and whispered, "I like what I see, man." He grunted. "This has to be her first time at family game night. If she's going to be at the next one, I'll never skip out on another invite. Count me as a regular."

Holding up his hands, Parke stepped back. He wasn't about to play assistant to the matchmaker. That was a woman's job, and his wife was betting on Imani, not Josephine, for Ellington. Plus, Parke doubted any woman would be impressed with a man who couldn't find a pair of socks. Tonight was the latest example.

"Any updates?" Ellington muffled his question; his expression was no longer playful as his eyes followed Josephine.

"No." Parke frowned and stole a deep breath. He refused to let Gilbert Ann's lack of response ruin a good time. Still, Parke wished his son was present to experience the Jamieson love.

The identity of the next guest wasn't a mystery. Malcolm's signature Morse code ring was the prelude to his entry. He and Cheney never locked their doors when entertaining, but the Jamiesons claimed it was proper etiquette to knock or ring a bell before walking in.

Cheney excused herself from Josephine. Walking to the front door, Cheney snatched it open. Peeping over her shoulder, Parke could see Hallison and Malcolm locked in a slow kiss they should have finished in the bedroom.

"Humph. Our hotel is booked for the night," he heard Cheney tease when he came up behind her. Ellington had ditched Parke so he could mingle with one particular guest—Josephine.

Hallison giggled as the couple broke apart. She tried to take a breath, but Malcolm tickled her lips a few more times before glancing at Parke and Cheney with flaring nostrils.

"Do you mind, sister-in-law?" Malcolm feigned annoyance as he reached for the door handle, hinting for Cheney to step back before he shut the door in their faces. A second later, laughter commenced outside on Parke's porch.

Shaking her head, Cheney turned around and bumped into Parke's chest. "When they get tired or hungry, they'll come in," she mumbled, "or when Hali needs to use the bathroom." Her eyes twinkled with mischief.

Wrapping an arm around Cheney's waist, Parke smothered a kiss in her hair. "I'm glad they got their act together. I dread to think what almost happened once they split up."

She agreed.

Malcolm and Hallison were happy now. At one time, salvation separated them, but in the end, it was all a part of God's master plan. Before Parke dated Cheney, Malcolm and Hallison had a sizzling affair. Since his saintly conversion and after they tied the knot, the flames between them blazed.

The couple's gazes and caresses seemed to scorch anything or anyone who came near them. Hallison broke off their engagement when the Lord Jesus warned her to get her spiritual walk together alone. Malcolm almost lost his mind literally while jumping from woman to woman.

It took a while, but eventually Malcolm caved in to the Lord's terms, after his new love interest showed no compassion in the hospital emergency room when Cheney delivered her baby stillborn.

Parke slipped his arm from around Cheney's waist and linked

his fingers through hers. "You okay?" He searched her face for any hint of sadness that might leak through her emotional bar-riers during some game nights. The close-knit Jamiesons always reminded her of what she wanted with the Reynoldses. "One day it'll happen. Your family will be here alongside mine, bat-tling out the right answer to an outrageous question."

Sniffing, Cheney bobbed her head in agreement. "I know. I know. I believe God promised me this whole fiasco would bring us closer. Maybe I'm too impatient. Then I keep thinking about Grandma BB. I can't believe she's actually sitting in jail. I hope she's playing low."

I doubt it. Suddenly, Cheney's admission echoed in Parke's mind. Didn't God call him out on that very thing earlier? *Patience is on double duty,* he reflected on his personal circumstances.

Cheney must have sensed the change in his mood. Facing him, she frowned with concern as she searched his eyes. "Are you okay? I know your soul won't rest until you know for a fact if that boy is yours or not."

"I know he's mine." He cleared his throat and glanced at members of his family to shake the melancholy. "Hey, we're the hosts." He winked and lovingly swatted her behind. "Let's get this party started."

In the blink of an eye, Cheney retaliated by reaching behind him and pinching his bottom. "It's started. Now, go get Malcolm and Hali."

"Yes, ma'am." He saluted his wife, clicked his heels, and turned to do her bidding.

CHAPTER 20

"I love that man," Cheney said, glowing before her mind switched to the scene playing outside her door with Malcolm and Hallison. They were happy, they were a striking couple, and they were pregnant—Hallison was, of course. As Cheney walked back into kitchen to check on her dishes, she tried to dull the pain of losing three fetuses, babies, pregnancies, or whatever was the politically correct term—they were all souls.

Hallison had been the one to give Cheney her first baby shower. Now the tables were turned. Cheney would be the one to return the favor. It was bittersweet because she wouldn't be able to exchange advice about diaper rash or breastfeeding or colic— nothing with Hallison.

When Kami initially arrived as a foster child, she was almost two, potty trained, and a ready made little diva. Cheney prayed Hallison would have a healthy baby. God knew she wouldn't wish her misfortune on any woman.

She was preoccupied after checking on her macaroni and cheese when Josephine came up behind her and whispered, "You okay?"

Cheney jumped as if Josephine had said boo. She patted her chest to calm her pounding heart. "Before or after you scared me?" She busied herself washing her hands then wiping off the granite counter. "What do you need?"

"I need you to be a good hostess and give me something to drink, or is it your custom for a guest to fight for herself?"

"Fend for yourself," Cheney corrected, laughing. Understanding her blunder, Josephine joined in. Months earlier, Josephine would have felt belittled if Americans corrected her as if she lacked intelligence. Once she put her pride aside and got to know Cheney better, she depended on Cheney to help her align idioms used in American culture. "I was waiting for a friend of mine to get here, but she doesn't stop the show. By the way, you look cute."

Like Cheney's brother, Josephine seemed to create her own fashion statement. She wore a lilac T-shirt with long, drooping lace sleeves that offset denim bell-bottom jeans with bluish-purple triangular inserts near her ankles. Like Cheney, Josephine wasn't intimidated by her height. The black patent leather stilettos were at least four inches high, and multiple straps climbed her feet from her blue-polished toenails to her ankles.

She nodded. "Thank you. I purchased this in Egypt a few years ago. When I return home, you must come to visit, and we'll spend the day shopping."

"Sounds like a plan." Cheney nodded, contemplating an adventure. "How do you think Grandma BB is doing?"

"You're praying for Grandmother B, aren't you?" Josephine asked, refusing to slang Mrs. Beacon's name. When Cheney nodded, Josephine continued, "Then we'll have to start counting the days until she's back with us."

"Amen," Cheney agreed. "She has a little less than two months now."

They continued chatting as they strolled from the kitchen, carrying appetizers to the table. "Okay, everybody, let's bless the food so we can eat." Her roundup was interrupted by the doorbell. "Ah, that's probably Imani now." On her way to the door, she saw that Malcolm and Hallison had finally come inside, but they were still huddled together. Instead of stealing kisses, Malcolm was meticulously stroking Hallison's make-believe belly as if his touch would cause their child to grow.

Ah, the doting father-to-be syndrome: pathetic, annoying, and sweet. Cheney had enjoyed those moments with Parke. After their third failed attempt to have a baby, both agreed their efforts were too traumatic. They shifted their priorities to pursuing custody of Parke's biological son and rearing Kami. Their perfect plan had cracks from the beginning. God had other diversions with Mrs. Beacon's and her father's trials.

Cheney had her hand on the doorknob when the bell rang. "Hold on, Imani," she mumbled under her breath. Opening the door, Cheney was stunned and elated. It wasn't a mirage. Standing on her porch in the flesh was a long-ago prayer answered.

"Hey, sis," Rainey greeted. If possible, his smile reached beyond his eyes and passed his hairline before landing in his shoes. He twirled his car keys around one finger like a hula hoop before depositing them in his pants pocket. Rainey stepped over the threshold, edging pass her still body. He initiated a ten-second hug and moved on.

"Rainey, what are you doing here?" she stuttered, blinking as she pushed the door closed.

"This is family night," he stated with a shrug, as if she needed to be reminded.

"It is," Cheney confirmed almost in a whisper, wondering how he knew. Did it matter? she asked herself. *No.*

"I hope I'm invited," he asked cautiously, but the determination in his eyes dared anyone, including her, to tell him he had to leave.

"Always."

"Great. I'm glad to be here." Grinning, Rainey spun around. He began a mission of mingling, starting with Parke's parents, as if they were old acquaintances instead of his sister's in-laws.

Arching a brow, Cheney watched in wonder as the shock and uneasiness diminished. Aside from being suspicious, she really was happy to see her twin. Rainey Reynolds was actually in her living room for family night. She chuckled at his unusual attire of expensive cuff links with a starched denim shirt and jeans. The aftermath of some designer cologne tickled her nose. Rainey probably thought he was dressed casually, but the cuff links were a dead giveaway he had money and ample attitude to go with it.

Cheney sighed. She could count the number of times he had actually been in her home during the past three years she had been married—five visits. Cheney smirked. Tonight was an encouraging development.

She had questions, like who invited him? How did he know about family game night? Cheney couldn't recall if Rainey enjoyed playing games. What happened to the scowl that usually hung off his face when he saw her? The Lord held her tongue.

At the same moment, Parke glanced up from talking to Malcolm and stopped mid-sentence. Parke's eyes widened in surprise before a smile stretched across his face. Leaving his brother's side, Parke met Rainey halfway and shared a hearty handshake, hug, and slap on the back. "Hey, man. It's good to see you."

"Thanks. I'm glad I could make it," Rainey replied.

Rainey wormed his way farther into the room, speaking to every guest as if he were a regular. Parke glanced over his shoulder at Cheney and mouthed, "Did you know he was coming?"

"Uh-uh." She shook her head. When Parke first became interested in Cheney, he didn't know what to make of her strained relationship with her family, although he assured her he would always be in her corner. No matter how awkward the situation, Parke went out of his way to treat the Reynoldses warmly, as if there were no contention.

Casually and comfortably, Rainey nodded as he methodically chatted with Malcolm, then Hallison. He lingered as he introduced himself to Ellington. Somehow, their conversation included professions, and the two of them engaged in an abbreviated Q and A about if there was an age limit for adults to wear braces. Before the discussion was over, Rainey and Ellington exchanged numbers.

Next, Rainey tugged on Kami's ponytails then winked when she was about to protest. Rainey's eyes rested on Josephine's face. As he made her his final destination, he slowed his steps.

Thrilled in her new role as a self-appointed busybody for her brother, Cheney was annoyed when the doorbell rang, interrupting her internal plotting process. Blindly, she opened the door and didn't bother greeting her next guest.

"Well, hello to you too," Imani said dryly as she swayed into the room, closing the door behind her. She tilted her head back enough for her hair to bounce. When Imani planted her hand on her hip, she struck a pose as if she were a show headliner.

Cheney rolled her eyes. Rainey's arrival had thrown her off. She actually had forgotten Imani said she was coming late. "Sorry." As customary, whatever Imani wore, she looked great. Tonight, she was dressed in a red off-the-shoulder short dress and red sandals. Cheney hoped her friend had the night off, because she didn't look like she was going to work as a repo woman in that getup.

"Well, well, if it isn't the gorgeous little car thief," Ellington said snidely, strolling their way. With his hands stuck in his pants pockets, he stretched the fabric enough to lift the legs to flash his bare ankles. "Please tell me you don't have my truck hitched outside."

Imani's eyes widened. "Oh, was that your truck? I hauled that thing away an hour ago," she taunted. When Ellington appeared as if he were about to explode, Imani laughed. "Just kiddin'."

Cheney rolled her eyes. Imani had her going there, too, for

a moment. Typical Imani: she loved to keep men on their knees, seeking her attention.

Folding his arms, Ellington rocked on the backs of his heels. "As I informed you before, my payments are current and on time." Ellington snarled in a way that made it hard to decipher whether he was teasing or threatening.

Imani, all five feet seven inches of her, inched closer to his face. The move caught Ellington off guard, causing him to step back. She thumped her chest before pointing a red manicured nail in his face, then changed her mind and faced Cheney. "Did someone actually invite this guy?" She twisted her nose in disdain and nodded her head toward him. Imani attended less often than Ellington, and then only when Parke and Cheney were the hosts. "What do you know about black history?"

Ellington snickered. "Well, Miss Can't Read Numbers, unless you're *passing* yourself, once again you have the wrong address."

He referred to the time period between the 1940s and 1960s, when light-skinned blacks who could pass as whites were afforded better jobs because their employers thought they were Caucasian. Practicing a secret code of "don't ask, don't tell," blacks never corrected them, so that they could enjoy the benefits denied to people of color. Some movie houses, restaurants, and stores didn't encourage black patrons.

Imani wanted attention, and Ellington's remark gave it to her. It didn't take long for the pair to become the spotlight. Parke and Cheney were about to intervene when the elder Parke commanded the floor. "The Duke is our guest, Imani, as well as you. If you two want to fight, take it to the board games. Now, let's eat." The elder Parke clapped his hands as Kami jumped up and down, rubbing her stomach.

"Something tells me we'll all need our energy to watch the resurrection of *Crossfire.*" The popular CNN current event news show that ended in 2005 was known for heated debates among its four hosts.

Ssshing her husband, Charlotte slapped his wrist. "Honey, it's not our house." She frowned.

"It's okay, Mom. I'm ready to eat too." Parke patted his stomach. "Cheney has everything set up. Let's bless the food and the cooks."

Everyone moved to the next room. Kami latched on to Hallison as they circled the table. As Cheney linked hands with Josephine, Rainey broke their link. Without saying a word, he took their hands, bowed his head, and waited for the prayer to begin. Again, Cheney lifted her brow, squinting. *Who is this guy?*

After a few minutes, when no verbal prayer was offered, guests peeped at Parke for directions, but Kami had already started.

"Lord Jesus, in your name, bless my mommy and daddy, bless me to like everything on my plate, bless my grandma and grandpa, Uncle Malcolm and Auntie Hali, and bless Uncle Rainey." Opening her eyes, she stared at Josephine. "Ah, are you my auntie or something?"

Josephine smiled at the innocent question. "Back home, in my village, we are all one family. We are all related."

Satisfied, Kami nodded. "Okay. Amen."

"And Lord, please bless and sanctify our food. Amen," Cheney added.

The adults chuckled as they broke the chain. Plates clattered for the next twenty minutes as the guests sampled hearty portions of the soul food potluck dishes, including cornbread-stuffed chicken, and Meeting House potato salad. They *oohed*, *ahhed*, and moaned over Cheney's secret recipe meatballs and three-cheese macaroni and cheese.

Even Kami asked for more seven-layered salad. When there was a slight respite in eating, Cheney went into the kitchen and returned with three rich, guilty desserts. Parke waved her off, fearful of the Death by Chocolate cake, gooey butter cake, and sweet potato pecan pie.

"My wife is trying to kill me," he said, patting his stomach.

Per the family rules, after the meal was finished, the men cleared the table and loaded the new dishwasher they called Big Bertha. Even Rainey joined in on the designated duties. Parke squinted at Cheney. She admitted she was just as perplexed by her brother's behavior as Parke. At times, Rainey seemed preoccupied with Josephine. Evidently, Josephine was unaware, as she engaged in a conversation with Imani about the latest neighborhood news. Ten minutes later, the table was cleared for the board games.

Malcolm and Hallison, as usual, couldn't keep their eyes and hands off each other. Ellington refused to openly look at Imani, but when he did, he snarled. Cheney wasn't buying his indifference. Shaking her head, Cheney sighed. *Has the entertainment already begun?*

Rainey asked, "What kind of games are we playing?"

"The black ones," Imani volunteered. Instead of addressing Rainey, she glared at Ellington. Cheney recognized the look that had instilled fear in bullies on the playground. After a few scuffles during recess, no one questioned whether she was black enough. As far as Cheney knew, Imani's descendants were from Australia.

Cheney recognized the challenge and stood. Whatever her friend was up to, Cheney needed to spray pesticide on the plot. "Imani, can you help me for a moment in the kitchen?"

Josephine got up. "I can—"

Cheney waved her off. "Nah, I need Imani for this."

Seemingly clueless, Imani excused herself. Trailing Cheney into the next room, Imani sauntered across the hardwood floor with a rhythm meant to garnish a man's attention. Cheney glanced over her shoulder. Imani had accomplished the mission with Rainey—who never held a personal interest in the woman he considered a play sister, but never minded looking—and Ellington, who appeared in agony for looking. Parke and Malcolm dared not to sneak a peek.

Once they were behind closed doors, Cheney didn't waste a second. "What is wrong with you two? Parke told me what happened with the repo mix-up, but good grief. That's been a while ago. Ellington needs to get over it, and you need to stop baiting him. Parke attended Lincoln University with The Duke, and they're frat brothers."

Imani folded her arms and appeared bored.

"I even had the silliest notion of introducing you two."

"That was silly. Thanks, but no thanks," she said, offended. "Look at him."

"Okay?" Bewildered, Cheney shrugged. She twisted her lips, confused, waiting for her friend to explain.

Imani stomped her heel. "He's white."

"Ohh . . ." Cheney said as if a mental light bulb came on. She rested her fists on her hips. "Look in the mirror, Imani, so are you."

"Since when?" Imani jutted her chin as if she were back on the playground; then she backed down. "Okay, but it's our secret. If anyone asks, I'm Puerto Rican, or another black ethnic group."

Cheney threw up her arms. If Imani had been on the same bus with Rosa Parks, there was no doubt she would've encouraged Rosa to stay where she was, and Imani would've handled it. "Girl, God has a whole different group with your name on it."

Imani huffed. "I know, I know—the saints."

"As long as you know. C'mon. We'd better get back in there."

"The only thing I've got to say is Ellington better not miss a car payment on my watch." She turned to go back into the dining room then twirled around. "One other thing. Who dressed him?"

"I don't know."

Imani shook her head in pity. "Whoever did forgot to put socks on him."

CHAPTER 21

What is up with Imani? Rainey lifted a brow. As a first-time guest, he wasn't about to referee the ruckus as he did when they were growing up. Imani had her claws out, and Rainey was glad he wasn't her target. Although she had always been a looker when they were in high school, Imani had too much attitude for any man. Rainey thought about warning Ellington to be on guard, but decided against it as Rainey glanced at Josephine again.

The moment Cheney and Imani returned to the room, Ellington blurted, "Well, I'm ready." He snorted at Imani.

"You think I'm not?" She glared and flopped in her seat. Rambling through her purse, she yanked out a stick of gum. Once she managed to finally unwrap it, Imani balled it up then stuffed it in her mouth. She popped it a couple of times and cracked her knuckles. "Shuffle the deck, roll the dice, or pull a number. Whatever. Bring it on."

Rainey restrained himself from falling out of his chair, laughing. He had forgotten how much fun it was to witness Imani's antics in full throttle. The only thing missing from her dramatics was her signature backward baseball cap. Blinking, Rainey had to refocus. She was not his object of concentration. Josephine held that distinction, and it irked Rainey that she did. Refocusing, he scrutinized a worn board game, *What Black Folks Know*, as Parke laid it on the table.

"This is my wife's favorite. She doesn't think I know she plays it solitary to expand her knowledge about Black America when I'm not home." He winked at Cheney.

His sister blushed. The lightbulb of acknowledgment seemed to flash in Rainey's head before burning brightly. Parke really did love her, and she was truly happy. The few times he had been around Parke, he summarized the guy was okay, but to make his sister blush—whoa.

"The maximum number of players is six, so pick your partners," Parke gave the instructions. "And don't fight over Cheney," he added.

"Josephine, would you like to be on a winning team?" Rainey asked nonchalantly. He had to tread carefully with the unpredictable woman. He wasn't about to supersede Imani's show-stopping performance as the night's attraction to get Josephine to take notice. His ego could only be bruised so many times.

"Thank you for your invitation, but I've decided to join forces with my neighbor."

Shrugging, he accepted Josephine's answer, but he chided himself for asking. That left Rainey no choice but to be partnered with the sockless bandit—Ellington. Rainey hoped the guy could back up the words he was smarting off at Imani earlier, or they would be the biggest losers.

"Okay, then it's settled. The object of the game is simple. Roll the dice and pick a card. If you don't think the question is enough of a challenge for your opponent, then you may substitute with one of your own." Parke raised his hand. "It can't be fictional, and it will be verified by others in the room, dictionary, or Internet. In order to win, you must stump every team with a question. The first pair to baffle the others for two rounds is the champ."

"Sounds easy enough." Rainey relaxed as others sat straighter, leaned forward, and waited for the game to begin, as if a gun would pop and start the first lap.

Imani was the last to roll the dice, but had the highest number. She pulled a card for her team. After a few moments, she transformed a snicker into a mischievous grin. She angled her head toward Ellington. "I think this is a preschool question—"

Kami intercepted and raised her hand. "Miss Imani, I'll be in kindergarten next year. Ask me." She jumped up and down.

Rainey was amused by his niece's eagerness. As children, he and Cheney had high IQs. He wouldn't be surprised if Kami had inherited it too. Wait a minute, he shook himself. That quickly, he had forgotten Kami was adopted.

"It's okay with me," Cheney approved.

Ellington leaned back. "Yeah, ask the little diva princess in the house," he challenged. "And see if you're smarter than a preschooler."

Rainey hoped Ellington was as fast a learner as his nemesis, Imani. Would Josephine become Rainey's archenemy in the game? She didn't bait him as Imani did to Parke's friend; neither did they see eye to eye. As a matter of fact, Rainey was convinced Josephine had forgotten about his presence.

Ignoring Ellington, Imani twisted her lips. She appeared to be pondering a difficult question; then she snapped her finger. "Ready?"

Kami nodded. Her eyes were wide with eagerness. She gripped the edge of the table so she wouldn't miss a word. Clear nail polish dotted with sparkles covered her tiny fingernails.

"Name the first black President of the United States."

"Barack Obama." Kami clapped and hopped in place.

The Jamiesons cheered her on. Rainey chuckled. The answer was a no-brainer to anyone not in Pampers.

"You cheated," Imani playfully scolded.

"Um-um." Kami shook her head. "Daddy makes me watch the news every evening."

"Name his wife."

"Michelle," Kami proudly told Imani, giggling. Again, Kami clapped excitedly as if she were a pet that earned a treat.

Imani put on a game face. "His two daughters."

"Sasha and Malia."

By this time, the family got rowdy. "Go, Kami. Go, go . . ."

"The dog's name?" Imani challenged, reclining in her chair with a "gotcha" smile when Kami paused.

"Bo. I won. I won." She pranced around, fanning her two long ponytails from side to side.

Frowning, Imani stared, bewildered. She jerked her head from face to face, seeking confirmation. "Is that right? Is she right?"

When everyone nodded, Imani groaned.

Ellington barked, "Not only can't you read addresses, but you just got whipped by a preschooler." His amusement was infectious as others ribbed the questioner.

Imani sneered and eyed Kami. "Show-off." She winked to lessen her blow.

Parke pulled his daughter aside and gave her a tight hug. "That's a Jamieson."

Rainey was impressed. At moments like this, he felt a tinge of sadness. Would his birth child have been as smart? He didn't have time to reflect on the fantasy. It appeared Imani wasn't going down without a fight. She turned to her intended opponents, Team Rainey and Ellington.

"Okay, since you're smarter than a four-year-old, Ellington, you can answer this one for your team. Name five cities that were once, and possibly remain, a sundown town." Imani crossed her arms.

"Thanks a lot, partner," Rainey mumbled sarcastically to Ellington for stirring the wrath of Imani. "Hey, I'm a first-timer. Can't I get a medical term or an oral procedure? I'm clueless to what a sundown town is, so I can't name any."

"Too bad your big-mouth cohort can't help. Give up?" Imani reached for her pen and pad, chuckling. In exaggerated movements, she tilted her head and poised her finger, ready to mark the first loser on the paper.

"At one time, there were more than fifteen hundred sundown towns, including most suburbs across the United States. There was no doubt of the town's allegiance; like Anna, Illinois, hinting, ain't no niggers allowed after sundown. They were common along the East Coast. There was one sundown town in Warren, Michigan; even the Los Angeles suburb of Glendale was once considered one to avoid."

Imani was shocked. Her jaw dropped as Rainey's eyes bucked. "How do you know that?" She chomped on a new piece of gum she stuffed in her mouth.

"I do know how to read. There is even a book called . . . hmm . . . called *Sundown Towns*!" Ellington baited her.

Rainey was way out of his league. He did not come to be shamed, especially in front of a woman who already seemed to think very little of him. He straightened his shoulders; he was Dr. Rainey L. Reynolds, a third-generation doctor and prominent orthodontist.

"Okay, that's enough, you two." Parke pounded his fist on the table like a gavel. "Rainey, I believe you're next. Pull a card."

So much for the pep talk. Rainey swallowed. He was no match for a Jamieson game night. He flipped the card and seemed to muse over the question before directing it at the lovely, but egotistical Josephine. "This may be too hard of a question, since you're not originally from here. I'm not trying to ambush you."

"Don't concern yourself about my intellect. I'm ready." Josephine smiled and tapped her manicured hands on the table.

"Name the oldest cemetery in St. Louis, and anyone famous who could be buried there." Rainey didn't make up the question, and frankly, he had never been to the landmark.

Josephine bit her lip, thinking, then stretched her mouth into a smile. "It's a toss-up between Bellefontaine and Calvary Cemetery."

Rainey looked to Parke. "She can't guess—"

"It is rude to interrupt. I was thinking aloud to myself." She held up her hand. "I'll pick Bellefontaine because playwright Tennessee Williams is buried there, as well as beer pioneer Adolphus Busch."

He shook his head in amazement as he read the answer on the card. "How did you know that?"

"I'm a library science graduate student. We are trained to locate and absorb information on just about anything. Search engines are endless."

Rainey twitched his mustache as if he didn't believe her.

"Plus" Josephine paused, lifting a finger. "I assisted a high schooler who was researching local epidemics after the health authorities warned of a swine flu pandemic. We both became fascinated with St. Louis's 1849 cholera outbreak that ironically delayed the completion of the cemetery, so that the grounds could be used to bury the dead. About one-tenth of the city's population died from the epidemic in one summer."

After two rounds, Rainey realized the games they played were about more than intellect; pride seemed to beam through everyone's face as they correctly recited the answers.

Parke's brother, Malcolm, and Hallison were one point ahead at the beginning of the third round. They threatened to go in for the kill when Hallison read the card. "Okay, Papa P," she said, grinning at the elder Parke. "What was the name of the first black trade union? I'll give you a hint."

The elder Parke snickered. "Save your hint, daughter. That union was formed at one of the largest employers of male ex-slaves. Oddly, in those days, one requirement was the darker your skin, the better your chance of getting hired."

Rainey, along with others in the room, was quiet. Still clueless, he hoped Parke's father would explain. Even Josephine's expression seemed to consider an answer. Good. At least he wasn't the only one stumped.

"The Brotherhood of Sleeping Car Porters with the Pullman Company," the elder Parke said with a nonchalant flair.

Rainey couldn't resist leaning across the table and whispering to Josephine, "Did you know the answer?"

When she shook her head, Rainey wanted to pump his fist in the air with a "touchdown" stance.

"I guess I'd better be the one to check a book out from the library," Josephine admitted with a sheepish smile. Rainey was hypnotized. Man, he wished he was granted a closer inspection of her perfect teeth.

"Maybe I will, too," Rainey said.

"If you're a resident of Ferguson, then I'll be happy to assist you."

Rainey wished the woman would at least flirt with him a few times. If only he could take her up on the offer. Ferguson wasn't his home, but that didn't mean he couldn't stop by. Ideas were already percolating in his brilliant mind.

An hour later, after snacks were reduced to crumbs, Cheney intervened. "Okay, everybody, no doubt we're a studious bunch and not much can slip by us."

"Cheney and Parke," Rainey interrupted, tilting his head toward Kami, who was knocked out, "you've done a great job with my niece."

"Thank you," Cheney mouthed as her eyes teared at his compliment. Clearing her throat, she recovered to finish her announcement. "I'm tired and getting grouchy. Sorry, we'll have to pick up where we left off next month, or start with a new game."

The guests murmured, stood, and stretched. Rainey was

happy he didn't have to rack his brain anymore that night. Halli-son and Malcolm, appearing contrite, mumbled they were close to winning. Wearily, Cheney and Parke hugged everyone and thanked them for coming. Rainey was almost out the door when Cheney embraced him and dragged him to the side.

"Not so fast, Rainey Reynolds. Not that I'm not glad to see you, but what inspired your impromptu visit?"

Folding his arms, he baited her. "Are you saying I wasn't in-vited, or I'm not welcomed?"

Cheney didn't back down. "So, now you want to play games? As long as I've been married and invited my family, no one ever accepted."

"Josephine invited me. Will that work?" Rainey grasped for straws. He would let his sister figure it out, because he really didn't know why he had come.

"Invited you? She was a first-time guest herself." She put her hands on her hips.

"Actually, she mentioned it." Swallowing, Rainey scanned the room. He didn't make eye contact as he confessed, "So I invited myself to check things out."

Cheney grinned. "You invited yourself, huh?" She squinted as if she was piecing two things together. "You were checking out Josephine." When Rainey didn't respond, Cheney teased, "What's wrong? Cat got your tongue?"

"Am I on the witness stand?" Wrong choice of words. Sud-denly, his good mood snapped. He didn't want to revisit the situation that caused the contention between them. He tried to push the incident behind him and move on, but at times, like now, he still brewed. Cheney had no idea the anger that was boiling to the top.

"Speaking of trial," she said softly, "God is going to bless Dad for accepting responsibility for his bad judgment."

"Yeah, but that's your personal decision. I'm still convinced it was an accident that should've stayed buried."

"Umm-hmm. Well, since you're not admitting you're here because Josephine is here, then you probably would never admit that without Grandma BB, there would be no Josephine. There are no coincidences in our lives. To be attracted to Josephine, who is very beautiful, that would make you as much a traitor as me, since she's connected to Grandma BB."

"A traitor? Absolutely not," Rainey said, fuming. His nostrils flared.

Lifting a brow, she challenged him to continue. "And the reason is?"

"Forget it. You're guilty by association. I don't want to join your club." Rainey was about to stalk out, confused that after a fun-filled night, he had reverted to a person he was battling to shed.

Cheney smiled as if she knew what was going through his head. She kissed him on his cheek and turned to walk away, leaving him to close the door behind him. "Oh, by the way, you're guilty by infatuation, so come back anytime."

CHAPTER 22

On day one hundred and twenty, Mrs. Beacon was released from jail. Cheney had missed her presence and couldn't wait to give her a crushing hug. They chatted on the phone as soon as Mrs. Beacon was escorted home by a van full of red hat ladies.

"Give me a day or two to sleep on my water bed, and I'll be back to my old cheerful self," Mrs. Beacon told Cheney. They agreed to enjoy a picnic in Wabash Park, since Kami was officially out of school for the summer.

Cheney had taken the day off work, using one of the few remaining vacation days she had left after attending the trials. She couldn't explain her emotions. Her surrogate grandmother did the crime and served the time. Now it was time to move on. She prayed her father would be given probation.

She was minutes away from Mrs. Beacon's house when red and blue flashing lights in her rearview mirror alarmed her. Without its siren blaring, a patrol car was silently advancing. Panicking, Cheney prayed she hadn't exceeded the speed limit, rolled through a stop sign, or committed any other infraction. She immediately clicked on her right turn signal. Drivers obliged, allowing her to pull over.

When the Ferguson police car sped by, she breathed a sigh of relief; then Cheney did a double take. A woman in the passenger seat of the patrol cruiser waved frantically out the window, trying to get her attention. Her mouth dropped open. "Grandma BB!"

Cheney's heart leaped in her chest. The woman was barely out of jail, and already she was in police custody. Cheney grimaced. Once the coast was clear, Cheney maneuvered back in traffic to trail them at a lawful speed and respectable distance. They headed toward Mrs. Beacon's house, where two police cars had blocked off the street. Her heart pounded in her chest. She didn't know what to think.

Cheney parked as close to the area as she dared. Turning off the ignition, she almost strangled herself getting out of her car. She had forgotten to unbuckle her seat belt; Kami's too. She quickly released both restraints.

The passenger door of the police car swung open with force. Polished Stacy Adams shoes were the first things to slap the ground. The hem of a red housedress followed, but Grandma BB didn't get out. Ignoring the high heels she was wearing, Cheney almost jogged to the cruiser. Kami's pace was unhurried.

"Grandma BB, are you all right?" Cheney squatted, making eye contact with her friend, who was still in the passenger seat, unrestrained by handcuffs. At least it meant she wasn't under arrest again. Cheney was more than confused. "What's going on? What did you do?"

"Grandma B!" Kami shouted when she saw Mrs. Beacon.

"Shhh, chile." Mrs. Beacon frowned at both of them, placing a finger on her lips. "They've got the house surrounded."

House? Whose house? Cheney looked up and scanned the block. She recognized the house of her former neighbor, Kenneth Dawson, as the center of commotion. His decorative beveled glass front door was slightly ajar. Two officers had their weapons drawn. Cheney's heart pounded in fear. "Oh, dear God. I hope Mr. Dawson is all right," she whispered as she began to say a prayer.

Shaking her head, Mrs. Beacon twisted her lips in disappointment, an expression Mrs. Beacon displayed when she felt Cheney lacked sleuthing acumen in crucial situations. "Of course Dawson's all right. He's not even there. He left for the barbershop about an hour and twenty-three minutes ago. You know Dawson's like clockwork, rain or shine. Every Thursday at three-fifteen, he leaves for a haircut. Don't know why. He doesn't have enough hair to run a fork through it. " Mrs. Beacon returned her concentration to the unfolding scene. "Looks like I got out of jail just in time."

"Grandma BB," Kami said loudly, giving her a hug.

Mrs. Beacon quickly returned the hug, fiddled in the oversized pockets of her housedress, and pulled out a wrapped sucker. She stuck it in Kami's hand. "Go sit down. We'll play a game of cards later."

With a wide grin, Kami quietly followed Mrs. Beacon's instructions as she tore the plastic off the lollipop. Her friend didn't make a move to get completely out of the car. She seemed content to use the passenger door as a shield.

Details from a true neighborhood watchwoman, Cheney thought. Someone needed to suggest to Mr. Dawson that he change his routine. Clearly it was predictable if Mrs. Beacon had it down to the minute.

"Whew!" she whispered. "For a moment, you had me worried that you had violated your parole," Cheney admitted. Lifting her brow, Cheney felt there had to be more to the story. She cautiously touched Mrs. Beacon's arm. Startled, the woman almost jumped out of her Stacy Adams.

"What, girl?" Mrs. Beacon gritted her teeth, annoyed. "We've got an active crime scene. Be quiet or we'll miss something. Although . . ." She paused, thinking. "I guess technically, I've violated my parole when I drove away in those thugs' get-away car. Can you believe I didn't have my license and an insurance card?

Anyway, that's not even part of the story." She peered again at Mr. Dawson's house.

Cheney was growing impatient as she tried to pry out bits of information to no avail. A few minutes later, she checked on Kami, who had begun playing hopscotch on the sidewalk. No doubt, her candy was gone. Becoming restless, Cheney wanted answers, and she wasn't getting them fast enough. She was inches away from tapping Mrs. Beacon's shoulder when the police shouted, "Drop it!" Cheney obeyed, releasing her purse and keys, which crashed to the pavement.

Mrs. Beacon peeked over her shoulder at Cheney and grumbled. "Not you. Them." She pointed.

Three men, who could easily be eligible for a football draft if weight and size were the only requirements, threw their goods on the lawn: a microwave, flat-screen television, and a tricycle. Cheney wondered at the street value for heisting a kid's bike.

The robbers' arms flew in the air in surrender. Their legs gave way as they dropped to their knees. The police raced toward them. It didn't take long for them to cuff and haul them off Mr. Dawson's property.

About fifteen minutes later, the officer who drove the cruiser with Mrs. Beacon suddenly reappeared. Cheney hadn't realized he had left. He returned the gun to his holster and complimented her former neighbor. "It was dangerous, but you took down some big ones. Thanks, Grandma BB. Next time, don't tamper with the evidence, or I'll have to inform your probation officer."

"Yeah," Mrs. Beacon replied nonchalantly as she struggled to stand, ignoring the warning.

Standing, Cheney assisted her friend before bending down to pick up her purse and keys off the ground. She checked on Kami to make sure she was still in eyesight, then tugged Mrs. Beacon aside.

"Okay, I don't need to ask how you knew about the break-in. I'm sure your minute-by-minute watch from your front window saved the day. Now, what evidence is the officer talking about?"

"Oh, nothing really. He's complaining about me stealing their get-away vehicle, but I took them crooks down, didn't I?" Mrs. Beacon shook herself free. "You sure are nosy, and you don't even live on our block anymore. This is how it went down. I was in the house, minding my own business, when I sensed something was amiss."

Cheney crossed her arms and lifted a brow. "Right. You can smell trouble coming a town away," she exaggerated.

"You know it. Okay, I was conducting my half-hour neighborhood security check. That's when I noticed this black van pull up across the street." Mrs. Beacon leaned in and winked. "Evidently the dudes had cased the joint. Then two guys jumped out the back of the van. They were dressed in all black, like in those spy movies. Anyway, they shoved black caps over their faces and took off toward the house. Now who wears a knit cap in June?"

Raising her hand as a student, Cheney answered dryly. "Burglars."

Mrs. Beacon huffed and rolled her eyes. "Smart mouth. That was my cue they were up to no good. I documented the time then reached for my binoculars. When the crooks hurried around the back of Dawson's house, the driver got out of the van. As he strolled to the front door, the man was constantly looking both ways. Let's say they weren't delivering any *Watchtower* pamphlets."

Cheney's head was starting to spin as she checked her watch. "Grandma BB, can you give me the short version of how you ended up in a patrol car? I need to go home and start dinner."

"Don't rush me. Humph," she snapped. "Anyway, while they were inside, I ran across the street to write down the license plate number. That's when I noticed the motor running. Now, this part I'm not making up. That hussy next door, Imani, pulled up in that monstrous tow truck. She was about to repo the van. Can you believe that?" Mrs. Beacon asked incredulously. "What kind of stupid criminals get their getaway car repo'd?"

Only Grandma BB's truth is stranger than fiction. It was drama Cheney didn't mind missing. She massaged her temples. "Can this get any worse?" She turned to leave when Mrs. Beacon stopped her.

"Well, it could've been. Thanks to quick thinking on my part, I stole their get-away car and drove it to the police department with Imani hot on my trail. I left her at the station. She's trying to convince them she has an order from the bank to repossess the thing. The last I heard was the lieutenant arguing the impounded vehicle was now evidence." Mrs. Beacon laughed. Her thrill was to gain the upper hand on her annoying neighbor. "I came back to the crime scene with backup."

"Yep, that's you. Always a mastermind."

Mrs. Beacon grinned wide. "Yeah . . . I bet this gets me the highest neighborhood watch medal they have," Mrs. Beacon said excitedly. "I may have to nominate myself." She winked. "Go home and start dinner. I gotta go change my housecoat and polish my shoes. You know there's nothing like a fresh shine on a pair of Stacy Adams!"

"What about the picnic?"

"Take it to Parke. I'm still on duty. He'll eat anything you cook." Mrs. Beacon grinned and sighed. "Ah . . . it's great to be back."

CHAPTER 23

"Happy Father's Day, Daddy," Kami yelled, jumping on her parents' California king bed, dragging her present.

Parke moaned, scooting Cheney over to make room, not for Kami, but for her gift. Whatever it was, he didn't want to get poked. Parke managed to lift an eyelid. The wrapping paper missed a spot. The need for guessing was unnecessary. It was a fishing pole.

He held in a chuckle. His daughter was slick. Kami knew he didn't like fishing. Parke preferred eating them, instead of catching, cleaning, and trying to convince his wife to cook them. Of course, if he had a son, he would be forced to change his way of thinking.

Celebrating Father's Day with a son might not ever happen. Parke berated himself for blatantly giving Gilbert the heads-up of his intentions to take legal action. In hindsight, that probably wasn't the best time to be truthful. A few days ago, his hope was dashed when Twinkie called with the heart-wrenching news. Parke slept badly as the conversation replayed in his head.

Kami Jamieson would be his only child, unless he and Cheney chose to adopt again. Parke decided to face the facts he was rearing a tomboy. "Ouch," he yelled as Kami kneed him, causing his abdomen to throb. The distraction didn't stop him from recalling his conversation with Twinkie.

"Parke, I'm sorry to bother you, but you've been patient.

You've backed away from calling me daily. Four days is your new record." Twinkie had released a heavy sigh. "Through Gilbert Ann's attorney, the Anns won't agree to a paternity test. If that is your son, we may never know."

He was speechless as his heart plummeted. "It was one simple request," he whispered. As far as he was concerned, the law owed him that much. Parke was confident he heard God's voice telling him He had his back, but what did that mean? The Parke Jamieson legacy would end with him at the number six—seven, if Parke considered the previous son who passed away before he took his first breath.

So, that was it. Their decision was final. Parke couldn't bring himself to tell his wife the mission was over. Cheney was still bubbling over the fact that Rainey had come to family game night a few weeks ago. In spite of Rainey's recent animosity relapse, Cheney rejoiced, believing it was part of God fulfilling His prophecy of drawing the Reynoldses closer, even if it was one member for now.

"Parke, are you there?" Twinkie had asked hesitantly.

He adjusted the cordless phone on his ear. "Yeah," he said more forcefully than he wanted.

"There is one more thing. His attorney advises you against making any further contact with them, or you'll be slapped with a restraining order."

"I see." Parke remembered his thumb hovering over the END button after he mumbled thank you. He didn't care if Twinkie heard him or not. His attempt to blink away the moisture building in his eyes was futile. He silently cried for another child he believed was his, but couldn't have.

Later that night, while Cheney took Kami to a birthday party, he talked to God while on his knees; then he sat still, praying. Finally, Parke paced throughout his bedroom, speaking in unknown tongues. It was always a comfort, knowing that it was God's New Testament evidence that He was listening.

He was physically, mentally, and spiritually drained when he retired to bed much earlier than his normal eleven o'clock. Twice during the night, God woke him and reminded him he was already blessed with a daughter who would bring him joy.

"Ouch," Parke shouted. That joy was now kneeing him in the chest.

"Daddy, it's what you wanted. We can go fishing after church." Kami's excitement was contagious.

Parke banished his pity party as he scooted up in the bed. He yanked the covers off Cheney's head. "Hey, if I have to get up, so do you."

"No," Cheney rebelled, squeezing her eyes shut.

Briefly, Parke thought about the sweet revenge of connecting a hook to the pole and snagging it on Cheney's lacy underwear. She would wake up then. He grinned as he pinched her behind. Cheney screamed and shot up, gripping the covers. Thank God Cheney always slipped into a T-shirt before going to sleep just in case their daughter paid them a night visit.

Not waiting for him, Kami laughed as she ripped off the paper for him to inspect her gift. Exaggerating his surprise and pleasure, he grabbed Kami in a bear hug. She squealed her delight and he held on, knowing she was the true gift from God to cherish. "Okay, princess diva. What's the first morning rule in our house?"

She twisted her lips before her brown eyes widened. "Pray!"

That was not the answer Parke was looking for. He nodded. "Okay. The second rule."

Kami grinned. "Brush our teeth."

"Right. Last one to the bathroom has to rake the leaves in the fall," Parke challenged as the three scrambled off the bed.

***

The Jamiesons were late for church, courtesy of Parke not following instructions to assemble the fishing pole. They walked in as the praise team ended the worship segment. It was one of those special days when their church didn't complain about the crowd. Fortunately, Malcolm and Hallison held them seats.

As the three entered the pew, Parke smirked. It wasn't the first time he wondered if the couple shopped online. He had never seen two people dress so much alike. It was almost sickening. If Hallison wore black, so did Malcolm. If she was decked out in red, he wore something in the red family—masculine, of course. Today, they were dressed in white from Hallison's hat to her shoes. Malcolm was wrapped in so much white he resembled a groom ready to walk down the aisle. Both were all smiles.

Parke hoped God would sprinkle some of their jubilation on him before church ended. As Parke knelt to pray, he whispered, "Lord, help me get through this, because I know how to pray, but I don't know what to pray anymore. Thank you. Amen."

Getting up, Parke sat at the same time as Cheney. He guided her closer. Kami was occupied, rambling through Hallison's purse for candy. Children's church was closed so that families could be together on Father's Day.

Malcolm frowned and nudged Parke. "It's Father's Day, old man. You okay?"

"Yeah."

His brother eyed him, but didn't address his doubts as the pastor walked to the pulpit.

Parke grabbed his Bible and began flipping the pages. He desperately needed God to help him reconcile that his attempts for verifying the boy was his were over. Parke needed to get it together before he shared the disappointing news with Cheney. He had to convince her he was all right and would accept the outcome with dignity and grace. That didn't even sound like a Jamieson.

"Praise the Lord, family, and happy Father's Day." Pastor Scott waited as the congregation responded. Nodding afterward, he opened his Bible, but didn't direct his congregants to the passage. He hesitated in quoting a scripture and removed his reading glasses. The pastor looked back out in the audience. "You know, becoming a father is the easy part, and it doesn't take love for it to be accomplished. Being a dad, on the other hand, requires love, strength, and forgiveness. It's a privilege worth the headache. I commend dads who strive to rear their black boys to be strong black men, mentally and spiritually. It's Father's Day, yet it's no guarantee that our children will do and say the right things to make us happy."

Leaning against the podium, Pastor Scott shrugged. "We can lead by example, good or bad. In the Old Testament, there are plenty of cases where kings served the one and living God. That was the example. When their sons took over the reign, some worshipped the God of their fathers. Others chose wickedness, but the most important thing I want you to understand was they had an example . . . ."

Parke listened. He struggled not to twist what the preacher was saying. Parke might possibly never know if he was the father to the boy. His black son would be reared by a white man. Parke could only pray the child would learn his black roots.

Pastor Scott cracked his reverie. "Today is a happy day, regardless of your relationship with your son or daughter. I don't know what battles you're fighting right now. I don't know how submerged you are in your valley, but Psalm 34:1 says, *I will bless the Lord at all times. His praise shall continuously be in my mouth.* You can read the other verses." He shook his finger at the audience. "When is the best time to extol the Lord?"

The congregation responded, "At all times."

He nodded. "You've gotten the worst news you've ever received about your child. When you open your mouth, what should come out first?" He cupped his ear, listening for their answer. "Complaints are not an option. God expects more from us than lip service. Your soul, spirit, and body should be in sync. Read Luke 19:40. Praise is the one thing we're not supposed to contain. It's automatic . . . in good times, in bad times. Everything that God created will praise Him. The wind, the sea, the water, the grass in the pasture, even the stones give off praise. It's all about being in the presence of God, showing off his handiwork."

Parke agreed with everything his pastor preached, but lacked the mental strength to give the Lord Jesus more than lip praise. He was angry, disappointed, heartbroken, and confused. His mind wandered.

"I need to get through to you today. It's simplistic, but praising the Lord works. If He tells you something, believe it. Remember, the devil likes attention. Don't give it to the snake. Focus on God, and He will speak encouragement, peace, salvation, promises, prosperity, and more to your spirit.

"Life is not a cartoon where a scene can be rewound when it comes to God's blessings. Once the impartations of blessings leave His mouth, His words penetrate to the intended targets on earth. According to Isaiah 55:11: *So shall my word be that goes forth from my mouth. It shall not return to me void, but it shall accomplish what I please, and it shall prosper in the thing for which I sent it.* That sounds pretty definite to me."

Without formally labeling it, the pastor had preached his Father's Day sermon. Closing his Bible, Pastor Scott took a deep breath and walked from behind the pulpit. "Now, this is the part of the service where there is an uneven exchange. If you surrender to God today, He'll give you more than what you walked in here with."

Pastor Scott lifted one arm while holding the cordless mike in the other. "This is your altar call. Open to anyone, especially fathers. This is your day to repent where you are, ask God for His mercy and forgiveness, then come and walk down the aisle to the altar where there is a change of clothing for you if you're ready for a wash cycle in your spiritual life. The baptismal pool is ready, and God's expecting you. Lead the way for your children and they will come."

Malcolm nudged Parke. "Hey, look over there." He waited for Parke to follow his line of vision. "That's one of the researchers at my firm. I've been inviting him, but like me, some folks are stubborn. His mother was killed by a drunk driver and he's been mad at God ever since."

What is it with the drunk drivers? Parke frowned. He watched the young man stroll to the waiting minister at the altar. Parke wondered if the man was temporarily swayed by the message, or if he really wanted salvation.

God spoke, *I'll judge the hearts of men.*

CHAPTER 24

Monday morning after breakfast, Cheney was straightening the kitchen before she had to drop off Kami for a weeklong stay at Christian summer nature camp less than forty miles outside the St. Louis area. Parke teased her more than once, "Let the honeymoon begin." When the phone rang, she glanced at the time on the wall clock. Cheney hoped Parke would grab it. By the third ring, she answered. "Hello?"

"Is this Mrs. Jamieson?" the voice was polite, proper, and hesitant.

"Yes." Cheney tried to recognize the caller. She grew impatient. It was too early for solicitation. Plus, she and Parke were registered on the Do Not Call list, and their bills were current. "May I help you?"

"My name is Gilbert Ann."

Cheney's breath froze; her heart had a tantrum in her chest. Although she was momentarily speechless, Cheney managed to swallow. The previous night, after getting Kami to sleep, Parke seemed distant as they were lying in their own bed. Through her persistence and coaxing, Parke reluctantly admitted why he was so distracted after what seemed to be an enjoyable Father's Day.

"It's over, Cheney. There can be no more attempts to validate he's my son," Parke had barely whispered.

It was one more setback, one more hurt, and one more time they had to run back to God for counseling. They cried about what they had lost, but eventually laughed, reminiscing about some of Kami's antics. Blinking, she focused on the man on the other end of her phone.

"If you and your husband have time today, my wife and I would like to meet with you," Gilbert requested. The cockiness Parke had pegged on Gilbert Ann was absent in his voice.

On cue, Parke strolled down the back stairs. He appeared refreshed. The cleansing of their souls seemed to rejuvenate him. His nostrils flared in appreciation of her long, flowing blue-and-green skirt and blue top. He twisted his mouth in a flirt. When he acknowledged the worried expression on her face, his pending seduction went cold turkey. He nearly leaped down three steps trying to get to her.

Parke mouthed, "Who is it? What's wrong?" His stare indicated his concern.

When he stepped closer, Cheney covered the phone and mumbled, "It's Gilbert Ann. He and his wife want to meet with us."

Huffing, Parke not so gently plucked the phone out of Cheney's hand and slapped it against his ear. Cheney winced. That had to hurt, but Parke didn't seem fazed. He put his game face on before saying a word.

"Good morning, Gilbert." Parke listened as conflicting emotions played across his face. After a few minutes, he finally gave Cheney a hint of an outcome. "Give me the day, time, and place, and Cheney and I will be there." He glanced at Cheney. "In an hour?"

Shaking her head, she tapped her wristwatch. "I've got to get to work. I have trouble tickets stacked on my desk from Friday. It's top priority," she said in a hushed tone as Parke listened patiently.

"Oh, baby, I'm sorry, I forgot," he whispered in her ear then returned to his phone conversation. "Gilbert, this afternoon would be better for us. Yes, I'm sure our meeting is important, but my wife and I have commitments this morning that can't be rescheduled." Parke paused, nodding. "Yes, one o'clock is fine. Let's meet at Hendel's Market Cafe and Piano Bar on Saint Denis in Old Town Florissant. We'll see you there."

Cheney exhaled when Parke disconnected and met her gaze. She tried to gauge his reaction to the call. He didn't have the same jubilance and anxiety he had after his very first conversation with Gilbert. Today, Parke appeared a tad annoyed. Childishly, she wanted to cheer when her husband actually made demands. Next, she wanted to pop him upside his head for taunting Gilbert again. "Well, what do you think that's all about? You don't seem happy."

Resting his fist on his waist, Parke looked away, grimacing. "It's because of God that I haven't developed hypertension over this situation. I refuse to let this man jerk my chain. If I can't have the child who may be my son, fine. This Gilbert will not dangle the boy over my head like a mistletoe, where I'm supposed to get warm and fuzzy feelings every time he calls because he feels I'll gladly do his bidding because of the boy. Next thing I know, he'll want to extort money from me if he mentions the boy. It ain't going to happen."

He pounded his fist on their granite counter. "Enough is enough." The engraved determination on Parke's handsome face was confirmation he wasn't bluffing.

"We'll find out," she said in an attempt to comfort her husband.

Snapping out of his reverie, Parke kissed Cheney. "I'm really feeling God's leadership on this one. I'm heading to the office; then I'll pick you up at your office in a few hours. We're a team, baby."

He kissed her again, lingering a few moments.

Cheney grinned. At times, she loved her husband's stubbornness, especially when it came to them as a family. "Watch out Anns, the Jamiesons are coming."

At 12:51, Parke and Cheney were shown to the patio seating at Hendel's. Parke considered the century-old former grocer's storefront as an intimate hideaway for lunch or dinner. Trees towering over the brick-covered ground and bells tolling from a neighboring church added to the historic atmosphere. It was close to their home and Cheney's work.

After Parke pulled out the chair for his wife, he took his seat. Relaxing, Parke squeezed her shoulder as he looked around. He didn't try to hide his smirk. In a sense, Gilbert was doing Parke's bidding by driving across the city to his turf. Once they indulged what their adversaries had to say, he could enjoy lunch with his wife.

Cheney took a deep breath. "This time next year, Daddy could be in prison. It's funny; when Grandma BB was in jail, I worried, but deep down inside, I believed she could hold her own. I'm not getting that same feeling if Daddy is *incarcerated*. It seems so surreal." Cheney's voice cracked as she searched for any focal point besides her husband's face.

Parke teased Cheney's chin with his thumb. Leaning over, he brushed a kiss against Cheney's lips. "God gave me you, and we're going to make it despite this drama that's more twisted than what's on a soap opera. You have me, Cheney, whenever you need me."

Gilbert's appearance interrupted the love zone Parke was enjoying with Cheney. An attractive woman, evidently Gilbert's wife, accompanied him as a hostess escorted them through a rose-covered archway. Standing, Parke nodded a greeting then shook Gilbert's hand when the couple reached the table.

After the pleasantries of introducing their wives, Parke got to the point. "Is something wrong with my son?"

"Relax, Parke. GJ is fine—if he is your son." Gilbert met Parke's challenge.

Gilbert's attire was low key. The suit was absent in favor of a tan short-sleeve shirt and brown trousers. His wife was fashionable, but conservatively dressed in a casual suit.

Parke cringed. The child's rename was really starting to grate on his nerves. "Then what is this about? Last I heard—as a matter of fact, a few days ago—I was instructed not to contact you, yet you practically summon my presence. Man, if you're setting me up . . ."

Cheney forced her fingers into his clenched fist, loosening the tension. Parke held his tongue.

After the strained formalities, Gilbert and Harriett sat without an invitation. A waitress approached them. This time around Parke had an appetite. Without scanning a menu, he ordered a seafood stuffed mushrooms appetizer for him and Cheney.

"Would you like to see the menu, sir?" the young girl asked the newcomers.

The Anns shook their heads and asked for water. "I won't waste anyone's time. I'll consent for Gilbert to take a paternity test. If it is confirmed that you're his biological father, I'm willing to terminate custody for you to adopt him."

Cheney gasped. "What?"

"Just like that." Parke snapped his fingers. He squinted and drummed his fingers on the white plastic-covered wrought-iron table. This sounded too easy. "Umm-hmm. How humbling, how magnanimous, how—"

"Parke!" Cheney nudged him, but he didn't look her way.

"I've got this, babe. Now, why would you want to do me any favors, Mr. Ann?"

When Gilbert was about to explain, the waitress returned with four glasses of water, giving their guests a few minutes to stall. Whereas the others took sips, Gilbert gulped down a large portion.

"Mr. Jamieson, Harriett is four months pregnant." His wife reached across the table and covered Gilbert's hand. "We couldn't believe it after six long years."

Parke was dumbfounded. Too many emotions whirled in his mind. Although congratulations were probably in order, Parke didn't see that as a reason to throw a child back into a broken system. He glanced at Cheney. Her eyes were glazed with tears, but Parke couldn't decipher what her reaction meant.

The waitress returned with Parke and Cheney's order. Although she said earlier she was hungry, Cheney didn't touch her plate. Parke silently said grace and took a bite, trying to digest the new information along with his food. Parke chewed slowly as all eyes around the table remained on him. Wiping his mouth, he nodded for Gilbert to proceed.

"Three nights ago, God spoke to me in a dream. I was on a beach with a baby in my arms. For some reason, I lifted it up to the sky as in a form of worship. As I lowered the child—I couldn't tell if it was a boy or girl—a pair of large, strong hands were waiting to take the baby. I placed the infant in a makeshift cocoon. It seemed as if God's fingertip scripted the words, using the light in the sky against gray clouds: *Give him up.*"

Parke wasn't ready to break open the bottles of sparkling white grape juice. Doubt began to seep in. What if he wasn't the father of Gilbert's adopted son? Parke pushed aside his plate. His appetite was quenched as his spirit bore witness, and his heart pumped in recognition of what Gilbert had revealed.

Gilbert swallowed. "Parke, I know that even without a paternity test that you are Gil—I mean the boy's father. God gave me one more confirmation. That was Friday night. Sunday morning, Father's Day, marked the third day Harriet hadn't been feeling well. My wife's mother, also a great woman of God, phoned early with the strangest request: take a pregnancy test.

"What was so odd about it was she knew the diagnosis doctors had told us more than ten years ago. It took some convincing, but finally Harriet did as her mother suggested."

Parke could feel Cheney's leg trembling under the table. She pinched the tablecloth and refused to make eye contact with him. When he discreetly laid his hand over her thigh to still her movement, his hand shook from the intensity.

Gilbert chuckled. "Actually, we retook the test five more times after the first one came back positive. We can't believe my Harriett has been with our first child for four months!" He grinned at his blushing wife. "The doctors confirmed it this morning."

Not to be outdone, Parke spoke up, "Yes, *my* Cheney and I have been on the receiving end of the Lord's blessings and miracles." He squeezed her knee and the shaking ceased.

"It didn't take the doctor's confirmation about the pregnancy for us to release Gilbert Junior. God was getting us ready. We'll initiate the termination process of our parental rights immediately so you can legally adopt the son God gave you."

Parke never thought he would ever hear Gilbert willingly give up custody of the boy. The building of an engaging smile was crushed when Gilbert held up his finger.

"I do have one condition."

I knew it! Parke couldn't speak as he tensed in his seat. He fought back steam coming through his nose.

"I want to be a part of his life from afar. I want to know how he's doing, and I want to be his self-appointed godfather."

As the second-born son, Malcolm would be designated as the godfather. Parke couldn't allow his brother to be robbed of that right. Parke folded his hands and adjusted his shoulders. "I'm afraid I'll have to deny one of your requests, and it has nothing to do with being vengeful. The Jamiesons are a tight family. My brothers and I have positions we are destined to fill as descendants of Prince Paki and Elaine. The firstborn son must carry the Parke Kokumuo name. Male uncles, if any, become his godfathers. They also have to marry women with strong character who can nurture a prince."

Parke had his own chuckle, pointing his thumb toward Cheney. "Brains and beauty," he teased then choked with emotions. Despite all he didn't have, he would be considered a blessed man by this tenth great-grandfather's standards. "Gilbert, the bottom line is you and your wife don't need titles to be part of our family."

"Amen," Cheney spoke for the first time.

"Thank you," Harriett whispered with a smile.

After a moment of silence, the couples took deep breaths as Gilbert reached in his back pocket. Pulling out his wallet, he opened it and picked through several business and credit cards. Mixed in the stack was a lone picture. When Gilbert slid the picture toward the Jamiesons, it stopped in front of Parke. Mesmerized, Parke's mouth dropped.

"That's me . . . oh my God, that's me." Parke was in awe as he stared into the eyes of the little boy he'd helped create.

Cheney leaned over. "He's adorable. Parke, the resemblance is uncanny. He's definitely another Jamieson."

"That's what I thought the first time I saw Parke," Gilbert confessed. "Of course, I wasn't going to tell you that."

The men exchanged chuckles as Harriett reached across the table and covered Cheney's hand with hers. "We know you'll love him."

"There's no doubt we have plenty of love for him," Cheney assured her.

Gilbert slapped his palms on the table, grinning. "Time to eat."

The waitress appeared immediately. Gilbert ordered enough food for everyone at the table. Parke was too excited to put another thing in his mouth. As he examined the picture, Parke further scrutinized the eyes, mouth, nose, and the shirt he wore. He looked for scars, birthmarks, and insect bites. He wondered at the brand of the blue-and-orange plaid shirt that clothed the child. *His boy.*

Parke was still grinning when the Anns's orders arrived. The strained mood turned festive, until he sensed Cheney's silence. Her shoulders shook. Lifting his arm, he engulfed his wife and snuggled her closer to him.

"Mrs. Jamieson, are you all right?" Harriett asked.

Cheney nodded, but Parke wasn't so sure.

CHAPTER 25

What was Rainey thinking to allow the twins, Peter and Paul, to challenge him to almost two hours of reading a day? Their bickering started outside in the waiting room and followed them into his office.

Initially, Rainey assumed their squabble was over whose turn was next to play one of the electronic games he stocked in the lobby. He was flabbergasted when they were set to wrestle over who would read the lone *Time* magazine on the table.

Curiosity got the best of him. It was normal for the boys to be boisterous, but to be disrespectful to each other? He had never seen it. "Hey, what's the ruckus about? If you two act up like that again, I'll leave your braces on your teeth until after you're old and gray." Rainey strained a stern expression, but a grin slipped out.

"Paul knows I want to win the iPod, but he keeps taking my books from me," Peter, the younger twin, tattled, elbowing his brother.

"Hold still, Peter, so I can inspect your teeth." Rainey blamed himself for asking questions during an examination.

"Dr. Rainey, Peter got the cool prizes last time. I want the iPod this year," Paul argued, vying for attention.

Rainey nodded, completely confused. "Open wider, Peter, then bite down." His brother was still hyped. "Is there a coupon for a free iPod or something?"

Peter shook his head as Rainey tried to get a good look at his back braces.

"Nope," his twin answered. "You have to be in the summer reading club to win. I'm going to beat everyone. The library has some cool stuff at different levels, and I want to win them all." Paul mimicked a sinister laugh.

Finishing with Peter, Rainey decided to get the full story, or he would never get through with Paul's examination. "And you have to read an hour a day to win prizes?" They nodded. "Humph, when I was a little boy, our school had a summer reading program. My twin read enough books for both of us. Who's going to keep track?"

Puffing out his future biceps, Paul pointed. "It's an honor system, and Momma says we'd better not cheat. I'm going to beat him anyway." He pointed to his brother. "I could probably beat you, too, Dr. Reynolds."

Rainey laughed and tweaked Paul's nose. "No, you can't."

"I bet I can," Paul challenged.

And that's how he got tricked. Before Rainey knew what happened, he had boasted he could read twice the required reading time. Minutes later, he eyed the angelic-looking, double-crossing faces that taunted him. For a fleeting moment, he couldn't tell them apart because they were dressed alike in tan shorts and black T-shirts. The ten-year-olds were a unified front.

Three hours later, the reading challenge was Rainey's excuse for sitting in his BMW in the Ferguson Library parking lot. It didn't matter that he passed two larger and newer libraries on the way, and he wasn't a Ferguson resident. The others didn't employ a certain librarian named Josephine.

He glanced at the two boxed lunches stacked on the seat next to him. Rainey had thought about Josephine since Cheney's family game night a week ago, but he didn't have a reason to see her. It wasn't like she was giving him any encouraging signs.

Thanks to another set of twins, Rainey had a plan he was setting in motion. Everything was falling in place. Surprisingly, his patient load was light for the day, so he had left work early, stopped by the Honey Baked Ham store, and purchased two sandwich combos: one turkey, the other ham. Whichever one Josephine didn't want, Rainey would devour.

He took a few minutes to primp. Pulling down the sun visor, he patted his hair, rubbed his fingers across his brows and down his goatee. Lastly, he checked his smile at all angles. White, gleaming teeth grinned back at him. Satisfied, he reached for a sugar free mint from his cup holder and popped it in his mouth. Returning the sun visor to its position, he straightened his tie and climbed out of his BMW. After shutting the door, he flexed his muscles as if cameras were waiting. Once he realized he had forgotten his bribe offering, he rounded the car to get the food and activate his car alarm.

In command of his swagger, he headed toward the library's entrance. Mentally editing the fine points of his spiel, Rainey shifted the lunches and entered. His visit would also serve another purpose—to refresh his memory on Africa, African-American and local history, and other tidbits he should know as a black man. The next time the Jamiesons had another game night, whether Cheney asked him or not, Rainey would have no qualms about inviting himself again. If Josephine attended the next game night, if he didn't pique her interest, then he surely would amaze himself.

He frowned as he strolled to a help desk that appeared to be vacated. Did he really want to impress a woman who didn't acknowledge and respect the complexities of Rainey Reynolds, DMD? At the moment, he had no answer. Resting the lunches and his keys on the counter, Rainey scanned the area for the person he wanted to see.

"You can't eat in here," a voice ordered, shattering his concentration.

Looking in both directions, Rainey couldn't locate the owner of the voice.

"Young man, I said you can't eat in here," she repeated in a sterner tone.

Rainey glanced down. On the other side of the counter, a woman stood maybe four feet tall with a book in her hand. Her head of white hair was overpowering the gray. Although she was thin, her face was chunky with wrinkles, and she wore bright red lipstick.

"Oh, I'm sorry." He gathered his light load in one swift movement. "This is for Josephine." Showcasing perfectly aligned teeth, Rainey grinned.

The woman wasn't impressed as she ignored him. She spied the glass-covered counter, inspecting for smudges. "She's at lunch."

"Do you know when she will return?"

"When she's finished." Dismissing him with a curt nod, she scuffled to the other side of the desk to assist a teenage girl.

Now what? Rainey doubted the librarian would tell him Josephine's whereabouts. She could be in a back room, taking a walk, or sitting in a McDonald's drive-through line.

Rainey mumbled his thanks to the woman's back. Surprisingly, she replied without turning around, "You're welcome."

On the way out, his stride was reduced to a frustrated walk. It seemed as if his master plan had crumbled to a dumb idea. Rainey didn't have an answer for why he was running circles around Josephine. Shrugging, he tried to convince himself she was nothing more than another pretty face. He grunted. "Yeah, pretty face, great body, and high and mighty."

He refused to waste his day. Although it was almost July, the

St. Louis humidity hadn't begun to punish its residents. The community park across the street seemed inviting. Once again, he invited himself and headed for it.

Using the stone retaining wall that guarded wildflowers, Rainey created a makeshift seat. He sighed in a flash of bliss, staring at pedestrians in a crosswalk. He forced his mind away from his dysfunctional family: Janae, who was starting to annoy him; his mother, who was near a mental collapse; his father, a pillar of the society, was going to jail; and his twin sister . . .

The more he was around Cheney, the harder it became to find fault. Somehow, she was fast becoming a bright spot in his life with her easygoing mannerism and eagerness to forgive others' trespasses. Rainey blinked and reached for one of the lunches. Opening the box, he stared at his ham sandwich, small serving of potato salad, and bottled water.

He silently said grace. Before he could swallow his first bite, he trained his eyes on a colorful vision of loveliness in the distance. Once he locked in on the woman, he recognized it was Josephine. Today, she wore a yellow dress that seemed to dance with the wind. Her feet were protected in dainty athletic shoes. She walked with her face to the sun, and her lips moved as if she were talking to it.

He swallowed and tore off another bite. Watching her approach afforded him a moment of lustful entertainment. She moved with a degree of confidence, while maintaining a beat to an inaudible tune. Rainey wiped his mouth, relaxed, formed a cocky smirk, and waited. He counted down the seconds until her approach: five, four, three, two, one . . . then she strolled right past him. Frowning, he scrambled to his feet. "Josephine?"

When she didn't stop, Rainey laid his box on the wall. "Josephine."

Twirling, her skirt twisted around her as if she were the Statue of Liberty. With a mock salute, she shielded her eyes. "Rainey?" She backtracked, meeting him halfway. "What are you doing here?"

"I came to share lunch with you."

Dropping her hand, she exposed a line of perspiration above her lip. "Why would you do that?"

Why? Rainey fought the urge to grit his teeth. The gesture would have flattered most women. *Why?* Why wasn't he surprised that she was surprised? She actually expected a reply. "A peace offering."

"For?"

Rainey angled his head, stretching his neck muscles. A smart woman asking dumb questions. Wasn't it obvious he was trying to make up for his slip of the tongue during game night? He didn't owe her an explanation. "Josephine, I happened to be out this way and had a taste for a homemade sandwich. I happened to think about you when I was at the Honey Baked Ham store, so I brought an extra one for you."

She gave him one of those smiles that would put him out of business. "That sounds thoughtful; however, I've already eaten."

Of course. He nodded. "Do you have any time left to relax and sit with me, maybe talk?"

Josephine checked her watch as he led her back to the wall. Rainey dusted the space with his hand and waited for her to take a seat before he sat beside her.

"Would you like a bottle of water? It comes with the lunch."

"Sure." The one word seemed to soften her features, as if that were possible. She accepted and then prayed over her water. Twisting off the cap, she took two conservative sips and sighed. "Thank you, Rainey."

He couldn't stop staring. If he knew women from Africa were this beautiful, he would have signed up to work with Dentists

Without Borders, a non-profit organization that provides dental care to less privileged people around the world.

Josephine took a gulp and looked into the sky. "Are you ever in awe about—"

"You have no idea how much I'm in awe with . . . you."

"I'm flattered, but I was referring to God's handiwork. I love living in this area. It's beautiful. Whether I'm on campus or at work, whenever I get a chance, I get out and walk and enjoy the things God created without a blueprint." She chuckled and leaned closer. "I'll tell you a secret. I even like walking in the rain. I guess if I'm still here when it snows, I'll enjoy doing that."

Rainey rolled up his long sleeves and shifted on the brick wall, but there wasn't a comfortable position, so he gave up. "What do you mean if you're still here?"

"I'm from Ghana, Africa. That is my home. My family is there."

Somehow, Rainey could feel Josephine's magnetism. He didn't want to rush the moment. "How does an African woman get a name like Josephine?"

"From my mother." Scrunching up her nose, Josephine elegantly fanned her hand in the air. "Names are not limited to a country. That is supposed to be my Christian name. It's one of three names bestowed on me. In Ghana, children aren't named until their eighth day on this earth. Since I was born on a Tuesday, all girls are called Abena. If I were a male, I would've been named Kwabena."

"That's the oddest thing I've ever heard. Nameless for eight days is like you don't exist."

"Biblically, Adam didn't give Eve a name right away, and we see how much damage they did before then. In Luke chapter two, our great Savior was circumcised and named Jesus on the eighth day, so I guess you can say Ghanaians follow tradition."

Rainey would never attest to being a Bible scholar, but he would have to go find that for himself. Josephine was as fascinating as she was beautiful. "Okay, Abena," he teased.

Josephine lifted her chin in pride. "A baby's second name is after a very influential and good citizen in the community. Finally, we are given a third name from the Bible, our Christian name. Josephine is close to Joseph. I believe that was my mother's excuse to secretly name me after Josephine Baker."

"You know St. Louis is Josephine Baker's birthplace." He was afraid to look at his watch. He didn't want her to go.

"It's not a coincidence that the University of Missouri is known for its great curriculum in library science either. There are thirty-eight other states that offer that program in your country and Canada, but God has already ordered my footsteps in the place where I am supposed to be. I'm filling the shoes."

Rainey nodded. The conversation was getting too deep for him. "Ever thought about a detour?"

"Not really."

CHAPTER 26

Parke could barely contain his happiness. The paternity test was scheduled for the following afternoon. God had already revealed to Gilbert that Parke was the father, but Parke doubted the court would go along without the physical evidence.

On the flip side, Parke had been observing his wife. Cheney still smiled at him the same way, but sadness outlined her happiness. She had asked for some alone time after they had met with the Anns, and Parke had granted it. Intermission was over.

On the way back from the restaurant, she explained her emotional breakdown. "I know God loves the sinner and the saints alike. In Matthew 5, God says, *He makes His sun rise on the wicked and on the good, and makes the rain fall upon the upright and the wrongdoers.* I wanted to be in on a blessing and got a little overwhelmed. That's all."

She recovered and beamed at him. With a twinkle in her eyes, Cheney had absorbed a deep breath before patting Parke's hand. "I'll be all right. I had the same reaction when I learned Hali was pregnant, and now this Harriett lady. It's like invasion of the pregnant women," she joked.

He hadn't laughed. He had no idea she felt that way.

"Parke, I do have mixed feelings about them tossing Gilbert back into the system. I've never heard of the adoptive parents giving a child back. Foster parents, yes."

Stopping at a red light, Parke tightened his grip on the

wheel. He took a deep breath. "Babe, until he's officially ours, call him PK, Parke, Little PJ, whatever, but if I hear that name again, I might crash my SUV; and honestly, I don't care what their reasoning is as long as I have our boy."

Shifting in her seat, Cheney remained silent. Parke glanced at her. He couldn't see it, but her agony seem to pound in his ear.

Now, days later, Parke was still replaying the scene in his head. Parke closed his eyes, shutting out the daydream, and refocused on the conversation with his client on the phone. He glanced at the clock one last time—twenty hours away from seeing his son.

When he hung up from reassuring Mr. Cole that his Nike stocks were holding steady, he leaned back in his chair and drummed his finger against his mustache. Cheney's mood pulled at his heart. His joy battled with his helplessness that somehow he had to remind her and himself how much he loved her.

Cheney couldn't believe it. When she walked outside to the company's parking lot, she thought a flock of birds had attacked her vehicle. Upon closer inspection, she recognized white hand-prints on her side windows and windshield. Without a doubt, the stunt was a Parke trademark.

Before she could ID the culprit, she realized there were plenty of clear spaces left for driving. Still, she wasn't in the mood for a neighborhood prank. Missouri Telephone's tactic was to plant buildings near residential areas, so in addition to a security system, neighbors could keep a watchful eye on the property.

Cheney groaned as she reached over and snatched a sheet of floral stationery from under one windshield wiper. She almost gagged on a whiff of cologne, which was drenched on the paper—Parke. The next was his message: A MASSAGE AWAITS YOU. Lifting a brow, she smiled before she balled up the paper. "Umm-hmm.

A car wash awaits you, Parke Jamieson." Marvin Sapp's "Never Could Have Made It" ring tone that matched hers announced her husband's call.

Before she could load into him about messing up her Altima, he asked, "Are you coming home now?"

Planting her hand on her hip, she fussed, "Yes, I'm on my way home, and you better wash my car. Parke, what possessed you to—"

Click. She looked at her phone. "Did he just hang up on me?" Stamping her heel, she walked around to the driver's side and disengaged her alarm. As she got ready to slide in, a bunch of miniature roses held court with a note: I BET YOU'RE WONDERING WHAT I'M UP TO, HUH?

She picked them up and sniffed. Getting in, she turned the ignition, shaking her head, impressed. "Yep, I am," she confided in the petals of the flowers. She never knew what was going on in her husband's head.

After strapping in, Cheney located a graffiti-free space on the window so she could back out. It wasn't the first time Cheney was glad she lived nearby.

Minutes later, she pulled in front of their renovated historic house on Darst. Her mouth dropped open. Posing in the driveway was Parke, dressed in a loose T-shirt and shorts. In one hand was a hose with streaming water. By his sandal-clad feet was a bucket topped off with thick, soapy foam.

Acting as a parking attendant, he directed her to a designated spot. Dropping the hose, Parke came around and opened her door. He reached inside, turned off the ignition, and unfastened her seat belt. Grasping her hand, Parke gently guided her outside. Unexpectedly, her heel smashed the top of the hose, and they squealed together after getting briefly sprayed. Cheney was mesmerized by the intensity of his stare.

Parke brushed a kiss against her lips. "You know I love you, don't you?" His husky voice lingered.

At the right moment, his tone would have made Cheney faint. Although she was enjoying his seduction, she had to get out a few remarks about her car, but she couldn't resist him.

"You know," he paused and nipped his lip before pulling back. "My car didn't need washing until you dirtied it."

Shrugging, Parke nudged her out of the way so he could slam her car door. "Sorry about that, baby. I'll wash your car while you relax in a long, hot bath. It's waiting."

"Ooh, you've been reading Proverbs 31 again, haven't you?" She puckered her lips and blew him a kiss as she strolled to the porch. Cheney was about to step over another section of the water hose. Instead, she picked it up, careful not to get wet except for her hand.

Grinning, she turned around. Parke appeared to have read her mind. He walked forward anyway as she aimed. He yelled for her to stop, but she was having too much fun. Satisfied she had paid him back for her car, she took off running toward the door, predicting Parke would give chase. Breathless, she reached for the knob and looked over her shoulder. Parke hadn't moved as water dripped from his soaked clothes. "Not Proverbs," he corrected, referring to the passage about a virtuous woman. "Song of Solomon."

The love book of the Bible. Cheney's heart leaped with desire for her husband. Sighing, Cheney opened the door and practically bounced up the stairs, praising God for a Bible-reading, Bible-believing, and Bible-living husband. "Hmm. Thank God for summer camp and Grandma BB picking Kami up."

An hour later after Cheney's bath and Parke's shower, they lay snuggled in bed. Parke took time to whisper the words he needed to say and that she needed to hear.

"You are the most important person to me, besides Christ. I had no idea God would take us on this journey, but I couldn't find my way without you," he said, playing in her hair.

She rubbed his smooth jaw. "I had no idea my life would be this complicated once I stepped over on the Lord's side."

"Humph. I don't want to even think how confounded we would be without Him."

"Yeah. You're telling me."

They talked and kissed and frolicked late into the night, courtesy of Mrs. Beacon. The surrogate grandmother wanted Kami to spend the night, so they could get up the next morning and make Kami's favorite—Mickey Mouse pancakes.

Saturday, they woke early, and Parke demonstrated part two of what he had planned, aided by small gifts and handwritten poems. By early afternoon, Cheney was still lounging in bed and dozing. The last thing she remembered hearing was Parke praying for her.

On Sunday, Parke's attentiveness didn't fade. He fed her breakfast in bed, although their virtual weekend getaway was over one minute after Kami Jamieson came home. Mrs. Beacon pointed out that Kami needed to go to Sunday school, and Mrs. Beacon was going to play bingo.

Evidently, her surrogate grandmother's stint in jail wasn't enough to persuade her to return to Christ fully committed. What would be Mrs. Beacon's breaking point before running to God? For Cheney, it was the guilt that consumed her about the abortion.

Kami begged to be served breakfast in bed too. Cheney granted her permission, and Parke did his ladies' bidding.

Finally, when it was time to dress for church, Parke selected a dress he liked for Cheney to wear. Briefly, he tried his hand as a stylist. In vain, he fussed over her hair. Thank God she had a hat to match. Cheney drew the line when he wanted to assist with putting on her stockings.

Once inside the sanctuary, Parke held Cheney's hand as they got on their knees to pray, thanking Jesus for another day. Cheney heard Parke murmur, "Bless my wife, Lord," before he said, "Amen." When they sat, Parke placed his arm possessively around Cheney's shoulder. She was content to stay in his co-coon and clap her hands as others stood to worship. Although Cheney embraced the choir's full throttle of praise, she craved a message from God. While Pastor Scott was making his way to the pulpit, Cheney was already unzipping her Bible cover.

"I'm going to share with you, baby," Parke whispered, taking her Bible from her.

Cheney couldn't look into his eyes because she was always mesmerized with his lips when he called her baby. "You brought your own."

"I'd rather read with you. You know the saying: a family that prays together stays together."

Cheney smiled. She recalled Philippians 4:11: *Not that I am implying that I was in any personal want, for I have learned how to be content (satisfied to the point where I am not disturbed or disquieted) in whatever state I am.* She allowed peace to settle in her spirit. She was content, knowing that Jesus had placed Parke in her life.

"Good morning, saints and friends," Pastor Scott greeted the congregation. "Today's message from God is so simple that even a fifth grader can understand, because it's about taking tests. I'm entitling it 'Temptation is a Test.' There's one thing I want you to remember. You can't pass a test unless you study.

"In the Amplified version of 2 Timothy 2:15, it reads, *Study and be eager and do your utmost to present yourself to God approved and tested by trial, a workman who has no cause to be ashamed, correctly analyzing and accurately dividing—rightly handling and skillfully teaching–the Word of Truth.* Why do you think teachers give students a pop quiz? It's to see if students are ready. Sometimes your temptations are pop quizzes.

"One mistake we make is thinking we can recognize a temptation, but temptation comes in many forms, not just lust. Doubt is the biggest test, next impatience, and don't forget envy. The list is endless. Remember, we are tested by trials . . . ."

Cheney began to identify the low points in her life as temptations that were testing her faith. Opening her purse, Cheney raked the bottom of her purse for a pen to take notes. She tried her best to be discreet as she shifted keys and paper wrappers.

"Baby," Parke whispered to get her attention then slipped a pen from inside his suit jacket and winked. She didn't know how he knew what she needed.

Only Parke K. Jamieson the Sixth could make her heart melt. She made himself comfortable under his stretched arm. Yes, she was content.

In less than an hour, Pastor Scott was bringing his sermon to a close. He lifted his hand to the congregation. "Are you ready to be tested? Are you really prepared? There could be a pop quiz any minute. If you know you haven't studied long and hard, then it's time for you to repent and come to be baptized in Jesus' name to clear your mind. Follow God's directions and you'll pass."

CHAPTER 27

Cheney was summoned to the Reynolds mansion by her father. The two months the judge gave Roland to set his affairs in order before sentencing had dwindled down to five weeks. Parking in their circular driveway, Cheney dreaded the visit. She closed her eyes. "Lord, we're running out of time. Please have mercy on my father and help us all bear this phase in our lives. Amen." Opening her eyes, she got out of her car and counted each step to the front door. Miss Mattie was already stationed there, waiting for her.

Once inside the foyer, Cheney expected her father to be in the study. Her pace to the room was even slower. She found him, but didn't expect to see him reading his Bible. As if sensing her presence, Roland looked up with brightness shining in his eyes. He stood and greeted her at the entrance.

"Hi, Daddy," she said seconds before he smothered her with a hug.

"I'm so glad you're here. I wanted to have a private talk." With her arm wrapped around his waist, they strolled to the sofa. He sat first then patted the space beside him. Cheney sniffed back tears before joining him. "Listen, I've made so many mistakes, baby, and I can't say I'm sorry enough." His voice cracked as Cheney squeezed him tighter.

"Have you read the part in the Bible that says we all have sinned and fallen short of the glory of God?" Cheney reached for his opened Bible to see what passage he was reading. She fingered the scripture he had highlighted. Matthew 9:12: *Jesus said, It is not the healthy who need a doctor, but the sick. But go and learn what this means: I desire mercy, not sacrifice. For I have not come to call the righteous, but sinners.*

He remained silent until he thought she was finished, then chuckled. "I guess that's me, huh? Righteous, as I led others to believe, but in reality a big sinner."

Cheney closed the Bible and her eyes. She didn't know what to say without crying. He touched her shoulder.

"It's going to be all right. I have to pay the piper. Your mother, on the other hand, has retained the services of a high-powered prison consultant. Personally, I think it's a waste of money for a so-called specialist to offer me a crash course on prison politics."

"What?" Cheney squinted.

"He left me a pamphlet to study about the dos and don'ts behind the bars. One is to play cards and talk sports so I don't come across as anti-social, although the most volatile place inside there is the TV room. The big no-no is never to cut in front of others in the food line. No worries there. I'm sure the food isn't worth fighting over."

"Unbelievable, but I guess that does make sense. It's all about survival."

"Evidently, celebrities like Michael Vick, Martha Stewart, and Bernie Madoff have used those prison consultants and they made it out— well, except for Bernie."

Her father's casual attempt at humor made her want to cry. Confinement of any kind was a loss of freedom. She concentrated on the scripture her father had highlighted. *God, your Word is truly medicine for whatever ails us. Lord, I know my father has sinned, but just like you marked Cain's forehead in Genesis 4 after he killed Abel, so that no one would touch him, please cover Daddy with your blood, so that he will not be harmed if he goes to prison.*

"Mentally, I've been imprisoned for a long time." Roland interrupted Cheney's private thoughts.

"I'm sorry—"

He held up his hand. "No, let me finish, baby. Your mother and siblings want to blame you for this. They can't accept I've been living a lie. I'm the one who set the chain of events in motion years ago by one single act—leaving that accident." He looked away, appearing to struggle for the next words. "I thought I was hiding under my name and profession. I guess like Adam and Eve thought they were hiding their nakedness with a scrap of leaves. Ridiculous, isn't it?"

Roland took a deep breath. "But God knew how to make me come clean. It seemed as if He was using you to carry my burden. I'm sorry you had to endure the fallout from your decision until it broke your spirit and you ran to God for deliverance. In a sense, your salvation caused me to repent. Baby, you didn't stay away from your family on your own will. The Lord sent you back at the exact time He wanted and placed you where He wanted you to live . . . ."

She was amazed at the wisdom her father was imparting. He broke the scenario down in sections and connected the dots. Would God really make her pay for the sins of her father? She felt somewhat indignant for being used as a pawn.

I chose you to bring your family together, God whispered.

Cheney recognized His voice as she clasped her hands together, resting her forehead on them. She wasn't sure if those words were comforting.

I chose Jesus to shed His blood. I chose you to bring souls to Me, God reassured her.

That's when she realized her burden really wasn't about her. God's mission was much bigger. She faced her father with a weak smile, recalling 1 Thessalonians 5:18: *Thank God in every-*

thing (no matter what the circumstances may be, be thankful and give thanks), for this is the will of God for you (who are) in Christ Jesus (the Revealer and Mediator of that will). She sniffed. "It's going to be all right, Dad."

Roland nodded. "I know, baby. I have no fear in going to prison. I've made sure your mother is financially secure, and my attorney worked out a plan of restitution to Mrs. Beacon, your Grandma BB, in the event."

"But Daddy, it's not a done deal. Maybe you won't have to go at all." Cheney pleaded for him to think positive.

He shifted on the sofa and scooted closer until their knees touched. Roland loosened her clutched hands and wrapped them in his. "I want you to promise me that if I'm not around, you won't give up on our family. Talk to your mother, sister, and twin. Don't let their anger discourage you. Keep talking to them about Jesus."

"I promise." Cheney sniffed through a smile as her spirit leaped with victory. "It sounds like you've already repented. How about sealing the deal with the baptism in Jesus' name?"

"I wouldn't have it any other way," he agreed.

Cheney relaxed, pleased as she grinned. *The devil's mad. He's lost a soul he thought he had,* she silently said in a sing-song melody.

CHAPTER 28

Parke and Gilbert stood before the judge. The frustration on Judge Davis's face was apparent. "I am furious," she said, snarling as she pointed a finger at the Anns and their attorney. "Do you have any idea of the impact of your actions on the child? Do you know how much court time was wasted?

"This entire scenario is unprecedented. Never in my time on the bench have I seen such indecisiveness. Attorney Lindell, I can't help but wonder if a crime has been committed on someone's part. How and why did your clients come to a conclusion to give up custody of a child whose adoption is still wet with ink? Were Mr. and Mrs. Ann bribed, intimidated, or threatened?"

"That is not the case, Your Honor," their attorney responded, appearing somewhat uncomfortable in his position as the bearer of bad news. "After much prayer," he stuttered, "my clients felt it was in the best interest of Gilbert Junior . . ."

Parke cringed. His first order of business would be to officially give the boy the name he was destined to have.

A few days earlier, the paternity test verified what God had already told Gilbert. The moment had been surreal. Anyone who met Parke knew he was a man's man, but that hadn't kept him from tearing up after learning the results. In a day or so, Parke would have his son all to himself—at least that's what he thought.

The judge shook her head, glanced down at a document before her, and trapped Parke in a stare. "What's your story?" Judge

Davis asked as if she didn't already know it. Her tone wasn't as threatening, but she didn't seem glad to see him again either.

Clearing his throat, Parke nodded as Cheney squeezed his hand. "As you are aware, Your Honor, a paternity test has verified I am the biological father, and since the Anns are giving him up, I would like to take immediate custody of my son," he said very matter-of-factly.

New to the mix in the courtroom was the person representing Parke's son. "Your Honor, as guardian ad litem for Gilbert Ann Junior, I, too, am disappointed at the turn of events, but in light of what has already transpired, I recommend a thorough investigation to make sure Gilbert can be placed in a loving, stable home. I do have other concerns," the representative, an elderly man, spoke for the first time.

"Which are?" Judge Davis prompted.

Yeah? Parke frowned, but dared not utter. Twinkie must have sensed his tension, because she slightly nudged Parke to stay calm.

"I propose that Gilbert Junior be returned to the foster care system. This is the most unfortunate situation for a child who needs not only a loving home, but stability. The court missed the mark by awarding custody to Mr. and Mrs. Ann. It's in his best interest that it doesn't happen again, with or without biological parents."

Parke was outraged at the audacity of the middleman. For forty minutes, the judge heard pleas and arguments. Cheney and Parke linked hands and silently prayed as they waited for the judge's determination.

"Since the biological father's parental rights were terminated and the parental rights of the child's adoptive parents are in the process of being terminated, Gilbert Ann Junior will be returned to the system until further notice." She hit the gavel and stood, adjoining the court.

Shocked, speechless, and rooted in place, Parke's heart sank with disappointment. Cheney massaged his hand. Twinkie's lips moved, but Parke didn't hear a word.

The next day, the mood was just as sober as Parke and Cheney made calls to the Division of Family Services to activate their status as foster parents. In his office, Parke threw up his hands in frustration. "I can't believe I'm going through this." He slammed his fist on his desk. From the corner of his eye, Parke saw his assistant back away from his doorway. "The test proved I'm the father, he's my son, and so what is the problem?" He didn't expect his assistant to have the winning answer.

Gilbert seemed to sense his vibes when he phoned, offering Parke his prayers. It was easier for Parke to accept Gilbert's gestures, knowing that he freely gave up Parke's son. Otherwise, they would have maintained their battle lines. His son had already been removed from Gilbert and Harriet's home.

"I'm convinced I did the right thing." Gilbert tried to console.

Parke toyed with a pen on his desk. "It's not your fault. At least you did what God instructed you. Now, it's a waiting game." God wasn't making it easy. First, the rumor that he might have a son; finding the son, verifying parentage, trying to reverse the adoption, now fighting to gain custody. *Unbelievable.* Parke could write a book with this much drama.

CHAPTER 29

On the last Sunday in June, Dr. Roland Reynolds walked confidently through the door and down the aisle of Faith Miracle Church. Trailing in his path were Cheney's mother, her siblings, brother-in-law, niece, and nephew.

Cheney sighed with happiness. Hallison grinned and gave her a thumb up as she and Malcolm scooted down the pew to make way for the visitors. Cheney's lips trembled with tears swimming in her eyes. She had hoped, but like the disciple Thomas, quietly doubted if the day would come when the Reynoldses would attend church as a family, as they had when she was a child.

Her mother, Gayle, and Rainey nodded their greetings. Contrite as ever, Janae refused to make eye contact. Her husband, Bryce, on the other hand, smiled as he carried their sleeping son. He appeared genuinely happy to be there. Their daughter, Natalie, was latched on to her grandpa's hand.

Parke pulled Cheney deeper under the cocoon of his arm and placed a kiss near her ear. "They're here. Relax. Only thing we can do is pray," Parke said before shaking his father-in-law's hand.

As the choir sang the last note of "How Great Thou Art," Pastor Scott stood and slowly stepped to the pulpit. Laying down his Bible, he hesitated. He removed his reading glasses and glanced into the audience, squinting as if he were searching for one person.

"God says whosoever will, let him come." He paused then opened his Bible. "In Revelation 22, God is letting us know the window of opportunity is closing, and He will not put us in a head lock to do anything. Although some of the consequences might cause us to wish we had made different choices, Jesus won't force His love or salvation. Consider verses 11 through 13: *He that is unjust, let him be unjust still: and he who is filthy, let him be filthy still: and he that is righteous, let him be righteous still: and he that is holy, let him be holy still.* Payday is coming in verse 12: *And, behold, I come quickly; and my reward is with me, to give every man according as his work shall be. I am Alpha and Omega, the beginning and the end, the first and the last.*" He closed his Bible. "That says it all.

"No person purposely tries to get lost in the woods or forest. That's why campers use markers to find their way out. If you were in the woods today, would you stay there, not knowing what dangers surrounded you, or would you scramble to get out? When you're confused about which direction to go, you might pray for a search-and-rescue team. Jesus is your search and rescue."

Pastor Scott held people captive, including Cheney's family. As he preached, Cheney remembered the day God spoke to her, urging her to find rest, comfort, and deliverance in Him. There was no guarantee that any of her family members would seek a fresh start today, but their willingness to come—well, maybe next time they would return under their own will. At least Cheney knew within her being that through the simplistic foolishness of preaching, they could be saved, recalling 1 Corinthians 1.

"Today, you don't have to be lost in the forest." The man of God interrupted her thoughts. "The forest is your life of sins. God knows where you are. Adam and Eve hid in a garden, but He found them."

Cheney's heart leaped. Her father had mentioned Adam and Eve the other day. She was sure it wasn't a coincidence that Pastor Scott was preaching on it for the morning sermon.

"It's time for you to come out the forest of sins. This is your invitation," Pastor Scott said as the congregation stood for altar call. The choir softly sang "Let It Rain."

Taking a deep breath, Cheney and Parke stood, leaving Kami on the pew asleep. Parke linked his hand through hers. Now, it was a waiting game to see if anyone in her family, especially her father, was receptive to the message.

"There are three beautiful benefits of salvation." Pastor Scott held up his hand, counting his fingers. "First, you don't need an appointment to talk to God. He's always on call, so repent right now.

"Second, remember the foolishness of preaching. Well, to some, to be baptized in water in the name of Jesus is foolishness. Can water really rinse a multitude of sins down the drain? Yes.

"Come on. Third, and definitely not the last of God's benefits, is infusion of the Holy Ghost. The evidence is speaking in other tongues—foolish to some, but wise to those who believe God. So, the choice is up to you to let Jesus cleanse your soul as He washes your sins away. We have a change of clothing for baptismal."

Roland leaned over and kissed Cheney's cheek. "Thank you," he whispered.

She stared at her father with questions. Cheney had her answer when he stepped out of the pew into the aisle. With pride and relief, Cheney watched his determined stride, heading to one of the ministers near the altar. Her family seemed to stare with curiosity.

Roland was not alone, as others followed him to the front. Unfortunately, no other family member left her row. While the candidates were in a back room dressing for the baptismal, the service continued with the offertory, until all candidates were ready. Finally, one by one, men, women, and a few teenagers began their descent into the pool, stirring the water. Roland was third in line. A minister also in a white T-shirt and pants instructed Roland to cross his arms.

"My dear brethren, upon the confession of your faith, and the confidence that we have in the holy Word of God, I indeed baptize you in the name above all names, Jesus, for the remission of your sins. According to the Book of Acts, you shall receive the gift of the Holy Ghost evident by the speaking in other tongues," the minister proclaimed with one hand raised. "God, show him the evidence." His other hand gripped the back of Roland's T-shirt.

As Roland was dipped, the water swayed until he was briefly buried. When he came out of the water, Roland released a loud shout, "Hallelujah!" As the congregation's praise increased to mingle with his, so did an explosion of tongues in Roland's mouth, which didn't stop as he came out of the water.

Cheney shouted for joy. Tears streamed down her face. Hallison reached for her and took her hand. The praise in the church was high as the congregation continued to witness soul after soul being baptized. A few others spoke in tongues. If the new converts desired, they would be ushered into a small chapel, where they would pray and seek God to fill them with the Holy Ghost as He had done for the apostles in the Book of Acts. Now, if only the rest of her family and friends would come.

Cheney leaned over to her brother. "Rainey, what Dad experienced was real."

Shrugging, Rainey appeared skeptical. "Maybe."

CHAPTER 30

Rainey didn't know what to make of what he had witnessed at church. He couldn't dispute the electrifying praise that engulfed him. The message was moving, but the sermon didn't scare him out of his seat to make a sudden impulse-buying decision.

He somewhat enjoyed himself. The preaching was simple, and it did leave a lasting impression, but Rainey would never admit that to his sister. He wasn't up to feeling pressured.

Forty minutes after service was dismissed and the church crowd thinned, Rainey and his family still lingered, waiting for his dad. He was eager to see if Roland was different in any way—looks, mannerisms, or speech.

His nieces and one nephew ran circles around Rainey as the adults spoke. Bryce and Janae were pulled away by one of Janae's sorority sisters who could possibly be a church member. Rainey tried to keep a straight face to see if the woman had any success in converting his die-hard stubborn older sister. If they could convince Mrs. Evil Eye to convert, then he would become a believer.

Be saved from this crooked, perverse, wicked, unjust generation. Acts 2, someone said from beside him, or was it behind him?

Startled, Rainey turned to his left and right. No one seemed to pay him any attention. Cheney, Parke, Malcolm, and Hallison were almost huddled together in an animated conversation. Rainey shook off the eerie feeling. As he casually observed the sanctuary, from a distance, he thought he saw Josephine. About to verify that assumption, he had moved in that direction when his father made his appearance.

His mother and Cheney raced to Roland, who opened his arms and embraced them. The grandchildren encircled Roland, vying for his attention. Finally, in a nonchalant manner, Rainey approached his father, who hadn't grinned so wide since the whole hit-and-run fiasco surfaced. Roland extended his large hand for a shake. When Rainey accepted, his father enfolded him in his arms and didn't let him go for what seemed like forever.

"Dad, is everything all right?" Rainey asked when he managed to disengage himself.

"Son," Roland said, chuckling, "I can't explain it, but an emotional weight has been lifted. God shoved it off my shoulders, so to answer your question, yes."

Roland didn't elaborate, and Rainey wasn't too eager to inquire, so he dropped the subject. When Cheney called his name, Rainey turned around.

"I'm so glad you came," she said, hugging him. Her embrace was almost deadening. "Rainey, do you think we can talk later?" Cheney asked with an angelic expression.

"Not today." He waved at his dad, kissed his mother, and nodded to everybody else then left.

A few days later, Rainey decided to try his luck again with Josephine. He had two choices: visit her at the library again or show up at Mrs. Beacon's house—and he had no intention of setting foot on that woman's property.

Rainey walked into Ferguson Library on a mission. He didn't want to be intrigued with the attractive, arrogant African woman, Josephine Yaa Abena, or whatever her name was. He took a chance, hoping she was working.

As he headed to the circulation desk, Josephine was poised, reading a thick textbook. Glancing up, she didn't seem surprised to see him. As a matter of fact, her expression relayed she had been expecting him; the beginning of a smile slowly transformed into a sexy smirk.

Today, her shapely figure was wrapped in a tan skirt. The silhouettes of African women, carrying loads above their heads, were splashed throughout the skirt. Gold was her choice of color for a sleeveless top. Tall, thick-heeled sandals supported her shimmering legs. The only thing that rang in Rainey's head was Josephine saying, *Come to Africa with me.* He recalled the phrase from when she conducted the storytelling session.

"Good afternoon, Josephine." Rainey came empty-handed. There would be no lunch today. His task was to determine if the attraction was one-sided, and he needed her full cooperation to find out.

"Good afternoon." She lifted her brow, closing the book.

Rainey drummed his fingers on the counter. He was the king of a stare-down duel, but that wasn't his intent. "I'm here to invite you to Fair St. Louis. It's one of the largest Fourth of July celebrations in the country. I haven't gone in years, but I think you'll enjoy it. Consider me your tour guide."

Eyeing him, Josephine didn't respond right away. "To be honest, I don't think you can handle me."

A snicker tilted his lips. Folding his arms, Rainey rocked in his loafers. "Oh, baby, I can handle you, all right."

"One moment, Dr. Reynolds." She lifted a finger as a patron came to the counter. Josephine directed her attention to a young girl whose head barely touched the top of the desk.

Although Rainey expected his dental degree to garner him

respect, he didn't welcome it when Josephine switched to the professional mode.

"Hi, I'm trying to get a book, but the shelf is too high. I need help. Will you help me?" the child with thick, long black cornrows whined.

"Sure, sweetie, I'll . . ."

Eavesdropping, Rainey unfolded his arm and walked around to the other side. "I got it, Josie." He squatted to meet the child's eyes. "Show me where it is." Standing, he followed the girl who skipped to a shelf across the room. Once Rainey assisted her, he strolled back to the counter. "Accept my invitation, Josie."

"Very few people call me Josie. I prefer Josephine, after Josephine Baker, remember?"

"Ah, yes, Miss Josephine Baker. My apologies." He tamed his expression to resist a patronizing tone that would probably offend her. "Will you attend Fair St. Louis on the riverfront with me?"

She sighed. "Rainey, I agree to accompany you, but I must warn you we have different outlooks. We may never be friends without you changing some things in your life."

Josephine did it again. Outrage began to spiral in the pit of his stomach, gathering speed as it raced to the surface. The woman wore arrogance like her beautiful, straight teeth. "Changes in my life?" he mocked. "Since we're baring our souls, we could be more than friends if you weren't residing with a criminal. I was giving you the benefit of the doubt as an exchange student. You had no idea what you were walking into." He balled his fist, but refused to slam it on the counter. *Do I really want to go out with this woman? If so, why?* he kept asking himself.

"Grandmother B has served her time and has been freed from jail. It's time for you to free yourself from the anger that has imprisoned you."

Rainey remained expressionless. He hated when someone was right and it wasn't him. "Is that a yes or no, Josephine?"

"I would love to experience the fair if you leave your attitude behind," she said softly.

Jingling his car keys, Rainey nodded. She had a lot of nerve. "I'll pick you up Friday morning." Spinning around, he headed toward the door. *I need to make an appointment with a psychiatrist, because I'm definitely becoming another person when I'm around Josephine.*

"Rainey," she called in a hushed tone.

Stopping, he glanced over his shoulder, still fuming. He didn't respond, but his mannerism said it all. *What?*

"I'll be ready." Her eyes sparkled along with a perfect smile, but the charm didn't work.

He finished his trek out of the library to his car. Once he was behind the wheel, he released his frustration in a string of curses. "This was a bad idea, bad idea," he mumbled, turning the ignition, knowing nothing would stop him from going through with the date.

CHAPTER 31

Cheney was running out of bonding time with her father. Parke was running out of patience. He wanted his son now, and Kami was running circles around both of them, demanding more "me" time.

Since Roland accepted the Lord's salvation, Cheney spoke with him almost every morning, sometimes more than once. Those father-daughter phone calls filled a hunger that had her starving for years. In her heart, Cheney murmured it wasn't fair that finally someone in her family came wholeheartedly to Christ, and now that person could possibly be taken away from her.

Leaving her office early, Cheney had walked into the Shop 'n Save grocery store to grab a few things to make tacos for Kami and more meat to barbecue when she got the call.

"Mrs. Jamieson, this is Lola Frances, the social worker with the Division of Family and Children's Services."

Cheney's heart raced. They had been waiting to hear from someone. Hopefully, they were one step closer.

"Mrs. Jamieson, as you are probably aware, since you and your husband have been foster parents in the past, your reinstatement request should take less time than normal. I still need to update your references and schedule a home visit. The sooner we take care of that, the sooner we can place Gilbert in your home for a trial visit."

Gilbert. She shuddered. Parke would have a fit hearing that name. "I'm off work now."

"I did have a cancellation today because of the upcoming Fourth of July holiday. If you can be at your home in, say about an hour, we can get that out of the way."

Cheney abandoned her shopping cart. "I'll be there in five minutes." She hurried off the phone and left the store. Once she was in the parking lot, Cheney fumbled for her car keys. She called Parke to give him an update, pinching the phone between her shoulder and ear.

"I'll be home in twelve minutes," he said, rushing her off the phone.

"Parke!" She paused in the aisle near her car, causing a driver to honk. "You're at least twenty or thirty minutes away. Take your time so you won't have an accident. I'm not up to spending the evening in a crowded emergency room along with parents who didn't supervise their kids while playing with fireworks. I mean it, Parkay," she said, referring to the pet name she used when trying to get her point across.

"Yes, dear."

She grinned. *Works every time.*

Friday morning, the Fourth of July, Rainey parked his BMW outside Mrs. Beacon's house and turned off the ignition. He scrutinized her oversized brick bungalow with a trail of colorful flowers circling the exterior. It was too much house for one woman. He grimaced; Josephine made two.

Shifting in his seat, Rainey huffed. "What am I doing here?" Since he probably wouldn't like his answer, Rainey got out of the car. Dressed casually in a coral polo shirt, white shorts, and his pedicured feet sporting designer sandals, Rainey forced himself to follow the walkway to the front door.

"I'm a traitor." He hoped Mrs. Beacon wasn't home. One-on-one, he didn't know how he would react to her. Cheney had forgiven Mrs. Beacon, his dad had forgiven her, but Rainey still had issues with forgiving people who wronged him or his loved ones.

He hadn't stepped one foot on the porch when the door opened and Josephine appeared, ready to go. Rainey's mouth dropped. How could one woman look good all the time? Josephine needed very little assistance with beauty supplies. A sleeveless dress with wild colors swayed at her ankles. Flat, comfortable sandals showcased her feet. It was the first time he had seen her without heels. She was still tall and beautiful. Most of her hair was stuffed under a straw hat. The look was cute, but the effort was wasted, since a lot of her hair was rebellious.

"Good morning. I didn't want to keep you waiting—in the car. I doubted you would come inside the house."

He wasn't used to a woman knowing his mind. It irritated him that Josephine did most of the time. Rainey couldn't seem to get the upper hand with her. "As always, you look pretty, Josephine."

Tilting her head, she looked pleased. "Thank you, and as always, you look very nice."

Hmm. Maybe, she doesn't have the upper hand if she noticed. Rainey waited as she turned around and locked the door. Going down the stairs first, Rainey offered his hand as an anchor.

Accepting his assistance, Josephine lifted her face to the sun, displaying confidence that Rainey had her as she glided down the steps. He held in a chuckle. Josephine was definitely African queen material. Once on the walkway, Rainey shoved his hands in his pockets and continued the escort to his BMW in silence.

Opening the passenger door, Josephine slid inside at the same time Imani came barreling down the street in her tow truck. She pulled into her driveway next door and jumped out with the motor running.

"Hey, what's up, doc?" Imani shouted, waving. She reminded him of a pet pit bull—loud and dangerous until the end.

So this was Imani in her new role as the repo woman. If his sister could convert Imani, her fierce friend, then he would really pay attention. Growing up, whomever Cheney liked, Imani admired. Imani applied the same principle for enemy combatants, as she called them. If Cheney hadn't been speaking to him, then Rainey wouldn't have put it past Imani to accidentally bump his car with her tow truck. For a while, Cheney was working overtime to mend fences, and as a loyal supporter, Imani was in her corner.

"Hey, yourself." He grinned. "You're working on a holiday?"

In her stilettos, Imani danced backward toward her house, mimicking football players in practice. "What can I say? It's the best time to crash a party. Most people are home during the holidays, and I need the money."

Laughing and shaking his head, Rainey got behind the wheel of his car. "Now, that's a woman who needs prayer," he mumbled to himself.

Josephine glanced out the window and waved. "I like her. She's funny, vivacious, and blunt, which I like."

"Takes one to know one," Rainey murmured, checking over his shoulder.

Reaching over, Josephine covered his hand as he shifted into gear. "Rainey, I should warn you I have very good hearing."

"Nothing gets past you, does it?"

"If that's a compliment, then I can't accept it. I'm not perfect, although I strive to be in God's eyes. If that was meant as an insult, then I take exception."

Rainey's roar of laughter competed with the sound of his motor. At least Josephine was consistent—complex. She didn't share his humor, but didn't balk either. It was his turn to let her to figure him out.

While en route to the riverfront, Rainey opted for jazz music to calm him, instead of trying to engage Josephine in meaningless chatter. Before the night was over, he would bet they would have some type of disagreement. Rainey planned to win a round.

He wasn't a big fan of crowds, free events, and St. Louis–style heat and humidity, but he was willing to risk the combination to get to know more about Josephine. Rainey had tried to plan a St. Louis tour about Josephine Baker, but that didn't pan out.

Finally, he picked up the phone and called the library's reference desk for the answer to whether Josephine Baker was born in St. Louis, Missouri, or East St. Louis, Illinois. Missouri, known as the Show-Me State, was the winner. The Black World History Wax Museum in North St. Louis city had an impressive exhibit of the exotic entertainer. Unfortunately, it was closed for the holiday.

"How does your country celebrate Independence Day?" he asked, stopping his car at a traffic light after exiting the highway.

Josephine adjusted the air vent to blow directly on her face, declining Rainey's hand to control the temperature. "The Republic of Ghana has been celebrating its Independence Day every March sixth since 1957. Ghana was the first sub-Saharan country to free itself from British colonial rule," she answered proudly.

Briefly taking his eyes off the road, Rainey scanned her from head to toe for the second time within thirty minutes. "That explains your accent, and you are truly beautiful."

She nodded and accepted his compliment. "Thank you, but it's the beauty of holiness I strive to ooze."

Rainey wanted to groan. He did not want to talk to Josephine or anybody at the moment about church. "Can't you separate the two?"

"I've been taught to never take credit for things I have no control over." She opened her mouth as if she was about to say something, but stopped. After a few minutes, she tilted her head. "Why do you want to separate yourself from God?"

Rainey gripped the wheel with his left hand and squeezed the clutch, debating if he wanted to answer, or if she deserved one. *Why not?* Turnaround was fair game. He had a few questions himself. "I think the Lord separated Himself from me years ago when I was in a relationship that went badly. God wasn't on my side. He didn't intervene when a girlfriend made a decision. The consequences cut through me. Since then, it seems like I can sniff out dishonest people," Rainey said bluntly.

He changed the subject. "Let's look for a parking spot. Hopefully, it won't be too far from the parade route. You'll enjoy the Veiled Prophet Parade. I think rain or shine, floats and bands have marched down Market Street for more than one hundred and thirty years. For some reason, the V.P Fair's named was changed to Fair St. Louis."

Josephine rode quietly, occasionally twisting her neck, looking for a parking space. She didn't comment on Rainey's revelation, neither did she interrupt his narrative.

"That guy's leaving," Rainey shouted in victory as he whipped between two cars as an SUV left. He turned off the ignition, got out, and trotted around the car to help Josephine. "Let's hurry. I heard a drum line and cheers." He armed his alarm.

Taking her hand, Rainey led Josephine in a power walk until they had reached a thunderous crowd. They wormed their way into a thin group, so at least they could see over the tops of people's heads. It didn't take long for the pair to join in with the screaming, clapping, and cheering at the floats and bands. Josephine laughed at some of the performers, and Rainey chuckled with her.

Almost an hour later, the last of the floats drifted by; sirens of emergency vehicles trailed with flashing lights, signaling the end of the parade and the start of the fair. The sun beamed high in the sky, shedding unforgiving heat.

"Feel like walking down to the riverfront?" Rainey asked.

"That's why I wore these shoes." She lifted her sandal-clad foot to remind him, attempting to balance on one leg. Rainey reached out and steadied her.

Their first stop was at a food booth. "Can I get you anything?" he asked, towering over her.

"Water—two bottles—please." Josephine released her magic by smiling.

Rainey observed her features through hooded lashes as he reached in his back pocket for his wallet. "You're breaking my bank, woman," he teased as he asked for three waters.

He exchanged money with the booth attendant, who reached into the bottom of a cooler and pulled out three bottles, dripping with ice. Josephine accepted, then bowed her head and blessed her drink. After twisting off the cap, she gulped down half the bottle.

The crowd increased as the couple carved their way to food and game booths. Live music blasted from speakers on the levee under the Gateway Arch. In previous years, organizers had attracted entertainers like Boyz II Men, Angie Stone, Hootie and the Blowfish, Sheryl Crow, and even the late James Brown.

By early afternoon, finding a place to rest was a premium. The heat was taking its toll, causing Rainey and Josephine to slow their pace.

"Tired?"

Face flushed, Josephine nodded.

Rainey spotted space at the top of the stairs on the Old Courthouse building. He grabbed Josephine's hand and practically dragged her to an inviting steeple of steps before someone else had the same idea. Once he knew she was okay and shielded from the sun, he went in search of food.

Josephine was leaning back on her elbows when he returned. She scooted over and Rainey rested beside her. "Here, I brought you a smoked turkey leg and another bottle of water." She accepted with her thanks.

As she blessed her food, she included Rainey. "Lord, thank you for today and this food. Jesus, please order my steps and Rainey's in your Word. Amen."

Rainey lifted a brow at her off-beat request, but he let it go. He was starting to accept the fact that Josephine and the Bible were synonymous, whether she carried the book or not. It was always her point of reference.

While fortifying their energy, they used each other as an anchor, shoulder to shoulder. Rainey learned that Josephine was a slow eater; not because she chewed her food thoroughly, but because she talked between bites.

"What inspired you to become an orthodontist when your father is a medical doctor?"

Rainey eyed her half-eaten turkey leg, wondering if she was going to finish it. He shrugged off the possibility of him eating it for her. "My father loves children. He always said the only way babies could have a good start when they take their first breath is to take care of their mother." Rainey looked away. "He may never practice again. It's up to the medical board."

She nodded and swallowed. "It's up to God."

Maybe, if God intervenes, Rainey thought but kept to himself. The Lord hadn't made a move in any crisis since Rainey could remember. "My dad drilled into me that a good doctor helps those in need." Which made the hit and run case out of his father's character. He kept the thought to himself.

"When I was younger, I knew two classmates whose families didn't have the money to fix their teeth. I remember whenever they smiled, they would cover their mouths. Although I never said it out loud, I always thought they had monster teeth. As I got older, I learned one of the boys had some kind of facial deformity. Since then, my stupidity has led to my dedication in my profession." He sighed. "The way a person smiles tells me a lot about their personality, whether they're shy, confident, mischievous, loving, or unfortunate."

"What about my smile?" Her eyes sparkled as she curled her lips, exposing a few teeth to examine.

He squinted. "Hmm. Your smile says, 'I'm flirting and I don't even know it.' "

She elbowed him and stood, brushing off any crumbs. They crumpled their trash as Rainey got up. Holding her hand, they descended the stairs. Once they reached the packed sidewalk, Rainey found a recycle bin.

"And I thought you were a professional, Dr. Reynolds."

Rainey threw back his head and laughed. "Hey, don't hurt me for being truthful. Come on." Wrapping his hand around Josephine's waist, he steered her away from some rowdy teenagers. Facing the towering St. Louis landmark and tourist attraction, they looked both ways before crossing Broadway Street, heading for the Arch grounds again.

Josephine shielded her eyes from the sun and peered upward. "It's amazing up close. How tall is the Arch?"

"I believe it's six hundred and thirty feet, the highest national monument in the world. It's more than twice the height of the Statue of Liberty, which you remind me of with your poise. It's more than a hundred feet higher than the Washington Monument, and even taller than the Bent Pyramid in Egypt." He rolled off the facts proudly, but enough of being a tour guide. He wanted facts on her. "Your turn. Why did you come to America? And why is library science your focus?"

"Everybody wants to come to America," she teased, scrunching up her nose. "Didn't you see the movie with actor Eddie Murphy? Plus, the United States is the land of the free and opportunity."

"Okay. I'm sold." He snickered. "But library science? I'm not an avid reader outside dental and orthodontist-related journals, but I do pick up a thriller or sci-fi novel every now and then. Is a career as a librarian worth"—he drew quotation marks with his fingers—"*coming to America?*"

Josephine stopped suddenly on the sidewalk, almost causing a domino effect with walkers behind them. "Dr. Reynolds," she said in a clipped British accent, "you amaze me by your lack of knowledge, concerning one of your finest educational institutions in your state. The University of Missouri at Columbia's master of arts in information science and learning technologies with an emphasis in library science, is the only master's degree program your state accredits. I take online courses, as well as satellite classes at the St. Louis campus and other sites—"

He held up his hand to close the floodgates of her sales pitch. "I stand chastened. I had no idea."

"But you should." Josephine continued her scolding. "Education is the source of wealth in your country. Librarians are more than bookworms. We're researchers for individuals and companies like television stations, law firms, and government agencies. Have a question? We know how to track down the answer." She raised her finger. "And God demands we pursue His wisdom. In Hosea 4, we perish without it."

Rainey snickered. *There she goes again.* Somehow, she could mention the Bible without blinking a curly lash. She picked up on his vibes.

"Is that offensive?"

He shook his head. *Offensive? No. Annoying? Somewhat.*

"It's a positive habit that doesn't make me ashamed. I want others to know it's not Josephine's wisdom that I speak, but God's."

Shrugging, Rainey resumed their walk, nudging her along. "Makes sense to me."

As the sun magically set, the expectation among the crowd intensified. At exactly nine o'clock, the much-anticipated fireworks show got underway. From the Illinois side of the Mississippi River, the cannons exploded, shooting a streak of rainbow colors over the river and across the sky. The illusion was splashes of blues, reds, and whites under the Arch. For the next thirty minutes, the designs and sounds were nonstop as the crowd *ooh*ed and *ahh*ed. Children, resting on the shoulders of their fathers, pointed.

It wasn't that the coordinated fireworks weren't phenomenal. Rainey preferred to let the reflection of the lights in Josephine's eyes mesmerize him. Every few minutes, she seemed to hold her breath. The crowd was estimated in the thousands; many were from neighboring states that had come for the annual event.

"Wow, I'm so glad you invited me," Josephine said, glancing at him.

"I'm humbled that you accepted."

"This is exhilarating and romantic," she said, almost breathless, quickly returning her attention to the fireworks.

Standing near Josephine felt intimate to Rainey. "Is this really romantic, Josephine? Is it exciting that we're here, sharing this moment?" Rainey doubted she would answer him, and she didn't right away.

"The experience is romantic." She waved an arm in the air like a wand. "If you're asking if this is a coincidence we're both here together. . ." She didn't blink. "No."

He nodded, stuffed his hands in his pants pockets and re-focused on the Arch. Rainey hadn't expected her to admit it. Maybe he was softening her up. "Josephine, I believe we can do better than this fragile friendship." When he turned back to her, she squinted as if she were searching for his sincerity.

"Two wide gulfs seem to separate us. You can barely tolerate your twin sister and Grandmother B. See, like now, the very mention of her name plasters a scowl on your face." Shaking her head, Josephine gave him a disapproving frown. "In my country, family is the most important relationship. We are bound until we die. Some believe the tie is never cut."

"I'm glad you understand the strength of the family commit-ment. That's what I've been trying to convey to Cheney. To be-friend Mrs. Beacon was traitorous."

She dismissed him and let the fireworks dancing in the sky woo her. "Make it three things that would make a serious relationship between us unlikely. You have to forgive, Rainey. Sometimes, pride prevents those who have wronged us from say-ing I'm sorry; however, too much pride is destructive and unpro-ductive."

The powerful, earth-shattering explosives could drown out what Josephine had pointed out. "I love my twin, and as for for-giveness . . ." He couldn't finish the statement because the times he felt he was making progress, an invisible rope yanked him back. He would never admit that weakness to Josephine. Never.

"Rainey," she said, rubbing his arm and waiting for his complete attention. "I'm not the woman who broke your heart; therefore, I'm not responsible to mend it. That's where God steps in."

CHAPTER 32

"We have to talk," Cheney said over the phone.

Rainey disagreed. His Sunday plans didn't include having a cozy chat with his sister, yet he was suspicious about the urgency he heard in her voice.

"You can come to dinner after we get home from church," she offered.

He wasn't up for a praise, preaching, and prayer session. Cheney wasn't guilty of forcing the issue of God on him, but after his father's recent conversion, Rainey was actually dreading that whatever moved his father to change might fall on him.

Sighing, Rainey conceded, but he wasn't changing his plans. Occasionally, he dined out on Sunday evenings. Sometimes he ate alone; other times an insignificant companion joined him.

Rainey could use their talk to his advantage. It could be an opportunity to uncover more information about the arrogant woman he was ridiculously attracted to. Since Josephine's brazen, unsolicited critique a few nights ago, they were back to square one: on opposing sides.

Refusing her culinary invitation, Rainey suggested Brandt's Cafe in the U-City Loop, where he could enjoy sidewalk dining and live jazz music after their talk. The Loop, as it was known, was a popular common ground destination between city dwellers and suburbanites. It boasted six blocks of entertainment, retail shops, and restaurants, all thriving on foot traffic.

Later that afternoon, Rainey already had a table when Cheney rounded the corner. Reclining in the chair, he stole a minute to observe her. Despite the adversities in her life with the pregnancies, Cheney glowed. She was still beautiful, and he was envious that she could find happiness. It was as if she blotted out the past. When she spotted him, Rainey stood. Once she was at their table, they hugged then sat.

"You told me not to order anything for you. Change your mind?" She shook her head, so Rainey added, "I hope you don't mind if I eat when my meal arrives."

Her response was unusual. Cheney bowed her head as if someone had slid a plate of food under her nose. Sighing, she looked up and folded her hands. He deciphered she was on a mission—him.

"Rainey, I love you, but I'm imperfect. As deficient as I am, I need you to stop judging me and love me despite all my faults. My medical file was compromised. At times, outsiders watching us wouldn't guess we've lost our camaraderie, until something sets you off and your blast of anger returns from nowhere."

A waitress delivered his walnut-and-apple salad. Rainey said a five-second blessing over his food and dug in. "That's when I remember how devastated I was when Shanice killed our baby. It's been more than ten years, and I'm still haunted about what happened. I wanted that child. Do you realize how many babies that Dad has saved over the course of his profession? Of course you do. You're a Reynolds. Then when I found out you had undergone the same procedure, I lost my emotional mind. I didn't know you anymore."

Cheney reached across the table and covered his hand. "Rainey, none of us knows what we're capable of doing until we're in a crisis. For me, I made a decision when I felt God didn't answer me in a timely manner." She frowned. "At that time, I chose an option that is legal, but to paraphrase what Apostle Paul said in 1 Corinthians 6:12, all things that are law-ful, aren't always expedited. In other words, just because some-thing is available to me, doesn't mean I have to take it. I don't want you to find yourself in the middle of a storm, and you make a decision that could be wrong for you.

"Come to Jesus before the storm picks up. You made Daddy so proud when you chose dentistry. Don't disappoint him now by being too bullheaded to seek the same salvation he found."

He took a sip of the water his waitress had brought before his salad. "I'll think about it."

She took a deep breath and smiled. "Thank you." She relaxed.

"Now, there's something I want to talk to you about."

"Sure," she said with a shrug.

"Josephine."

Confusion dawned on Cheney's face. When realization hit, she smirked. "It's going to cost you."

"How much?" With a six-figure income, he doubted Cheney or Josephine would break his bank.

"Salvation. Without a commitment, it may be a long road with Josephine, but that's my assessment. I don't know where that is on her priority list."

Rainey huffed. "I do."

Checking his watch for the third time was not a good sign. Parke wanted to appear calm and not impatient as he relaxed against his sofa. If he glanced at the minute hand one more time, it would definitely blow his cover. He tugged on one of his daughter's neatly twisted ponytails to annoy Kami.

"Daddy, stop."

"Okay." Parke pouted. He was stressed and couldn't help it.

In two more minutes, the social worker, Mrs. Frances, and Little Parke would be late for the designated drop-off time.

The previous week, for Mrs. Frances's first visit, she had arrived ready for their house inspection, targeting possible safety hazards. Since Parke and Cheney were approved years earlier for emergency foster care cases, it helped expedite Little Parke's placement. Their updated reference check came back clean, and the paperwork was filed. The Jamiesons were ready.

As Parke exhaled, his doorbell rang. He practically leaped from the sofa and tripped over Kami, racing to the door. Cheney blocked his path.

"Back off, Parke," Cheney warned calmly. She held up her hand and forced him back. "He's here. We don't want to scare him with your over-the-edge excitement."

Puffing out his chest, Parke flexed his muscles. "I'm his father."

"And I'll be his mother, so will you sit down?" Cheney ordered then opened the door. She looked from the social worker to the child then stepped back. "Please come in."

Little Parke was dressed in blue jeans, white sneakers, and a red Cardinals T-shirt and baseball cap. He didn't seem to be as tall as Kami, but with Jamieson blood flowing through his veins, the height, biceps, and abs would come later. Parke's son appeared oblivious to what was about to transpire.

Mrs. Frances's chubby face was void of any makeup, except for two thick streaks of a brown eyebrow pencil. Her short, gray hair was trimmed like freshly cut grass. It was the second time Parke noticed her nondescript black pants, black shoes, and a white blouse.

Cheney glanced over her shoulder, but Parke's eyes were fixated on his son. *His son.* Five years, almost five and a half years, and this was the first time Parke had seen his son. Parke's heart pounded harder with warmth as Kami made her presence known. She shoved her fist on her imaginary hip as if she were ready to lay down the rules.

The social worker nudged the child forward to make introductions. Parke squatted, resisting the urge to steal his son and sprint for a touchdown. He ached for some alone time with him, but he couldn't. This very moment was a family event.

It seemed Parke had dreamed, play acted, and replayed this very scenario in his head over the past year. What would be the first thing he would say to his son when he finally met him? He had practiced his speech, yet he couldn't recall a word.

"My name is Parke too. You were named after me because I'm your real dad." The child's stone expression failed to give Parke the encouragement he needed to say more. After a few moments of awkward silence, Parke reluctantly inched up to his full height and gave the child some space.

As if taking her cue to fill the lull, Mrs. Frances shifted the child's backpack, which hung from her arm. Squeezing Little Parke's hand, she continued the introductions. "This is his wife, Cheney," Mrs. Frances explained.

Cheney gave him a tender expression and winked, causing his first reaction. Little Parke blushed. *Like father, like son.* Parke called it the Cheney effect. *Why am I jealous?*

And this is their daughter and your sister, Kami." Mrs. Frances ushered him closer. The adults held their breath, hoping the boy would at least bond with another child. No such luck.

"I don't want a big brother. Do you have a younger one you can bring?" Kami asked Mrs. Frances, crossing her arms.

Parke grimaced. Leave it to his little diva to speak her mind. Normally, Parke would have swiftly scolded her, but he didn't think that would make a good first impression.

Mrs. Frances's eyes twinkled as she chuckled. "Maybe next time, dear. Now," she said, facing Cheney and Parke, "why don't we relax and get to know each other?"

Parke discussed throwing a big welcome home party, but his wife, the boss of his castle, said no. He relented on the party, but he wouldn't back down from purchasing a mini Indy car with a 3.5 horsepower Tecumseh Power Sport gas engine—a perfect companion for any child, especially a boy under ten years old. He angled the toy in the living room as if it were on a showroom floor. Cheney even allowed him to push some furniture to the side to give it the car dealership feel.

The child sat stoic. Any closer to Mrs. Frances, he would be in her lap. Little Parke took one peek at the car and two glances at Kami. He didn't move. Nothing his son did slipped by Parke.

". . . so you understand?" Mrs. Frances rattled last-minute details.

Parke nodded, tuning out Cheney and Mrs. Frances. *I should've dressed in my Cardinals slugger Albert Pujols jersey to match my boy.* The more Parke tried to coax Little Parke to come to him, the more guarded the child became.

Bored with the idle chatter of the adults, Kami soon forgot about her new houseguest. Slowly, she began tampering with the mini Indy car as if she were contemplating a car jacking.

"Kami, don't you even think about touching it," Parke stated firmly without trying to scare his son. Contrite, she marched upstairs to her bedroom. She shut her door loud enough to protest her displeasure. She fell short of slamming it, which would result in some serious punishments.

A half hour later, after a glass of homemade wild berry lemonade and cookies, Mrs. Frances announced it was time for her to go. Little Parke jumped off the sofa and clung to the social worker's chunky calf.

"Don't be afraid, Little Gilbert." Mrs. Frances tried to comfort.

"Little Parke," Parke correct. "Once the adoption is final, we plan to legally change his name back to what it should be, Parke K. Jamieson the Seventh."

"The Seventh is taken," Cheney reminded him in a no-compromise tone.

Mrs. Frances stood in a huff. "Maybe it's best to stick to Little Gilbert until you figure out your numbers." She looked down and patted the boy's head and spoke softly. "I'll be back to check on you. Your dad will take care of you, okay?" She smiled and said her good-byes as if knowing Little Parke wasn't going to respond.

Mrs. Frances almost made her escape when the boy spoke for the first time. "My name is Park Jamie. I don't like Little Gilbert."

His son made Parke proud. He tightened his lips to keep from smirking before Mrs. Frances squinted Parke's way. "Then Park Jamie it is," Mrs. Frances agreed with a warm smile.

A few minutes later, unrestrained, the social worker opened the door and walked out. Parke audibly sighed. He felt as if he had been holding his breath since Mrs. Frances arrived. Plastering his hands on his waist, Parke nibbled on his bottom lip. He stared at the boy, who hadn't stirred. *Now, on to the biggest trial of my life—getting to know my son.*

CHAPTER 33

Cheney thought being the center of attention wasn't all it was cracked up to be. The visible signs that Little Parke wasn't a mannequin were the rapid blinking of his long lashes and a finger slightly twitching.

The tension collapsed then reassembled when Kami, who had come back downstairs, was the first to speak as she crossed her arms. "All the other toys in the house are mine. Mommy and Daddy bought 'em. You can play with 'em, but you have to ask, and no boys are allowed in my bedroom. . . ." Kami rattled on to a disinterested boy. At that moment, Cheney appreciated the saying, *Silence is golden.*

"Little girl, if you don't hush, you won't see any toys for a week," Cheney scolded, pointing her finger. Kami pouted.

On the other hand, Parke wasn't having much luck either. He was too overbearing as he attempted to coax his son to the car. Cheney shook her head in pity. Now that Little Parke was before her eyes, Cheney searched the child's face for affirmation of the Jamieson genes she saw in the picture. He had his father's black curly hair, but thick, black eyebrows probably like his mother's. The boy's skin was darker than Parke's, almost a caramel shade, but despite the slight differences, there was no doubt the boy was a Jamieson. Little Parke followed Parke's every movement. Fright filled his eyes when he turned to Kami. Cheney had to break the ice; the quietness was becoming eerie to her in the comfort of her home.

Taking a seat back on the sofa, Cheney turned her attention to two three-dimensional wooden puzzles on a coffee table: a black stallion and reddish-yellow goldfish. She had bought it as a knickknack for guests.

Finally, Parke had enough sense to stop harassing the boy. Without warning, Little Parke left his post at the door. At a snail's pace, he inched closer to Cheney and the object, after looking in both directions, barely moving his head to accomplish the task.

Cheney had counted to one hundred by the time Little Parke was within inches from the sofa. He seemed spellbound with the figurines. Discreetly, Cheney and Parke watched him in silence. Kami had stubbornly returned her room when she realized she wasn't the object of their attention. When the puzzles no longer held Little Parke's fascination, his eyes began to droop.

"Hey, sweetie, are you tired?" Cheney asked in a soft tone, meant to be soothing.

His body stiffened as she removed his cap, exposing more curls. Little Parke relaxed and sat on the sofa.

Yawning, the child shook his head, but hesitantly laid his head on her arm. She snuggled him closer and stroked his arm, humming unrecognizable tunes.

Out of nowhere and not to be outdone, Kami made a beeline for her mother. Parke intercepted and scooped her up as her legs dangled in the air.

"Parke," Cheney whispered, "we have a slight problem. What *is* his name?"

"Why would you ask me that?" He frowned.

Cheney's heart pounded, hoping he didn't repeat what he said to Mrs. Frances. There was only one Parke K. Jamieson VI, and she married him. There could only be one Parke K. Jamieson VII, and she buried him. Depending on Parke's answer, their family reunion would remain happy. "Parke . . . I'm waiting."

With pit bull Kami still in his arms, he came and knelt before Cheney. She couldn't break their eye contact. "His name is Parke the Eighth." He grinned. "Although some people are going to think our family can't count."

"They can't," she whispered before Parke kissed her, referring to Parker I, II, III, etc.; then, after the Emancipation Proclamation, his ancestors dropped the last *R* and started with Parke I, II, III, IV, V, her husband, Parke the Sixth, and their stillborn son, Parke the Seventh. So finally, Little Parke the Eighth dozed beside her. "We've got to find a nickname, or learn a better system to keep track of all the P. Jamiesons in the world."

Once the boy was knocked out, despite her protests, Kami's nap time came early. They switched children; Parke cradled his five-year-old son as if he were a newborn.

"I'll put Kami in her bed, but I think we need to leave him down here and stay with him. At least when he awakes, he'll recognize his surroundings," Cheney instructed him.

"I knew there was a reason why I married you. You're a smart one." He pressed his lips against hers then returned his attention to his son.

Parke was still watching Little Parke sleep when Cheney returned. Grinning, she sighed. "Ready?"

"Yep. Let's do it." While Cheney punched in numbers on the cordless phone, Parke yanked his BlackBerry off his belt clip with one hand as he held Little Parke. In less than a minute, he was sending multiple text messages: MY SON IS HERE. I STILL MIGHT THROW A PARTY. He sent the message to his mom, Malcolm, Ellington, and Twinkie. Within five minutes, Malcolm texted back that he was on his way with Hallison; Ellington's reply was simple: I'M BRINGING THE BALLOONS.

Cheney convinced Parke to release his son and lay him on the sofa. Parke did, but remained at his side. A half hour later when the family began to arrive, and Little Parke hadn't awakened, Parke left his post. He *shh*ed them at the door, and made everyone tiptoe inside.

"I baked cookies yesterday," Mrs. Jamieson explained, distracted by her sleeping grandson on the sofa. She shoved the pan in Parke's hands. The elder Parke followed, wearing an exaggerated grin. He slapped Parke on the back. "Good work, son. You found him."

"Correction. I found him," Ellington said, bringing up the rear. True to his word, he held numerous colorful helium balloons that hid his face. If Parke had any doubts of Ellington Brown's ID, he glanced down at the sockless bandit.

"Let's get this party started," Ellington shouted.

"Be quiet, Bozo the Clown. He's still asleep," Parke fussed, smacking the balloons.

Malcolm and Hallison were the last ones to show up, since they lived about five miles away in St. Charles County. Parke knew they would've been there sooner if it weren't for Hallison's condition.

At six months pregnant, Hallison glowed as she walked through the door with her protruding stomach and her bodyguard, Malcolm, close behind. Since Little Parke was still sleep, Hallison suddenly garnered all the attention.

Parke observed his wife. He knew it was hard for her to see Hallison pregnant. It brought an onslaught of memories of what she had lost. He breathed a sigh of relief when he didn't see a touch of sadness cross his wife's beautiful face. As a matter of fact, Cheney and Hallison engaged in a whispered, animated conversation.

When Little Parke whimpered and stretched, conversations

hushed. Everyone moved closer to the sofa and peered down. Holding their breath, they waited. When it didn't appear he would wake, they backed off like dancers performing a rehearsed routine. Suddenly, the child opened his eyes and cautiously looked around. He couldn't have looked more frightened.

Despite the smiling faces surrounding him, his tiny fingers gripped the sofa. Everyone started talking at once. Recognizing Cheney, he relaxed about one degree. When his grandmother attempted to bribe him with a cookie, he shook his head. Ellington's balloons didn't hold Little Parke's interest either.

"Give him some breathing room, everybody. Let's give him an opportunity to come to us," Cheney ordered. They murmured, but obeyed. The result was Little Parke staying close to her the remainder of the evening.

CHAPTER 34

It took twenty-four hours for the word to spread to Mrs. Beacon about the new addition to the Jamieson family, courtesy of Parke. If he was excited, he made sure the whole world celebrated with him.

"I was there when Kami came home from the hospital," Mrs. Beacon scolded over the phone, referring to when Cheney got the call in the middle of the night. The social worker had asked Cheney if she could accept a toddler who was taken from her home. Cheney had never regretted that decision. "And I'm on my way over there now."

"Not yet, Grandma BB," Cheney told her.

"And who is going to stop me? If you'll remember, I've been to jail and got the outfit to prove it. So, unless you've got a S.W.A.T. team on your rooftop, I'm on my way. I ain't scared of no jail. I've seen what it's like inside . . . ."

Cheney removed the phone from her ear and just stared at it. She then placed it back against her ear and said, "Grandma BB, calm down. Little Parke is trying to adjust as it is. You are kinda high strung. Can you give us two weeks to bond?"

"Two weeks!" Mrs. Beacon shrieked. "If I'm high strung, it's because of my blood pressure medicine. I can always stop taking it—"

Shaking her head, Cheney rolled her eyes. She actually missed the drama when Mrs. Beacon was in jail. She chuckled silently.

Cheney wouldn't have her Grandma BB any other way. "Okay. How about a week and a half?"

"I can't believe you're pushing me away." Mrs. Beacon's voice trembled, followed by an exaggerated sniff.

Cheney wasn't falling for it. "You know I know all your stunts, so you might as well put away that personality. It doesn't work on me."

"Three days," Mrs. Beacon countered, not to be deterred.

"Grandma BB, I love you, but please, give us one week, and I'm not budging." She put her hand on her hip as if Mrs. Beacon could see her attitude through the phone.

"Humph. You've got one week; then try to stop me. Anyway, I'm leaving tomorrow for Jamaica, mon. Prison is murder on a woman's complexion, so my chapter of the Red Hat Society is treating me to a trip. I plan to get a lot of sun. I'll make my presence known to my great-godson when I get back." Mrs. Beacon disconnected.

"You've got to love her," Cheney said to herself with a smirk.

True to her threat, one week later, Mrs. Beacon phoned Cheney. "I'm ready to do my drive-by."

Cheney froze as a half-floured chicken breast dangled in the air. She almost dropped the cordless that was propped on her shoulder as she prepared dinner. Cheney wasn't in the mood for Mrs. Beacon's theatrics. "Tomorrow would be better."

"Humph. Try to stop me. You ain't shame because I'm an ex-con, are you?" Mrs. Beacon sound almost boastful. She was back from vacation in high definition.

Less than an hour later, Cheney had finished setting the table when the doorbell rang. Cheney cracked the door. Mrs. Beacon opened it wider to wrap Cheney in a hug tight enough to suck the breath out of her. It was a comical moment, considering the woman was more than a foot shorter than Cheney.

Kami came barreling around the corner, screaming her delight at seeing her surrogate god-grandmother, although "god" was definitely an endearment more than a religious commitment. Mrs. Beacon freed Cheney and squatted as far down as her arthritic knees would allow. When a bone cracked, she stood again. Kami latched on to Mrs. Beacon's leg and wouldn't let go. Unconcerned, Mrs. Beacon began walking with a limp as if she were wearing a cast.

"Kami, stop it." Cheney did her best to refrain from laughing. "I'd better go and set another place setting."

Mrs. Beacon waved her off. "Unless you've moved the kitchen, I know where everything is. You go on. I'll set my own place." Before Cheney could argue, Mrs. Beacon strolled into the kitchen, bumping into Parke, who was carrying a dish of mashed potatoes.

"Hey, Grandma BB, we've missed you. You've been in hiding or jail?" he teased, leaned down, and smacked a kiss on her cheek. "Seriously, it looks like you enjoyed Jamaica."

Mrs. Beacon shrugged. "You know it, but the only way I'll return to jail depends on who messes with me."

In her signature Stacy Adams shoes, she clunked across the floor. Her choice of attire was a black-and-white striped blouse and wide-legged pants. She had a black satin belt tied at her waist.

Cheney placed her fists on her hips. She had crossed a prison uniform with martial arts workout clothes. "Why are you wearing that? Didn't you have enough of the prison garb?"

"I put this together while in Jamaica. Fashionable, ain't it? Prisoners are issued orange jumpsuits. Ugh. It looked terrible against my skin color. It's a two-fold souvenir. Every time I wear it, I'll be reminded of the island and why I traveled there."

Shaking her head, Cheney walked to the table where the children were already waiting. Parke stood and held back Cheney's chair. She accepted his chivalry as Mrs. Beacon slammed cabinet doors in the background until she swiped a ceramic plate off a stack and fumbled with utensils. Parke grinned. Cheney shook her head.

Mrs. Beacon came into the dining room. Her eyes lit up when she laid eyes on their new family addition. Parke grabbed a chair in the corner. He was about to place it next to Cheney when Mrs. Beacon had a better idea. Squeezing herself between Kami and Little Parke's chairs, she scooted them apart.

"I'll sit right here," Mrs. Beacon said.

Without arguing, Parke repositioned the children's plates, made an opening, and planted the chair according to Mrs. Beacon's specification as she arranged her place setting. "Have you said grace?" she asked, looking around the table.

"We were waiting for you," Parke answered.

"Chile, you didn't have to do that. Don't worry about me." Mrs. Beacon fanned the air. When no one moved to eat, she looked on her right side at Kami, who was grinning, and then her left side to Little Parke, who wasn't. "Okay. C'mon, let's get this over with. I'm hungry." She reached for the children's hands, and they responded.

Knowing the routine, Mrs. Beacon bowed her head.

Parke began, "Lord, we thank you for your salvation today. We also thank you for every person at this table. I ask you to bless them and . . ."

Without opening her eyes, Cheney heard Mrs. Beacon mumble, "I thought we were blessing the food."

"Lord," Parke continued, "thank you for the hands that prepared it, sanctify it to strengthen our bodies, and bless those who have not, in Jesus' name. Amen."

Everyone picked up their forks and dug in. After a few minutes, Mrs. Beacon chewed and eyed Little Parke. "So, what's your name and what number are you?"

"Park Jamie," the child hesitantly answered. His eyes were wide in wonder at Mrs. Beacon.

"Uh-huh. You're a Jamieson," Parke corrected with a reassuring nod and wink.

Kami frowned. "He's not a Jamieson. I'm a Jamieson." She practically snarled at Little Parke. "You haven't been adopted yet."

Mrs. Beacon swayed her head back and forth between them as if she were watching a tennis match. Surprised by their behavior, Cheney glanced at Parke. "This girl knows too much grown folks' business," she mouthed.

"I'm a Jamieson." Little Parke raised his voice, but did a good job of controlling his temper. His small baby face turned red.

"I was a Jamieson first." Kami jutted her chin.

Mrs. Beacon grinned. "Whoa. I'm glad I didn't miss this."

Cheney hushed her as Parke stood to settle them down, threatening to take away video games. *Leave it to Grandma BB to stir up mess.* One small victory—it was the first time Little Parke openly bumped heads with Kami, concerning his place within the family. Sighing, Cheney finished eating.

Parke watched the dinner scene with interest. That had been the first emotion he and Cheney had seen Little Parke display. Parke had been careful not to overload his son with information about his heritage, but as another week passed, Parke felt it was time.

He loved his daughter. There was no doubt in his mind that Kami would be an independent woman, like her mother, when she grew up. The only problem was Kami was only four years old. *Lord Jesus, help me to survive the diva years.*

Since Little Parke's arrival, his son had been shy, and most times, withdrawn, but once Kami entered the room, the tension was thick. He wouldn't classify it as sibling rivalry, but it was a matter of time. Since Little Parke was coming out of his shell, Parke wanted to indoctrinate his son about his heritage.

In the sun porch on the floor, Parke raced Hot Wheels cars with the younger Jamieson. "Little Parke," he said as two toy cars collided, "I know you miss your mother."

The boy nodded as his bottom lip curved downward. "I've been sad. She used to play with me a lot."

Parke's heart broke. "Did she ever tell you about me?"

"Uh-huh. She showed me a picture of a man." The child shrugged and shook his head. "You looked real old," he said. Propping his elbow on the floor to rest his chin, he squinted at his father.

Old my foot.

Bored with the adult conversation, Little Parke resumed his playtime activity. His tiny hands raced his car from side to side then watched in awe as the purple vintage Corvette took flight.

Boy, I'm not even forty. Plus, Parke had only found a few gray strands. He could probably thank Kami for that. "Son, I know you've been sad since Rachel died, and you've had to live with new people. I'm sorry your momma died, and I know she loved you very much, and so do Cheney and I. You don't have to worry about any more daddies."

Little Parke squinted and tilted his head. "Yes, sir. I knew you were my daddy."

"You did?"

He bobbed his head. "We have the same name."

"That's right. We do." Parke chuckled, remembering that was

one of the first things he told Little Parke when he arrived with Mrs. Frances. "You want to hear a true story?" Little Parke lost interest with the car and gave his father his attention. "You are rich, son. You will grow up and be rich in knowledge, rich in character, and rich in heavenly and earthly possessions. Your ancestors came from the Diomande Tribe in Côte d'Ivoire, Africa. It's called the jewel of West Africa.

"Our family was made up of tribes: mothers, fathers, sisters, brothers, cousins, grandparents. King Dateh ruled the Akan Kingdom. His son, Prince Paki, was kidnapped and brought to America, but he was strong and escaped. Paki ran away with a beautiful woman. They were our grandparents about a hundred years ago . . . ."

Parke held off about the slavery part for another few years. Little Parke had to understand the institution of slavery before someone introduced racism to him.

CHAPTER 35

One month later, Dr. Roland Reynolds, in front of his family, members of the media, and onlookers, stood before Judge Davis, awaiting his fate. The mood had a strange feel to it. Cheney actually felt guilty for basking in personal happiness at home while the Reynoldses' lives were in turmoil. Her mother had aged a couple of years in the past months.

The prosecutor requested that Judge Davis give Roland the maximum sentence of five years. Roland's attorney asked the judge for leniency. Cheney held her breath when the judge addressed her father.

"Do you have anything to say, Mr. Reynolds?"

"Yes, Your Honor, I would like to apologize to Mrs. Beacon, society, and my family for the misjudgment I made years ago."

Near the back row with Josephine, Mrs. Beacon reluctantly nodded, although she appeared defiant and unforgiving. Cheney saw through the mask she wore. Cheney recognized compassion, as if Mrs. Beacon understood what fate could befall on Roland.

"Perhaps, if it weren't for my cowardly actions, a man would be alive today. I know my apology is long overdue and can't bring back Mr. Beacon, but I'm remorseful and accept my guilt. I have repented, and now, I'm at your mercy, Your Honor."

Expressionless, Judge Davis nodded. "The hypocrisy of your actions and the life that you allowed to die so that you can live is despicable. You have altered untold lives that cannot be reversed. I have taken into consideration your plea, your service to society, and the charge brought against you. Therefore, I sentence you to two years at the Algoa Correctional Center on No More Victims Road in Jefferson City, Missouri." Judge Davis explained it was a minimum security facility.

Gasping for air, Cheney exchanged a teary expression with Rainey. Janae and Gayle wailed their shock. Rainey wrapped his arm around his mother.

Before their father was taken into custody, he glanced over his shoulder and sent a genuine, encouraging smile. "All is well in my soul," Roland consoled them. "Cheney," he called, giving her a pointed look. Without saying another word, his expression silently reminded Cheney of her promise to continue sharing Jesus' redeeming love and salvation with their family. She planned to keep it.

Roland hadn't been processed as an inmate, but like she had with Mrs. Beacon, Cheney was already counting the days before his release. She wanted to delay her father going in and accelerate his coming out. For a fleeting moment, she wished his sin had stayed buried, but then he might not have repented and turned to God.

Cheney wouldn't trade years of motherhood for a day of singlehood for anything. Yet, after the morning's event, all she craved was cuddling up next to her husband. "God, only you would give Daddy the courage to say all is well in his soul. Now, please weave peace in mine, as well as my family, in Jesus' name. Amen." She continued to pray on her drive home. There was no way she could return to work and actually get something done.

Later that evening, after Parke gave her the comfort she needed, she phoned her mother. The housekeeper said she was rest-ing. "I'll take care of her, Miss Cheney."

"I know you will, Miss Mattie. I know."

The next day, after leaving Missouri Telephone, Cheney made the Reynolds mansion her first stop. Miss Mattie met her at the front door with a smile that she was paid to have; then she rolled her eyes and whispered, "Good luck."

Cheney had already been on the receiving end of her moth-er's fury since the story broke about Roland's involvement in the hit-and-run cold case. She could imagine what punishment her mother would bestow on her for the next two years. Walking into the study, Cheney wasn't prepared for what she saw.

Gayle was stretched out on the couch in her favorite silver pantsuit. It was so crumpled, it look like her body was wrapped in aluminum foil. Her hair, more pepper than salt, had three large curlers planted in it that formed the Bermuda Triangle. Cheney frowned, unable to determine if her mother was getting dressed or undressed. The conclusion was she needed help in doing whatever it was.

Stepping closer, Cheney peered at her mother. Gayle's per-fume of choice was replaced by liquor. The scent wasn't strong, as if she had downed a bottle, but it was a dead giveaway she had more than one glass of something.

Tentatively, Cheney nudged her. "Mom?"

Gayle moaned, but didn't open her eyes.

"Momma?" she called again. "It's me, Cheney. I came to check on you. Come on." Cheney bent and struggled with the noncompliant body, but she managed to get her mother in a sitting position. Cheney swiftly sat next to her as an anchor. Gayle's head automatically slid on Cheney's shoulder.

Tears welled in Cheney's eyes. She had never seen her moth-er drunk. Come to think of it, they didn't stock liquor in the house. "What's going on?"

She mumbled something Cheney couldn't understand, but the agony was apparent. Propping Gayle's head against the back of the sofa, she went in search of Miss Mattie, but the house-keeper was already in the doorway, carrying a tray with a pitcher of water and bananas.

"Who got my mother drunk? Who bought her liquor? She doesn't drink," Cheney ranted, flustered. "How much alcohol did she have? I need a pot of coffee."

Mattie shook her head. "Miss Cheney, your mother got her-self drunk. Considering she's over twenty-one, I don't think she needed to show an ID to make a purchase. As far as no liquor in the Reynolds household, Gayle seems to be making up for lost time—big time." She took a deep breath and kept an even tone. "Mrs. Reynolds needs water to dilute the alcohol in her system, and maybe a banana to give her some energy. I also suggest you have her walk it off," the unlicensed nurse lectured.

"Yes, ma'am. Thank you. How did you know all this?"

"TV. You can cut, suture, and administer drugs. Even learn the steps to perform autopsies on the cable network."

"I see." Taking the offering, Cheney went back to her moth-er. Sip by sip, Cheney coaxed her mother until she had swal-lowed most of the tall glass of water.

Gayle wasn't completely sober, but she was alert enough to hold a conversation. "Come on, Mom. Let's go upstairs to the ballroom, our favorite place to talk."

It wasn't uncommon for mansions in the Central West End to have ballrooms on the third floor, or bowling alleys in the basement. Gayle had spent many afternoons after school there with her daughters. Gayle loved music and she loved to dance. In their home, she and the girls had private lessons in ballet, tap, jazz, and even ballroom. It was considered the girls' room for slumber parties or to work through problems.

Cheney knew there would be no dancing that night. With each step, Gayle became more alert. She still slurred her words, but at least Cheney could understand most, which included *Roland* and *gone*. Questions swarmed in her head. Was her mother a casual drinker, a closet alcoholic? If this was her first drink, Cheney and her siblings would make sure it was her last. Roland would insist upon it.

At the top of the landing, they paused. Giving her mother a chance to rest, they sat on a plush white cushioned window seat the length of a queen-size bed. The stained-glass window above it was custom designed from a photograph of exotic birds.

When it appeared Gayle had become too relaxed, Cheney assisted her in standing again then proceeded down a short hall into a mirror-walled dance studio. It was off the main ballroom that was frequently used for parties. Pushing open the white French doors, Cheney guided her mother inside, adjusting the lighting on the wall sconces to cast a dim glow.

Once they sat in twin velvet-cushion chairs, Cheney rubbed her mother's hands. "Momma, Daddy will be okay and so will we. He's only a couple of hours away."

"You were such a sweet little girl. How come when you became an adult, you became a taboo?" Gayle rambled. Cheney didn't know if Gayle was sober, baring her soul, or if alcohol was having its way. "I know people make mistakes. I've made plenty of them myself, but this isn't fair. I refuse to believe it. Your daddy saves babies, you destroyed one. Roland admitted to being a drunk driver, but I don't recall him ever taking a drink, even at social gatherings. Your father is sitting in prison innocent. Men of his stature don't go to prison. People overlook minor indiscretions. This wasn't supposed to happen."

"And you blame me?"

Gayle nodded a few times. "You started it."

Cheney blinked. Was that the alcohol talking or her heart?

CHAPTER 36

Early one Sunday morning, Hallison phoned Cheney. "Sis, I can't seem to pick up energy this morning. It may be your turn to save Malcolm and me a seat at church."

Cheney laughed as she fingered through several outfits in her closet. "You really must be slowing down if a mother of two beats a pregnant woman to church."

"Two more months, and girl, this Jamieson will be out of here. I don't see how you did it. Whew. I feel ugly."

"Hali, with your height and your butterball bulge, models would make room for you on the runway." Cheney had enjoyed being pregnant. She was in awe, knowing a tiny life growing inside was God's miracle. Jesus had healed her womb so she could carry Parke's seed. Since Little Parke's arrival, the painful memories of losing those two babies were becoming distant. The child was reserved, which she and Parke expected, but he was also polite and well mannered. His mother had done a great job rearing him until her death, despite leaving his father out of the loop.

Kami was another story. The little diva was predictable. She demanded all of their attention. Some of it wasn't always in her favor, especially when she had to stay in her room as punishment. She sighed. The ready-made children were definitely the way to go.

"I meant to ask you, have you heard from your dad? How's he holding up?" Hallison inquired.

Cheney glanced up to see Parke escorting his son into their master bedroom. Little Parke didn't look too happy. The determined expression on Parke's face explained why. Cheney chuckled. The child was adjusting, although at the moment, Little Parke balked at the idea of hanging a tie around his neck.

Little Parke was positioned in front of a free-standing cheval mirror. Parke stood behind him, where Cheney could see both their reflections. Patiently and meticulously, Parke demonstrated how to tie a tie. *Again.* Cheney happily sighed.

After getting sidetracked, Cheney refocused on her phone conversation. "Daddy is doing remarkably well. Since he's in a minimum security prison, the other inmates seem respectable and come to him with medical questions. I guess you can say after he dispenses his advice, he talks about Jesus. In his last letter, Daddy said one man has even attended chapel with him a few times.

"It's definitely not a resort. He says there are some scary men in there. We're thankful for the prison consultants, based out of Nashville, who prepped him on how to fit in and not bring attention to his former affluent status in the outside world. He wrote he blew his cover a few weeks ago when a prisoner sprained his foot. Keep praying for him, Hali."

"I will. Jesus sent Paul into prison to preach to the captives, and look what happened."

Cheney sighed. "Umm-hmm. That sounds good on paper, but I want my dad home. Oh, and I did tell you that Momma's in therapy for her depression. Rainey made sure of that, fearing she would become an alcoholic and, God forbid, get behind the wheel."

"I can understand Rainey's fear."

Cheney yawned and checked her watch. She hadn't seen Kami in the past ten minutes. "Yeah. At least we got to Momma before this thing got too far. She chose alcohol to deal with the stress of the trial instead of running to God."

"Well, we both can attest that God isn't always the first choice."

"You know it. Let me go, Hali. If I'm supposed to beat you to church, I'd better get dressed and check on your diva niece."

"Okay, honey. I'm going to take another quick nap, and I'll see you later."

"Right." After they disconnected, Cheney chuckled. *Hali will never make it.* Parke was now brushing Little Parke's hair. "That was Hali. She says to save her and Malcolm a seat."

Parke smirked, amused. "This is what? The second time in a month?"

Nodding, Cheney snickered. "Well, she's getting close to her due date. Soon you and Malcolm will have sons."

"Yep, and my son will be better looking." Parke twisted his lips in confidence then winked at Little Parke. "Okay, go see if your sister is ready."

"Yes, sir." Clearly, the boy wasn't excited about the task.

Once the child left the room, Parke whispered, "I'll be glad when this trial period is over. The foster family visits remind me that he's not really ours yet." So far, they had passed three follow-up inspections.

"Well, babe." Cheney stood too fast and teetered with a momentary dizziness.

Concerned, Parke was at her side immediately. "You're doing too much." He cupped her chin with his hand then guided it closer to his lips. "What did I tell you? You don't have to prove your love for Little Parke. He knows, and I know. Even Kami knows she has to share you now. Slow down, baby, okay?" He searched her eyes for compliance. "I don't want a super mother. I prefer a super lover."

She laughed. "Get your mind out of the gutter."

"Hey, I'm married."

"I do recall saying yes at the wedding."

By the time she and Parke loaded the SUV with their children, Cheney was tired. At times, combing and detangling Kami's thick hair was a major task, then for some reason, Kami couldn't find her shoes to match her gold dress.

Cheney's exhaustion dissipated once they walked through the church doors. The praise team was singing one of Cheney's favorites, "How Great Thou Art." In sync, the four claimed a pew and on one accord, they knelt and prayed. One by one, they stood and shook out of their coats and jackets before taking their seats.

Since it was the Sunday for children's church, Kami and Little Parke raced off to their classrooms. Cheney and Parke smiled at each other as they lifted their hands in praise, joining the chorus. When Cheney thought about the goodness of the Lord, her eyes misted. It seemed surreal when her family entered the sanctuary for the second time since Roland's imprisonment.

Malcolm and Hallison arrived about fifteen minutes into Pastor Scott's preaching. The cat naps had done Hallison good. She looked refreshed and vibrant.

"Let's go back to Ecclesiastes, the third chapter." Pastor Scott waited as pages flipped. "Yes, time does bring about a change. It's supposed to. Whatever season you're in now, it's about to change. That's God's word. Now, don't go getting scared because things are going good right now. If you enjoy the snow of the winter, then you have to endure the ice and take precautions against the slippery roads. It's part of the season.

"If you see the spring flowers bloom, you must remember storms will come. The same goes for the summer and fall. To grow with God, we must suffer a little while down here. Endure the darkness because your season is about to change to light, but oh, when we see Jesus, that's when you're going to have a permanent, everlasting season."

Pastor Scott continued to preach how evilness likes to tag along with goodness, but how important it was to resist it and evilness's stay would be temporary. He segued into the call to discipleship. Even after several people repented and made their way to the altar, Pastor Scott didn't stop his appeal, but extended it until five other men from Cheney's section surrendered. They made their way to the aisle and walked to the front to the waiting ministers.

"That's right. Keep coming. God wants to save you now, at this very moment. God is on site now. He will not turn you away. Since tomorrow's not promised, come today. Don't put it off any longer. Come . . . there is no appointment to schedule." Pastor Scott waved his hand.

The altar call concluded when the candidates changed into white clothes. One by one, they stepped into the baptismal pool. With their arms crossed, the ministers supported their back as one minister lifted up his hand. "My dear brothers and sisters, upon the confession of your sins, and the confidence we have in the Word of God, we baptize you as instructed to the apostles, and they carried out in the Book of Acts, in the name of Jesus for the remission of your sins. Amen."

The crowd went wild when one man started shouting and praising God in the water. After church was dismissed, Mrs. Beacon came to Cheney's mind. The woman was just as stubborn now as she was before she went to jail. She still refused to attend church, fussing she'd rather go back to jail. "If you don't stop cutting up, the Lord, might just send you back there," Cheney always warned her.

***

By the end of the week, Cheney was convinced Little Parke or Kami had passed some type of bug on to her. Although she wasn't running a temperature, she was exhausted after waking up. Parke even commented more than once that she looked tired. "Don't worry about the kids. I'll make sure I'm off early enough to pick them up from school and drop them off at their martial arts lesson."

"Don't think I missed your insult about my great looks, but I'm too drained to argue."

"But you'll forgive me because you love me and know I'm always going to take care of you," he said a little too confidently for Cheney.

"Umm-hmm." She rolled over.

Parke packed the children's lunches; then Cheney checked their school uniforms. After her approval, Parke dropped them off at school before heading to his office. Thankful for his thoughtfulness, Cheney smiled and closed her eyes, hoping to get in thirty more minutes of sleep.

It didn't help. An hour later and still drowsy, Cheney got up and hoped an orange-cranberry muffin and a cup of decaf would jumpstart her day. It didn't. Her stomach felt queasy, so she didn't chance putting more into it. She barely put in a half day's work before going back home. Although the phone company had a generous benefit package of sick, vacation, and excused time off, her days were dwindling. The trials had taken a big chunk.

As she locked up her desk, she called Parke to let him know she was leaving early. Once at home, she climbed in bed. It seemed as if she had just closed her eyes when the phone rang.

The room was dimmed and the house was quiet. Normally she wouldn't have answered it, but she recognized Malcolm

Jamieson on the caller ID, and it was almost five o'clock. She picked up. "Hello?"

"Whew. What's wrong with you? Did I wake you?" Hallison rolled off the questions.

"Hey, Hali. Just tired, girl. I don't know if I picked up something from Little Parke or Kami. You know kids like to share everything. Plus, Parke isn't helping with his glowing compliments of 'you need rest,' or 'you look tired.' I haven't felt like this since I had morning sickness."

"Maybe you're pregnant," Hallison stated.

Fully awake, Cheney scooted up in the bed. "I don't think so." She wasn't in the mood for jokes. After all she went through, that would not be a welcome condition at this point in her life; but her sister-in-law had planted a seed. "Hali, that's not even funny. I've accepted the fact that I can't have children. God gave us two beautiful ones—well, almost. The home visits have gone well. We're still months away before we can officially apply for adoption."

Both were quiet as they fed off the possibility. Hallison cleared her throat. "Well, I called to see if you can tag along with me to my doctor's appointment in the morning. Malcolm has to be in on a client review. It's at nine. I was hoping, since you have flex time, you can go with me. If not, I'll ask my mother or Momma J, but you know those two. They would have a list of questions to ask the doctor about the health of my baby."

A bout of nausea hit Cheney. Rubbing her stomach until the uneasiness passed, she didn't want to commit if she was going to feel like this in the morning. "Hali, I would love to, but you'd better have your mother on standby. Maybe, whatever I have might pass in the morning, but pregnant? Nah."

"Okay," Hallison practically sang in the phone. "Take a pregnancy test for the fun of it," she teased and hung up.

Returning the cordless phone to its holder on the nightstand, Cheney took a deep breath. She dismissed the nonsense and slid back under the covers. As she closed her eyes, the next voice she heard was Parke's.

"I'm heading to Walgreen's for a pregnancy test." He closed the bedroom door that she didn't know he had opened. Evidently, he had heard enough of the one-sided conversation.

She moaned and frowned. "Lord, not again. I've had my quota of seasons."

Less than an hour later, Cheney woke again at the sound of excited little voices. Opening her eyes, Parke stood over her, dangling a plastic bag from his fingertips. Again she scooted up and threw back the comforter. "Parke, Hali's hormones were talking."

Parke's expression alternated between hope and trepidation. "And we're going to see if yours have anything to say. Take it, baby." He slowly offered her the bulging bag with three boxed kits.

Why did she dread the task or the outcome? She looked from Parke to the package. He hadn't moved.

"Okay," she whispered, accepting her fate. She dragged herself to the bathroom and closed the door in vain. As she knew he would, Parke followed. A few minutes later, when the colored bands appeared, they knew.

"You're pregnant," Parke stated.

"If so, thanks to you." She gritted her teeth. "I sure hope it's wrong," Cheney said and meant it. She had two children, lost two children, terminated one baby, and she was through. "I'll retake it in the morning."

Parke covered her fidgety hand. "I'm staying home."

Oh no, this man is not getting ready to drive me crazy, she worried. "That's not necessary. Hali wants me to go along with her to Dr.

Gray's office. While I'm there, I'll take another test," she said to pacify him and calm her nerves, although she predicted her nerves would still be frayed in the morning.

"You okay? Because I'm scared," Hallison admitted as she drove herself to the doctor, with Cheney in the passenger seat as if she were the patient.

"What's the matter, Hali? Is the baby okay?" Cheney panicked as her head whipped around from looking out the window.

"I'm talking about you. I'm scared for you." Hallison accelerated when the light turned green.

"Yeah, I'm scared for me too. What are the odds of me actually delivering a healthy baby? I really wanted a baby with Parke, but you know what? I even think I could pass as Little Parke's birth mother. I mean, after all, there are no such things as stepchildren, since I've never heard of a step-husband or step-wife."

"Trying to talk yourself into it, huh?"

"I hope I'm doing a good job convincing myself." Cheney sighed. "Hali, if I'm pregnant, I don't want you to tell anybody, not even Malcolm."

Hallison took one hand off the wheel. "Now, wait a minute. Malcolm and I don't keep secrets."

Cheney was about to say Hallison and Malcolm hadn't lost any babies, either, but she held her tongue. Hallison was still pregnant, and Cheney didn't need to plant a seed of doubt. Cheney decided to keep the news to herself. At least she could threaten Parke, knowing if the word got out, he would be the culprit.

She was fine in her perfect season. *I thought getting pregnant was by faith. It's keeping the baby that seems more trying.*

I have the power to keep you and your unborn child, God spoke.

An hour later, the Jamieson wives left the doctor's office. Cheney drove this time. Hallison and her baby boy were doing fine. Cheney wasn't, after the doctor confirmed her pregnancy. She honestly didn't know how she felt.

Later that afternoon while at work, her threat to Parke was ineffective. The string of phone calls she received afterward verified it. Cheney was livid. She wasn't ready for people's pity or others' guarded enthusiasm. A few hours later when she walked in the door at home, Parke was in the kitchen making sundaes for the children as a celebration. The real evidence of his betrayal was the box of gum cigars on the counter.

She kissed Kami's cheek and Little Parke's forehead. With a ridiculous grin on his face, Parke leaned forward and puckered his lips for a kiss.

Cheney seized the opportunity. She nipped him. "Big mouth."

CHAPTER 37

It was story time at Ferguson Library. Since the day Parke filled Little Parke's mind about Africa, his son couldn't get enough information. Already he showed early signs of becoming a history bookworm. When Cheney and the children walked through the door, Josephine was at her post at the counter, looking regal in black. Her hair was piled on top of her head.

Cheney tried to keep her pregnancy low key. The obvious sign was she couldn't get enough bed rest, but she didn't want to disappoint the children and miss storytelling. Parke would be tied up most of the afternoon at an MBA event, lecturing about financial investment and money management.

She claimed a seat in the back of the room and stretched her legs; legs that her husband had complimented the previous night as having well-toned calves. Relaxing against the wall, Cheney closed her eyes minutes before Josephine sat beside her. "Are you feeling well? Your face isn't showing your natural beauty."

"I don't know how I'm supposed to take that. I'm worn out because I'm pregnant, and right now my beauty is in a makeup bag at home."

Josephine squealed and clasped her hands. Cheney shushed her. "I didn't come to get attacked by a room of kids because they can't hear the tales. I'm glad you're excited."

"Don't be silly. You're married to a handsome man. Grandmother B summarized your prior difficulties having a baby. I say this is good news." Josephine smiled, reminding Cheney of her brother's livelihood as a smile perfectionist.

Rainey. She remembered his attraction to her. "I've been meaning to talk to you." Cheney lifted a brow. Nobody messed over her twin. "Cut my brother some slack."

"Excuse me?" Josephine looked genuinely perplexed.

"Rainey likes you." Cheney patted her chest. "If I had to set my brother up on a blind date, I would pick you."

"I am honored by your confidence, but I will not be a man's clean-up woman."

"What are you talking about?" Cheney was fully alert.

"I refuse to repair something I did not break. The bitterness I hear coming from him could only have come from a failed relationship. If he is attracted to me, then he must cut all ties with the past. If he gets a spiritual makeover, then . . . hmm . . . he might be a candidate.

"I've shared with you I want a Christian companion, someone to hold my hand during walks, someone to share a foot long Subway sandwich—club, of course. If a man can take me out to dinner and watch funny movies with me, he ought to be able to read the Bible with me. Does Rainey meet those requirements?"

At times, Josephine could come across as detached, but Cheney learned that was her personality. A scripture came to her. "That's a lot to expect from imperfect people. You may not be able to heal his spirit, but you can soothe him with encouraging words. Josephine, did you ever think you may be the only person to draw him to Christ?"

Josephine looked horrified. She shook her head. "God wouldn't do that to me."

Cheney chuckled. "Oh, yes, our God would. If you want all those things, make it happen—pray. It's no coincidence you accepted Rainey's invitation to Fair St. Louis." Cheney laughed at

Josephine's surprised look. "Yes, he told me about the warring frustration and attraction to you. I don't consider that a coincidence. God really could use you to bring him to Christ."

"What do I get out of the deal?"

Is this woman serious? Besides handsome and loveable—that is, once God gave him a makeover—Rainey was a respectable, highly sought after orthodontist in an elite society. "How about a spiritual crown just knowing your actions caused someone to escape the gates of hell to be ready for heaven?" Cheney suggested.

Josephine held eye contact with Cheney. "Dr. Rainey Terrence Reynolds's attitude isn't appealing. He's too arrogant, and he doesn't seem to have a sense of family loyalty."

Cheney did her best not to smile. *Arrogant? Now, who is calling the kettle black?* Interesting that very few people knew Rainey's middle name. There were perks to being a researcher. "Family loyalty? Josephine, that is only one of the things that enflamed my brother."

Josephine sighed as her lips curled into a smile. "All right. I'll call Rainey, but I need his number."

"I just so happen to have his home, cell, and work number already written out for you."

"What if I had said forget it?"

Cheney's eyes twinkled in merriment. "I know how to pray. God knows how to make us change our hearts and minds."

"Hmm. I can't argue with that. After all, Rainey is very good looking. I'll give him the benefit of the doubt since he's your brother. Speaking of family, where I come from, families are united." Josephine patted Cheney's stomach. "Why are you unhappy? You are increasing your family. Children are a blessing."

"I've been through so many what-ifs in my life." Cheney fidgeted with her sweater. "Don't misunderstand me. My pregnancies are miracles, but it's the outcomes that are devastating."

"I believe there is a scripture in Philippians I, where Paul and Timothy told the saints, *Being confident of this, that He who began a good work in you will carry it on to completion until the day of Christ Jesus,* which means to me, the same God that performed that miracle pregnancy is the same God who can finish the course." Josephine playfully knocked on Cheney's head with her knuckles then counted on her fingers. "God granted Rachel in the Bible two sons—Joseph and Benjamin. Eli's wife, Hannah, gave birth to Samuel after praying. Don't forget Abraham's wife Sarah."

"Okay, I get the message," Cheney said, laughing. Josephine would surely give her brother a run for his money. Cheney was putting her request in to the Lord for Josephine and Rainey to work out. They both would have to give, and it would be interesting to see who gave the most. She shoved Josephine with her shoulder, causing them to sway in rhythm.

Remembering the children, Cheney glanced in the direction of Kami and Little Parke. Miss Diva, Busybody Kami was liable to be anywhere, whereas Little Parke, who was bonding closer every day, would only move when he was instructed. "Little Parke's former adoptive mother, Harriett, is also pregnant."

"Then it's settled. We have to trust God, Cheney. You're not in this alone—"

"We? Don't tell me you're pregnant too."

"Of course not. I would not give a man the satisfaction of tagging me as a momma's baby."

Cheney bowed her head to hide a grin. She was always amused the few times the African woman couldn't get the African-American slang right. She didn't want to offend Josephine by correcting her with "baby's momma."

"What I mean is I'm here for you if you need a friend. As a matter of fact, I've been urging Grandmother B to get up earlier in the morning to be my prayer partner before her workout with Keyshia Cole's music blaring in the background."

"What did Grandma BB say?"

"Grandmother B says the best she can do is text a prayer in the morning."

"Text a prayer." Cheney shook her head. Somehow she wasn't surprised.

CHAPTER 38

I'm such a hypocrite.
Cheney wrote to her father weeks later.
I profess to having all this faith, but I'm scared, Daddy. Not so much for me, but for the baby. This is so hard . . . .
She scribbled on for a few more paragraphs before signing off:
Well, thanks for listening, Daddy. I love you.
Cheney sealed the letter, making sure she mentioned Gayle had progressed with the psychological sessions to help her cope with the stress. She dropped it in the mail on her way to work. She knew in a few weeks, she would receive a reply. Rubbing her stomach, Cheney always felt better after she vented to her father.

This pregnancy was so different from the others. Physically, she still suffered her bouts of nausea when she didn't eat regularly, and she still was zapped of energy. Little Parke and Kami were more than happy to help when they were instructed.

"Mommy, is our baby going to heaven again, or is she coming home with us this time?" Kami had asked more than once, always emphasizing her desire for a sister. Cheney tried not to cry after the innocent question.

Little Parke had his moments when he withdrew, but she and Parke gave him extra doses of hugs and attention. Cheney had become a pro at reading his moods.

As predicted, two and a half weeks later, a letter from Algoa

Correctional Center in Jefferson City was waiting for her on the kitchen table. She and Parke had visited him twice; Rainey and Janae once. Gayle said she wasn't ready to see him institutionalized. She faithfully wrote him letters, but had yet to mail any of them.

Apparently, Kami had gotten the mail out of the mailbox. The evidence was on a nearby chair, where some pieces of mail rested because Kami couldn't reach the counter all the time. Cheney opened the envelope then pulled back a bar chair from the counter. Once she had steadied herself, she began reading.

> Dear Princess,
>
> I know about being a hypocrite. You are not one. Sometimes, when we talk to others about Jesus concerning an issue, our heart is listening for direction too. Yes, you've shared with me how badly you wanted a baby. Even in my capacity as an obstetrician, I couldn't have done anything any different in treatment.
>
> Since I've been here, I've reread the Book of Isaiah, but I keep coming back to 55:8: My thoughts are not your thoughts, neither are my ways your ways.
>
> Keep talking about Jesus and His goodness to help you overcome the anxiety. Remember to get plenty of rest and exercise according to Dr. Gray's instructions. He's a good doctor. Don't forget to maintain a balanced diet, and most of all, pray for your baby. I love you, and I'll be praying too. After all, I want to see my new grandbaby when I get out of here.
>
> Tell Parke to take care of my daughter. Give Kami and Little Parke my love. Don't forget to pray for our family and check up on your mother. She told me you two have talked.
>
> Whatever you do, don't let Janae upset you. You may have to wait until after you have the baby to work on that

one. I don't want you to be stressed. Please extend my re-
morse to Mrs. Beacon again.

Love,

Dad,

One of the most converted hypocrites God has saved

His sign-off was the part that made Cheney teary-eyed. His
letters gave her encouragement until the next time.

Still holding the letter, Cheney got up and kicked off her
shoes before heading upstairs. She changed clothes then sat on
the chaise in her bay window and read it again. Parke walked
into the bedroom as she finished and was stuffing it back into
the envelope.

"Hey, baby. Was it a good message from Roland?"

Cheney nodded and sighed. "He quoted Isaiah 55:8. It's a
mystery about God's ways and His purpose. I've prayed for my
family's salvation since I came to know the Lord." She mustered
a chuckle. "The Lord saved him then sent him to prison. I don't
understand God's reason for that. Parke, would I be complaining if I said I feel cheated?"

"I would say you have some serious hormones working,"
Parke responded without giving her a direct answer. He came
closer and knelt by her side. "Sweetheart, you're four-and-a-half
months pregnant. If you thought I was overprotective and pam-
pered you before, you ain't seen *anything* yet." He wiggled his
eyebrows mischievously.

"Baby, I'm concerned about your physical welfare, but I'm
also praying for your soul and mental health. I guess this is one
of those situations in our lives that require fasting and praying.
It's time for me to go back to my regular weekly fast." He stroked
her cheek. "This affects me as much as you."

His cell phone chimed. Without looking at the ID, they both

knew it was Malcolm from the *Star Wars* ringtone. Cheney's heart pounded. Hallison was due any day, and that made Cheney anxious.

"What's up, bro?" Parke answered before different emotions raced across his face. Lately, Parke had decided to wear a thin five o'clock shadow, which made him and Malcolm look more alike, but Parke was more handsome. "Yep. I'll tell Cheney. We'll be praying, but I think we'll stay here and wait." There was a pause as Parke nodded. "Right. Right. You understand what I mean. Thanks, bro. Love you both. Remember to call us as soon as MJ makes his entrance."

Cheney was already shifting, ready to get up and dressed before Parke disconnected, but his firm arm stilled her. "Where do you think you're going?"

"To the hospital." She frowned, annoyed. Wasn't it obvious?

"Oh, no you're not," he said firmly. "We'll wait right here at home. I don't want you more stressed. Plus, it could be a long night." Parke reached for her hand. "Let's pray." He waited for her to bow her head.

"Father, in the name of Jesus, we come to you today totally dependent on your grace and mercy. Lord, even with our imperfect selves, we know you love us and expect us to strive for perfection.

"We ask that you bless my sister-in-law, Hali, and give Malcolm the strength to be right by her side. Let them have a safe delivery and healthy baby. There are so many people to pray for and so many needs, but, Jesus, let your perfect will be done in my life, my family, my unsaved but loving parents, my in-laws, Roland, Janae, Gayle . . ."

Parke was in no rush as he called out names. When he mentioned her name, tongues exploded and the anointing fell on Cheney. As tears streamed down her cheeks, she lifted her hands. "Hallelujah, hallelujah, Jesus, thank you for all that you've done. Lord, help me to trust you."

Without opening her eyes, Cheney felt Kami's presence. She imagined Little Parke wasn't far away. Kami was drawn to prayer like a Bomb Pop truck. The Lord hadn't given any evidence that He had filled her with the gift of His Holy Ghost yet, but Kami was determined to keep asking Jesus for it so she could talk to God in "the secret code," as she described God-directed speaking in other tongues. The requests and concerns were definitely secrets between God and the prayee, unless He interpreted the message or sent someone else to do His bidding.

As the tongues ceased, Cheney and Parke opened their eyes to find Little Parke standing in the doorway with an uncertain expression. Parke went over and lifted his son in one arm, anticipating Kami would leap into his other arm. Kami didn't disappoint. After Cheney had stretched out in their California king bed, Parke carefully placed his children on the opposite side before climbing in himself.

Cheney struggled to relax. Parke surfed the channels for a program to occupy Kami and Little Parke. Satisfied with *Sid the Science Kid*, he left the room and headed downstairs to make his dinner specialty—hot dogs and pork 'n beans. He topped off the two-course meal with leftover salad and chocolate pudding.

Twenty minutes later when he returned upstairs, the children were fascinated with Sid's latest experiment with light and rainbows. Cheney was waiting on him. "You think we should get an update on Hali?" Cheney asked, but her expression revealed it was a demand.

"Nope." Parke had already checked in with Malcolm while he was downstairs, and the doctors confirmed Hallison had dilated, but expected a long wait. He wanted Cheney to stay calm while he worried himself to death. This event was too big a deal. He

held no grudge against his brother for producing the first legiti-
mate Jamieson son—if the sonogram proved to be correct. As a
matter of fact, in Cheney's present condition, he was more than
confident this time that he and Cheney were next in line.

Parke didn't like Cheney making unnecessary trips up and
down the stairs, despite the doctor's assurance that Cheney was
healthy and didn't need to curtail any normal activities. Yet, he
brought the meal to her. "It's picnic time," he announced with a
plaid blanket in his arms.

"Yay." Kami bounced on the bed. Little Parke didn't take his
eyes off the TV, but grinned.

"Parke—" Majority rule drowned out Cheney's protests. She
had no choice but to comply and join the children on the blanket Parke had spread on their floor. He left and came back with
dinner. Parke mixed silverware with paper plates from Christmas and paper cups from Kami's last birthday party. For the
final touch, he blew up two discarded balloons branded with a
HAPPY NEW YEAR logo.

As far as Little Parke and Kami were concerned, dinnertime
was fun time, as Parke told them corny jokes. Cheney didn't
hide her boredom as she checked her watch several times. Twice,
she nudged Parke and nagged him about calling Malcolm. His
response was always, "Patience."

When they were finished eating, Parke cleaned up the mess as
Cheney helped prepare Kami and Little Parke for bed. An hour
later, Cheney was snuggled next to Parke in their own bed.

"It's been a long time and we haven't heard anything." Cheney
yawned.

Shifting, Parke anchored himself on his elbow and came
clean. "Nothing's changed. I've spoken with Malcolm a couple
of times. Hali's still pregnant, and Malcolm's still a nervous
wreck." He grinned.

Cheney sighed. "You think we'll ever experience that?" She toyed with imaginary lint on her pillowcase.

"What?"

"A normal delivery with you going nuts and me screaming for drugs," Cheney said, her lids fluttering with a smile.

Parke probably saw through her. There was no amusement behind Cheney's tentative smile. She was hurting and there was nothing he could say to make her believe this pregnancy wouldn't end like the others. They had prayed and quoted every scripture on faith, but Cheney couldn't shake the underlying doubt that crept up from time to time. Parke prayed harder for the words to comfort her and strengthen his faith.

It was ten minutes past one in the morning when Parke's cell phone chimed the theme to *Star Wars*. Parke fumbled for the noisemaker on the nightstand and had barely said hello when Malcolm screamed into the phone. "He's here. My boy is here!"

"Congratulations," Parke murmured, disconnected, and drifted back to sleep.

CHAPTER 39

Cheney welcomed the arrival of Malcolm Danso—meaning reliable—Jamieson Junior. The Jamiesons and Hallison's mother *ooh*ed and *ahh*ed over the baby, who weighed seven pounds and ten ounces at birth.

If it weren't for breastfeeding, Hallison may have been pushed to the back of the line to hold her own child. Even Malcolm insisted on diaper changing and sponge baths. Cheney wondered how long Malcolm would vie for those tasks.

"You can hold him, sis." Hallison lovingly offered Malcolm Junior. to her sister-in-law a few weeks after his birth.

"Oh, I know I can . . . ah, okay." Cheney gnawed on her bottom lip, removing the thin layer of lip gloss.

A hush spread among the family members who waited for their turn as they relaxed in Malcolm and Hallison's living room. Cheney sighed as she accepted God's gift to the family. Closing her eyes, she sniffed the freshness of the baby's scent before cuddling him close to her breast. He immediately turned his face, expecting a meal.

The baby inside Cheney's womb began to move, stretching like it never had before. It was as if the baby felt the presence of another infant.

Cheney chuckled. It was the most movement she had felt since the fluttering began a few weeks ago. As she held her nephew, Cheney didn't emotionally fall apart. Evidently, God had her hormones in check.

"Ah, Cheney," Hallison said as she shooed her niece and nephew out of the way and scooted next to her sister-in-law, "you can give him back if you're tired of holding him."

Content, Cheney shook her head. "I'm not."

Without asking for it, Cheney received too much advice and not enough prayer from Imani and Mrs. Beacon about what she shouldn't and should do as an expectant mother. Most were old wives' tales, such as if Cheney craved something sweet, she was having a girl, versus wanting sour juices or food would indicate a boy. Neither of them had ever had babies, but that didn't stop them from becoming mother hens. Apparently, they had forgotten this wasn't her first pregnancy.

Cheney's spiritual encouragement came in large doses from Hallison, Josephine, and Parke. Through his letters to Gayle, Roland encouraged her to check on their daughter regularly. As Cheney strived to spend more time with her mother, they began to mend their shattered relationship, but the stitching was still fragile.

Her pregnancy progressed into the sixth month without incident, but that didn't mean Parke eased up on his pampering. He enforced new rules of the house, which were created every day, like one-hour visiting hours, or not allowing Cheney to stand more than fifteen minutes. Parke even restricted his mother's visits to the weekend, unless Cheney needed her sooner.

Finally, one Sunday morning after church, Cheney reactivated her status as the queen bee of the house. "Honey, the doctor says the baby's heartbeat is strong and I'm maintaining my weight. I don't appreciate you keeping people at bay because you're afraid I'm going to catch germs. I'm fine."

"That doctor doesn't know what he's talking about. Viruses are lurking in the air, waiting to attack you. It ain't going to happen on my watch!"

Somewhere during the seventh month, Parke had renewed his club membership at every major bookseller, including the African-American bookstore. Although Parke and Cheney already had some of the same books from the last pregnancy, he insisted on newer editions. At the rate he was buying books, they would be forced to convert their spare guest room into a home library.

The only real peace of mind Cheney got was behind the closed doors of her office, where she had daily heart-to-heart talks with God. She welcomed going to work and enduring her male crew, who complained more than chatty women. She had to give them credit. They did show her some compassion. Instead of bickering among themselves, and then griping to her, they bypassed Cheney and resolved their own spats.

About a month later, she had awakened with a slight abdominal pain. There wasn't any bleeding, and the baby seemed to be moving, so she wasn't alarmed. She refused to allow fear to take root in her mind. Before she had dressed for work, she reached for her bottle of holy oil in the bathroom medicine cabinet. By faith, she dabbed a little on her stomach and prayed. Afterward, she chuckled as the baby shifted on her bladder, as if it recognized the power of prayer.

By mid-morning, Cheney was exhausted after she ended a four-way teleconference with other telephone managers. She yawned a few times then opened her top drawer to grab a snack bar. She glanced at the small desk calendar she had hidden there. Each day of her pregnancy had been crossed out. "Lord Jesus, I know you're concerned about my every doubt and fear. I'm in the home stretch now, and I thank you. I'm two weeks farther along than I was with Parke the Seventh when you took him back. Lord Jesus, please help me to make it this time with my baby."

Trust me, God spoke.

"Lord, I don't have a choice."

Parke was a mess. His nerves were shot, he had aged ten years, and one time, he passed up his house, forgetting where he lived. They had three weeks to go. It was Cheney's last day at work before starting her maternity leave. He fed her breakfast in bed. When it was time for her to get dressed for the office, he stayed in the bathroom, in case she needed him, and then dropped her off at work.

For the next eight hours, he called Cheney every hour. A few times, she hung up on him. "Parke, I'm busy. Unless you want me to have our baby in this office with a telephone representative assisting in the delivery, let me get my work done."

Thank goodness she had only slammed down the phone once. The last time he called before he left to pick her up, she actually talked to him.

"Parke, we're so close. Do you think we'll make it?"

"We say we believe in miracles. The world taunts us and says there are no more miracles. This is not about us. Remember what Pastor Scott preached on last Sunday?" He didn't give her time to answer. "If God can't get the glory out of our lives, then why are we here? Galatians 6:9: *Let us not be weary in well doing—* which is God's will—*in due season, we shall reap if we faint not.* No matter what, it's God's will that will prevail."

As Cheney's due date inched closer, Parke issued one last decree, and he refused to take no for an answer: The Jamieson and Reynolds families were ordered to his house for a group prayer over his wife.

Surprisingly, Gayle was the driving force behind Janae's compliance. Her husband, Bryce, on the hand, thought it was a good idea. Parke and Malcolm's youngest brother, Cameron, flew into town from Boston for what Parke called the impartation of blessings. Cheney was glad to see her youngest brother-in-law.

Cameron's quiet intellect earned him a four-year scholarship at Massachusetts Institute of Technology (MIT). A lucrative job after graduating with a degree in mechanical engineering kept him on the East Coast.

Cameron had shocked Parke with his declaration. "I'm thinking about moving back home permanently, PJ." The surprising revelation was a contradiction to Cameron's earlier statement that he would never move back to St. Louis, and so far, he hadn't broken his resolution. Evidently, something had changed his mind.

Parke beamed. "It would be like old times. What's stopping you?"

"The bad boys from Boston." Cameron sighed. "Ace and Kidd said if I leave, they're coming with me."

"Humph, then you better stay there. Our first cousins are the worst bunch of the Jamieson men. Hanging with them makes anyone guilty by association."

"Who are you telling? But I will be there for the prayer. I'm really pulling for you and Cheney this time."

"I know. Everybody is except for the devil," Parke had told him as they ended their call.

Within two days, Cameron arrived as he said he would. Thank God their cousins hadn't tagged along. Cameron must have mentioned a family prayer, and that killed it for the brothers.

Mrs. Beacon was a no-show, stating she was off to a Red Hat Society event. Ellington said he would send positive thoughts when he learned that Imani would take a break from playing cat and mouse with bill dodgers to be in attendance. Nothing could

stop Malcolm and Hallison, along with their baby, from partici-
pating in the family prayers.

Cheney was adamant that her brother be in attendance,
whether Josephine could be there or not. Although Josephine
had extended an olive branch to Rainey, he had declined. A few
times when Cheney met Rainey for lunch, he didn't hold back
pointing out everything that was wrong with Josephine.

"But she is beautiful, right?" Cheney had baited him, grinning.

"Absolutely," he had reluctantly admitted.

Scheming to get them together kept her mind off what
could go wrong with her pregnancy. In her mind, she was writing a romance novel where Josephine and Rainey were the main
characters. They both came—together. What a surprise.

CHAPTER 40

When Parke anointed Cheney's head with holy oil, he knew if the group was of one accord, the Holy Ghost would descend upon them as it did in the upper room on the day of Pentecost in the Book of Acts.

The prayer had knocked Cheney out. She was so deep in her sleep that she was snoring. Parke would have thought it was amusing if he wasn't so tired. Praying was a job. It took concentration and determination for the group to be in sync, but finally everyone cooperated. Their guests said their good-byes with hugs and kisses.

Hours later, Parke put his children to bed then returned to the sitting area in his bedroom. Although he was beat, he was too keyed up to sleep; but he wanted to stay close to his wife. He grabbed a baby book off a stack of others and began to thumb through the pages.

As soon as he began reviewing the labor symptoms, his lids felt heavy. "Figures." Frustrated that his body couldn't make up its mind about sleep, he closed the book and turned off the lamp. Getting up, he went into the bathroom and disrobed. Thirsty, he gulped down a big glass of water, got on his knees by Cheney's side, and said his prayers before climbing in bed.

Some time during the night, Cheney had stopped snoring. He stirred and opened his eyes. Cheney was smiling in her sleep. Parke stared at his wife before drifting back to sleep. Soon Parke

298   **Pat Simmons**

was dreaming of taking the children to a water park. He was about to dive into the deep end when Cheney started shoving him. "Parke, wake up. You peed in the bed."

His eyes were too heavy to open. "I didn't do it," he slurred and turned over.

That's when a pillow slapped him upside his head before Cheney yelled out in pain. "That's me. Wake up. My water broke. The baby is coming."

Parke shot up from the bed. He turned and looked at Cheney, who was writhing in pain. "Oh my God. Oh, Jesus . . . Lord, help us."

"Honey," Cheney said calmly before gritting her teeth, then huffed, "if you can get me to the hospital, the Lord will help us."

"Yeah, right." He ran around the room, flipping through books to review what to do next. He couldn't breathe. At that moment, Parke wished he had agreed to brush up on the breathing techniques they learned in the Lamaze class for the last pregnancy. *Stupid.* It was bad timing for him to lose control. He pulled on his pants and slipped on his shirt that he had inadvertently turned inside out.

"Parke, if you don't help me get cleaned up, I'm going to have our baby here with our daughter acting as the nurse and Little Parke the doctor."

"Right. Right." He huffed, momentarily confused. "Okay . . . where are my shoes?"

Twenty minutes later, Parke was in his SUV driving to De-Paul's hospital. Cheney moaned while holding her stomach. Their children were sleepy, dressed in their pajamas and raincoats because Parke was too distracted to grab their jackets out of the dryer.

Using his vehicle's OnStar hands-free calling phone service, Parke pushed one button, recited Malcolm's number, and waited while the number was dialed. Less than a minute later, Malcolm answered. "Cheney's in labor. Cheney's in labor. Call everybody else," he barked and disconnected. He wiped the sweat off his forehead and prayed nobody got in his way en route to the hospital.

Seven hours and five minutes later, Parke couldn't help but stare at the most handsome baby in the nursery. This was what life was all about. This was proof of God's promise. Parke wasn't leaving his post. He would stand guard at the window and watch his son until Cheney woke; then they would all bond together.

He was so focused that the slight poking in his leg was nothing more than a minor annoyance.

"Daddy? What's his name?" Kami asked as she stood on her tippy toes to get a look.

"Huh?" Parke frowned, not too pleased with the interruption.

"I'm going to still be the oldest," Little Parke stated without looking away.

Their bickering began, until Little Parke repeated Kami's question. "What's his name, Daddy?"

Parke sighed and looked from his two children to the third one sleeping in the nursery's bassinet. He actually couldn't remember how many times or when his son had begun to call him Daddy, but each time, Parke wanted to grab Little Parke and never let him go.

EPILOGUE

Parke ogled Cheney, who was nursing Paden—meaning royal—as Cheney sat in the rocking chair in their bedroom. The eight-pound, two-ounce boy was not only bigger than Malcolm's son had been at birth, but just as healthy. The moment he was born, Parke lifted his son up to the Lord as his tenth great-grandfather had done. Unlike Prince Paki, Parke knew the real and living God through Jesus. He praised God for His promise, blessing, and the measure of faith he held on to, at times with uncertainty.

"Thank you," Parke whispered to Cheney. He had uttered those two words almost nonstop for more than a month. "Our life has been a miracle. You truly have given me more than I could've ever hoped or dreamt. I'm—"

A thump on their bedroom door interrupted their tender moment. Kami and Little Parke "Pace" were arguing again. Parke and Cheney usually chuckled and refereed their spats. He loved the noise of children under foot.

They had begun to call him Pace to keep the confusion down at gatherings; plus, he boldly informed his father, "I'm not little, Dad. When I grow up, I'll be taller than you, Grandpa, and Uncle Malcolm."

There was another knock and the door opened. Parke blinked away the memory of that special moment to concentrate on their present crisis.

"Daddy, I told Pace that I was the princess of the house, and he said uh-uh because he's the prince." Kami pointed then crossed her arms. "Tell him, Daddy. He can't be the prince."

Parke stood from his kneeling position in front of Cheney then squatted to be eye level with his children. "Kami, your brother is a prince, but you're still a princess."

Pace grinned. "I told you, and I'm older than you too. One day, I'll be the king," he said to antagonize his sister before racing out of the room. Kami ran after him, crying, in denial that she wasn't the only royalty in the house.

Parke sighed. The joys of parenthood. He and Cheney had faith in God's Word. Hebrews 11:1: *Now faith is a substance of things hoped for, the evidence of things not seen.* Their children were the substance of everything they could have ever hoped for, and judging from their grocery bill, the evidence of what they had not seen years earlier.

About the Author . . .

Pat Simmons is the recipient of the Katherine D. Jones Award for grace and humility presented at the 2008 Romance Slam Jam in Chicago, IL. She is a Jesus baptized Believer and received the gift of Holy Ghost by the evidence of speaking in other tongues. She has worked in radio and television for more than fifteen years; been married for more than twenty- five years; and has a son and daughter.

Pat Simmons handles media publicity, including author interviews for the yearly RT BOOKLOVERS Conventions. She holds a B.S. in Mass Communications from Emerson College in Boston, MA. Her hobbies include sewing almost everything she wears; she developed a passion for genealogy after her great-grandmother, Minerva Brown Wade, died at the age of 97 years old.

In her honor, Pat creates characters in her stories from her genealogy tree. In *Still Guilty*, Ellington "The Duke" Brown's name was for Ellis Brown, twin to Louis Brown, the only brothers of Minerva Brown. Her great-grandmother, Minerva Brown Wade, also had a younger sister, Hattie, who Pat never found in any other census besides 1900.

The author found a newspaper article on Ellis while surfing the Internet. It read: 100 YEAR OLD MAN PERISHES IN HOUSE FIRE. Unfortunately, the last trace of Louis was in the 1910 census in Arkansas. He was sixteen, Minerva was nineteen, and they were living in the household of their uncle, Wyatt Palmer.

Pat Simmons is the bestselling author of her debut novel, BOOK I: *Guilty of Love*. Other titles include award-winner *Talk to Me*; BOOK II: *Not Guilty of Love*, and BOOK III: *Still Guilty*. For 2011, she is planning to release *Crowning Glory*. Look for the next installment in the *Guilty* series with *Guilty by Association*, featuring one of the bad boys from Boston, Kevin "Kidd" Jamieson. For more stories in the *Guilty* series, keep your ideas coming.

Pat welcomes your emails at pat@patsimmons.net or snail mail:
Pat Simmons, 3831 Vaile Ave., Box 58, Florissant, MO 63034.

Be blessed always !

BOOKCLUB DISCUSSION . . .

1.   I know many readers were happy that Cheney and Parke finally had their baby. Discuss your faith when it appears your request has gone unanswered from God.

2.   The Lord was about to bless Cheney. Was she justified in not wanting to go down that road again?

3.   Cheney's father, Dr. Roland Reynolds, committed a crime, repented, and God forgave him. Should he still have served prison time?

4.   Talk about Cheney's feelings toward her sister-in-law, Hali, when she learned that she was pregnant.

5.   Has God ever told you and someone else different messages concerning the same situation?

6.   The Lord allowed Little Parke "Pace" to be adopted. What do you think was God's reason for doing that? Discuss a "Grandma BB" personality: someone who won't go to church, but will quote scriptures to others and urge them to go.

7.   In some states like Missouri, it is a man's responsibility to know if he fathered a child. Talk about the court's power to terminate parental rights if the father and mother want the child.

8.   Could a relationship between Josephine and Rainey work without either one of them compromising?

9.   Why did Cheney's mother, Gayle, blame her daughter for Roland's plight?

Excerpt from *Crowning Glory*

CHAPTER 1

Without a test, there can be no testimony, Karyn Wallace reminded herself five minutes after she agreed to a date with Levi Tolliver. She wasn't Cinderella, and Karyn doubted the widower would be her prince.

Yes, she was affected by the most beautiful dark chocolate eyes she had seen in a long time. Even camouflaged behind designer glasses that were angled perfectly on a chiseled nose, they were hypnotic. His thick, wavy black hair and thin mustache were nice, but it was Levi's dimples that seemed to be on standby, waiting to smile. He was buffed, at five feet and eleven inches, but Karyn wasn't intimidated by Levi's height as he towered over her petite statute.

"Karyn, I've surrendered to God's subtle urging to learn more about you. You might as well surrender to what God is stirring between us," Levi stated as if he had sealed a business deal after his fifth visit in a month to Bookshelves Unlimited where she worked.

"What am I surrendering to?" At twenty-seven, Karyn was too old to play games. Was Levi challenging her, or was God diverting her from resolve to live for Christ regardless of any obstacles hurdled her way? She didn't have time to test the waters to see if she could survive another relationship gone awry.

"If you're expecting some smooth lines, you'll have to take a rain check. My heart has been listening, waiting for God to move me to the next phase." He paused as if debating what to say next. "Karyn, God has designated you as someone who should be in my life. I don't know in what capacity, but I guess God will let us know sooner than later." As he leaned closer, his lashes mesmerized her. "Deny the attraction."

Anchoring her elbows on the table in the store's café, Karyn rested her chin in her hands. She took pleasure in delaying her response. "I'm attracted to flashy cars, white kittens, black-eyed peas, and—" She owned neither, but couldn't get enough of peas at a soul food place near her apartment.

"My Buick LaCrosse is new, but not flashy, my daughter is allergic to cats, and my mother can throw down on any beans, peas, or greens." A dimple winked as he stretched his lips into a lazy grin. "Add me to your list, Karyn, because we could find out that we're perfect as a couple, or make close acquaintances, although friendship is not on my run-down."

ORDER FORM
URBAN BOOKS, LLC
78 E. Industry Ct
Deer Park, NY 11729

Name: (please print):_____

Address: _____

City/State: _____

Zip: _____

QTY	TITLES	PRICE
	16 ½ On The Block	$14.95
	16 On The Block	$14.95
	Betrayal	$14.95
	Both Sides Of The Fence	$14.95
	Cheesecake And Teardrops	$14.95
	Denim Diaries	$14.95
	Happily Ever Now	$14.95
	Hell Has No Fury	$14.95
	If It Isn't love	$14.95
	Last Breath	$14.95
	Loving Dasia	$14.95
	Say It Ain't So	$14.95

Shipping and Handling - add $3.50 for 1st book then $1.75 for each additional book.

Please send a check payable to:

Urban Books, LLC

Please allow 4 - 6 weeks for delivery

ORDER FORM
URBAN BOOKS, LLC
78 E. Industry Ct
Deer Park, NY 11729

Name: (please print):_____

Address: _____

City/State: _____

Zip: _____

QTY	TITLES	PRICE
	The Cartel	$14.95
	The Cartel#2	$14.95
	The Dopeman's Wife	$14.95
	The Prada Plan	$14.95
	Gunz And Roses	$14.95
	Snow White	$14.95
	A Pimp's Life	$14.95
	Hush	$14.95
	Little Black Girl Lost 1	$14.95
	Little Black Girl Lost 2	$14.95
	Little Black Girl Lost 3	$14.95
	Little Black Girl Lost 4	$14.95

Shipping and Handling - add $3.50 for 1st book then $1.75 for each additional book.
Please send a check payable to:
Urban Books, LLC
Please allow 4 - 6 weeks for delivery

ORDER FORM
URBAN BOOKS, LLC
78 E. Industry Ct
Deer Park, NY 11729

Name: (please print):_____

Address: _____

City/State: _____

Zip: _____

QTY	TITLES	PRICE
	A Man's Worth	$14.95
	Abundant Rain	$14.95
	Battle Of Jericho	$14.95
	By The Grace Of God	$14.95
	Dance Into Destiny	$14.95
	Divorcing The Devil	$14.95
	Forsaken	$14.95
	Grace And Mercy	$14.95
	Guilty & Not Guilty Of Love	$14.95
	His Woman, His Wife His Widow	$14.95
	Illusion	$14.95
	The LoveChild	$14.95

Shipping and Handling - add $3.50 for 1st book then $1.75 for each additional book.
Please send a check payable to:
Urban Books, LLC
Please allow 4 - 6 weeks for delivery

ORDER FORM
URBAN BOOKS, LLC
78 E. Industry Ct
Deer Park, NY 11729

Name: (please print):_____

Address: _____

City/State: _____

Zip: _____

QTY	TITLES	PRICE

Shipping and Handling - add $3.50 for 1st book then $1.75 for each additional book.
Please send a check payable to:
   Urban Books, LLC
Please allow 4 - 6 weeks for delivery

Notes

Notes

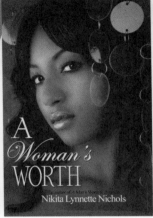

The Morning After
Kendra Norman-Bellamy &
Hank Stewart
978-1-60162-941-8
1-60162-941-9
(trade paperback)

A Woman's Worth
Nikita Lynnette Nichols
978-1-60162-874-9
1-60162-874-9
(trade paperback)

Me, Myself and Him
E.N. Joy
978-1-60162-844-2
1-60162-844-7
(mass market)

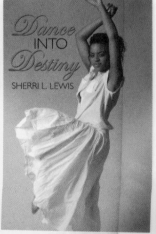

**She Who Finds
a Husband**
E.N. Joy
978-1-60162-875-6
1-60162-875-7
(trade paperback)

Desperate Decisions
Marilyn M. Anderson
978-1-60162-846-6
1-60162-846-3
(trade paperback)

Dance Into Destiny
Sherri L. Lewis
978-1-60162-847-3
1-60162-847-1
(mass market)

STILL
Guilty

Cheney Jamieson made a difficult decision in the past, and now it's affecting the lives of three men she loves in surprising and unexpected ways.

Cheney's twin brother, Rainey Reynolds, is bitter after a former girlfriend terminates a pregnancy that he welcomed. When he learns that his sister made the same choice, Rainey lashes out at her with disdain. Can the new Christian woman in his life help him understand that forgiveness is the first step toward healing?

Cheney's husband, Parke K. Jamieson VI, is expected to sire the next generation of Jamiesons, but complications from Cheney's botched abortion makes carrying a baby to full term impossible. The only hope is Parke's illegitimate son, who was in foster care until he was recently adopted. Parke needs a couple of miracles, but he has to wait on God's timing.

Cheney's father, Dr. Roland Reynolds, has had his own past indiscretions. Could Cheney be paying for the sins of her father?

Still Guilty, the third installment in Pat Simmons' popular *Guilty* series, reminds us that sometimes we don't have any control over things that are set in motion, but God is always there to help us weather the storms.

U.S. $14.95 / CANADA $17.95

ISBN - 13 : 978-1-60162-851-0
ISBN - 10 : 1-60162-851-X

PRINTED IN U.S.A.

EAN

9 781601 628510

51495

DESIGN BY SMILEY GUIRAND

URBAN CHRISTIAN

The finest in Christian fiction
www.urbanchristianonline.net